LOSING LENORE

PRAISE FOR JOE KLINGLER

Praise for RATS
International Rubery Book Award - Fiction Short List

"Klingler's debut is an intelligent, non-stop page turner."
—Manhattan Book Review (5-Stars)

"A deep logistical jungle sure to entertain buffs and newcomers to
the techno-thriller genre."
—Kirkus Reviews (Featured Selection. Recommended List)

Praise for Missing Mona
London Book Festival Winner

"Reads like a good old private investigator novel from years ago."
—San Francisco Book Review (5-Stars)

"Klingler's Chicago…was exciting and gritty."
—Manhattan Book Review

Praise for Mash Up
Winner National Indie Excellence Award—Thriller

"Effortlessly clever prose…a thoughtful, well-constructed tale."
—Kirkus Reviews
"The perfect detective read…a classic addition to the noir genre."
—San Francisco Book Review (5-Stars)

Praise for Tune Up
Winner Pacific Book Awards—Thriller of the Year

"A spiderweb of secrets, sex, blackmail, and murder."
—Kirkus Reviews

"Recalls the work of James Ellroy. Suspenseful mastery in its best form. Not to be missed."
—Seattle Book Review (5-Stars)

Praise for Burn Up

Winner New York City Big Book Award—Multi-cultural Fiction

"Surprise after surprise…players come alive on the page."
—The Pacific Book Review Starred Review

"Crisp and edgy writing…enhanced by cliffhanging chapter endings."
—Clarion Reviews

Praise for Lock Up

Eric Hoffer Book Awards Finalist

"If you like writing which reads easily, plots that force your pulse to quicken, and characters you enjoy spending time with, go ahead and commit yourself to Lock Up."
—Pacific Book Review

"If you are looking for a good mystery/thriller, look no further than Klingler's Secrets of Mylin trilogy!"
—Manhattan Book Review (5-Stars)

Praise for FLEE

Independent Press Awards—Distinguished Favorite

"A gripping race-the-clock tale featuring savvy female supporting characters."
—Kirkus Reviews "Recommended" Book

"Klingler dispenses with a drawn-out preamble in getting to the thick of an adrenalin-rich plot."
—San Francisco Book Review (5-Stars)

ALSO BY JOE KLINGLER

RATS
Mash UP
Missing Mona
Tune Up
Burn Up
Lock Up
FLEE

For the latest news, please visit

www.joeklingler.com

LOSING LENORE

A Tommy Cuda Mystery

JOE KLINGLER

CARTOSI LLC
Stateline

Cover design by Karen Phillips and Ansel Niner

ISBN: 978-1-941156-17-9

www.joeklingler.com

Published by:
CARTOSI LLC
P.O. Box 3329
Stateline, NV 89449

CARTOSI is a registered trademark of Cartosi LLC

*To the memory of Martha Goddard,
pioneering developer of the sexual assault evidence collection kit
(rape kit)*

CHAPTER 1

The inside of my eyelids glowed like red-hot coals as I drifted in that limbo land of sweet joy between deep sleep and slow awakening. I fought to hang onto the remnants of my last dream: a warm breeze off the waters of the Mediterranean stroking my face, voices chattering around me, topless swimmers hopping into ocean waves, and volleyball players wearing vanishing bikinis kicking sand and smacking balls over a red, white, and green net; while I sipped an Italian beer I had never heard of before, feeling the cold brew slide down my throat. I stretched out on my lounge chair facing the ocean…

My head banged hard into an immovable object. My eyes popped open.

Sunshine blinded me.

In an instant, the Riviera dream vaporized, replaced by a cinder block building painted a sad gray. A sunbeam sneaking between window blinds pierced my eyes. I was on my side on a tile floor patterned to look like marble. I began to remember; her voice filled my head.

"Too bad we can't wait for the back seat."

I smiled and rolled onto my back.

Paper rustled. I looked down. I was swimming in money. Literally. Ben Franklins aligned along my body as if someone had dealt seven-card stud down my leg.

I remembered her clearly.

But I could't remember the money.

I stood. The bills fluttered to the floor. My clothes lay folded on top of the desk. I put on nearly black blue jeans, a red T-shirt, and a black leather jacket with a mandarin collar. A lump in the jacket pocket proved to be my car keys. But my car had seen some hard times and was being refurbished by my friend Chin.

Why would I have the keys?

I got down on my hands and knees and collected fifty bills. Five thousand in cash.

Source unknown.

The room was empty except for a blonde wood desk and a black wastebasket. Blue painter's tape held a sheet of paper to the inside of a closed, windowless door. A pair of hand-drawn curves suggested a woman's body. A fat arrow pointed right. I moved closer. Drawn with a black crayon. Or eyebrow pencil.

Where was she taking me?

I stepped into the hallway. Same tile. Same paint. A fluorescent tube buzzed above me. I turned right. The hallway ended at a service elevator. I pressed the only option: down. The doors slid open. The panel inside had three choices:

2

1

B

A stickie beside the B displayed the same suggestive curves of the first note. I pressed B. The elevator clanked and took its time descending. A single gliding door revealed a room the size of a four-car garage filled to bursting with rows of green steel shelves. Narrow windows near the ceiling, gray with dirt, fought sunlight. Dust motes floated in the two sunbeams that had managed to sneak in. The aroma of "only books live here" surrounded me.

I traversed the book maze, back and forth the length of the room, until spying double curves taped to wooden doors between two windows.

An arrow pointed up.

I opened the door on the right. A railing made of gray pipe surrounded a scarred plank floor. A black box hung from the railing by a thick wire. A curved bar ran overhead. Sunlight seeped through a long crack above me. The box had two unlabeled buttons: red and blue.

I pressed the red button. Nothing.

I held it down. A whir filled the space. The plank floor shuddered. I reached for a railing.

The floor, railing, and overhead bar rose as one. The bar tilted the ceiling into two hinged rectangles. The morning sun roared through the open space between them.

The platform shuddered and stopped. I squinted at a Chicago street from the middle of a sidewalk. Ten yards away, a turbo-bronze metallic Plymouth Barracuda sat parked at the curb. My grandfather had left me his Barracuda—the one he had wanted to see the country in before obligations interfered. His was turbo-bronze, too. Chin was retrofitting mine with a red leather interior after vandals had searched it with sharp knives. I didn't think there was a second one in the Universe.

I circumnavigated the car.

Under the rear glass window rested a guitar case with a Santana sticker across it. Beside it, a cardboard box looked a lot like my vinyl record collection.

How?

I inserted the key from my jacket pocket into the driver's door. The lock popped up. I slipped into the driver's seat and banged my knee on the steering column. Fumbling for the adjustment knob, I pushed the seat backwards until it accommodated my six feet plus frame. A note displaying the double curves hung from the dash. It read, "Turn me over."

She had said that too. More than once.

Hi Tommy,

We stayed up all night helping Chin finish your car. Then we chipped in from the rewards you gave us to provide traveling cash. We figure that if you don't leave right this instant, you will never get west of Chicago.

Marvin says: "Use the Les Paul, man. Guitars are made to be played. What are you saving it for?" He returned the knock-off to its previous owner, who is thrilled to have it back, even though he won't be able to play it for a few more months.

We are all pursuing our dreams as hard as we can. We wish you mucho luck chasing yours. Let us know when you dip your boot into the Pacific.

Until then,
— Your new Chicago friends

That explained the five grand. They were trying to make me leave, knowing I wanted to stay. Good friends for sure.

Two guys in light tan suits, both wearing red ties, split apart as they walked around the freight elevator blocking the sidewalk.

"Stupid to leave that open," one said, loud enough for me to hear.

I went to the box, held the black button for five seconds, and stepped back. The elevator rumbled down. The sidewalk slabs dropped into place like a tomb being sealed. My friends were right. The city was holding me in orbit like the gravitational force of a nearby planet. I needed to reach escape velocity before it was too late.

I hopped into the driver's seat and turned the key. The big Hemi rumbled to life. I drove directly into the sun until reaching Lakeshore Drive, then turned south toward Interstate-80 West, a marvel of astonishing engineering that ran all the way to the Pacific Ocean. But I had no interest in riding a ribbon of concrete that bypassed most of America. I wanted Route 66. The Mother Road that had settled the West.

I just had to find what was left of it.

I drove with the sun on my back and the Alpine radio Chin had chosen tuned to WDCB Chicago. They were broadcasting Hambone's Blues Party from the back of his black Cadillac parked at the corner of Blues Boulevard and Jazz Avenue. Hambone was spinning a version of Red Rooster by a 14-year-old YouTube star named Thunder Kid when I glided into a rest stop somewhere between West Chicago and the Route 66 that I hadn't found yet.

I parked beside a maroon mini van with an Ohio license plate, locked the Barracuda, and headed for the restroom. On the way I passed a green metal box selling the Chicago Tribune, the New York Times, and USA Today. Sitting on the sidewalk beside the machine was a young woman with a blue and gray blanket spread out in front of her. She was dealing cards onto the blanket, face down. An upturned white hat with a 360-degree brim held a pair of one-dollar bills. A note pinned to the hat beckoned:

Your Fortune $5

I stopped and watched her purple-fingernail hands place cards in a semicircle with me at the center. The temperature had been warming all morning and was nearing 80 degrees F. Yet she wore a black cape that reminded me of a rain poncho. The hood hid her eyes as she bowed over the cards. She stopped dealing, placed the remainder of the deck in front of her crossed legs, and passed her hand over the blanket.

"Your future is in these cards," she said, tilting her head back and looking directly into my eyes. Hers were black against skin the color all the girls tried to get each spring at Daytona Beach. But hers was no suntan.

The hood hid her hair. Her full lips weren't smiling or frowning, just waiting. She had the gentle expression of an inquisitive child and could be as young as 16, or maybe as old as 25. She didn't appear to be wearing makeup, though I knew there were secret ways to look "natural" with special techniques. But I'd vote that she was just born beautiful.

She blinked long black eyelashes at me.

"Does this really work?" I asked.

"This…" she waved both hands quickly over the cards like a magician about to turn them into rabbits, "can change your life." Her calm expression remained frozen.

I wasn't sure I wanted my life changed, but I was on an adventure.

"Can you break a hundred?"

Her lips spread into a wide smile revealing shiny teeth that could do toothpaste commercials.

"If I could change a hundred, I wouldn't be sitting at this newsstand telling fortunes. Will you take an IOU?"

I dropped a hundred into the hat. She produced a pen and what appeared to be a gum wrapper from inside the poncho, scribbled, and handed it up to me.

IOU $95 — Leni the Leviathan

"Leni the powerful?" I said.

She winked.

I placed the wrapper carefully in my brown wallet. It was made of Kevlar and looked new, even though it was a gift from my father for high school graduation almost a decade ago. He told me on more than one occasion, "If you take care of your money, it will take care of you." I sat down on the sidewalk cross-legged.

"You're going to tell me to pick a card, aren't you?"

She smiled close-lipped.

"Focus your eyes," she pointed at her own eyes with the index and pinky of her left hand, "right here. Touch a card with your non-dominant hand using only your peripheral vision. The results are more accurate than if you select a card with your full attention. Your brain gets in the way of the forces of nature."

Her smile didn't change. Her eyes held the stillness of a doll waiting for someone to pick her up.

I roamed my left hand over the semicircle of cards while gazing into Leni's black eyes wondering what they had seen that led to her sitting on this sidewalk. I moved my hand slowly trying to feel a tingle, a force, an urge—something that would separate one card from the other even though I thought this was all mumbo jumbo.

That one, third from the end on the left, was pulling my hand. I touched it with two fingers.

"Don't move your hand," Leni said. She placed two fingers of her right hand on the card and slid them until they touched mine in mirror image.

She whispered, "Let's listen," and motioned at her eyes again.

A pickup truck started up behind me and the driver sat and revved the engine over and over. Traffic whooshed on the Interstate not far away. A woman passed behind me complaining, "You always wait too long before taking a break." Probably talking to her husband. He didn't comment. Maybe not stopping was his comment. Footfalls clopping toward me from my right were accompanied by a child's gleeful screaming. The child brushed my back as he or she went past, pushing me toward the card.

"Ah," Leni said. "The sounds of civilization." She put her fingers under the edge of the card and nodded at me.

I slipped my fingers under the card and together we lifted it like it was a heavy weight that needed two people. I followed her movement until the card was between us at the level of our hearts.

She gazed into my eyes, so I gazed back.

The poncho still hid her hair. Her eyes glistened like pools of ink. Her lips held the promise of the Mona Lisa. She didn't speak. Or blink. Her skin was so smooth it could have been AI generated. The card lay balanced on our fingertips. I half expected it to levitate.

"What are your thoughts?" Leni said.

"I was admiring your beauty."

Her smiled widened, but only slightly.

"Be specific. The universe lives in the details."

"Your skin is smoother than the turbo-bronze paint on my classic car."

Her eyes left mine and landed on something behind my left shoulder. They registered recognition. Alarm. Fear. She pulled her hand away and swept up her blue blanket with the remainder of the deck and the white hat in a single motion. Then she was on her feet and running.

My tarot card dropped into my lap face down.

CHAPTER 2

glanced over my left shoulder. A Cadillac sedan the color of a clear noon sky cruised slowly behind the row of parked cars. A dark tinted window revealed a thirty-ish white male with a ducktail haircut behind the wheel.

Leni the Leviathan was gone.

The Cadillac continued around the building toward the lot where eighteen-wheelers sat idling. One trailer was loaded with rolls of steel the size of an SUV, another advertised Ding Dongs, and a third promoted Walmart. The Caddy cut between the Ding Dongs and the steel.

Traversing the truck lot would bring the driver full circle around the building. There were plenty of parking spots available, so the only reason to circle was because he was looking for something. Or someone.

I didn't need a private-eye license to figure out that the Caddy had spooked my five-dollar fortune teller. Glass doors let me into a lobby adorned with life-size black and white photos of the raccoons and snakes that inhabited the fine state of Illinois. The men's room was to my left, women's to my right.

No sign of Leni.

I stopped in the men's room and considered the future that the card inside my jacket would predict. I had cash, a loose plan to reach the Pacific Ocean at some point, and no commitments to be anywhere at anytime. Nothing to do and nowhere to be gave me the freedom to improvise. Just like in music, sometimes the improvised parts of life were the most exciting.

I remembered a red-headed hitchhiker who told me her name was Mona. But she lied. Maybe I should hop into my Barracuda and escape while I still had the chance.

But where was the adventure in that?

I paced back and forth in the lobby counting my steps. Then I went outside and paced some more. The women's restroom had an elevated outside window of frosted glass. It was wider than it was tall, and tilted out at a 45-degree angle. The screen covering the opening was torn in the top right corner.

I pulled the card I had chosen from my jacket and looked at its face for the first time. A figure in a red robe held a staff aloft. Or maybe it was a candle burning at both ends. An infinity symbol hovered above his head. A sword and a chalice and a staff and flowers and the words The Magician all appeared on the card.

The Caddy was out of sight. Standing on my toes I held the card up close to the screen in the middle of the window.

"Psst. Leni. You in there?"

The screeching sound of two hard materials that didn't like being rubbing together came through the window. Hands arrived behind the screen.

The hood of the Caddy came into view to my left.

I tucked the card away and spun around to lean casually against the building. I wished for a cigarette to add realism to the scene, even though my experience with smoking was limited to trying to impress girls in bars.

The screen fell out against the tilted window. Metallic crunching accompanied the window folding outward until it was nearly horizontal.

"Wait," I said to the tree ten feet in front of me. "A Cadillac is circling the rest area."

"Bastard."

Not much to go on, but it sounded like Leni.

"I'm leaving to bring my car around. I'll be right back."

The Caddy passed again while I moved my Barracuda as close as possible and still be in the parking lot. Then I went back to the window. It was a good seven or eight feet drop to the ground.

"You ready?" I said.

"For what?" came through the now screen-less window.

"I'm traveling west in search of a fortune teller." I walked over to the tree and leaned against it to get a better view of the Caddy coming around the corner. Based on the first two laps, we had less than a minute to escape.

A bundle appeared on the windowsill.

"Wait," I said, as I stared at metallic blue shining in the morning sun. "Ten seconds." The Caddy flowed toward the two tractor-trailer rigs. "Five seconds."

The Caddy disappeared.

I took three steps to be directly beneath the window.

"Now!"

The bundle tumbled out. I caught it and dropped some kind of padded backpack at my feet. By the time I looked up, Leni's head was poking out the window. She was struggling to wiggle through the opening, still wearing her hooded black poncho. She stretched both arms toward me.

We interlocked the fingers of our hands. I pulled. She slid out the window and came at me head first. I grabbed her around the waist before her head hit the pavement. Her feet found the ground. She stood upright and pulled the hood around her face.

No Caddy.

I grabbed her backpack, put one arm around her, and whispered, "Bronze Plymouth." She buried her face into my shoulder as we walked fast toward my car.

Still no Caddy.

I opened the passenger door, wrangled her inside, and handed her the pack.

"Lean forward and stay low," I said.

I closed the door and looked past the building. The front bumper of the Caddy was coming into view. I forced myself not to run around the front of my car and jump into the driver's seat. Instead, I leaned my backside against the passenger door, obscuring the view inside. Then I lifted my left hand and tapped at my palm with my index finger like someone absorbed in 21st century texting.

The Caddy rolled by, passed between the trucks and out of sight around the far edge of the building.

I moved fast around the front bumper. The Hemi started first try. I pushed in the clutch, slammed into reverse, and backed out. Leni's face was pressed against her knees, the bag between her feet.

"Is west okay?" I said.

The hood nodded. "I can't pay you." Pause. "I already owe you."

We passed the parked trucks. I accelerated toward the highway. Before I reached it the shiny blue Caddy became visible in my rearview mirror. It was pointing straight at us for a brief heart-pounding moment, then it made a hard left to pass between the trucks as it had before.

"That's okay. I'm going west with or without you."

I waited until the Caddy was out of sight, then stomped on the Hemi and flowed into highway traffic.

"Is the coast clear?" Leni said.

"A blue Cadillac is circling the rest stop."

She sat up and pushed her hood back. Her black hair was arranged in a dozen braids, some of which reached her shoulders. Each braid had a brightly colored string woven through it: red, purple, green, pink.

She stared straight ahead.

"You're not one of those gas or ass guys, are you?"

"Do they still exist?" I said.

"Don't take this personally," she said, "but men are pigs."

"You're generalizing."

She didn't turn. What I could see of her expression through her dangling braids hadn't changed.

"Humans categorize to survive. That's how the brain works." She paused again. "So?"

I shook my head. "No charge. That seat and I are going west. Unless my fortune says differently."

She smiled, but not enough to show her teeth.

"I'll finish predicting your future when we can sit still and concentrate."

A smartphone the size of Whopper appeared in her hand. She tapped. Scrolled. Tapped. Smiled broadly showing bright teeth any dentist would be proud of. The flash fired. She tapped some more.

We rolled down the highway with the sun shining through the long rear window of the Barracuda onto my Gibson guitar case and sealed box of vinyl albums that I had collected while being educated as a night-shift radio DJ. I checked the mirrors for a blue Caddy.

"Does it work?" I said.

She turned slowly to face me. I watched the road and stole glances her way. Her dark eyes were calm, but her eyebrows were clenched. She stared.

"Do you mean, is your future in the cards?"

I nodded.

"They have their role," she said.

I changed the subject. "What are you studying in college?"

She faced forward and raised the hood of the poncho.

"What makes you think I'm in college?"

"Young female traveling west from Chicago. No car. No bus. No money. But knows stuff. Like how tarot cards work. And—" I pulled out to pass a Winnebago towing a trailer with a bright red Harley-Davidson on it that gave meaning to the term land-yacht. "Someone is chasing her."

"Are you a cop?"

"Wannabe private eye. But a license is required."

"So what are you?"

"A guy driving to the Pacific Ocean because he felt…" I shrugged.

She turned toward me again. "Adventure?"

"A life-changing one, I hope." I reached between the seats for my aviator shades and slipped them on to emphasize that I only half-knew what I was doing, but was trying to do it boldly.

She pulled out her phone and tapped again. While she was tapping she said, "Meanwhile?"

"Meanwhile, live off the land and take each day as it comes." I checked the mirrors for the Caddy, but saw only the flat white front of the Winnebago.

She pushed her hood down and chewed on her lower lip as she tapped a drum solo on her phone at a hundred beats per minute.

"Sounds fun. It's hot in here."

The temperature seemed just right, but I wasn't wearing a poncho.

"I can turn on the AC. Or maybe your poncho is holding in too much heat."

"Typical guy, trying to get my clothes off." She laughed. I couldn't tell if she was insulted or pleased. But she stuffed her phone into her navy blue pack and wiggled around under the seat belt Chin had installed with the new interior. It was charcoal colored and looked fine against the red leather interior. In 1965, Barracuda's didn't have seatbelts. And certainly not the custom one Grandpa had scored in a story he had never entirely explained.

Leni rolled the poncho around her left arm and tucked it on the floor behind her seat. She was wearing a snug white sleeveless sweater over a white bra. Her breasts would be noticed anywhere. Her jeans had been razored so much that I could see her thighs, strong and lean like a dancer or yoga instructor.

I held one eye on the road and the other on Leni. Her left arm was sleeveless, but her right arm had a sleeve covering half her biceps. The collar on her right side was pulled down over her shoulder.

Unusual design? Didn't seem likely, but I was a long way from being on top of fashion trends.

"Feel better?"

She nodded. "Waterproof clothes make me sweat."

"I thought princesses glowed."

She laughed again. I still couldn't decode what emotion was escaping. The sound was happy, but her demeanor was withdrawn.

"So who wants to know what I study in college?"

I extended my right hand.

"Tommy Cuda, at your service."

She slapped me five and said, "Nice to meet you, Tommy. As you know I am Leni, short for Lenore. I was a college student up until this week. College is really expensive."

"One point seven trillion dollars in student loan debt in the United States supports your observation."

"Trillion?" She blew a stream of air at the windshield. "And I was just thinking about taking out a loan to stay in school."

"What do your tarot cards say?" I grinned.

"You jest, but the suggestions made by the cards can cause a person to take an action that they otherwise wouldn't have."

My speedo had crept up to 90 mph so I eased off.

"And therefore reach a different outcome," I said. "And the victim will claim that the cards had a secret insight."

"Yep."

"Do they?"

"Have insight?" More laughing. "They're pieces of cardboard with ink on them. What do you think?"

"I think you're a psychology major," I said.

She grew quiet for a moment.

"You should get that license. You'll be a good private dick."

I glanced in the rearview.

"Blue Cadillac, half mile back."

She started to turn around. I put my arm between the seats.

"He might see you. Maybe peek out the side view mirror."

She leaned forward and shifted around to get the right angle on the mirror.

"You trying to avoid him?" I asked.

She nodded, eyes glued to the mirror.

"Is he following us?" she said.

The caddy was slowly closing the distance between us.

"Hard to say. He might remember my car from the rest stop. Classic cars stick in people's minds. If they're the kind of people who notice cars. Or, he might have given up the search and headed this way on the assumption that you were also moving west. If we let him pass, he'll see you unless you duck out of sight. If we don't let him pass, he might conclude that we're running from him."

She bent fully forward with her head so low that her knees touched her ears. Maybe she really was a yoga instructor.

I eased my foot off the accelerator a bit to let the Caddy catch us. When it did, I stared straight ahead at the highway as the Caddy pulled out to pass.

"Here he comes," I said.

Leni nodded from between her knees and scrunched into an even smaller ball.

The bright blue hood of the Cadillac pulled alongside. It didn't appear to be in a hurry. Likely he was on cruise control and flowing along thinking about his prey. As his passenger's door approached, I reached for the volume on the radio to block his view of my passenger seat with my shoulders. In case he was curious. In case he remembered me or the Barracuda from the rest stop. He had circled enough times to memorize the entire lot.

A rectangular tag swung from his rearview mirror. Dangerous to block the driver's view out the windshield. But lots of people had been doing it since the days of fuzzy dice.

The Caddy cleared my front bumper. A maroon "Chicago Maroons" decal stretched across the bottom of the rear window. I sat up and recited the Illinois license plate number to Leni, who rummaged in her pack and scribbled it into a notebook with a red dragon on the cover.

His seat back was too high for me to see anything except dark hair that reached the collar of a tan dress shirt. I shifted left in an attempt to see his face reflected in his inside rearview mirror, but the most I got was sunglasses with a black frame.

He hung close in front of us, blowing up my cruise-control theory. That suggested he was examining the interior of my Barracuda for any sign of Leni. Maybe he remembered my car, or maybe he was checking every vehicle he passed.

A long minute later, he accelerated away. I debated how far he would have to get before it was safe for Leni to sit up. All he had to do was recognize that there was now a person in what had been an empty passenger's seat.

"You OK to wait a couple more minutes?" I asked.

CHAPTER 3

I've held this position before," Leni said. "But never in a car." She didn't laugh, although she might have been grinning. Maybe she meant yoga class.

"We could exit," I said. "But he might think that was too much coincidence and backtrack."

The Caddy grew smaller.

I checked my inside rearview. A kid who could barely see over the dash was biting into a candy bar in a white SUV five car-lengths behind us. Probably from a vending machine at the rest stop. Probably something I should have done. The driver was eating a round sandwich with two hands, apparently trusting in self-driving technology to keep the vehicle on the road.

A red truck with a polished chrome grill visible over the roof of the SUV pulled into the left lane, moving fast. As it went by I read, "Bowling Transportation, Fostoria, OH" in white, hand-lettered paint on the passenger door. Turn signals blinked and it pulled in front of us with plenty of room to spare.

"You can sit up," I said. "We have a blocker." There was no way the Caddy driver was going to be able to see through a tractor-trailer rig and two rolls of steel big enough to crush a house.

Leni eased herself upright and stretched her back.

"That's huge," she said.

"I bet you say that to all the truckers."

Leni shook her head, then burst out laughing.

"Sorry," I said. "Something serious is going on. I assume you do not want that Caddy driver to find you."

"Correct."

There was no point in recreating the wheel.

"Do you have a plan?"

"Nope."

"How did you get to the rest stop?"

"Hitchhiked." Leni stared straight ahead. "A gas or ass situation got me tossed out at the rest stop. I was hoping to tell a few fortunes so I wouldn't be broke."

I matched the speed of the steel hauler at a safe distance to keep that mountain in front of us.

"How important is not meeting Mr. Cadillac?"

"At the moment, super very. I don't want to talk to him. I don't want to see him. I want to forget that he exists." She paused. "Even better if he disappeared forever."

On the radio Hambone introduced a new record by Kingfish entitled, "They don't make 'em like they used to." It opened with a bent guitar string screaming for its life.

Leni smiled at her phone, flashed a photo, then went back to tapping.

I said, "To quote Sir Paul, 'I'm a man in the middle of something that he doesn't really understand.'"

Leni's eyes turned toward me. Slowly, like she was scared to look. Her face followed.

"Sir who?"

Working at the Oberlin College radio station had been a voyage through the history of popular music. Most people didn't listen to anything more than a month old.

"It's a line from an old song."

"Was it in a movie?"

I shook my head. "I don't think so."

The steel hauler cruised in the low seventies.

"What don't you understand?" she said.

"I'm in a car with a voodoo girl who tells fortunes. What happens next?"

She faced forward. "I could tell your future."

I pulled The Magician card out of my pocket and handed it to her. "Do you need this?"

"No, but it won't hurt." She took the card and stared at it. "Let me see. You will travel west. Hmm." She turned the card upside down. "You will not be alone." She squinted at the card and hummed a tune I didn't recognize. "You will befriend a companion. She…yes, it is a she…will travel with you for…" She paused. She hummed. "For two full tanks of gas. For which you will not charge her."

"Does the card show where we'll be going?"

She turned it sideways. The magician's head pointed at me. She stopped humming.

"An obstacle blocks your way."

The steel hauler in front of me slowed, so I eased my foot off the gas. A white Mercedes coupe passed on my left doing close to 90.

She rotated the card so the magician's head pointed out her window.

"The view is cloudy beyond the obstacle," she said.

"What can you tell me about the obstacle?"

"It's moving."

"Can you see where it's going?" I said.

She looked out the windshield. The trailer with tons of steel on its back had six license plates.

"I suspect it knows the address where I grew up."

"And that's where you were going before you ran to hide in the ladies room?"

She nodded and said, "Where were you going?"

"Like the card says, west. But I'm not in a hurry. I can spare a couple tanks of gas."

She tucked the card into the middle of the deck, stuffed the deck into her pack, and returned to staring out the windshield. Her shoulders slumped forward. A dark cloud seemed to emanate from her. If we had been in a movie, the music would shift to a minor key.

I followed the six license plates on the trailer, thinking about how to run from a guy who knew where you lived. Maybe knew your family. Friends. Hangouts. Hard to know how deep the knowledge went. Or how hard he would dig.

"Do you have a place to stay in Chicago?" I said.

"A room through the end of the month."

The right blinker on the steel-hauling trailer flashed. I checked my mirror and pulled partway into the left lane to see around the truck.

No Caddy in sight.

Maybe the truck driver was headed to a good place for lunch. I flicked my turn signal on and followed the license plates off the highway and to a diner with rows of fuel pumps. The name "5-Star" blinked in orange neon over a white building.

"Are you hungry?" I said. "I haven't eaten yet today."

"Me neither. But I'm not in the mood."

"I'll get take—"

The truck turned toward the fuel pumps, which gave me a clear view of the parking lot. Three spots to the left of glass doors with '5-Star' painted in yellow across them sat the Cadillac, tangling tag and Maroons included.

It was empty.

Leni ducked. I turned and followed the truck to the parking area for oversized vehicles where I hid my Barracuda between the Bowling steel hauler and a pure white tractor trailer whose long-haired, pale-faced driver was leaning against the rear doors sucking on a blue stick. By the time I turned the engine off, the steel hauler was standing outside my window.

He was over six feet and at least 250 pounds, much of it solid muscle. Tattoos covered his left arm from his wrist to the edge of a black T-shirt with the sleeves cut off. The outline of a Harley-Davidson bar-and-shield logo covered the front of the shirt. But it didn't say "Harley-Davidson." It said, "If you can read this, get out of my way."

I cranked the window halfway down.

"Are you following me?" he said. No hello. No smile.

"Hi. We're using your truck as a blocker so someone doesn't see my friend here."

Leni was leaned forward hugging her knees. She turned her head and smiled.

The guy squinted like the sun was in his eyes but didn't say anything.

"It's a long story that I only know part of. A guy in a blue Cadillac is following her. She doesn't want to talk to him."

The squint turned to a smile. Then he started laughing.

"I've been in a few lover's triangles myself." His eyes flashed to Leni. "She's a pretty one, for sure."

From her leaned forward position, Leni's eyes flashed to his face. Then to my eyes. Then back to his face.

I thought about a book I had found in the public library in Chicago: The Complete Idiot's Guide to Private Investigating. It discussed the pros and cons of carrying a weapon. Thus far, I hadn't acquired one.

The trucker's smile vanished. He walked to the rear of his trailer, scanned the horizon for a few seconds, then returned.

"Only one blue Caddy," he said. He glanced back and forth along the length of my car as if assessing the quality of the paint. "Weird color. What you got in this thing?"

"Hemi," I said.

He nodded knowingly.

"Tell you what. I was on my way to grab lunch. I like to keep the steel rolling while I eat. You skedaddle and make time." He gestured with his head. "When the Caddy tries to pass me later, I'll..." a different sort of smile spread his lips, "discourage him. Give you lovebirds some breathing room."

I looked at Leni, who was looking at me but not saying anything.

"That's mighty kind of you," I said. "Could I buy you lunch?"

"Sure, that'll help my daily budget. The boss watches every damn penny."

I fished a bill out of my pocket and rolled the window all the way down. When he took it, I noticed a smiling sun tattoo on the inside of his wrist.

"This'll buy a lot of lunches," he said. "And dinner and a couple of imported beers."

"We appreciate your help," I said.

Leni nodded and softly said, "Thanks."

"My pleasure, little lady." He moved two fingers of his right hand toward his eyes. "I'll keep an eye on that Caddy."

He dug into a pocket and came out with a pair of wraparound sunglasses with reflective lenses, slipped them on, waved goodbye and headed for the main building.

I started the Hemi.

The trucker turned around and gave me a thumbs up, so I revved the big V8 a couple of times.

His smile grew wider.

Then I dropped the Hurst shifter into gear and we hit the road.

CHAPTER 4

We rolled onto the Interstate. I accelerated to 85, trying to put distance between us and the Caddy while avoiding a visit from the Illinois highway patrol.

"Coast is clear," I said.

Leni sat up. She stared out the windshield at nothing in particular, her eyes tearing.

"There are napkins in the glovebox," I said. "I stash the extra ones from diners."

Her mouth twitched toward a smile.

"You like diners?" she said.

"Key component of the American Dream. Traveling the country by car. See the U-S-A in your Chevrolet. Ride the Mother road."

Leni popped the glovebox open.

"How old are you?"

"A lot younger than this car. My grandfather gave it to me. He had a great appreciation for the way America formed around its highway system."

A roadmap flopped out. Leni dug around and found one of the tiny napkins that Dairy Queens hand out with ice cream cones. She dabbed at her eyes.

"What's a Mad Map?" she said.

"They guide you to the places in the country that will make you angry, rather than the beautiful ones."

Leni looked at me with her mouth slightly open. Her full lips gave me ideas that I kept to myself.

I laughed. "I don't know. I didn't even know it was in there."

"You have a map and don't know it?"

"My friend Chin just put a new interior in this car. Maybe he left it for me."

"Rides of a Lifetime, it says. "Twenty-four hundred classic miles." She looked at me. "Why?"

"Because he knows that I blew out of Ohio to drive my grandfather's classic car to the Pacific Ocean and try to find America along the way."

Leni reached into her backpack and pulled out her phone.

"America, like the rest of the world, is in here," she said.

I flicked my blinker on to pull around two guys in a red Corvette convertible with the top down—an older model, when the engine was still in the front. I knew about the ancient Route 66 TV show, so far back it was broadcast in black and white. I wondered if those guys did. As soon as I pulled in front of them, the Vette's engine roared and it pulled up beside me. I held up my left hand showing three fingers. The blonde guy in the passenger's seat laughed and shouted. I couldn't hear him, but his face was happy.

Two fingers.

One.

I slipped the Hurst down a gear.

No fingers.

I floored the Barracuda, opening up dual four-barrel carburetors into a 426 cubic inch Hemi with a finely tuned exhaust system and custom heads developed by Chrysler in a limited edition run of prototypes way back in the 60s.

I pulled a couple of car lengths ahead.

In short order we were doing 120 mph and the Vette's nose was opposite my shoulder and gaining. I eased off the gas, hoping there wasn't a speed trap ahead and held up a thumb as the Vette flashed past. The guy in the passenger's seat was still laughing.

Leni was breathing like she had just stepped off an inverted roller coaster.

"Boys," she said.

"And their toys," I added.

"Why did you do that?"

"He wanted to race. Probably recognized the exhaust sound and knew there was something fancy under my hood."

"Men are idiots."

"That's a generalization," I said.

"It applies, generally."

I laughed, but not too loud. She had a point.

"We could end up in jail," she said.

I nodded. "Yep. But what you just experienced can't be accessed from your phone."

She looked at me like I was speaking Swahili.

I shrugged. "Maybe we should get off the highway. Just in case there's an airplane tracking us. Do you think your friend in the Caddy will stick with the highway?"

She shrugged and said, "Not my friend."

"When our trucker buddy blocks him, he'll want to make up time," I said. "I'd guess Interstate."

She shrugged again, this time with just the bare shoulder.

I considered for a moment. "Do you want to talk about it?"

She shook her head.

"Do you know where he's going?"

She nodded. "The home address I gave the University."

"How would he?" I stopped my mouth. "Sorry, you don't want to talk about it. Are we going to the same place?"

"I was," Leni said. "But not now." She picked up the Mad Map. "Are you really going to drive all this way?"

"Unless I run out of money."

Leni unfolded the map, held it up with two hands blocking her view out the windshield, and stared at it. Then she lifted her face to gaze out the window at the farmland going by on both sides.

I waited.

Her nose curved up at the tip. Her eyes were moist but she wasn't crying. A row of splotches along the back of her neck glowed red, visible even against her dark skin.

We rode in silence for minutes.

"There," she said, pointing at a green and white road sign. "Two miles to our exit."

Route 53.

I stopped at the end of the exit. Leni pointed. We headed south, hopefully on a road the blue Caddy wouldn't be thinking about.

"Do we have a destination?" I said.

"The Launching Pad."

"What are we launching?"

Leni turned to me and smiled. "Lunch."

I swung into a parking lot beside a two-story high statue of a spaceman holding a rocket. A plaque named him the Gemini Giant. We walked into a brick diner filled with Route 66 signs, patches, cups, and bobble head dolls of the Giant that advertised the diner: "It's Outta of This World." I learned that the Giant was 28 feet tall, made of fiberglass by a company in California, was named for the NASA Gemini space missions, and was originally a muffler salesman before acquiring a space helmet and a rocket.

Mid-morning the diner was empty except for one guy in a black leather jacket having coffee and talking to a waitress wearing a snug silver dress. The dress reached to mid-thigh and had a Launching Pad patch where the NASA logo would be on a spacesuit.

I ordered the Rocket Burger and a chocolate shake: the perfect breakfast. Leni ordered deep fried pizza puffs called Rocket Spheres and a Coke. Then she began to tear a red paper napkin into tiny squares and stack them in front of her on the red Formica table.

I waited for her to start the conversation.

She didn't.

I finally said, "We're in Wilmington, Illinois. Is it on the way to someplace that you want to go?"

She shook her head. "I don't have any place to go." She tore off a piece of napkin and let it flutter onto the pile. "And if I did, I don't have anyone to go there with."

I considered what it might feel like to not have a family member or a friend where you were welcome to rest your head. I didn't like the feeling. A pang of not communicating with my family enough zigged through me.

"Cadillac man is messing things up for you?"

She looked up. Her eyes were moist again. Or still. She shook her head slowly.

"You have no idea."

The waitress arrived with our food. Her silver dress stretched tight and rode up her thighs when she leaned forward to put the plates on the table. She looked at us.

"Do you sell postcards?" I asked.

"Sure do." She pointed to a rotating rack holding something like 100 different cards. "Can sell you stamps for them too."

"Would you choose a dozen for me? Stamps too."

"Who are the Rocket cards targeting?"

"Mom, Dad, high school friends."

She winked and left without bothering to straighten her dress.

The first bite of the Rocket Burger reminded me how long it had been since I'd eaten. Leni was correct, I had no idea what was going on. I started running through in my head what every private eye I had ever read about would do in this situation.

Leni offered me a Rocket Sphere. It was hot and crispy and tasted like a pepperoni pizza genetically modified by a fried chicken.

"Leni, imagine this," I said. "You're a young lady with a problem. You have a stack of money in your backpack. You walk into the office of a professional investigator," I pointed at myself. "What would you want me to do?"

"Turn back time," she said.

I nodded. Clearly a solid clue something bad had happened.

"Let's say this isn't science fiction. What else?"

"Kill him."

I choked a little on my milkshake. But I was getting calibrated.

"Private investigators investigate. I don't think they assassinate people."

"They should. It would solve a lot of problems."

She was probably right. But that wasn't how the law worked.

"Is there a third choice?" I said.

She rotated a Sphere around and around, examining it from all sides before popping it into her mouth.

"Revenge," she said.

I took a big bite of my burger to buy time to think. Payback, rage, revenge, wrath, whatever you called it, was a prime mover behind a great deal of human activity, maybe even a majority of it. Along with the other six deadly sins.

"Do you have something specific in mind?" I said.

She shook her head while sipping Coke and examining another Sphere.

"Not yet."

I compared the inside of my burger to a Frisch's Big Boy layer by layer. The Rocket was thicker and juicer. And the sauce was flame orange instead of creamy white.

"Would you like to go back to Chicago?" I said.

Leni looked away from her food and directly at me.

"He'll be there."

I debated between burger and shake. Getting the right mix was important.

"What will happen?"

"He'll find me. Tell me I'm acting like an overly sensitive little girl. What's one more time? We were meant to be together. How much he loves me. All that patronizing romantic claptrap men spew when they have a hard-on."

"Mansplaining the situation since you clearly don't understand it?"

She smiled ever so slightly. "Right."

"What if he can't find you?"

She shrugged that bare shoulder.

"I can't attend classes. So why be in Chicago?"

I could think of several good cultural reasons to be in Chicago, including a club called the Pink Monkey. But none of them would help Leni or move me closer to the Pacific.

"How about attending remotely?"

She shrugged again. "Why stay in Chicago to stare at a computer?"

"We could stalk Cadillac man," I said. An idea squirreled its way into my head. Chin would know how to do it. And Chin was in Chicago.

Her lips pursed and shifted as she thought.

"Why?" she said.

"Revenge."

Her smile grew a bit larger.

"Why would you help me?"

She couldn't pay me. It would likely take me in the wrong compass direction. And I had no idea what her problem was.

"It's in the cards," I said.

CHAPTER 5

"I can't go home," Leni said.

"But you want to?" I said.

She nodded, said nothing.

"We can't go there because…"

"He'll find me."

"You don't have to talk to him."

"Then he'll talk to my mother. And tell her lies. And she'll push me to go back."

I cruised the Barracuda along at 66 mph in honor of our Route. The Rocket postcards with hand applied stamps were lying on the back seat in a white bag with the Gemini Giant printed on it.

"Has Mom met Mr. Cadillac before?"

Leni shook her head as she tapped out messages on her phone, which she had been doing on and off since we left The Launching Pad. Sometimes she would smile and take a selfie. I figured she had lots of friends who all lived through their phones like my friends back in Ohio. I was alone in concluding that a device on your person that could interrupt you at any time was a horrible idea. Like a doggy shock collar where anyone with your phone number had a button.

"Why would your mother listen to a stranger?"

Leni looked at me quizzically.

"You ever been to a doctor?" she said.

"Sure, when I was born."

She shook her head but didn't laugh.

"Okay, for vaccinations. Blood work. Annual physical. All that stuff."

"The first time you met him or her. Were you strangers?"

"For sure. Feels weird to have someone of the opposite sex touch you that you've never met before."

"Yet you trusted her?"

"As far as I trust anyone in the medical profession."

She laughed. "Yeah, I get that. Okay, so why did you trust her?"

"She's a doctor. She knows stuff that I don't. I depend on her to explain my body to me."

"That's why my mother would listen to a stranger."

"Mr. Cadillac is a doctor?"

"Of sorts," Leni said.

I pulled off the road onto a gravel lot of the oldest gas station I had ever seen. A lone pump beneath a Standard Oil Company sign sat in the shade of a gray shingled canopy. The glass top actually held gas.

"We need gas?" Leni said.

"Nope. I just want to see the history of this road. Not sure this place even sells gas anymore."

I parked the Barracuda in front of the pump and walked around the tiny building. Built in 1932. Two work bays had been added later, but it was still small. It had been Standard Oil, then Phillips 66, and Sinclair, and now Standard again.

Leni walked around and pointed her phone here and there. I wondered if she saw anything or just took pictures.

I read a document in the window.

"This place was modeled after a station in Ohio," I said. "It's made like a house to make customers feel comfortable." I studied a black and white photo of the station in its heyday. There were six people posed in front of the pump; some of them looked to be about about my age. I wondered where their lives had led.

Leni was out of sight.

I started the car and revved the Hemi. In a few seconds she came trotting around the corner of the work bays and slipped into the passenger's seat. Gravel crunched as we rolled out of the lot.

"That place is almost a hundred years old," she said.

"Feels weird thinking about how much has changed," I said.

"And keeps changing. Humans must adapt."

I glanced her way. She was completely serious.

"Adapt?"

"Of course. Our environment keeps changing whether we like it or not." She appraised me and her face implied that I wasn't getting a passing grade. "Look at you. No smartphone. No Apple CarPlay. No Bluetooth anything. How can you even function?"

"I eat. Sleep. Burn gasoline in my machine. I get by."

I sounded defensive. What was I defending?

"That's barely survival. How are you going to thrive in the coming world of virtual reality? Don't you read Meta's advertising? Have you even heard of AI?"

I was thinking about experiencing a historic road to the ocean and Leni was dreaming of spaceships in the Matrix.

"Do I need to thrive?"

"Only if you want to eat, sleep, and drive your gas guzzling machine."

I laughed.

"What's funny?"

"Nothing," I said. "You sure are serious about Meta's fantasy."

"Pisses me off that people are so cavalier about our society. Humongous changes fall on us just because some dweeb in California has a techno wet dream."

"I thought you liked technology?"

She squinted at me.

"I said 'humans must adapt.'" She grew quiet for a moment, then spoke softly. "Like I'm trying to adapt moving from a teeny town in Missouri to a major competitive private university in the big bad town of Chicago."

I had just spent some crazy weeks in Chicago myself. I wasn't sure if I had adapted or barely survived.

"So Mom's place is out. What's our second choice?" I said.

"Suicide."

The car was filled with engine rumble and tire whine and wind noise. But it felt eerily quiet.

"Seems a bit final. What if you don't like it?"

Her eyes drifted toward me, their darkness becoming a deep shocking blue in the sunshine. Her face had no expression. Then she burst out laughing until she was in tears. I couldn't tell what was causing them. When she finally calmed herself she turned back to the windshield.

"You're supposed to tell me I shouldn't think such things. How horrible it is to contemplate the end of my existence. Intervene. Instead, you ask me what happens if I don't like it?" She shook her head. "Fresh approach."

I shrugged. "You're young and beautiful and in college. You have a lot of life to enjoy. Why end it over a 'sort of' doctor?"

"You're right. He ain't worth it."

"Good attitude."

"But..." she said.

I waited. The tires rolled. Fuel disappeared at about twelve miles per gallon.

"It's not okay," she said.

"Will revenge make it okay?"

"It'll make it better. Not sure it will ever be okay."

"Only one way to find out," I said.

She leaned her head against the back of the red leather seat and stared at the tan headliner.

"That's how life works, doesn't it?" she said. "You have to try things to see how they turn out."

"I believe that idea was at the heart of the Enlightenment: Knowledge comes only from observation." I checked the rearview for the hundredth time. Still no Cadillac.

"You a science geek?" she said.

"I was thinking about music."

She reached over and flipped the radio on. Then fiddled with the tuner until she found electronic dance music. She rocked forward and back with the throbbing bass. We rode without speaking. I went through the options she had outlined in my head and didn't come up with a good idea.

"How long will this guy stalk you?"

"Probably forever. I remind him of someone 'special' in his life. I'm like no one else he has ever met. We are meant for each other. Unquote."

"So we can't just lay low for a few weeks and then sneak back to Chicago?"

She shook her head aimlessly.

"He'll find me fast. He has spies all over campus."

"Can we hide someplace until we come up with a plan?"

"We?" she said.

"I'm curious."

"Remember that cat," she said. She was quiet for almost a mile. Then, "I can't pay you. But I know a place." She tapped a message into her phone and stared at it. We drove a couple of more miles. Her phone beeped. She turned to me and smiled. "Got a place we can crash that Mister 'I need you in my life' doesn't know about."

"So now we avoid spies?" I said.

"I don't think he has any this far from Chicago."

CHAPTER 6

eni's head lay wedged between the seat's back and the window as she slept. I drove with the radio off, listening to tires hum and the Hemi throb as we wound our way along less than perfect blacktop toward St. Louis. As I passed the city limits for yet another small town I had never heard of, something conjured her awake. With sleepy eyes, two yawns, and a pointed finger she directed me along streets that grew narrower and narrower for almost three miles.

"That one," Leni said.

The two-story house of white brick hadn't seen fresh paint in a decade. Except for the front door, whose gloss black finish reflected like a pond at midnight. There was no driveway so I parked on the street in a black-hole shadow directly beneath a failed street lamp. A tree with Mardi Gras beads hanging amongst sparse leaves on scrawny limbs stood between us and the black door.

The white house was shoulder to shoulder on one side with a similar house painted pale blue. On its other side a narrow dirt path disappeared behind a rust-spotted iron gate. Both houses had a small front yard paved diagonally with gray bricks. Two wooden steps, also painted white long ago, led to the shiny front door. Beside the steps a two-foot bronze chimpanzee contemplated a bone white human skull in its right hand.

Leni knocked.

The door was opened by a tall, slender black guy wearing round John Lennon glasses with matte black frames. His hair was brush-bristle short. He matched the door: jeans, loafers, tight T-shirt. Except for a silver smartwatch with a gray band. And a splash of color from a half-dollar sized padlock dangling from a gold chain around his neck. A single stone at the center of the lock could have been a diamond. An engraving might have been a fire breathing dragon.

"Lenore," he said. "Been months, girl. You're looking good."

They hugged for half a minute, Leni's backpack dangling from one hand. They unclenched.

"Prof, this is my new friend Tommy. We met on the road."

We shook hands. His grip was firm but gentle, like he was holding something that might break.

"Is that Prof, like a prophet predicting the future?" I said.

He shook his head and smiled.

"Most people guess professor."

"I figured a guy with a polished black door wouldn't be so predictable."

His smile held. He stepped aside and gestured for us to step into the house.

"The name is for Profit, king of capitalism. People consider it a dirty word, as if making money from an endeavor taints it with evil."

"They often travel together," I said.

"Love of money," Prof said.

"Is the root of all evil," I finished for him.

He smiled. "Leni knows she is always welcome. Follow me."

Prof led us to a living room that was dimly lit even by dead streetlight standards. Most of the light came from three, curved, panoramic computer displays arranged on a silver desk in a twenty-foot semicircle. A black and white gaming chair sat at their center. A black couch lined one wall.

"Command central," he said.

"What do you command, a Starship?" I asked.

Leni shook her head.

"Have a seat," he said.

Leni sat on one end of the couch. I took the other. Prof spun the gaming chair around and settled into it.

"Does your mother know you're back in town?" Prof asked.

No small talk. If Leni was at his house, something wasn't quite right.

Leni shook her head. "Just got into town." She glanced at me and back to Prof. "I have a little problem."

"At least it's little," he said.

Leni sighed.

"Okay," Prof said. "How can I help?"

Leni's face scrunched like she had just heard bad news.

"Do you have room for us to hide here for awhile?"

"I can get a hotel," I said.

Leni turned toward me. "Then I won't have a chauffeur."

Prof laughed.

"I'll be available." I grinned.

"But how will I reach you?"

She had a point.

Prof waved his hand. "I have room for both of you. I live on this floor. There's a bath and three rooms upstairs. One of them is storage, but the other two are inhabitable."

"Thanks," Leni said softly.

Prof's dark eyes were gentle, but alive with the look of a guy playing a championship chess match.

"Should I ask?" he said.

Leni looked at her sandals. The nails on her big toes were painted white. The other nails were light blue. She was quiet for a long time, then shook her head slowly.

"I…I'm not ready to talk about it," she said.

"Whatever it is, better if your Mom's not involved?"

She nodded.

The room was quiet. A fireplace in the back wall held flickering flames behind glass but made no sound. White curtains covered all of the windows. The only color in the room besides the computer screens was an embroidered rug on the floor. It was gray with a green and gold dragon standing on the Earth staring up at me.

"I work a lot," Prof said. "Come and go as you please. I'm a lousy host."

"Thanks," Leni said.

"That's a lot of computing power. What do you do?" I asked.

"I have three jobs at the moment."

"Any you can talk about?" I said.

He half-smiled. "I work for Meta Corporation."

"Zuckerworld?"

He grinned. "Yeah. Facebook, Instagram, etcetera."

I surveyed the panoramic landscape across his desk. The only people I knew with setups like that were…

"Virtual Reality development?"

"Nope. Care to guess again?"

"With that much glass? You must need to see something important."

"Content moderator," he said.

"No!" Leni said. "Is that what you do with that huge computer?"

"It's actually three computers and I switch between them."

"And you use three so they don't contaminate each other," I said. "Like keeping utensils for raw meat separate from everything else."

Prof laughed. "Exactly."

Leni said, "We read an article in class about moderators. You can get PTSD from that job."

"Some people might. But I have tricks. Plus," he paused. "I'm me."

"I almost forgot," Leni said, and laughed. It sounded genuine. Maybe it helped her forget her troubles for a few seconds.

Prof swiveled his chair to face me. "I'm an outlier on most any statistical analysis you care to do. I played chess. Was a bit of a prodigy. Won a few bucks. School bored me. Dropped out. Focused on being an autodidact. Got inspired by Zuckerberg reading a book a week. Figured I would need more to succeed, so I read two. Learned to speed read, both text and video. Started my own company."

"I didn't know it was possible to speed-read video," I said.

"Couple ways to do it. Easiest is to speed up playback but keep the audio at the same pitch. Lots of apps can do that now. So I can review two, three times the video of someone running at standard speed."

"And not miss anything?"

"Nothing important. A moderator simply classifies content: harmful, not harmful. Once you memorize Meta's rulebook, it's straightforward. Another way to do it is to only show every tenth frame. Then I'm ten times faster. Still don't miss much."

"I'm betting you get paid per review."

Prof smiled. "Sort of. Another secret."

I had a guess he was paid by volume, but let it pass.

"And you speed read?"

"Only way I don't get bored," he said. "One thing I like about text. When the information content slows down, I simply read faster. That's where I got the idea for the high-speed review of video."

"And you're always in a hurry," Leni said.

He shook his head. "I'm never in a hurry. I'm efficient. I force the world to move at exactly the pace I want."

"Moderator is one of your three jobs?" I said.

"Yeah. The one I report to the IRS." He laughed and spun his chair in a full circle and arrived back holding a silver glass with a black lid and a straw in his hand. He sipped. "Can I get you two anything? Eat, drink? Have you had dinner?"

"We ate at The Launching Pad. I don't know if I need to eat again for a week," Leni said.

Voices reached us from the street.

Prof went to the window and parted a curtain with one finger.

"Are you driving a turd-brown heap?" he asked.

"Turbo bronze metallic. Sixty-five Plymouth," I said.

"Couple guys are interested in it."

Leni ran to the window and peeked around the curtain.

"Damn." She didn't elaborate.

"Damn?" I said.

"If they see me, they'll tell my little brother."

"And then your mother will find out," I said. "And she will want to know why you haven't visited."

"She'll ask questions. She doesn't trust me."

I knew better than to go down that path.

Prof stroked his chin with long, thin fingers: a guy thinking about a chess move.

"They might steal it," he said.

"Not good. First, it's not an automatic and the Hurst shifter is finicky. Second, my guitar and records are in the back."

"Those they can pawn."

I hopped off the couch and headed for the front door.

"Tommy," Leni called from behind me.

A guy wearing a green satin jacket with a team logo on the back that I didn't recognize had his palms flat on the roof as he stared in through the passenger window. A second guy, almost invisible in a black hoodie and black jeans, was leaning over the rear window without touching the car. The cool evening air found my spine.

"Hey, guys. How do you like it?"

They jerked upright, like they had been doing something wrong and the teacher had entered the room. The guy in the green jacket spoke.

"Shoulda known this was a white guy's ride. Ain't much to look at."

"Original paint," I said.

He looked at the car, then back at me.

"Maybe looks better in daylight," he said.

The other guy laughed. "Hard to look worse."

"Turbo bronze metallic is an acquired taste," I said. "I didn't choose it, my grandfather willed the car to me."

"How old is this junk?"

First guy again. He was facing me now so I couldn't see the logo on the back of his jacket.

"Sixty-five. But the red leather is newer." An image from Chin's garage of my car with the seats stripped out intruded. "Had a little fire in Chicago that destroyed the interior."

The guy in the hoodie actually looked interested.

"Electrical failure?"

I shook my head. "Security failure. Some boys thought I had booty stashed in the doors. When they didn't find it, they torched it."

He shook his head. "You pissed them off."

"By accident," I said. "I was…helping out a friend."

"Must have been a good friend," guy in the green jacket said.

"Her name's Mona."

They smiled. All guys understood doing stupid stuff for pussy. I walked around the front bumper to the driver's door and placed both hands on the roof where they could see them. No threat.

Guy by the rear bumper said, "Guitar case."

I nodded. "Gibson. I play blues."

"Kind of oxymoronic," Jacket said.

I smiled. "Yeah. White guy trying to channel Robert Johnson and B.B. King. But it's great music. And it gets inside of you."

"Appropriating culture," he said. "Like Elvis did."

"Just absorbing America, past and present. You think Elvis couldn't sing the blues?"

"Oh, he could sing it all right. But he stole it all from black folks."

"You mean the way black folks stole fried chicken."

They looked surprised. Not mean. Not angry. Just surprised.

"Scots liked to cook their chicken in fat. Scots came to the East Coast. African-Americans borrowed the method but brought their magical spices to the party and voila, the incredible, crispy treat we enjoy today."

"Ain't no way," Hoodie said.

I nodded. "Check it out. Cultures mix and influence and blend and evolve. Sort of like making a good cocktail."

"Still stole it," Jacket said.

"Elvis was clearly influenced by what he heard in Memphis. Anyone would be. How could a musician as talented as Elvis not be influenced by all that great music?"

"Ain't right," Jacket said.

I shrugged. "Let me ask you something. Do you think the integration that exists in the music industry today would have happened as fast, or at all, without Elvis?" I straightened. I loved history. And studied a lot of it in college. Almost majored in it. Still read about it. It excited me to see where things came from. "Or better yet, do you think rock and roll would have happened without 'That's all right, Momma?'"

They both grinned at me.

"Hell of a song," Hoodie said. "Written by a black guy."

"Yeah, Arthur Crudup, who some consider the Father of Rock and Roll. Who lifted the lyrics from Blind Lemon Jefferson. Might have been the first ever guitar solo. Look what happened there."

They both stayed quiet.

"Blending," Hoodie said.

I nodded vigorously. "Information wants to flow. Music is information. Hell, culture is information."

They met my eyes for a second.

"So what's up with this junker?" Jacket asked.

"Grandfather's ride. He always wanted to drive Route 66. Got married, had my mom, worked. Never had the chance."

"So you're doing it for him?"

I nodded solemnly. Knew I wouldn't be doing this trip without my grandfather's dream. Grandpa was right, there was adventure on the road.

Hoodie squatted near the rear bumper.

"What's with these tires, man? They like twice as wide as mine."

"Lotta horsepower. Need to get it to the ground," I said.

Jacket spread his arms wide.

"In this tin tub? It's as aerodynamic as a coffin."

"Four-twenty-six Hemi. Dual four-barrel Hollies. Hurst shifter. Positive differential. Blueprinted. Hot cams. Chrysler only made a handful of them."

Jacket whistled.

Hoodie laughed and said, "You could run moonshine in this thing."

"You got a name?" Jacket asked.

"Tommy Cuda."

"Jake," Jacket said. He gestured toward his colleague. "Ramone. What you doing on our turf?"

I nodded toward the house.

"Staying with Prof. We're working on a project."

They nodded knowingly. Apparently Prof had worked with white guys before. And it was okay.

"What's in that box?" Ramone said, pointing through the rear glass.

"You won't believe me," I said, smiling. I waited a couple of beats. "Vinyl records."

They looked at each other and shook their heads.

"You a time traveler," Jake said. "Going backwards." He reached inside his jacket, pulled his hand out and slapped the corner of my windshield. Then he gave me a small salute and walked away. Ramone followed him without a word.

I walked around the front bumper. A black oval sticker occupied the corner of the windshield. A white circle the size of a dime sat in the center. The image of a silver chain ran around the outside edge. I stared at it. I turned to look after Jake and Ramone. They were specks in the distance, strolling along as if they didn't have a care in the world.

Prof would know.

CHAPTER 7

I was lying awake upstairs at Prof's house in the back bedroom. Four in the morning, feeling restless, thinking about that piece of cardboard with Magician printed on it. Strange day. New bed. New people. New neighborhood with new sounds. Moonlight coming through the window made the room feel like something mysterious was about to happen. I got up for no particular reason except to feel my body move. Stood by the window. My Barracuda sat directly below beside a weathered garden shack. A narrow, gravel alley passed behind the house. The chattering of insects filled the night. I listened to my own breathing. The blue Cadillac weighed on my mind. I thought about cultural appropriation, melding, integration, influence, inspiration and where it all came from. I wondered why Mr. Crudup never got the royalties owed to him for recording all of that great music.

Unloading the Barracuda—guitar, records, clothes—had revealed a trapdoor in the floor beneath the long rear glass window. I hadn't found a way to unlock it yet.

A huffing sound rose above the insects.

I stepped into my jeans, crossed the hardwood floor barefoot and eased the door to the bedroom open. The sound grew louder. I stepped into the hallway. The bathroom was to my left. Leni's room was at the far end of the hall.

The huffing became moaning. Or sobbing. If Leni were lying awake crying, would she want me to comfort her? The floor creaked with each footstep. I stopped outside her door.

A buzz sounded like a huge bee. Or hummingbird.

Then moaning. Definitely moaning.

I wondered how well Leni knew Prof.

Not my business.

I headed back to my room. The floor creaked. A clicking noise cut through the insects. I stood still and listened to the recognizable rhythm of a fast typist.

I made my way to the stairs, stayed to one side to minimize creaking, went down half a dozen steps, and squatted. Prof was sitting at his panoramic workstation wearing a pair of chrome headphones and typing away at the center keyboard. Rows of numbers on the screen shifted and scrolled like the missile control screens in war movies.

Prof wasn't with Leni.

The keyboard clicked. The voice moaned. The hummingbird hummed. Insects chattered outside. I went back to bed and closed my eyes and imagined what it must have been like to be in that tiny studio in Memphis when a nineteen-year-old Elvis was laying down "It's All Right, Mama."

What felt like only minutes later a broad stripe of sunshine was warming the bed and arguing birds had replaced insects. As I lay there letting my brain defrost, the sun disappeared behind a cloud and a quiet sigh made me aware that Leni was under the blanket and curled up along my right side. The head of a stuffed turtle stuck out from beneath the blanket and touched her nose.

Had I seen that turtle before? Maybe. An object had been dangling from her backpack when it came out the restroom window. I hadn't realized it was a turtle. I eased out of bed and snuck to the bathroom where I showered and shaved and put on a fresh T-shirt with a Fender amplifier silkscreened on the back.

I peeked into my room. Leni was still hugging the turtle. The sun hadn't come back.

The stairs creaked as I descended. Prof was standing barefoot in the kitchen scrambling eggs and sipping orange juice. He was wearing black sweatpants and a matching T-shirt with a logo on the left breast I didn't recognize. He was hunched over the stove, moving slowly. Like maybe he hadn't been to bed since I saw him typing.

"Welcome to a new day," he said.

The kitchen was organized like a buffet brunch: utensils and plates at one end, knives and cutting boards standing in an orderly fashion on a separate counter. The cupboards were white, the floor was gray tile. The only color in the room were the yellow eggs.

"Good morning," I said. "You sure look organized."

"The five Esses of Lean Manufacturing," he said. "Sort, set in order, shine, standardize, sustain. They sound more impressive in Japanese."

"Lean Manufacturing?"

He nodded. "A system for identifying and eliminating waste. I apply it to my life so I can get the most done with my allotted time on this planet. People who are fond of silly 'life-hacks' should study the system. The most important one is standardize. Doing a thing the same way each time pays huge dividends over time."

"Do you mean like, build good habits?" I said.

His head bobbed. "Build any habit at all, even a bad one. Once you have a habit established, you can Kaizen it until you're satisfied with the result."

"More lean manufacturing?" I said.

"Oh yes. Lean is a deep philosophy based on Buddhist principles. It has applications far beyond manufacturing."

I looked around. There wasn't a dirty dish in sight.

"You use this in your kitchen?"

Prof moved the eggs around in the pan.

"For sure. Tools. Shining. Efficiency. It's a perfect testbed." He wagged his head at the endless opportunities.

"Seems stressful," I said.

"Au contraire. Stress is caused by…" he waited.

"Um…other people," I said.

Prof turned to me and smiled. "As is hell. Sartre. No, stress is caused by expectations. I must do this. I have to finish that. Yet…" Prof swirled the eggs and dumped them onto a plate beside two pieces of nearly burnt toast. "It is not the expectations themselves. It is the uncertainty around our ability to meet them that creates stress."

"Do you mean," I said, "that if I have a habit I know will deliver results, then I can predict the future?"

"And stress vaporizes like the morning mist," Prof said. "Control is everything. Without control, life is…" He looked at me while holding the pan in one hand and the spatula in the other.

"Chaos?" I said.

"You're smarter than your car makes you look. Would you like some eggs?"

"I'd like whatever you got. And please allow me to contribute to the grocery kitty."

Prof shook his head. "Not necessary. Start with these. I'll keep the griddle warm." He placed a white plate imprinted with a leafless tree in winter on the table and returned to the stove. I found a glass in the cupboard, orange juice in the fridge, and sat down to butter the toast.

"I'll wait for you," I said.

"No way. The eggs will get cold. Eat while the eaten's good. I'll join you in a few minutes."

He popped two pieces of bread into a gleaming white and chrome toaster, checked that the dial was at maximum, and pushed the lever.

"Thanks for letting me stay here last night."

"Any friend of Leni's," he said. "I look forward to hearing about your adventures."

I tasted the eggs: fluffy and smooth.

"Leni knows more than I do. But I have a question. After I talked to Jake and Ramone yesterday, Jake put a sticker on my windshield."

Prof turned to face me. His blank expression seemed to hide surprise. "An ellipse," he said. "Circle in the middle." He motioned with his index finger. "Chain border?"

"You've seen this before."

"Gang calling themselves the Eye Chain. Wordplay on the I Ching, one of the five classics of Confucianism."

"Jake and Ramone read Confucius?" I said.

He laughed. "Jake fancies himself a Buddhist."

"I bet there's a story there."

Prof stirred the eggs. Two pieces of nearly black toast popped up from the toaster.

"One guess," he said.

"A young, strong guy seeking the way. Either a bad LSD trip or," Prof turned toward me, our eyes met, "he met a woman."

Prof laughed. "The two have similarities, don't they?" He continued laughing. "Or maybe he met a woman during a bad trip?"

"I think he met a woman who talked Buddhism, got interested in both, and one day saw how to apply the 'Four Noble Truths' to a gang."

Prof paused his spatula. "Interesting to think about reincarnation and a bunch of hoodlums carrying semi-automatic weapons, isn't it?"

"And a little scary. Any idea why Jake put that sticker on my car?"

Prof watched the eggs. "He adopted you. No one in this neighborhood will touch you or your car once they see that sticker."

I thought back. Would Jake consider his becoming a Buddhist cultural appropriation? I tried to put one and one together from our conversation beside my car.

"Is Jake a musician?" I asked.

"You bet. Crazy fast drummer. He has lightning reflexes, and man can he transfer them to the skins."

"Transfer what?" Leni said, as she drifted into the kitchen unannounced.

"We're talking about Jake's drumming," I said.

Her lopsided hair dangled over dark slits of eyes. The colored ribbons and braids were gone. A black T-shirt with the same logo as Prof's draped to mid-thigh. She was barefoot. What showed of her legs could win a Miss Illinois pageant.

"Jake's an animal," she said, and placed her stuffed turtle on the table at the chair opposite me. The turtle's beady black eyes seemed to evaluate me.

"You hungry?" Prof said.

Leni looked at my plate.

"What did you do to the toast?" she said.

"I carbonize it," Prof said.

"Does that contribute to global warming or reduce it?" she said.

I laughed.

"It's carbon neutral," he said.

"You got cheese?"

"Bottom drawer of the fridge. Is scrambled okay?"

Leni nodded and plodded toward the fridge. She came back with an unopened block of white cheddar and a brown bottle of Sierra Nevada Hoptimum. Handcrafted in Chico, California according to the label. She twisted off the top.

"You going to eat both of those charcoals?" she asked.

I pushed my plate across to her. She glanced back and forth between the two and took the one that was five percent lighter.

"Thanks."

"Courtesy of Prof," I said.

Leni carefully sliced the cheese with a butter knife and place strips across her toast.

"Why so dark?" she said.

"I like crispy," Prof said.

Leni bit through the cheese and toast. "They are that," she said with her mouth full. Leni chased the cheese toast with beer. Prof stirred eggs. I chewed. The toast was indeed crunchy.

"How did you sleep?" I said.

She looked directly into my eyes. "What do you think?"

"Bumpy night?"

"Stalker. Too many people wanting stuff. Then I got…" She hesitated for a few seconds. "Cold."

I nodded, wondering if cold was code for lonely or scared. I ate some eggs. Prof filled a fresh plate with eggs and black toast, grabbed his orange juice, and came over to join us.

"The motherfucker raped me," Leni said flatly.

My fork froze mid-air.

Prof stopped mid-stride.

I started to ask "Are you okay?" but stopped myself. Of course she wasn't okay. While I was trying to figure out the right words, Prof jumped in.

"At the university?"

Good guess. Leni was a student and rape was nearly a national pastime on college campuses. The feds had even passed Title IX to force colleges to pay better attention.

Leni nodded.

Prof moved in slow motion to a chair. The kitchen suddenly felt big and empty, like a cathedral. Or courtroom.

"The Eye Chain will take care of him for you," Prof said.

Leni shook her head slowly as if hypnotized.

"No?" he said.

She continued shaking. "It's very complicated."

"When?" I said.

Her eyes moved toward me. Dampness made the deep blue almost black.

"Yesterday morning."

I had met her yesterday morning. Perhaps only hours after…

"That's why he's chasing you?"

She nodded. "One reason."

"So you came here," Prof said. Not quite a question.

She nodded.

I stacked some eggs on toast and stole a piece of cheese and put it on top. Took a bite. Prof forked eggs into his mouth and bit into the toast. The crunch was audible. Leni sipped her Hoptimum beer.

"He's angry with me," she said.

I choked. "Shouldn't it be the other way around?"

"I'm pissed too. I reported it."

I waited. She didn't elaborate.

"To the university?" I said.

She nodded.

"Does he know this?" Prof asked.

She shrugged.

"Ah, he wants to know what you did," Prof said. "Did you name him?"

Leni looked to Prof and then to me and back to Prof.

"Not yet. They told me I could name him later and the DNA would prove it." Leni ate her cheese bread. Prof and I ate our eggs. I drank some orange juice.

"Test kit?" Prof asked.

"Sort of," Leni said.

CHAPTER 8

Leni hadn't wanted to talk about it. Not the event, the kit, next steps, nothing. So we finished breakfast discussing Prof's job guarding social networks and how what most people considered extreme behavior online was really more like "baby, you ain't seen nothin' yet." Then Leni's eyes started to close and she wandered upstairs for a nap.

I went out back behind the house and opened the trunk. What looked like a trapdoor in the trunk floor sat beside the spare tire well. Two hinges across the top were nearly hidden by the thick tan carpet Chin had installed with the new red leather seats. There was no visible lock, or pull strap, or button along the side. Nothing at all. I pressed down on the door to see if it would pop up and release. No reaction.

I needed to think like a master mechanic moving quickly to finish a project. But why would Chin install a door at all? There wasn't much space under the floor; the gas tank and spare tire were in the way. Secret storage? For what?

Cash would be a good guess.

I already had my cash strategically distributed: pocket of my jeans, pocket of my leather jacket, guitar case, glovebox, luggage. Even a few hundred under the driver's side floor mat. I fingered the two metal keys for the Barracuda. The ignition was too far away. The only other keyholes were the two doors, also distant, and the trunk.

I closed the lid and inserted the second key. A quarter turn to the right popped the lock and the lid released. I held the key turned, lifted the lid, and reached inside. The trapdoor wouldn't budge. I straightened the key. Before a fluke impulse made me rotate the key to the left. I hadn't expected it to turn that way. But it did. And the trapdoor popped up a quarter inch.

"Chin, my friend, how do you come up with this stuff?"

Chin was back in Chicago. Probably lying under a car in his repair garage. He didn't hear me. No one else was around to hear me either.

I removed the key and slipped the double six ring into my jeans. It had been my grandfather's too. Each six held a key. The key ring itself held a dream. And a perspective on America. What it is. What it means. What it can mean. I checked the alley; no one in sight. I eased the trapdoor upright and let it rest against the security board between the trunk and the back seat.

I shook my head.

Chin, Chin, Chin. A Pioneer direct-drive turntable hovered just below the floor of the trunk. The inside of the door had an aluminum plate engraved with the words "Now Playing." A chrome trough held an album upright. The album clipped in the trough was named Blue China. Three guys stared unsmiling directly into the camera. They looked like angry martial artists, except one was holding a silver Stratocaster. They called themselves DragonZone. One word.

I slipped the album out of the cover. It was bright red vinyl with a gold label. The first song was titled "Silk Road Blues." I put it on the turntable and dropped the needle.

And heard nothing.

A brief search revealed audio controls along the right side of the turntable. Cranking the volume woke up speakers embedded in the trunk lid. They drove sound outward into the alley.

The drummer opened with a simple shuffle, except that it would completely skip a beat now and then, like a motorcycle trying to start, but failing. The guitar player, from the "more notes are better" school of playing, was super fast, and precise. The vocal was in Chinese, or what I thought might be Chinese, and sung in a mumbling style that made me think that there had been some bad times along that Silk Road.

"What you doin'?"

Leni appeared beside the rear fender of the Barracuda. She was again wearing a logo T-shirt as a dress, but this one was dark blue. She was still barefoot.

"Listening to records," I said. "How was your nap?"

She looked into the trunk and stared at the word DragonZone spinning round and round at the center of the record.

"Couldn't sleep. You must be a lot older than you look."

I laughed. "Boatloads of people listen to vinyl. The format is making a comeback."

"In their cars?"

"Sure. Why not spin vinyl at tailgate parties?"

She shook her head.

The sky was the gray of old concrete. The absence of sun kept the temperature around 65. I was comfortable without a jacket, but Leni wasn't wearing much. We listened to DragonZone for two songs. They were quite skilled and would occasionally morph to a bridge straight out of Shanghai with monster bends and plucked strings at the speed of light. I thought about a group of Asian guys playing instruments designed in Southern California, land of white-boy surfers who had borrowed the sport from native Hawaiians. The Stratocaster had been designed over half a century ago, and was now being used to play music invented by African-Americans, but twisted to fit Asia. I wondered where cultural appropriation began and ended.

"Thanks," Leni said.

I wasn't sure what part of the last twenty-four hours she was thinking about.

"Sure," I said. "My pleasure. Thanks for finding Prof. He's got a nice place here."

"Prof's into a lot of stuff," she said, but didn't elaborate. She leaned her hip against the car and listened.

"Do you like the blues?" I said.

She sucked on her lower lip, playing with it like it tasted good, and nodded slowly.

"I don't want him to find me," she said.

"What about school?"

She shook her head. "Can't go back."

"Ever? That's a lot to give up."

"He took a lot."

I was on a slippery slope leading to quicksand with a traumatized girl I barely knew, standing in a neighborhood sans white boys. I should shut up. But she seemed to want to say something.

"Any way to avoid him?"

She shook her head, her eyes following the red record.

"I work for him."

She had said it was complicated.

"Isn't he a professor?"

"He is." She paused and watched the arm lift and carry the needle away from the vinyl grooves that held so much magic.

"So you work for the University?"

She shook her head. "No."

"It's complicated," I said.

Her lips grinned, but her eyes stayed sad.

"You want a beer?" she said.

We had just finished breakfast. But I didn't want her to drink alone.

"If you're having one. Will Prof mind if we raid his supply?"

"Prof has lots of supplies."

She trotted off over gravel like it was soft grass. In bare feet.

I flipped the record over and read the English translations of the song titles.

"Beijing Bling"

"Draw Me a Dragon"

"Shoot the One You Love"

"No More Meditation"

I hoped that third song was about photography.

Leni returned with two bottles of Hoptimum in one hand, a bag of Fritos under her arm, and a foot long submarine sandwich in the other hand. She handed me a beer. I nodded thanks and lowered the needle. Apparently her cheese toast had been an appetizer.

With the food on the rear fender, we clinked bottles and toasted Prof for taking us in. Beijing Bling opened with screeching feedback.

The beer had a hint of orange creamsicle and bubble gum floating in a dank cave.

"He runs his own company," she said.

I frowned. "How does he have time to teach?"

"He doesn't do much."

I smiled. University jobs must be nice.

"What's the company do?" I said.

She tore the paper off of the sub, separated the pre-cut sections and took a huge bite of one half. She chewed for a moment and washed it down with beer.

"I'm not sure. I only know my job."

"How many employees?"

"No idea."

"How many did you work with?"

"None," she said.

I ate some sub and thought.

"It's a delivery service," she said.

"What do you deliver?"

"Amazon boxes."

"He works for Amazon?"

I drank some beer. Definitely creamsicle.

"Unclear," she said. "I never talked to anyone from Amazon. In fact, I never talk to him. Except for that first time to get trained."

"Sounds like Amway," I said. "My mother sold Amway for about six months. She liked having the parties." I grinned. "Actually, she was really into their Zen Plus skin care products. I remember the name because I was curious how anyone could put Zen into a product."

"Marketing," she said. "My job was pickup and delivery."

"Amazon boxes?"

She nodded while drinking from the brown bottle.

"Yep. The HappyBox app tells me where to pick up the box and where to deliver it. One end was always an Amazon locker place."

I got it.

"Amazon delivers to the locker. You pick up at the locker and deliver to the customer. Or vice versa."

She smacked her lips.

"That's good beer," she said. "Yes. Always from or to a locker."

"And the app gives you the code for the locker?"

"Right again."

"But why not have Amazon deliver right to the house?" I said.

"Well first, Amazon doesn't pick up if you're doing a return. You have to mess with UPS or someone. But the real reason is that lots of people steal Amazon boxes off of porches."

DragonZone started "Draw me a Dragon." It sounded like an old Robert Johnson single played on 78.

"So you pick up and deliver Amazon boxes," I said.

She drank her beer and nodded.

"Do you have a car?"

Leni tilted her head and looked at me like I had asked if the Earth were flat. If she had a car, she wouldn't have been telling fortunes at a rest stop.

"I have an electric bicycle in my room. It has touring bags to hold the boxes. Even goes in the snow with its fat knobby tires. I'm almost as fast as a motorcycle courier because I can flip a switch and use sidewalks whenever I want to and a motorcycle can't."

I finished my sub, thinking about riding a bicycle in Chicago traffic in winter.

"Clever," I said. "Does it take a lot of time?"

She shook her head.

"I cover the Amazon lockers close to campus. I go to the lockers, then ride a loop dropping and picking up and then back to the lockers."

Her bottle was empty. She opened the Fritos.

"Would you like another beer?" I said.

She nodded.

"Let me get it for you."

I finished mine on the way. As I walked into the kitchen, the doorbell rang. Prof's chair squeaked in the next room, so I grabbed two beers from the door of the fridge, leaving about ten more, and headed back out.

DragonZone was shouting "Shoot the One You Love" in English as I reached the trunk. Leni was staring at her cell phone. I wondered where a barefoot girl in a T-shirt carried a phone that size. She tapped in a message, then slipped the phone behind her and under the shirt. I handed her a Hoptimum.

She tilted her head.

"Why don't you have a cell phone?" she said, and sipped from the bottle while reaching into the Fritos bag.

"Saves money for gas," I said.

She tilted her head to the opposite side and stared at me as she flipped Fritos into her mouth one at a time.

"Look at it this way," I said. "Imagine back to a land before cell phones."

She squinted. I could see that the thought was hard for her.

"Really. Humans roamed the earth before cell phones," I said. "Think of being in that world. And an inventor comes along and says, 'I can put this little box in your pocket, and anyone who knows your number can make it interrupt you anytime they want. And your friends will become angry if you don't respond fast enough. And the box will record everything so the government can access it and read your messages and know where you are anytime of the day or night.' Think about that. Hundreds and hundreds of people who can reach out and touch you anytime they want, regardless of what you're doing. Your entire life recorded by an unseen entity."

Her cell phone buzzed for attention. Not the same buzz I had heard from her room. She glanced down.

"One sec," she said.

She drifted away from the car to stroll down the alley, holding the phone up, and speaking directly at it.

Video call.

I popped Fritos and sang "Shoot The One You Love" along with DragonZone each time they reached the chorus. I wondered what story the lyrics were telling. And why they had chosen to sing the chorus in English. I sipped beer and enjoyed the lack of sunshine. I had no important places to go or people to meet. I didn't really have to do anything until my money ran out.

Rape was hard to not think about.

Leni seemed sort of okay. But what was really going on inside her? She could be in shock. Maybe the worst was yet to come. How could a guy she had just met help? I sipped a fine brew I had never heard of and contemplated the multi-cultural nature of DragonZone.

"Sorry," she said. "You were fantasizing a world without smartphones when my smartphone interrupted." She giggled.

"Just imagine that no one in the world could interrupt you."

"How would I talk to anyone?"

"You could see them at the local pub." I smiled.

"So I have to leave my house to talk to people?"

"Stunning concept, isn't it? The mere idea that you have to be at the same space, time coordinates to communicate."

She laughed the way teenagers laugh at their parents.

"What was in the boxes?" I asked.

Leni shrugged. "No idea. Never opened one."

"Did you get good tips?" I asked.

She shook her head.

"Nope. Never saw a human. To pick up from the locker I just enter the code and pull out the box. The box has a number on it. The app tells me where to take that number and gives me instructions on where to leave it. Usually under a bush or behind a porch chair." She took a long swallow of beer. "Or it works the other way. The app tells me where to pick up the package and the locker to put it in. Super simple."

"You could be your own boss."

"Yeah. Except the app complains if the box isn't delivered on time, or goes to the wrong place."

I grinned. "Big brother."

"More like bitchy big sister at the wrong time of the month."

I laughed. "So how's the pay?"

"Flat rate. Andy Jackson for each delivery. Sometimes there would be four or five to the same locker group and I made out like a bandit for fifteen minute's work."

"How often you get paid?"

She wagged her head and the beer bottle at the same time as she drank.

"Each box has a twenty taped to the bottom. That's for me."

"Hmm. Did you carefully record every transaction so that you can accurately pay your taxes?"

Leni stared at me with a frozen expression, then she laughed and spit a little beer on the rear bumper. "Sorry," she said. "So if we are not standing in the same geographical location like time travelers from the 20th century, how do I reach you?"

I didn't have a good answer to that.

"I don't know. In Chicago I stayed at a B&B where they took messages for me."

"I don't think Prof will run an answering service." She upended the Fritos bag but it was empty. "How about a service on the Internet? You can get a bot. Or there are some that use an actual live human to answer the phone for you."

"Then they call and interrupt me?"

She shook her head.

"Only if you want them too. If you had a smartphone, it could notify you. But since you don't, you'll have to call in and check messages."

"Like an answering machine?"

She pointed at the sky.

"Up in the cloud. Where the Internet lives."

The needle lifted off the red record.

"Did you know," she said, "that stressed is desserts spelled backwards?"

I laughed. She smiled slightly.

"Hungry for something sweet?" I said.

"Are you coming on to me?"

"Would a white guy with an old car and no cell phone be crazy enough to come on to a princess like you?"

She laughed.

"How about a scone? We're in the United States, there must be a Starbucks nearby," I said.

"Better," she said. "Ma Pumbles. Let's go."

She plodded down the alley.

I closed the trunk lid and followed.

"Will Ma serve you barefoot?" I said.

Leni stopped and looked down at her feet. She made a burbling sound with her lips like a motorboat running out of gas.

"How about flip-flops from a drugstore?" I asked.

The store was two blocks beyond Ma Pumbles. A few cars slowed as they passed us on the way, but none were the blue Cadillac. The store had pink flip-flops for kids that fit. They also had a white cotton hoodie on a circular rack of hoodies. It had a logo on the arm that looked like a blood splotch. Leni liked it. The cashier took my hundred, frowned, and look at me like I was a convict. Then she checked the bill under a special light and accepted it as payment without a word.

Leni's face was hidden inside the hoodie and deep into her smartphone on the walk to Ma Pumbles.

"How many letters in Barracuda?" she said.

"Nine. Two Rs."

"Hmmm. What year is that old thing?"

"Nineteen sixty-five."

Tapping away on the phone she failed to stop at the corner. I reached out an arm and blocked her so she wouldn't step off the curb into traffic.

"Whoops," she said. "How do you like six five B A R A C U D A for a phone number? Only one R."

"Easy for me to remember," I said.

"What do you want them to say when they answer the phone?"

"Who's they?" I said.

"Your answering service. What are you?" she said.

"A wannabe private eye. But I don't have a license."

"You need a license to be a wannabe?" She laughed. "How about private dick?" She laughed harder. "Okay wait wait." She frowned in thought. "Something that goes well with Cuda."

"Cuda Consulting?"

"Yuk. Sounds like a bunch of ancient white guys with a stick up their butts. We need pizzazz."

A word from a college history class came to me.

"Freelance. Before you say 'yuk,' that word comes from a 'free lance', two words. Meaning a lance that was free to hire and not tied to a single kingdom. Essentially a mercenary in medieval times."

Leni stared at me. "Mercenary? That's kind of cool. Cuda Freelance it is." She tapped at her phone for half a minute.

"Okay, you're all set up. They'll start taking calls immediately. Your personal assistant is Tina Retrina. She will answer during standard business hours on the east coast. After that, a robot using a recording of Tina's voice will answer and take messages."

"You're kidding," I said.

She shook her head.

"Just like that?"

"Smartphones are smart," she said, and winked at me.

"How do I pay for this service?"

"You don't, I do. It's ten dollars for a hundred calls per month. And I already owe you ninety-five dollars. Plus—"

She started across the street. I hustled to catch up.

"Plus?" I said.

"I want to hire you as my private dick."

CHAPTER 9

I was sitting at a table for two looking at Leni over a maple-blueberry muffin the size of a softball. We were drinking coffee—hers black, mine with cream—and sharing the muffin. Ma Pumble's place was a narrow restaurant with artwork from local painters, mismatched tables and chairs, no tablecloths, self-service, and the aroma of baked goods that attracted people for miles. Two middle-aged women worked behind the counter. Neither admitted to being Ms. Pumbles. Four twenty-something guys sat at the far end eating cookies and passing a basketball back and forth behind their backs. So far, no one seemed to have noticed that I was the only white person in the place.

"Let me test my understanding," I said. "You want to hire me as your personal private investigator, which I can't do because I don't have a license. But even if I did, you don't know what you want me to investigate. For this service, you will pay my daily fee, which we haven't negotiated, and a bonus when and if we achieve the goals of the project. Which we haven't discussed."

Leni popped a chunk of muffin into her mouth and nodded.

"Okay, I'll take it," I said.

She smiled. "Knew you would. You're the curious type."

"Adventure doesn't come in and sit on your lap. You have to go out and hunt it." I ate some muffin and sipped my coffee, savoring the robust flavor of real cream and genuine Columbian.

The four guys stood up to the sound of metal chair legs screeching across well-worn linoleum.

"Where do you want me to start?" I said.

She shrugged.

"How about if we avoid the guy in the blue Cadillac whose name you refuse to reveal."

"Markus Corolla," she said.

My breath caught a little.

"Professor Markus Corolla," she said. "But he likes to be called Doc C. Like he's a rapper."

"I bet you're going to tell me that he likes college girls."

"That would be an understatement," she said.

"What would be?" The four guys had stopped at our table on their way out, casting a chilly shadow across it.

"Her professor likes college girls," I said.

The guy who had spoken looked to his friends and smiled wide.

"Don't we all."

I nodded agreement.

"So." He shifted his body weight to be even on both feet, like a soldier moving to at ease. "What's a white boy doing in Ma Pumbles?"

"Meeting with my employer," I said.

His eyebrows lifted. Not the answer he expected.

"And what is this little lady employing your white ass to do for her?"

All four laughed.

"A professor is stalking her. Followed her here all the way from Chicago. I'm helping her hide."

He looked at his buddies again. "Don't look like you're hiding very good to me."

I made a quick assumption.

"A thirty-something white guy probably wouldn't venture in here on his own."

Leni looked at me with a how did you know? expression.

The guy nodded. "Smart move. But what about you?"

"My client suggested the location. And the customer is always right." I sipped coffee to see if my hands were steady. So far, so good.

"Maybe it wasn't a good suggestion," he said.

My dad always said to play the cards you held. Of course, he had been talking about high-frequency trading on Wall Street. But the wisdom seemed to apply.

"Prof is busy with visitors, so we didn't want to bother him. And I haven't seen Jake or Ramone today. They might have a better suggestion." I shrugged. "I'll ask them tonight."

All of the names registered. Now he had a decision to make. If they were really my friends, then he probably wouldn't mess with me. But if was lying, he would be doubly interested in messing with me.

I waited. I had mouthed off enough. And Leni was staying quiet, which I took to mean that these guys were dangerous and she didn't want to mess with them either.

"You seeing Jake tonight?" he asked.

He was a quick thinker. I nodded and improvised.

"Prof said he would find out where Jake's playing. We're going down to check out his drumming."

The guy smiled. "He's a madman on drums, man. You gotta see it." He looked around at his buddies then back at me. "Maybe we'll see you there."

They laughed as one and drifted out of the restaurant. Apparently they found the idea of a white boy watching Jake drum amusing.

"You know those guys?" Leni said.

"No, I have no idea who they are."

"Then how could you talk to them like that?"

Talk to them!

I jumped out of my chair and reached the four guys just as they opened the door.

"Excuse me?" I said.

The other three cleared out of the building so that the guy who had spoken with me could turn and face me. He met my eyes with a challenge in his, but didn't speak.

"Thanks for stopping. I have a feeling that you and your friends are well connected."

He nodded. Of course he was. What idiot wouldn't understand that.

"The guy stalking her." I gestured with my head and didn't use Leni's name just in case he didn't know it. "He drives a bright blue Cadillac."

"Lots of Caddy's around here. They're sweet-ass cars."

"For sure. This is a late model with a University of Chicago Maroons decal across the back window."

He grinned. "Ain't many of those."

"I think that if you wanted to find that car, it would be easy for you."

"You're smart for a honk…white guy," he said. "What's it worth to you?"

"A Benjamin. Up front."

He held out his hand, palm up.

I dug in my pocket and peeled a bill off my fold and handed it to him.

"How do I reach you when I find him? Which should take about ten minutes."

"Would you mind leaving a message with my secretary? Call six five Baracuda. One R."

His face tightened. His eyes narrowed.

"The fish or the car?"

"The car," I said.

"You the guy driving the Hemi that Jake's been talking about?"

"Turbo bronze metallic. Wide rear tires for the drag strip. That's me."

He held out his hand.

"Tron," he said.

I shook. His grip was strong and insistent.

"Tommy."

"Pleasure doing business with you."

He turned and left.

When I reached the table Leni had stolen the rest of my muffin.

"Are you crazy?" she said.

"They seemed like guys who would know the neighborhood."

"Yeah, they sure do," she said. "What was that all about?"

"I hired them."

She stopped chewing my muffin. "You're serious."

"I was planning to drive around the neighborhood and look for that blue Cadillac. But Corolla might recognize my car. And it would be slow and tedious and prone to error."

She waited.

"I explained our problem to Tron and he was confident he could find the Caddy in ten minutes."

"How's he going—" She stopped.

"Yeah, that's what I think too. He's got people on every street corner. All he has to do is put the word out. If all of those eyes don't find the Caddy, it's not here."

"How much?"

"A hundred bucks."

She nodded, agreeing with something.

"And when he finds the Caddy," I said, "he'll call Cuda Freelance and leave a message."

A grin formed slowly along the right side of her mouth. But she didn't say 'I told you so.'

On the way back to Prof's with the muffin expanding in my stomach I remembered something Leni had said at breakfast.

"Leni, if you don't want to talk about this just say stop, okay?"

She was walking along beside me in her new white hoodie. She turned her head; I could see one eye.

"Go ahead."

"You said the university had done a, uh, test kit, sort of. How does 'sort of' come into play?"

Leni took a deep breath in, and let it out slowly. She continued to look at me as we strolled towards Prof's place. Then she looked away and spoke softly.

"As soon as he let me go, I ran out of his place." We walked a dozen paces. "It's on campus in faculty housing. So I ran crying back to my dorm. But—"

She wiped the sleeve of her new white sweatshirt across her face and was quiet for few moments.

Her phone buzzed.

She stopped on the sidewalk in front of a French Laundry that was running a 30% off special. Or perhaps had been before going of business. It was hard to tell looking through a dirt-caked window at an empty counter. Leni tapped a message into her phone and started walking again. She sniffled.

"I reached the building that houses student medical services. I had pain. My arms. Shoulder. Between my legs. Inside. I realized he might have hurt me bad."

I kept my mouth shut.

She stopped and faced me. "So I went in."

I nodded and tried to feel her pain so it would show on my face.

She turned and started walking again.

"Then things happened fast. They swept me into a little room that was white and bright and claustrophobic. I waited and a white woman with red hair wearing blue medical garb came in and said she was a rape specialist. Had been a victim herself years ago. I hadn't even told them that I had been raped, they just somehow knew. How did they know?"

"College campus in a major city. They've seen it before," I said.

She nodded trance-like as we walked.

"She asked me. I said yes. She got out this, this, thing. Told me it was a formal way of collecting evidence. Told me it was good that I came in right away and hadn't taken a shower or changed clothes or… anything really. I was plenty scared."

"Of her?"

She shook her head.

"Of the evidence?" I said.

"Yeah. I didn't know what it could do?"

"Put him in prison is the goal," I said.

She shook her head.

"Not to him. To me. I didn't want to fuck up my life."

We passed a corner gas station with a large M logo that was open but only half the lights were working. One pump had cobwebs floating from the pump handle.

"I refused to give her my name."

She moved toward me until our shoulders touched. Not knowing what else to do, I took her hand. She didn't look at me, or even slow down, she just squeezed it tight.

"I wouldn't give his name either."

I waited for her to say more. She didn't.

"What did the specialist do?" I said.

"Told me that she could take all of the evidence and file it as a 'Jane Doe' kit. It would have a number. No name. No identifying information. The DNA in it would prove that it had come from me. Nothing would be done with it unless I went to the police."

"So you're a Jane Doe at the clinic?"

"That's why I said 'sort of.'"

"It's good that you let them collect evidence. Just in case you want to file a report."

She shook her head.

"No way. I can't do that."

I squeezed her hand and walked for a bit.

"Do you want to talk about why?"

"What then? He fires me from my delivery job. Maybe I lose my other job too. He knows nothing about that one. My mother doesn't either. The defense tries to make it look consensual in court. Drags my past in." She paused. "Drags my present in. I'm destroyed and he gets a slap on the wrist."

"The university will fire him," I said.

She shook her head. "Not unless the court makes them. He brings in too much money."

CHAPTER 10

eni fled Chicago in a hurry with only what she could carry in her backpack. So we spent the rest of the day driving from store to store. At one point she modeled a silver, sleeveless top that looked fantastic on her. But it revealed scratches along her neck and bruise rings around her biceps. It was almost midnight by the time I turned into a strip mall on a boulevard a couple miles from Prof's house. The parking lot was empty except for a cluster of cars near the end furthest from the street. Two shops were boarded up, the boards covered with rattle-can graffiti in neon green and orange. I cruised the length of the lot and back.

No blue Cadillac.

I parked between a lowered Chevy from the 1960s and a tuned Acura. As I pulled up, blue lights came on beneath the Acura, turning it into a hovering UFO. I shut off the Hemi and we sat in the silent pulsing of the multi-colored sign for Toucan Sam's.

The bar featured a human-size, hand-painted toucan on the glass beside a list of Happy Hours by day of week. They were longest on Monday. None on Saturday. To its left, behind gray-smoked windows, a 24-hour vape shop displayed rows of colored pipes the way a jewelry store shows off rings and necklaces. An orange OPEN sign on the door was lit but flickering. To the right, six-foot posters of dark-skinned supermodels with super hairstyles streaked with rainbow colors blocked the view into a beauty salon called The Black Widow. The models all wore clothing that shined like it was made of metal.

I was wearing a black T-shirt with Gibson emblazoned on the front along with blue jeans, a leather jacket, and black boots with rubber soles that were comfortable for standing.

Leni was wearing the results from our day of shopping. A day Prof and I had funded in an effort to help her mental state. Strappy black heels that showed her new silver pedicure, skintight black pants that looked like leather but stretched, and a long sleeve shirt maybe even tighter than the pants of blue-toned snakeskin. A silver bracelet encircled her left wrist. A silver necklace with a tiny copper key on it floated above the snakeskin. Her hair was straight and shiny with random copper streaks that reflected. She wore stud earrings with a blue stone. For some reason, she reminded me of the old Virginia Slim TV commercials showing women who would rather fight than switch. Commercials that I only knew about because they had been the subject of much criticism in sociology class for their portrayal of females, violence, and smoking.

Leni looked at me and smiled. Something she hadn't done much since I met her.

"You ready to party?" I asked.

Her lips danced with each other a little as she thought.

"I'm here for the alcohol," she said.

I nodded and held up a finger for her to wait. I got out, locked my door with the key, walked around the front of the car, and opened her door for her.

She was still smiling, but shaking her head as she stepped out.

I locked the her door. My guitar was hiding in the trunk.

As we approached the purple door to Sam's place, a sticker on the window below the Toucan's left claw caught my eye. It matched the one on the windshield of my car. Only this one was the size of a basketball, and the eye in the center was bloodshot.

Leni pulled the door open with both hands and the stop-time groove of "Hoochie Coochie Man" rushed past us like a sirocco. We entered a room full of light, sound, smoke, and sweat. I naturally checked out the stage. In the back left corner Jake sat surrounded by a double bass drum set and a zillion cymbals. A thin guy in profile bent like a comma over a Hammond organ. A orange synthesizer sat on top the organ, making for a third set of keys. His feet, wearing something like ballet slippers, danced on the organ's bass pedals. The two musicians were wedged between towers of speakers on either side.

Dozens of shimmying bodies spilled off a wooden dance floor. Bar seating on the right faced rows of liquors bottles standing in front of a mirrored wall that made the place feel wide. Tiny tables barely adequate to hold drinks and vapes were jammed everywhere.

A handful of dancers glanced our way. One couple stared. Leni took my hand and dragged me toward the bar. I was the second white person in the room. The first was the muscular guy behind the bar wearing a tan, open-collared, button shirt and camo pants with a wide black belt that held something in a holster. A gun. Or maybe a Taser.

The shirt had an embroidered logo of the toucan in the window. It also had a dark blue name patch with white letters: SAM. His shirt sleeves were rolled up, revealing tattoos on both forearms.

Leni waved. Sam looked up, smiled, and pointed at two unoccupied stools at the far end of the bar.

"Did you call ahead?" I said loud enough to be heard above the music.

Leni shook her head. "I texted," she said, and laughed.

"Hi, Leni," Sam said, his voice like a sergeant shouting at new recruits. "New friend?"

"Hi, Sam. My friend with wheels, Tommy. Tommy, my friend with alcohol, Sam."

Sam nodded but didn't put out his hand. So I nodded back and said, "Pleasure to meet you, Sam. Cool that you have live music".

"Three nights a week. Other nights is a DJ." He grinned. "And sometimes we have Motown karaoke night." He glanced at Leni. "What'll it be?"

"Manhattan," she said. "The perfect one you make."

Sam looked my way.

"Beer. Whatever you recommend."

"I have twenty in bottles. Got a menu if you want. Bud and Sierra Nevada on tap. I recommend the latter. However." His eyes floated to Leni. "If you're going to keep up with this one, I have something better."

"Sierra on tap?" I said, surprise sneaking into my voice.

Sam grinned. "They're pushing east and incentivize me. Want to try something you've never had? Now how could I know that? Because I invented it."

I gave him a thumbs up.

His hands dropped below bar level. He poured from a clear glass bottle. He poured from a green glass bottle. A low-ball glass appeared with a lime slice on the edge, and a dark liquid on the rocks that was close to turbo bronze metallic.

"Do I want to ask?" I said.

"Only if you want to know," Leni said, then laughed.

Sam smiled.

I sipped the drink and a dozen flavors burst alive in my mouth. I was no connoisseur of cocktails. But I was certain I had never tasted anything like it.

"Nice."

"There's a story behind it," Sam said.

Jake hammered through a four-bar drum break displaying some intricate syncopation. When the organ came back in, I said, "For sure I'd like to hear it."

"A white kid dropped in here late one afternoon. Was dead on his feet. Said he was driving solo from Alaska to Washington D.C. Needed some food quick. Asked for a Dr. Pepper. Didn't look to me like he should be on the road. So I gave him the doctor and slipped in a bit of this." He held up a green bottle.

I read the label.

Jameson Irish Whiskey. Product of Ireland.

"He was asleep on the bar before he got halfway through the cheeseburger he ordered. I carried him into the back room and let him sleep. Got him back on the road about midnight with a promise to stop at a hotel by three A.M."

I sipped the drink again. It was flavorful without being too sweet. Had a certain smoothness that made me think I could drink a whole lot of them.

I said, "Does it have a name?"

"My idea is to call it a Black Jeep. That's what this kid Jonny was driving down from Alaska."

I held the drink up to the light. It certainly wasn't black, but I surely appreciated naming it after a vehicle.

"My problem," Sam said, "is if I call it a Black Jeep, people will think it's made with Jack Daniel's Black Label." He shook his head. "That's the wrong choice. The Jameson is more open, leaves room for the 23 flavors of the Pepper."

"I have a Barracuda out there painted the original turbo bronze metallic."

"Saw you come in. Classic cars stand out. They have style that's lacking today." Sam frowned. Then nodded. "Yeah, Bronze Jeep is better. Sort of like a Brass Monkey. Think I'll make it Toucan Sam's signature cocktail."

"I love it," Leni said as she reached over, took the drink out of my hand, and downed half of it."

We watched Sam mix Leni's drink while the band played behind him in the mirror. Jake was indeed an intense drummer. Combined with the organ and the solo now drooling out of the synth, they had a sound that lacked for nothing. I marveled at how many drums, cymbals, woodblocks, and cowbells Jake would hit in a single measure. Then I marveled at the thin guy playing bass with his feet, rhythm with his left hand, and soloing with flying right fingers.

They went into the next verse.

"What do you think?" Leni said.

"I think the band's great."

"How do you feel being the only white customer?"

I felt isolated and off balance. But nothing had happened to cause it.

"Like I shouldn't be here."

She looked directly into my eyes. Under the bar lights, hers appeared deep sea blue.

"That's how I feel every single day at the University of Chicago. Like an outsider. Maybe even a fraud."

"But—"

She cut me off with a raised hand.

"I shouldn't, right? They admitted me based on my performance. Gave me a partial scholarship. I have as much right to be there as anyone else."

I nodded agreement.

Sam placed her drink on a black paper napkin with a colorful Toucan on it.

Leni spoke toward her glass.

"I am not going to let that bastard take this away from me." She spun on her stool to face me. "He tells me I'm beautiful. How I remind him of someone special from his past, only I'm smarter and he loves me even more." She stopped to swallow a third of her Manhattan. "We have a disagreement. Yes, about other women. We talk over dinner. He claims he loves me. Won't happen again." She laughed. "Says I should trust him." She drank again, less than the first time. "Then I answer a video call, he screams about my cell phone and rapes me. He knows no means no. Doesn't give a goddamn."

She chugged the rest of the drink and placed the empty martini glass on the bar. She looked up and caught Sam's eye. If he was surprised, he didn't show it.

"Now I'm the one who suffers. I told him no at dinner. I told him no after dinner." Her voice grew softer. "I told him no while he was inside of me with his hand around my neck. I was screaming no as I ran out of the room dragging my jacket and backpack. No, no." Almost a whisper. "No." She stared into her empty glass. "I can't go back to his class. I can't work for him. There goes one of the two jobs that barely pay my bills. And I'll probably need counseling that I can't afford to deal with the trauma."

Sam swapped her second Manhattan for the empty glass. She reached for it, changed her mind, bent forward, and sipped from the glass sitting on the bar. Then she turned to me.

"Got any ideas?" she said.

"Leni, this is heavy stuff. I'm no shrink. Hell, I'm not even a private eye. I'm happy to share my thoughts if you want the uninformed opinion of a guy that hasn't been through anything like what you're talking about."

She stared at me with eyes that froze me in place.

"That's why I like you, Tommy. You don't pretend to know everything." She picked up her drink and sipped like it was the nectar of the gods. "OK, tell me your thoughts. Maybe you'll give me an idea."

I drank some of the Bronze Jeep. Where to start?

"Well, after such a huge…um…inflection point in your life, getting back to a normal routine might be a good first step."

She nodded. "I'm on my way. Drinking and dancing are a huge part of my life. Hell, I'm in college, right?" She smiled. Then frowned deeply. "My future sucks."

I chose my words with care.

"You have a lot of control over your future."

She laughed lightly. Then out loud and shook her head as her eyes grew moist.

"You think? I didn't do so well at that dinner."

The song ended. The band segued into a ballad I didn't recognize. The synthesizer moaned a haunting baritone sax line.

Someone tapped my left shoulder. I turned around and faced a linebacker-sized guy with short hair and a black shirt with black buttons and a button-down collar. He wore a midnight blue beret that made me think of a Green Beret gone to the dark side. Mirrored sunglasses hid his eyes.

"You know any Hendrix?" he said.

Know? As in: Able to play?

"Fire, Foxy Lady, Crosstown Traffic," I said. "Purple Haze when I'm lucky."

He smiled. "You're into the blues, aren't you?"

"I do what I can. But, I'm limited by circumstances."

His face grew serious. "How so?"

"I was born white."

He laughed loud and clapped me on the back so hard I nearly fell off the stool. Then he spoke to Leni.

"Where did you find this guy?"

"Stray cat," she said. "Picked him up on the street."

He turned to me. "I'll tell Jake. He wants you to sit in." He turned and headed for the stage.

I faced Leni. "Stray cat?"

She shrugged. "That's what came to mind." And she laughed.

Leni laughing was for sure better than her crying.

"I'll be right back," I said. "Please guard my Jeep."

"With my lips." She pulled the glass toward her.

I stepped outside. The door slammed. Silence washed over me. Not quite silence. Music leaked out of the club. A truck shifted gears in the distance. Car tires squealed against asphalt somewhere. I took a deep breath of the cool night air and headed for my Barracuda.

I put the key into the trunk lock and looked around to see if anyone was watching. In the back row, beyond the Black Widow hair salon, sat a blue Cadillac that hadn't been there when we went in. The lot lights weren't bright enough to show me if it was occupied. But a tag dangled from the inside rearview mirror.

I wondered how he found us, and realized that he might have his own eyes on the street. He found me the same way I had tried to find him.

I lifted the lid and grabbed my guitar case. Nothing moved in or around the Cadillac. I scanned along the storefronts. No one. I slammed the lid and headed toward Sam's. About halfway to the door, screeching tires drew my eyes toward the road. A pair of tuner cars had swung in and were coming straight at me. Their under-frame lights glowed red. I looked over my shoulder. The driver's door to the Cadillac stood open, but the interior light wasn't on.

I yanked the door to Sam's open with one hand. The band had finished the ballad and was grooving to the Moscow beat with a Red Elvises song called "We Got the Groove." I had spun it on college radio and been amazed how four Russian guys could channel Motown funk from Detroit. Appropriation? Inspiration? Tribute? It even had an organ solo.

I hustled to the stage and right to Jake's ear.

"Tuner cars racing into the lot. Riding on red frame lights."

His eyes told me I had done the right thing.

He stopped playing.

The organ screeched to a stop a couple beats later.

"Everyone on the floor," Jake said into his microphone. "We have visitors."

Chairs shuffled and people dropped low. No one complained.

Jake held up four fingers of his left hand and pointed to the front door with is right. Then he spun an index finger and gestured toward the back door. Half of the men in the bar moved.

The front door opened and a white guy walked into the club. He was wearing a dark suit, white shirt, red tie, and large dark glasses.

Jake and half a dozen guys exited via the back door. Four guys moved out the front door, shoving the newcomer out of the way. The lights went out except for rows of LEDs in the floor, like emergency exit lights in an aircraft.

It happened so fast I was still standing on the stage holding my guitar case. I stuffed it behind an amp and searched for Leni. Found her still sitting at the far end of the bar where I had left her.

The intruder scanned the club, saw Leni, and moved quickly along the length of the bar. He reached her before I did and said something that I wasn't close enough to understand. Leni tossed what was left of my beer in his face and then backhanded him with her fist. He took a step away, didn't fall, then came forward, put his hands around both of her biceps, and shook her the way you're never supposed to shake a baby. Her head rocked. He shouted at her: Do this, don't do that, can't leave, keep quiet.

She didn't struggle, just shook like a rag doll.

A gun blast hit the front window. Maybe a shotgun. The glass didn't break. A second blast tried again with the same result.

The guy was still holding Leni by both arms, probably bruising her. He leaned forward and spoke close to her ear. I couldn't hear him even in the now eerily quiet, nearly pitch black bar.

At least he had stopped shaking her.

I stopped behind Leni so he would see me. His eyes lifted but he didn't stop talking. He released her and wagged a finger in her face.

"Are you finished?" she shouted.

It was a misunderstanding. Had she reported the incident?

Leni didn't answer. He grew more agitated.

Gunfire popped outside. Handguns like at a firing range. Two or three shots. Silence. Two or three more shots.

After what seemed like an hour, but was probably less than a minute, tires squealed outside. Jake and his guys came in the front door. All looked healthy. I hadn't counted who had left, so I wasn't sure if they were all back.

The guy stared at Leni.

"What do you want to do?" I asked her.

He turned to face me.

"Get him away from me," she said.

I started to step around her to escort him out of the club, but Sam appeared.

"Sir, I'll have to ask you to leave for harassing the lady."

The guy spun toward Sam, who was taller and wider than Mr. Cadillac.

"Who the fuck are you to tell me what to do?"

I could see Sam's tattoos now. The left forearm was a dancing woman not wearing many clothes. The right one was an automatic rifle.

Sam waved a thumb at the window.

"I am Toucan Sam. This is my club. You are trespassing. If you don't walk out of here in the next ten seconds, I will break both of your arms."

"Like you could," the guy said. "I have resources you can't even imagine." The guy turned back to Leni and started to speak.

Before he got the second word out, Sam grabbed the guy's elbows and pressed them together behind his back. He was still swearing when Sam pushed his face into the heavy door to open it and dropped him in the parking lot. The door swung closed behind Sam as he returned to his place behind the bar.

Jake looked at the door, at Sam, at Leni, back at the door. Said, "Stupid honky."

The lights came on. People got up from the floor and returned to their tables. No one asked what happened.

So it had happened before. Maybe happens often.

Jake held out his hand. I shook it. He had plenty of strength to play drums.

"Good eye. You helped keep that simple."

I bowed my head slightly.

"Do you think it was related to the stupid honky?"

Jake grinned. "Too big a coincidence on the timing." He looked at Leni and the door. "He planned to grab her. But you and Sam got in the way."

"He wanted me to leave with him," Leni said, reaching for her drink. "In his dreams."

Jake met my eyes.

"That was a major vibe disruption. You ready to put this place back in the groove?" He gestured at the stage. "Slug has a bunch of amps for his synth. He'll set you up. What do you want to open with?"

I knew the drum part I wanted to hear Jake play.

"Fire," I said. "By Hendrix."

CHAPTER 11

Tron's messages said no one had seen him," Leni said. We were cruising through town on empty streets at low speeds, heading back to Prof's place. The short set I had played with Twice-As-Nice, Jake's two-piece band, had gone better than expected. The crowd loved Hendrix. Jake was as tight as a Swiss watch. And Slug, the keyboard player, covered for me like we had played together for years. Not one person told me that a white guy shouldn't be playing Hendrix or the blues or even be in the Toucan. Although one guy scowled at me from the dance floor when he thought I was looking at the red dress stretched over his girlfriend's body. He was right. I was. She was worth looking at.

"What time did his last message come in?" I asked.

Leni consulted her phone. "Eleven thirty."

"Is there any way he could have been in the area and Tron's people somehow missed him?"

Leni shook her head hard enough to make her hair wave.

"Only if he were invisible," she said. "Or not using his own car."

"He drove the Caddy to Toucan Sam's."

"So we conclude he wasn't in the area," she said. "He was out rounding up support from those guys who shot at us."

"Jake seemed to know who they were as soon as I mentioned the red underbody lights."

Leni's eyes widened. I'd swear they had a hint of purple.

"Red?" she whispered.

I nodded. The lights clearly meant something special.

"The local gangs run red for self-preservation," she said.

I attempted to put one and one together. Got three. She sensed my confusion.

"When they're on a run that includes violence, they show red."

"They warn everyone?"

"Yeah," she said. "The citizens. The cops. Usually the cops stay out of the way until the shooting is over. Fewer nice people get hurt. And no one, including the cops, care if the gangs get shot up. The more dead the merrier far as they're concerned."

"In Ohio we have sirens that warn when a tornado is coming so everyone can take shelter."

"It's like that," she said. "Only with bullets."

"All the gangs do this?"

"If they don't, the other gangs, um, teach them how it's done," she said.

"Eliminates the element of surprise."

"Yeah, but the overall outcome is better for everyone."

I made a left turn through an empty intersection. No one was out walking.

"Even the gangs?" I said.

"Especially them. The cops and citizens get out of the way. Fewer dead citizens mean less media and less cop pressure. This way, the gangs can do what they do in peace."

I turned toward her. The copper in her hair sparkled. Her face was luminous in the light of the night. And completely serious.

"Peace?" I said.

"Of course. Nothing brings peace to the soul like controlling your own destiny."

I drove in silence for a couple of blocks.

"You're in college, aren't you?" I said.

She laughed. "Too preachy?"

I shook my head. "Not at all. Just thinking different. Sort of like 'keeping the peace' in the old west."

"If there ever was an old west."

I turned up the gravel alleyway that led to Prof's house, pulled in close to the back door, and switched off the engine. We listened to the moonlight. Leni made no move to get out of the car, so I waited. Her phone beeped. For the first time since I met her, she ignored it.

She stared down at the knuckles of her right hand. The one she had used to smack Mr. Cadillac. They were scraped.

"How did it feel?" I asked.

She rubbed the knuckles with the thumb of her other hand.

"Great. But the feeling didn't last."

"Still, you have a good memory," I said.

She smiled slightly.

"Yes."

I waited. Insects that had gone quiet at the arrival of the car began to chirp again.

"Do you want to talk?" I said.

She shrugged. "Not sure where to start."

"How about we work backwards? What did he say to you just before he left?"

"'You can't leave now. You're in too deep.' Unquote."

The branches of a craggy oak tree to my left swayed in a sudden breeze.

"Do you know what he meant?" I said.

She shook her head dreamily.

"Care to speculate?"

"He pretends to be in love with me. Thinks I can't live without him." She stopped rubbing her knuckles and clasped her hands together. "He's wrong. I don't need him. I need to finish college and move on from this craziness."

I admired her consistency.

"A college professor shouldn't be banging an undergrad," she said. "I wanted to. He wanted to. But…" Her voice trailed off.

"Unlikely to have a good ending," I said. "But sometimes."

Leni's head bobbed slowly.

"Sometimes sunshine and rainbows," she said. "Sometimes."

"Do you see sunshine peeking through anywhere?"

She stared out the windshield. Prof's peeling white house was still in the moonlight. No lights showed, although I suspected Prof was inside sitting at his computers.

"Graduating," she said. "Getting a job. Never seeing this crappy little city again."

"You grew up here, didn't you?"

"Yeah. I feel like I'm in Death Valley dying of thirst. I know there is water on the other side of that mountain over there. But I can't climb it."

That sounded like the reason I was heading to the Pacific Ocean.

Leni's phoned pinged. She pulled it out of her purse, smiled at it for a few seconds, then put it away.

"You have a lot of friends," I said.

"Or maybe I don't have any."

She didn't elaborate.

I was still buzzing from playing with Jake and Slug. The high energy of making music took a long time to subside.

"Do you know the organ player?" I said.

"His name's George. But everyone calls him Doc or Slug."

"Like he's a doctor of music? He's a great player."

She shook her head. "More like what a regular doctor does," she said. "And he loves baseball. Slug is short for slugger."

I stared out over the bronze hood of granddad's car. A regular doctor prescribes…

"Should I ask?" I said.

She laughed. "Only if you want to know."

Convenient. Doc was where people could find him. Have a beer and a simple conversation. I'd bet drugs never changed hands inside of Toucan Sam's. But it would be easy to set up a meet. Or maybe have the goods delivered faster than Amazon Prime. Drug users were not ones to wait. Plus, he was sitting in a roomful of protection.

"Doc sounds smart," I said.

"And obsessed. All he wants to do is play music. But he, uh, has champagne tastes." She paused. "Especially in women."

"He sure has a lot of amps," I said.

"Obsessed."

We sat quietly. Leni's phone didn't buzz.

"Anything you want to do first?" I asked.

"Kill him."

"Do you think you could finish college from prison?"

"I know it's idiotic," she said. "But it feels good to say it out loud."

"Have a second choice?"

She pulled out her phone and tapped at it sporadically, like a pigeon trying to find a seed in the grass.

"Stay in school. Make enough money for tuition. Find a way to finish the bastard's class. I've spent weeks on his book Finding Hidden Meanings. I don't want to have to repeat the whole class with a new instructor." She leaned forward and gazed up at the moon. "I know it sounds stupid. But repeating things drives me nuts. Like I climbed a hill, slipped, fell, and slid all the way back down. I'm lying at the bottom cringing at the lost time and energy, knowing I have to climb it again." She turned to me. "What do you want to do?"

I considered the short and long term. And all of her problems that I knew about. I figured there were plenty more that I didn't know about.

"I want to know what's in those Amazon boxes you deliver."

She appeared to be in deep thought as she stared silently out the windshield.

"Because we don't know," I said. "And not knowing doesn't help us get the bastard."

Leni's lipped twitched towards a smile.

Her phone buzzed. She looked down to read it.

Tall shadows climbed the back of Prof's house. Leni's head spun around to look between the seats and out the back window. Her right hand shot out, grabbed the collar of my jacket, and yanked my head down until I was level with the gearshift.

"Don't move," she said. "No matter what." She tossed her smartphone into my lap and whispered, "Eight seven seven two one one." She popped the door handle and pushed the passenger door open with her high-heeled foot. The dome light blasted the interior white against the night.

The shadows stopped moving.

Leni stepped out of the car. Her own shadow rose up the back of the house like an awakening zombie.

"I knew you would come," she said. "I've been waiting."

No response.

She pushed the car door closed. Gravel crunched under her heels. Slow, careful footsteps.

"No resistance?" Male voice.

Probably the guy from the bar. Her teacher. Markus Corolla. But it was hard to be sure from inside the Barracuda. I studied Leni's shadow as it moved against Prof's house. Multiple edges suggested more than one car was parked behind my Barracuda with its headlights on.

"Did you deliver everything?" the voice asked.

No verbal response from Leni. Then.

"Get in."

She had said don't move no matter what. Was this her plan? Was she protecting me? Prof? Didn't she see other options?

The shadows shrank and vaporized. Shortly, there was nothing but me and moonlight. I counted to thirty. Had they left a sentry behind? Maybe a car sitting behind me with its lights off?

I inched up in the driver's seat while trying to remain invisible and peeked at the side mirror. A black coupe parked in the alley blocked my exit. One person with a hoodie up around his or her face was leaning against the front fender sucking on a vape. The tip glowed orange. The car windows were too dark to know if others were waiting inside.

The figure stared down at a smartphone. The light from the screen illuminated the hood, but I still couldn't see a face. In a few moments, he or she tucked the vape into the hoodie and walked around to the driver's side, got in.

Soon I was alone.

I stared at Leni's smartphone. The screen was dark. Why leave it with me?

She didn't want Cadillac man to see what was on it?

She didn't want me or Prof or Jake to track the phone and show up to cause trouble.

Or maybe she wanted me to do something. How was I supposed to know what?

I checked the alley one last time. It was empty.

The insects returned to quarreling.

CHAPTER 12

I wasn't about to forget it, but I wrote 877211 down on Prof's grocery notepad attached to the fridge. Then I tore off a back page, wrote the number down again, and put the slip of paper into the back pocket of my jeans.

Had Leni delivered everything?

An undelivered box could be in Chicago, or here in town, or hidden in the ladies' room of the rest stop where we met. I made my way up to the second floor and sat on my bed with Leni's phone in my hand. I hadn't tried to unlock it. But why would she give me her phone at all?

Because she wants you to do what she hired you to do.

She never actually said why she needed a private eye. Opening her phone seemed intrusive. And how would she exist without it? She had been on it constantly since we met.

Only yesterday?

When things happened, they sure happened fast.

I lifted the phone. 3:31 A.M. Battery half full—or maybe half empty. I slipped it under my pillow and thought about the word 'deliver' while staring at the moon. I was tired but still energized from Jake's locomotive drumming. Far as I could see, I had two choices: search the phone or search Prof's house for an Amazon box. Sitting here thinking about why Leni would return to Chicago with a guy who had raped her–allegedly–wouldn't get me anywhere.

I started in the shared bathroom. Tank on the toilet: water, rust stains, and a floating black ball. Cabinet under the sink: three rolls of toilet paper, plunger, bowl cleaner in a green bottle. Nothing in the tub except hair caught in the drain. A couple of towels on a silver rack. Unless Prof had a secret compartment, there wasn't any place to hide an Amazon box. Even a small one.

I stood in the hallway, exhaled, and listened. The rapid tap-tap of typing dominated. Prof working late. I walked to the closed door of Leni's room. Knocking seemed beside the point.

The knob turned. I pushed. The door didn't budge.

I returned to my room and studied the latch. There was no locking mechanism. And no deadbolt.

Back at Leni's room I put my shoulder against the door and pressed. The door popped inward and shuddered on its hinges. The bed was made. No scattered clothing. Cool white light from a distant streetlamp filtered through a partially drawn curtain and landed on the stack of bags from our shopping trip.

I started with a dark walnut dresser that had lived a long life. All four of the drawers were empty. The nightstand held a charger, a white USB cable, and a pink egg-shaped object with a tiny Bluetooth logo printed on one end. The closet was empty except for a screen the same size as the window. It had a ten-inch tear right in the middle.

I squatted, looked under the bed and right out the other side at the varnished baseboard of the far wall.

Leni's backpack sat on a winged chair upholstered with picnic scenes. It contained her blue poncho and the tarot cards. I flipped through the cards until my Magician gazed at me.

"Are you going to help me?" I asked softly.

The Magician suggested that the bed was the only thing large enough to hold a box. So I stripped off the blankets. Checked both pillows to be sure they contained nothing but feathers and felt every inch of the bare mattress. I began to put the blankets back on when the Magician prodded me to be more thorough.

I wrestled the full-size mattress onto the floor, turned it over, and found nothing. Then I tilted the ten-inch-thick box springs off the bed frame and lowered it onto the floor upside down. I ran a hand over the thin black cloth stapled to the wood frame, searching for an opening. I didn't find one. But a dark spot caught my eye. A box the size of a softball had been wedged between two springs. Closer examination revealed four staples in a row that were bent in the middle.

I returned to the bathroom and opened the drawer of the vanity. The toenail clipper had meant nothing to me when I saw it the first time. But it had a file that rotated out from one end. The file had a point.

The four staples pried out easily. I worked the box through the opening. White Amazon logos on black shipping tape sealed its top. The label had a first name, no address, and an eight-digit number with a dash in the middle. The box was sealed on the bottom with brown shipping tape. A twenty-dollar bill folded in half had been tucked into a translucent envelope and stuck over the tape.

I folded the clippers and slipped them in my pocket. I put the staples in the drawer of the nightstand. Then I reassembled the bed, grabbed the box, and went downstairs to sit in the kitchen and sip a beer.

It was 4:11 A.M.

My bottle was half empty when Prof wandered in. He glanced at the box and read my expression.

"Leni stole a delivery?"

"Corolla, the Cadillac guy, asked if she had delivered everything."

Prof went to the counter and started heating water.

"What did she say?"

"Don't know. She made me stay out of sight. I think she nodded yes, because then they left without a struggle."

Prof found an orange box of teabags and a white mug emblazoned with a blue rectangle enclosing a lower case f.

"She lied to him," he said.

I half grinned. "Sure looks that way."

"Do we want to know what's in the box?"

"Might help us understand why she kept it. She claims ignorance of what's inside." I turned the box over so Prof could see the bottom. "When I met Leni at the rest stop, she was trying to raise a few bucks by telling fortunes on the sidewalk. Yet, there's a twenty right here."

"Curious," he said. "Must be off limits."

"But she takes it before putting the box in the locker," I said.

"So she could have spent it and then put the box in the locker. Therefore—" he said.

"She had no intention of putting it in the locker. And needed that twenty to still be there if someone found it in her possession. So she could say that she was going to deliver it, but, um, circumstances prevented her."

Prof smiled, tore open a wrapper, and dropped the tea bag into the mug. "Or maybe she was going to dump it and claim that she never saw it. In which case, the money had better be there when it was found."

"I agree. We don't really know anything," I said.

Prof poured hot water into the mug.

"Including what's in the box," I added.

"Shall we guess before we open it?" he said.

"Are you confident it's not a bomb?"

He laughed. "Seems unlikely that Leni would be carrying a bomb. But then, lots of things about Leni are unlikely."

"She gave me her phone before she left."

Prof turned around with the steaming mug in his hand and leaned against the counter. He frowned for the better part of a minute. I sipped my beer. He blew across the surface of his tea.

"Why did she leave?" he said.

"Didn't say. Just tossed the phone in my lap and gave me a six-digit number. I think it's the passcode, but I haven't tested it."

"But she was running away from this guy. Doesn't make sense to go with him. Unless." He paused and sipped. "She's protecting us."

I remembered the gunfire at Toucan Sam's. And Leni smacking Corolla. And her pushing my face into the gearshift.

"Things that bad?" I said.

Prof blew across his tea longer than the last time.

"Usually are." He gestured with his head at the box. "How heavy is it?"

I hefted my beer bottle. "More than two beers. Less than a six pack."

Prof stepped over to stare at the box. I rotated it so he could see the bottom.

"The top will be easier," he said. "There's an Amazon warehouse in St. Louis. I'll arrange to, uh, obtain official tape."

He placed his cup on the table and pulled open a drawer beside the fridge. When he returned he handed me a blue folding utility knife.

"Where did you find it?" he asked.

"Hiding inside the box springs in her bedroom."

Prof nodded slowly. "Smart. She went to some effort to be sure a casual search would miss it."

"So she was expecting someone to look?"

Prof sipped his tea carefully. "Yes. But she doesn't know what's inside?"

I opened the folding knife and extended the blade a quarter of an inch. "Says she never opens the boxes. Like the US post office sending the mail through, but not reading it."

Prof squinted one eye. "Three-letter organizations never read our mail?"

We both laughed.

I examined the box. The label was off-center. If I were careful, I could cut the tape without damaging anything but the tape. I was careful.

I retracted the blade and folded the knife. The box sat on the table with the top tilted up. I looked up at Prof, who was still sipping his tea.

"Amazon is the everything store," he said.

"You have a guess?"

"Too small for a book. Based on the weight, I vote liquid. Laundry detergent. Motor oil. Perfume. Maybe something in a glass container."

There would be a lot of fingerprints on the box from all of the handling. But inside? I unfolded the knife and used the end where the blade retracted to lift the flaps of the box one at a time.

Prof leaned over to peer inside.

Neither of us spoke.

The box contained a black plastic bag closed at the top with a green twist tie.

No visible markings.

No receipt.

CHAPTER 13

We debated.

Not knowing wouldn't help us help Leni.

Knowing might.

We didn't have surgical gloves, so I undid the twist tie using needle-nose pliers. Three 180-degree twists. I spread the mouth of the bag open with the nose of the pliers, glanced inside, and leaned back so Prof could look.

"Amazon," he said.

"How?" I asked.

He shrugged, but remained silent.

"Have to insert it into the supply chain somehow," I said.

Prof's left eye squinted.

He was maybe thinking what I was thinking.

"How much does Leni get for delivering this box?" he asked.

"Twenty bucks. Cash. Taped to the bottom. That's hers. She takes it before putting the box in a locker or delivering it to a house."

"A clever ruse," Prof said.

"Yeah. The innocent mule doesn't know what she has. And if something goes wrong, she can't identify where it came from, where it's going, what it is." I paused. "Or who sent it."

A smile slowly brightened Prof's face.

"Like an Internet Service Provider that doesn't know a thing about that blockbuster movie you're stealing, even as they send gigabytes of data so you can watch it on your computer."

He pulled a teaspoon out of a drawer and dipped the tip into the black bag. Then he placed the spoon on a dinner plate on the table. We both stared.

"Amazing this is flowing through an Amazon warehouse," he said.

It was in an Amazon box sealed with logo tape. It had an Amazon label but no address. Something felt off.

"Leni says that she picks up from houses and delivers to lockers. Or picks up from lockers and delivers to houses. Uses an app called HappyBox."

"So people never have to get up off the couch. To borrow from H.L. Mencken, 'Nobody ever went broke underestimating the laziness of the American public.'"

"How much?" I said.

"In Chicago?" He shrugged thin shoulders that were slightly hunched from leaning over computer consoles. "Thirty grand. Maybe forty if it's special."

"It being?"

"If I recall my evening Wikipedia reading," he said, "this is the second most popular illegal recreational drug in the US, behind only our good friend Mary Jane."

I hummed the first few bars of "Cocaine" by J.J.Cale. Although most people had only heard the Clapton version.

Prof's smile was wry and knowing.

"Let's build a chain of inferences and see what we have," he said. "First, we are looking at a kilo of cocaine in an Amazon box."

"The possession of which will land us in jail on an intent to traffic charge," I said.

Prof didn't disagree.

I continued, "Leni hid this box inside her bed. Presumably last night."

"Which implies that she brought it with her from Chicago," he said.

"How did she get it?" I considered what Leni had told me about her last night in Chicago. "Was it a standard delivery?"

"Or did she grab it?" he said. "And no one knows that she has it. But the Cadillac driver suspects."

Prof sipped his tea. I went to the fridge for another beer. We were quiet for a minute.

"I think she would finish her deliveries for the day before having a romantic dinner with the boyfriend," I said. "They had dinner. They quarreled. He raped her."

"Leni knows where the to-be-delivered boxes are stored at his place. So she secretly grabs one just to mess with him."

"Wait a minute," I said. "Leni told me that she picks up the box at a locker and deliveries it to a residence. Or she picks it up at a residence and delivers it to a locker."

"Therefore," Prof said, "the boxes, and thus the evidence, are never in the possession of our man Cadillac."

I nodded. "So she couldn't have grabbed one."

"Which means," he said, "that she didn't deliver one prior to the romantic dinner."

I drank some beer, then said, "Leni held one back from the day's deliveries as insurance if the dinner didn't go well."

Prof returned to the counter, put the teabag back into his cup and poured hot water over it.

"So our man might not know it's missing," he said. "Maybe it should be in a locker. When the intended recipient complains, all fingers point directly at Leni."

"Who will claim that she has never seen it," I said. "But the sender will claim that the box was picked up."

"He said, she said," Prof said. "One of them is lying, but there's no way to know which one, unless she was unlucky enough to be caught on a surveillance camera."

I drank more beer. "Which leaves us where?"

"Sitting in my kitchen trying to help Leni and stay out of jail. I propose that the recipient has already complained. Assuming there is a complaint channel. The way this is set up, everyone is anonymous."

"Leni used HappyBox to find locations. It would know."

Prof shook his head while blowing on his tea.

"Not necessarily. I would use a zero-trust system so no one can know what it said to whom and when. The Feds hate tech like that. But it exists. It's easy to use. And it's cheap."

I started to think about how a society based on zero trust could work, but stopped myself before going down a rabbit hole.

"That would mean," I said, "That no one knows what happened to that box. Except the person who has it."

Prof nodded with his back to me. He was staring out the window at clouds moving across a half moon. Sunrise wasn't far away.

"So Leni steals the box. Doesn't know what's in it. Hides it. Then voluntarily returns to Chicago with her rapist. Why go back?"

"She kept talking about finishing her degree," I said. "And not losing the semester. How she had to go back and finish his class. Hated repeating things."

Prof spoke toward the moon.

"Do you remember The Girl with the Dragon Tattoo? Popular novel. The heroine went back to her abuser and made a recording of him abusing her. Then used the video to destroy his life."

"You don't think?"

He turned around slowly. "Leni is an intense lady. You have to meet her mother."

"Just to get a video?"

He shook his head. "No, to eliminate the uncertainty that permeates a rape case. Personal history. Establishment of consent. Most of that goes out the window when a jury watches a woman being raped. That's if it gets to trial. Once the rapist's lawyer sees the video, a plea bargain becomes likely."

I contemplated his words and drank before responding. "Leni told me she didn't want a trial because they would dig into her life."

"A student and a college professor?" he said. "Lawyers would be all over her. The university would protect itself. Guess who would have better lawyers?" He tested his tea.

My heart felt heavy, like it was pumping SAE 50 motor oil instead of blood.

"But to live through it a second time?"

"We're guessing," Prof said. "Maybe she's confident she can win a second round."

I considered another beer. I considered dawn was near. I considered that I had no idea what to do. So I asked, "How is she going to function without her phone?"

Prof placed his teacup on the counter and crossed to the black and stainless stove. He pulled open a drawer, stared into it for a moment, then reached in and tossed a dark object at me.

I caught it with two hands. Flipped it over.

"Burner," he said. "Only make phone calls or use Telegram secret messages. Nothing else. Don't surf the web."

"I've heard of these. Never used one." I glanced at him leaning against the stove. "You keep a drawer full of burner phones on hand?"

He smiled wide, said, "The drawer isn't full," and laughed.

I tapped in 65BARACUDA. A woman's voice told me that I had three new messages and how to listen to them.

"Tommy, Tron. Nothing in our territory. No one has seen this dude or his shiny blue car."

I pressed 1 for the next message.

"Tommy, Tron. Heard about the Toucan. We tailed them. They went north and kept going."

I pressed 1 again.

"Tommy." A whisper. "Be me."

The last message was 43 minutes old.

I ended the call.

"What?" Prof said.

"Tron followed the Caddy north three hours ago. But that Caddy ended up here."

Prof shrugged. "Simple tactic. Make us think they're leaving after the raid. Then backtrack on country roads and show up here to grab Leni."

"Last call was from her," I said. "She said 'be me.' Less than an hour ago."

Prof's forehead wrinkled, but only for a moment.

"That's why she gave you the phone. There's something she needs to do that she can't do with Corolla around."

"Their fight started because she was using the phone during dinner."

Prof grinned. "A lot of that going around," he said, and picked up his tea.

CHAPTER 14

atigue overcame desire as first light flowed around the bedroom curtains and my eyes dropped closed. I knew the next step was to login to Leni's phone and determine what she had meant by 'be me.' Prof had offered to help, but advised that I look first. He was her friend. Maybe she was more comfortable with a stranger, who would soon be gone, seeing the inside of her virtual life.

I slept.

I woke at noon and took a shower. I wasn't well rested, but I felt energized. I found a full breakfast on a plate in the fridge with a note stuck to the side.

9:09 A.M. Long night. The world gets crazier and crazier. See you for dinner if you're still around. Bon appetit! — P.

I wondered if Prof thought that I might head back to Chicago. Or maybe bail out while the getting was good.

I stuck the breakfast in the microwave. While waiting, I poured a glass of orange juice and sat down.

I lifted Leni's phone.

Three-quarters charge. The lock screen photo was the student view of a classroom. A professor was drawing a brain on a whiteboard with a red marker, his face in profile. Might be the guy who came into Toucan Sam's; the face was too small to be sure.

I entered 877211 and bit into some bacon.

The home screen appeared with four apps along the top and four along the bottom. In between was photo of a handwritten poem:

These are our days

These are our nights

Only time can separate

Wrongs from rights

No signature. Perhaps there hadn't been one. Or Leni had cropped it off to keep a secret.

The reheated scrambled eggs were surprisingly fluffy. Prof must know some food tricks.

Icons across the bottom:

Mail Photos Messages Browser

Standard stuff. Except the browser was DuckDuckGo. Leni opting for privacy.

Across the top:

Instagram Telegram Signal Oleace

Instagram showed 40 messages. Telegram 15. Signal 3. Oleace 27.

Eighty-five messages in one day? I had gone batty with a fraction of that. Mail showed only 1.

How to "Be me?"

I barely knew anything about her. I didn't know how old she was, or where she was born, or what she liked to drink at Starbucks. I started with Mail.

loverboy34@pm.me had written:

Leni, it was a misunderstanding. Let's talk. Please call.

The message was a day old. Unsigned.

I searched a little. PM.ME was Proton Mail, encrypted email from a company in Switzerland.

I opened Instagram.

Her most recent posts were a selfie on the rest stop sidewalk with the tarot cards splayed out in front of her and a selfie in my car with a red seat back visible over her shoulder. I scrolled back in time. Leni at the beach. Leni at a museum. Leni in the shower hidden by steam. Leni dancing in dark glasses, yoga pants, and a tiny, clingy green top. That one had 287 likes.

She had 2,800 followers. And was following 39.

I felt like a peeping Tom, closed the app, and stared at the home screen. I knew that Telegram and Signal both supported messaging and video chat. Chin had told me they used encryption for security. I took a deep breath and moved on. I searched for 'Oleace' with the DuckDuckGo browser and found a brand of massage oil, a restaurant in Lebanon, and 700 kinds of flowers in the olive family, including ash, jasmine, and lilac.

I launched the app.

The app wanted the password for an account named SallyHoliday. I gave it the six digits that I knew and was suddenly looking at myself on the screen surrounded by controls to set prices, activate camera, turn on audio, and adjust screen colors.

I finished the eggs and drank some orange juice.

For sure Tommy Cuda couldn't pass for SallyHoliday. I found electrical tape in a kitchen drawer filled with hand tools and stacked three layers over the selfie camera. The window went black except for a bit of gray along the bottom edge.

A message from spideyman22 popped up in a chat window beside the black video.

Hey, Sally. I just got paid. Let's play!

A blinking cursor awaited Sally's response. A tab in the corner of the black video read LIVE.

Your video feed isn't working — sm22

I fabricated an excuse.

My network is wonky.

Restart the app. Or move closer to my house. LOL.

Good idea. See you soon.

I located the right icon and logged out of the app. A few seconds later a notification told Sally that she had a new message from spideyman22.

If I was going to be Leni, I would also have to be Sally. I started reading the 28 messages piled up in her inbox. Most were only one line.

-Hey, answer me, bitch.

-Fantastic twenty minutes!

-Oh Sally Sally Sally, you make me cum so hard!

-I want you I want you.

-Don't leave so fast next time.

-I live in Colombia. Where are you from?

-You move like a flowing river. Flow to me.

A few were letters pouring out everlasting love for Sally's eyes, breasts, feet, butt, skin, smile, hair, fingers, fingernails, and even eyebrows. Two guys and one woman proposed marriage.

I read old messages to see how Leni had dealt with so many strangers making demands, wanting attention, asking to schedule a date, begging for photos of her body. Each message generated income. The ACCOUNT page showed the status of her earnings for a two-week period. She was doing a lot better per hour than I had as a mechanic at Walmart.

I touched a tab labeled CONTENT. It contained photos of Leni/ Sally in a trench coat, lingerie, bikini, no bikini. A handful of videos featured the same outfits, but with energetic music and a clever ending where the video stopped just as an article of clothing was about to reveal something special. No wonder Leni was always on her phone. She was in high demand from paying customers.

The screen pulsed. A yellow banner that reminded me of DO NOT CROSS police tape scrolled the words VIDEO CALL across the bottom of the screen. I ignored it.

I wondered how many virtual friends Sally had when I noticed a rating system in the corner. She was four point six stars out of five with 1217 ratings. How many hours per day must she be online to keep this world engaged? When did she study? How did she have time to deliver Amazon packages?

I suddenly felt lazy in comparison.

A folder labeled OUT TO LUNCH contained 20 videos. I tapped one called, "Thanks for contacting me." It showed Sally lying face up on her bed: full make up, bare shoulders. She thanked the viewer for their interest and promised to shower them with affection as soon as she was back online. The way she said the word 'affection' made it seem like more than a hug and a lollipop. I sent the video to minstrel55, who claimed to have something that he desperately needed to show Sally.

A chime bonged. Front doorbell. Prof was asleep. Maybe the visitor would go away. The bell bonged twice in a row. I debated. If I let it keep ringing, it would wake Prof–who may or may not want to wake up after working all night.

It rang again.

I shut off Leni's phone and attempted to not worry about where she was, who she was with, and what they were doing. I pulled out Prof's burner to call my service, disturbed by how difficult it seemed to be to escape technology in the twenty-first century. Not all technology. I rather liked the internal combustion engine, radio, beer, contraception, and vinyl records. But interpersonal communication devices made life feel like being in a cage at the zoo with visitors poking me with electronic probes.

The doorbell rang again. Persistent.

I was Prof's guest. The least I could do was help him sleep. He wouldn't even let me pay for food. I scrubbed the chair back across the floor as I stood. As I reached for the dull brass knob to open the front door, the bell bonged again.

I cracked the door open to peek out.

No one was on the porch poised with their finger over the black button beside the door. I stepped out onto the concrete porch in my bare feet. The sky was gray, but not the kind of gray that promised rain. The street was as empty as the porch, except for parked cars. I stared at the doorbell like it would give me an answer as to why it was ringing. It rang again, the chime reaching me through the open door.

Maybe it was broken.

A car horn yelped two short beeps.

Three cars sat along the near curb. White smoke was visible behind a hatchback, the furthest car to my left. The driver was motioning to me. I debated getting my shoes, but didn't want the doorbell to ring more and wake Prof, so I headed down the steps and along a walk made of individual smooth stones in my bare feet.

Her car was a small SUV in a bright red I had seen on hotrods. She was 20-something, with a puffy Afro containing a brilliant reddish-gold streak down the right side. The passenger window motored down.

"Hi, I'm Naomi. Where's Prof?"

"An emergency kept him up all night. He's still sleeping."

"That poor little skinny man needs a woman to give him stamina. Now what am I going to do?"

"My name's Tommy. I'm a…acquaintance of Leni. I'm staying at Prof's place."

"That little bitch is mooching off Prof again? Where is she?"

"On her way back to Chicago, I think."

Naomi leaned closer.

"Are you the guitar man folks are talking about? White boy that plays Jimi like the devil himself spread holy water on him?"

I laughed. "Never knew the devil to use holy water. I played at Sam's Friday night."

"You did something right. Heard it was good times."

I thought back. "It had some disturbing moments."

"I have a question," she said.

I tilted my head and smiled.

"How do you do Jimi on a Gibson Les Paul?

I laughed.

"Surprised you, didn't I?" she said.

I nodded. "You sure did. Short answer: cheat. My Les Paul has a switch that converts the humbuckers to single coil pick-ups like Jimi's Stratocaster had. Lots of people don't know that back in Jimi's day, the Strat only had a 3-way switch, so Jimi could only use one pickup at a time. Not like the five-way on modern Strats."

"Makes you wonder what Jimi would give us if he were alive now, don't it?"

"Sure does."

"You own shoes? You can't go into Shey's without proper attire."

"Boots and brothel creepers."

"Either. Can you spare an hour to cover for Prof?"

I considered how many messages 'Sally' would receive in the next hour. And what 'covering' for Prof might entail.

"I'd be happy to. But Prof is an awfully smart guy."

Her laughter revealed bold white teeth with a slight overbite.

"This requires dumb muscle and counting in small integers. Grab some footgear, let's go."

◇

Naomi blasted away from the curb with a tiny chirp of rubber the moment my seatbelt clicked. The right corner of her windshield held a sticker like the one Jake had given me. She stared straight ahead and rotated a wheel on the spoke of the steering wheel with her thumb, like she was tuning a radio. But no radio played. Naomi was wearing white yoga pants and white sneakers and an orange top that revealed a figure most guys would long to touch. She broke the silence.

"Do you always wear black?"

I glanced at my black T-shirt under a black leather motorcycle jacket that I felt comfortable wearing, even though I had only ridden a motorbike a few times. My roommate wrenched on his four-cylinder Honda in our living room and let me ride it when my Barracuda was non-operational.

"I have some blues and grays."

"Bold," she said. "How about yellow? Or lime green?"

"I played a lime-green guitar made by Reverend Musical Instruments once."

"Where?"

"As a prop for a theme party called 'black and green.' It was usually 'black and blue,' but the host changed it up that year."

"From what I hear about Friday, you're not such a drab guy."

All I recalled from Friday was trying to keep up with Jake's drumming and gun shots. The situation had demanded concentration.

"I strive to not be drab. But I'm a fan of efficient." I smiled.

Naomi glanced at me, then returned to fondling the thumbwheel. The car accelerated.

"Black is 'efficient' because it doesn't show stains," she said. "You can wash it less often."

She was right.

"Good point," I said. "But imagine if all of your clothing—shirts, pants, socks, underwear, hoodies—could all be washed together."

Naomi glanced my way again. Drove for a city block. Turned left. "That's brilliant. No sorting. No partial loads. Do you just stand there naked watching while everything that you own gets washed?"

"Of course not." I paused. "I usually practice the guitar."

She burst out laughing and swung the car to the curb across from a wall of glass frontage under an LED sign.

SHEY'S GYM

XX & XY Welcome!

Naomi had parked in front of a coffee shop named Star Sense that also sold fruit smoothies, vegetable blends, and protein drinks.

"Breakfast?" I asked.

"After," she said, pushing the driver's door open.

I stepped onto the curb wondering when I might see the sun again. There was something about dull light filtered through smoky gray clouds that seemed to pass through my skin and into my soul. Probably millions of years of evolution at work.

Naomi's back faced me. Her body leaned right against the steering wheel. She tilted her seat back forward and reached around behind her. A passing bright blue pickup truck with huge mud tires honked as it roared passed, giving his opinion of her car door swung out into traffic. I strolled around the back of the car to see if I could assist whatever it was we needed to carry.

I stopped by the left rear quarter panel.

Naomi was scooching herself with upper body strength from the driver's seat into a maroon wheelchair with a low back and solid wheel covers like a bicycle racer prepared for a time trial. The cover facing me was printed with a black and white photograph of Martin Luther King preaching. The handrail for spinning the rear wheel was neon pink.

Naomi spun the chair out of the way, slammed the driver's door, beeped the car locked, and did a wheelie on the chair's back wheels in a beeline toward the gym. I double-checked for traffic. A motorcycle with twin headlights was bearing down on us. I hightailed it after her. She reached the double glass doors to Shey's and touched a round silver plate with her elbow. The doors flung open, she rolled through, and I tailgated in behind her.

The place smelled like hot breath, sweat, wet socks, and determination. It had all black exercise equipment and a rainbow stripe six feet wide wrapped around the perimeter. Not a straight line, but climbing and falling in jagged steps along the wall like a crazed river.

A mass of foot-square lockers sat to our right. A huge silhouette of a pistol the size of a horse emblazoned on them had a red circle around it and a slash through it. A small sign beside a slotted black box read:

LOCKERS ARE FREE — DONATIONS ACCEPTED

Vertical metal detector poles, like the TSA entrance at an airport, separated the lobby from the gym.

Naomi slipped something into a locker and closed it. She turned a key and dropped it into a white purse slung from the side of her chair. I didn't get a good look, but a handgun in a black nylon holster was my first guess. She rolled through the detectors. They beeped and blinked green. A figure in the far corner of the gym waved her in.

I tailgated again.

"You've been here before," I said.

"Three times a week for the past two years. I wouldn't miss it for anything. I love this place."

I hadn't seen the inside of a gym since mandatory Physical Education class in college. But Naomi's enthusiasm made being here seem like a good idea.

"I haven't been to a gym in a long time."

"Don't worry. It's like riding a bike." Her half-hidden laughter made me think I had missed a private joke.

"Prof doesn't strike me as a gym rat," I said.

She rolled up to a row of dumbbells on a black steel rack, put two on her lap, and rolled to an open area with rubber flooring.

"Prof is a man of the mind. Especially as the mind relates to the wallet. Making money is a hobby for him, the way some people play golf." She looked me over. "Or the guitar." She held out a dumbbell with two hands so I took the handle with one. It was heavier than a mahogany Les Paul. "He is also a true and loyal friend. One day I was lamenting that I needed a gym buddy so I could exercise better, he instantly volunteered." She handed me the second dumbbell. "However, he didn't warn me that every time, he would lecture me on the latest info he had come across that was about to change the world."

She held one hand just above each shoulder and nodded at me. I placed a dumbbell carefully into the palm of each of her hands and stepped back.

"Please stand directly behind me. Don't help me unless I say 'help help' or if I fall out of the chair." She laughed again. "And tell me when I get to ten reps."

She pumped the weights vertically over her head, back straight, arms stretching upward slowly and evenly. Over and over.

"Ten," I said.

She stopped with elbows bent. I took the weights and placed them on the floor behind her chair. She tapped a smartwatch whose orange wristband matched the shirt clinging to her body and handed me her phone.

"We wait two minutes and do it again. Then we change to heavier dumbbells."

Naomi took long, slow breaths. I studied the other people in the gym. Two linebacker-sized guys, one white, one black, were spotting each other at a bench press with weights the size of train wheels. Their skin glistened under long overhead lights that gave off a warm daylight feel. The other person was a slender woman with bold red hair doing dead lifts from the floor in a lifting cage that made me think of the zoo. Butt out on the way down. Butt in and hips forward on the way up. She was wearing a bright pink sports bra and pink and gray camo yoga pants. Her sneakers were black and looked a couple of sizes too large. A tattoo on her left shoulder, possibly a raven, curved around and under the back of the bra.

"You want to get some of that?" Naomi said.

"She's pretty."

"Yes. But remember, you're in Shey's place."

She didn't elaborate.

"Does Shey have rules against members dating members?"

Naomi laughed and checked the time on her watch.

"If this place had that rule, it would be empty. But there are rules for sure."

"Need to be safe around heavy equipment," I said.

Her phone buzzed in my hand like a giant bee. Naomi positioned her palms again. I placed the dumbbells.

She exhaled through bright red lips and pressed her hands to the sky, then inhaled through her nose as she slowly lowered them back down. I counted.

"Five."

She kept going.

"Ten."

She stopped. I removed the weights. She shook out her arms. I started the two-minute timer on her phone.

"So much for warm up sets," she said. "Now we go for real weight." She popped her fingers open and closed.

"Forty-five pounds?" I asked, surprised. I returned the smaller dumbbells to the rack and returned with a 45 in each hand. These were heavier than a Fender amp. I lowered them to the floor.

"It's not the machines that are dangerous," she said.

"I noticed the symbol on the lockers."

She smiled. "No guns helps. But it's easy to hurt someone with heavy steel objects."

I glanced at the two big guys. They had moved to a different machine and were lifting a mountain of iron with their legs. The redhead was doing back exercises face down in a machine that suggested a medieval torture device. She faced directly at me and made eye contact with each rise of her body. A rise that also provided line of sight down her bra.

I smiled, then forced my eyes away.

"Her name is Tora," Naomi said. "I have her number."

Heat rose to my cheeks. I knew better than to notice another woman in the presence of a woman—no matter that we had met only hours ago. I changed the subject.

"If it's easy to get hurt, what does Shey do about it?"

Naomi shook her head, making her Afro bounce.

"There is no Shey. Leni's mom, Alexxia, owns this place. The name is a reminder of the rule."

The timer buzzed.

I handed her the heavier dumbbells one at a time. She managed eight reps before her arms started shaking like a hula dancer's grass skirt. I placed the weights on the floor and started the timer. Naomi's elevated breathing continued for a full minute. I was about to ask a question when she spoke.

"No prejudice is allowed in here. None. You make one off-color comment about another person and your membership is suspended until you prove you have taken EQ training. And passed. Stare at the name."

I stared for a few seconds and the word disassembled before my eyes.

SHEY
SHE
 HE
 HEY

"She, he, they," I said.

Naomi gave me a little golf clap.

"The English language," she said, "as rich and powerful as it is, lacks a generic pronoun for an individual of undefined gender identity. So Alexxia invented one."

"Clever," I said. "Seems obvious now that I've seen it."

I couldn't read the message in her smile.

"Lots of things are obvious after you figure them out. Like I have the same emotions as any girl. My heart didn't stop just because my legs don't work right. But obvious doesn't make it a reality."

I felt guilty as charged—focused on the wheelchair and not the lovely person in it.

"So Alexxia's simple message is: Everyone is welcome at Shey's?"

Naomi nodded. "Welcome. And to a large extent, protected. Between Alexxia, the cameras, and the gymnasts who call this place home who won't take shit from anyone, this is the safest place in the neighborhood."

"It even has gun laws." I smiled.

Naomi did too. "Sure does."

"Is that why the girl in pink is watching me? To make sure I follow the rules?"

The timer buzzed. Naomi shook her head.

"The two big guys keep looking this way too," I said.

"Natural curiosity. They see me with Prof. So they wonder. Are you my new physical therapist? Personal trainer? Sugar daddy? Why would Naomi be with a skinny white dude who dresses like a character from a goth comic book?"

I laughed. Perhaps I owned too much black. Was that even possible? I glanced at the men. They were engaged with the train wheels again and ignoring us.

"Next the legs," she said.

<>

I handed her weights, often with two hands, and operated the timer. Except for her leg routine. Then I was enlisted as an immovable object. She directed me to hold her leg in a particular position—straight, knee bent, angled in or out—and resist her efforts to move me. I paid close attention. Sometimes I could barely feel her effort. But I always smiled and cheered: "Push, push, you're doing great." The leg exercises seemed to make her muscles shiver more than lifting weights did. The complex movements, she told me, were designed to slow or possibly reverse the degradation of her neurons used for muscular control.

I sure hoped they worked.

Now Naomi sipped an orange drink so bright it appeared radioactive. She was eating special protein-packed pancakes with three eggs on them, over easy. She placed her glass on our table at the window and stared out at the street. The staff of Star Sense knew her and welcomed me. Except for the woman who brought Naomi's smoothie. She had looked at me like I smelled bad.

"If you lifted weights you would eat more," Naomi said. "I like eating. Needing to reach my calorie target for the day feels really good."

"I never think much about food. I just eat when I'm hungry."

She laughed. "A primitive. Live off the land. Survival as the prime directive."

She was right. I was living off the land: diners, friends, packs of hundred-dollar bills.

"Tell me," she said. "I know why I live in this excuse for a city. Why are you here?"

"Because it's between Chicago and Los Angeles."

She didn't laugh as she met my eyes and pulled pancakes from her fork with her tongue. Hers were glossy brown. Maybe even turbo-bronze metallic. And were clearly waiting for a more robust answer.

"I'm traveling route sixty-six from east to west."

"That's a song," she said. "I heard a rapper do it at a rave once."

"Bobby Troup wrote the song about his trip from Pennsylvania to California with his wife. He wanted to become a Hollywood songwriter. The King Cole Trio recorded it first. Nineteen forty-six. But many others have too: Bing Crosby, Chuck Berry, The Rolling Stones, Depeche Mode, Manhattan Transfer. Disney even used it in their Cars movie."

"Guitar player," she said, without further comment.

"Too much information?"

She shook her head. "Oh no, I love history. Most people don't bother to learn enough of it. Musicians," she paused, "especially electric guitar players, are full of tidbits of essentially useless information. For example, I bet you know what model guitar Chuck Berry used to record 'Get Your Kicks.' Maybe even which one the Stones used too."

I smiled. "I don't know for sure. But I could guess based on the guitars they favored around that time."

"Really? You don't have a vinyl of the Stones in your trunk?"

"You win. I'll check the liner notes."

"But," she said.

I waited. She sipped her smoothie.

"But?" I said.

"I'll bet 'who buys lunch' that you have no idea where you are going to make your next dollar."

I held up both hands in surrender. "You win."

"See. Guitar player."

"Are we so much alike?"

Her brown eyes roamed my face. She nodded slightly.

I felt like a cookie from a cutter.

"Oh yes." She smiled and I'd swear her eyes twinkled like in an animated movie. "You tend to be good with your hands."

CHAPTER 15

I waved goodbye to Naomi from Prof's porch, her little thank you kiss still warm on my left cheek. She had more joie de vivre than…maybe than anyone I had ever met. Not once did she mention why she used a wheelchair. I hadn't asked. If I had, she would have needed to tell a story she had told a hundred times about something she would rather forget. The chair just was, like the red-gold streak in her hair, or the metal-flake sparkle in her eyes.

The front door was unlocked. I found Prof in the kitchen having breakfast.

"Yo, Tommy. Saw your car out back but no you. Decide to take a walk in our little piece of the city?"

"I got hijacked by a beautiful woman on two wheels."

Prof's face was blank for a moment, then he glanced at a calendar beside the fridge. It showed photos of hot-rodded gaming systems. This month featured Lenovo. His shoulders sagged.

"Naomi?"

I nodded.

He shook his head. "Today isn't our usual day. She switched last week. I even have it logged on my DO NOT FORGET calendar."

"Humans are creatures of habit," I said. "Especially when sleep deprived."

He stood and rinsed his dishes in the sink.

"Thanks for covering for me. What do you think of her?"

"A beautiful person in a hundred ways."

Prof nodded.

"She requested day after tomorrow," I said. "I didn't know your schedule, and I sure don't know mine."

"Depend on Leni?"

I went to the fridge for a bottle of water. Just watching Naomi work out had made me thirsty. While I drank, I checked Leni's phone. Twenty new messages had arrived in Oleace. One account caught my eye.

turbobronze65

What were the odds?

I dig muscle cars. Cum find me. I'm lost.

No Signature.

"Hmm…"

"Something interesting in cyberspace?" Prof asked.

"I think Leni sent herself a message, hoping I would read it.

"You think?"

"No signature. No name," I said.

Prof stared out the kitchen window at the alley where they had grabbed Leni. "But you think it's Leni?"

"The account name is unique."

"You know the story about a hundred monkeys with typewriters eventually writing Shakespeare?"

"Yeah. But this is too much to be a coincidence. I told Leni that my car is a sixty-five Barracuda. Special Edition. And that the paint everyone thinks is brown is actually turbo bronze metallic."

"This account knows that?"

I nodded.

"What does Ms. Turbo want?"

"Says she's lost. I should, uh, come find her." I didn't mention her spelling.

Prof sat at the table, put his chin in one hand, and drummed the stone surface with the fingertips of the other.

"Not missing," he said. "Not kidnapped. Not back at school studying. But lost? Unusual choice of words."

"Lost," I said. "As in I don't know where I am. Or lost, my future is bleak."

"Or lost," he said, "someone found me, but has lost me again."

"The boyfriend?"

"Be a good guess," Prof said. "You possess Leni's phone. How did she post that message for you to find?"

"Laptop? Public library computer?" I held up the gray phone he had loaned to me. "Back up burner phone?"

"Tonight," he said. "Or tomorrow morning?"

"Your unstated analysis concludes that Leni is in some kind of trouble with Corolla and we should drop everything to go help her."

"Consider the possible outcomes. If she doesn't need us, we have a nice ride in your noble chariot. But if she does need us, and we don't go..." He shrugged.

"Easy choice. Let's go tonight. We'll need a place to stay."

"I'll handle it," he said, and headed up the stairs.

◇

Two stops for gas to feed the guzzler and another for snacks had us rolling into Chicago just before midnight. Prof had spent much of the time on his phone curating suspicious Meta posts. He would laugh occasionally, or shake his head, but he maintained confidentially and refused to tell me anything.

"Where did you get reservations?" I asked.

"I didn't," he said.

"I'm sure I heard you say that you would arrange for lodging."

"I did," he said.

"So where to. I need some shut-eye."

"Do you mean that we are not going to trip the light fantastic in the bustling cosmopolitan metroplex of Chicago tonight?"

"It's Monday," I said.

"All the better. People who party on Monday are more dedicated to the pursuit of joy."

The reference to 'joy' carried me back to a place called the Pink Monkey. I wondered if Mona was dancing tonight.

I made a sharp left.

Fifteen minutes of winding through city streets later, a valet was driving away in my Barracuda. The Monkey rose three brick stories above us, the windows blocked from the inside and glowing pink.

Prof laughed and shook his head.

"Fun name," he said.

I realized that I was standing on the very spot where I had been punched in the gut not so long ago.

Prof put a hand on my shoulder.

"You okay?"

"Yeah. Just a little flashback."

A waitress arrived wearing shiny black yoga pants and a white sports bra. Prof whispered an order in her ear, and we settled down to drinks the color of bananas with the texture of a milkshake. The sparse crowd was being worked by two dancers: a Filipino wearing the tallest heels I had ever seen, her shoes and lingerie both a shimmering silver that reminded me of liquid mercury; and a dark-skinned girl whose facial features suggested a princess from a powerful nation in Africa.

The stage was empty. The volume of the hip-hop tunes was subdued. The themes focused on lost love and lacked hot cars and drag racing.

I sipped the yellow fluid.

"How many natural fluids are yellow?" I asked.

"Several fruit juices," Prof said. "And mammal urine." He laughed.

A dancer emerged from a door in a far corner. Her Brazilian string bikini matched our drinks. Gray suede boots. Hair spiked straight out from her head as if an electric current were scorching through her lithe body. If her hair hadn't been red, I wouldn't have recognized Mona behind the alien-invader makeup. A few seconds later she was on stage tantalizing a gold pole and staring out over the heads of the audience as if we weren't there.

"What do you think?" I asked.

Prof held his drink in two hands, as if it needed protecting from thieves.

"What's to think? Good booze, nice ambience, lovely women. Life is good in the now."

"Sufficient intellectual stimulation?" I asked.

"I'm working on the Leni problem in the background to occupy that part of my being."

"Progress?"

"A rough draft of a plan." He raised the glass to his lips with both hands.

The African Princess approached our table. Up close, her dark skin was so perfect it looked Photoshopped.

"Hello boys," she said. British accent. Perfect diction. My better judgement began to flee.

"Would you care to join us?" Prof said. "My rich friend, who has enjoyed white privilege for his entire life, is studying the challenges of locomotion."

"I know that dance," she said.

Prof rose to pull out a chair for her, placing me to her right, him to her left, and all three of us able to see the stage where the red-headed alien moved.

She answered the question on our faces.

"My grandmother would sing 'Come on baby, do the loco-motion' while we were cleaning the house together. Someone clever added a hyphen in the title, so it was loco," she emphasized with a finger," hyphen motion on the record label. Sort of, um, changes the meaning." Her eyes turned dreamy. "Grandma made everything fun." She snapped back. "She told me the story behind that song when I was a teenager and made me promise to keep my wits about me my whole life long."

The waitress arrived. She nodded, I nodded, Prof passed, and the waitress was off.

"Thank you," she said. "I'm Ophelia."

Prof pointed. "Tommy, Prof."

She held her gaze on Prof for a moment.

"Nice to meet you both."

The yellow bikini stepped off the stage to converse with a guy in a tight black shirt that showed off his biceps.

"Will you tell us the story?" Prof asked.

She smiled. Her glistening teeth had just the slightest gap in front. More personality than gap.

"I haven't thought about this in a long time. So Grandma and I are cleaning and singing and I'm trying to do the dance moves in the lyrics. One day, she lifts the needle off the record and asks me, 'Do you know where songs come from?' I was maybe seven or eight years old. I said, 'the radio.'"

I smiled.

Prof gave a little toast of approval with his glass.

"Smart kid," he said.

"When Grandma stopped laughing, she explained how some people write songs and that other people sing them. She told me that 'Do the loco-motion,' was written by a girl named Carole King. Yes, she emphasized. A little white girl not much older than you wrote that song. Maybe her husband helped. I remember his name. Goffin, made me think of coffin. Even then, I knew this lesson was about girl power."

Ophelia's drink arrived in a plastic coconut that was doing a good job of faking it. It was filled with a white liquid and sported a red and white striped straw with a curlicue in it.

Ophelia smiled, held the coconut up, and proposed a toast to the inventors of rum. We all drank. She placed her fat coconut on the table.

"Then Grandma told me that Carole, the white girl, actually wrote the song for a singer named Dee Dee Sharp. Sometimes I call myself Dee Dee." She smiled. "When I'm not Ophelia. See, Dee Dee's a big time singer at the time. Has a smash hit called Mashed-Potato Time. A song about a dance. So little Carole offers her Loco-motion."

"I bet you're going to tell us that Dee Dee turned it down," I said, having a vague recollection of reading album liner notes at the Oberlin college radio station while spinning late-night vinyl from the school's massive record collection.

"That's right," Ophelia said. "Dee Dee passes on what will soon be a hit song and will go on to be in the Top 3 in America in three different decades. Can you imagine? That's longer than I've been alive."

"And the moral of the story?" Prof said, his eyes riveted to Ophelia.

Ophelia, aka Dee Dee, shook her head.

"We ain't to the moral yet, boy, we's just gettin' started."

We all laughed. Her British accent returned.

"Lesson number two. Be careful when looking a gift horse in the mouth. The world doesn't give you a mountain of opportunities. When one comes strolling along, reach out and grab that sucker."

Prof and I drank. Now focused on the moral of the story.

Ophelia sucked on the straw with her coconut sitting on the table. The straw was actually clear with a red stripe, so I could trace the rise of the white fluid to her lips, then watch it subside back into the coconut. A curved straw doesn't seem like it should be erotic, but Ophelia had her own ideas.

We watched the stage. Red and green lasers painted patterns on the girl wearing the yellow bikini, who had returned to dancing.

"Please go on," Prof said. "Your story is getting better and better."

Ophelia smiled. "So, Dee Dee passes on the song. Now our little white girl has a problem: a song about a dance that doesn't even exist, and no singer. What is she to do? As we now know, Carole eventually starts singing her own songs. Personally, I like Killing Me Softly, but she eventually has a whole string of hits. That all comes later. At this point in our story, Carole needs a singer."

Ophelia sipped.

I wracked my brain for the name of the singer who did Loco-motion back in the 60s. All I could think of was the letter E.

Ophelia watched my face as she sipped, a smile on her lips. Her knowing. Me trying to remember.

"Little Eva!" I almost shouted.

"Bingo. Know anything about her?"

Prof and I both shook our heads.

"Are you ready?" she said. "Eva Boyd was Carole's...are you really ready? OK." She paused. "Babysitter."

Prof choked on his yellow drink.

"You're making this up," he said.

Ophelia laughed. "Would my Grandma lie to you?"

"That's astonishing," I said. "Of all the available singers, they hired the babysitter?"

"They knew she could sing when they hired her. But yes, the babysitter sang the demo. The record company liked the demo and released it. Eva Boyd became Little Eva, R and B singer."

"And Grandma's lesson number three?" Prof asked.

"This one is from Eva's perspective, the little black girl with a lovely voice. In Grandma's words: 'Whatever you're trying to do, don't stand on the sidelines. Put yourself where the action is.'"

"That's a lot of great lessons from a story about a dance song," I said.

Ophelia leaned back with her coconut in both hands and sucked white liquid through a smile. With one eye I watched the yellow bikini flip upside down on the gold pole."

"What makes you think there aren't more lessons?" she said.

"I thought the release of the song would be the climax," I said.

"Hardly." Ophelia grinned. "Carole wrote another song inspired by Eva. But she never recorded it. Do you know about it?"

Prof watched the stage too. Even upside down the yellow bikini glanced at our table.

"Uh…" I said.

"The Crystals," Ophelia said.

I combed my brain for a 60s hit by the Crystals.

"Drawing a blank?" she asked.

"What year?" I said.

"Sixty-two. Same year as Loco-motion."

I sipped my yellow slush to buy time.

"The Crystals," I said, "were an all-girl group. They did Da-doo-run-run."

"Very good," she said, nodding.

"My grandfather liked fast cars and the music that went with them."

Ophelia laughed. "He might have like my Grandma."

I looked down at the back of my hand, wondering what shade it would be if that interracial marriage had happened back in the 60s.

"Then he kissed me," Prof said.

"You see that on Wikipedia?" I asked.

He nodded.

"Cheater." Ophelia laughed. "You're right. But that's not the song Grandma taught me."

"Did Phil Spector produce it?" I asked.

"Spector produced all of these songs."

"He was convicted of killing a woman," Prof said.

I remembered the trial. Strange things happened in the world of music. All that emotion near the surface and running hot.

Ophelia sucked her curlicue straw and released it.

"Give up?" she said.

Prof and I exchanged a glance, then nodded.

"Little Eva, the singing babysitter, had a boyfriend who beat her. She told Carole about it—including that that was how she knew her boyfriend loved her."

Leni's conundrum rushed into my head.

"You're going to tell us," Prof said, "that Carole wrote a song about it and the Crystals recorded it."

"You catch on fast," Ophelia said. "Are you ready for the title. It will blow you away."

The yellow bikini flipped right-side up and continued dancing. The music shifted toward electronic dance music.

Ophelia placed the coconut on the table. She smacked her right fist into the open palm of her left hand.

"He hit me. And it felt like a kiss."

"That's the song title?" Prof said.

"Sure is. Written by the little white girl documenting the life of her babysitter."

"What happened next?" I asked.

"According to Grandma, it started getting good airplay on the radio. Then people protested that it glorified domestic violence."

"And the song disappeared?" I said.

Ophelia drank, nodded, and wagged a finger at me, all at the same time.

"It's still here. Check Spotify."

"I suspect," Prof said, "that Ophelia's Grandma had an opinion."

Ophelia smiled and watched the yellow bikini dance for a moment.

"Grandma would play that song, then look me in the eye and say, 'If a man ever hits you, walk out and don't look back. That ain't no kind of love.'"

We all got quiet.

The music switched to a funky groove with a moaning saxophone.

"Smart lady," Prof said. After a long moment studying Ophelia's face, he added, "I bet there's more."

Ophelia laughed. "Grandma could bend your ear all night long with advice she wasn't shy about sharing." She made a peace sign with her right hand. "But only two more from Loco-motion."

The song started playing through the sound system. Little Eva's version from the 60s. Even on the ancient recording, the upbeat energy vibe of Spector's production was impossible to miss. I met Ophelia's dark eyes. They held a deep knowing friendliness, like a mom welcoming back her prodigal son.

She produced a smartphone and a smile.

"I'm good friends with the DJ."

Eva's voice filled the club with youthful energy. I tried not to imagine a young singer being smacked by her boyfriend but failed.

"Lesson five," Ophelia said, "do not let the world define you. Little Eva, stereotyped into the dance number category, never really got to sing anything else. Lesson six. Eva was making fifty bucks a week while the song ran up the charts and paid for Mr. Spector's cocaine habit."

"Own the rights," I said. "Tough to do back then."

"Tough to do anytime," Prof said. "You know what Jimmy Buffet said, 'Don't depend on the kindness of crooks.' Or something to that effect."

"Wikipedia?" Ophelia asked.

"Personal experience," Prof said. "The software industry has all of the same problems as the music business, with billion-dollar stakes."

"Maybe all of the lessons apply," Ophelia said. "Let's test your memory."

"Girl power," I said. "A woman can do anything she wants with her life."

She smiled her biggest smile all night. The little gap had a lot of personality.

"Don't look a gift horse in the mouth," Prof said. "The reason you sometimes call yourself Dee Dee."

Eyelash flutter from Ophelia, but no words.

"Number three, put yourself in the action," I said. "If you're an aspiring singer, get hired by a songwriting team." I grinned.

"Four," Prof said. "That ain't no kind of love."

"You guys are doing great for a couple of drunks in an exotic dance club." She laughed a tiny titter that barely cut through the song.

I suddenly realized that the yellow-bikini girl was doing the original Loco-motion across the stage. And I was being stared at.

"Um…" I said. "Don't let the world stereotype you and limit your options. Like the Army says, 'Be all you can be.'"

"And last but not least," Ophelia said, "keep your rights. Own the golden goose, not just a couple of eggs."

"Did your grandmother really teach you to own the golden goose," I asked.

"Are you kidding? She even bought me a fluffy stuffed goose to hug at night."

"No way it was gold," I said.

"Of course it was gold."

"Did she get you a gift horse too?" Prof said.

Ophelia tilted her chin down and her eyes up to stare at Prof. She sucked on her straw. Stopped. Sat up. Held her hands about ten inches apart.

"Unicorn."

◇

"Don't you wish."

The woman's voice came from behind my right shoulder. I would have recognized it anywhere. I twisted around in my chair.

The yellow bikini bottom was at my eye level.

"Tommy Cuda?" Mona said. "I thought you were going west. Driving into the sunset. Seeing the U.S.A." She gestured to the waiter.

Prof jumped up and pulled out the unoccupied fourth chair at our table.

"You're Tommy Cuda?" Ophelia said. "This girl has told me stories."

"And some of them are true," Mona added, as she scooched herself up to the table with an assist from Prof.

Ophelia smiled. "I wonder which ones."

"I was almost to St. Louis," I said. "Then I met some people. Mona, this is my new friend Prof. Prof, my dear friend Mona, who was missing when I found her."

"Pleasure to meet you," Prof said. "Tommy has been keeping secrets. Had I known you and Ophelia were in Chicago, I would have visited sooner."

Mona smiled. With her beauty and job at the Pink Monkey, she had likely heard every compliment that existed in thirty-eight different languages.

"Did 'some people' bring you to Chicago? Or you came back just to see me?" Mona asked.

Prof laughed, knowing I was trapped.

"We're in town on business. But this is the first place we stopped. Haven't even checked into our hotel yet."

Mona smiled an 'I think you're lying' smile. But it was the truth.

The bartender personally placed a coconut in front of Mona and left. Mona's coconut also had a twisty straw. But the stripe was blue.

"How long are you staying?" she asked.

"Unclear," I said. "My schedule is open. But Prof has a couple of real jobs."

"Nothing I can't do on my laptop in Starbucks," he said.

"Or the Pink Monkey?" Mona asked.

Prof smiled and licked his lips.

"Do you have good Wi-Fi?"

"Oh yeah," Ophelia said. "We've been streaming live shows since COVID nineteen hit. It's almost like being in the club. Everyone gets a table. Anyone can look around and see who else is here. Girls can discreetly approach any one customer and suggest a private show.

Dancers on multiple stages. You can even buy me a real drink and watch me suck on the straw."

"You folks are way ahead of Zuckerberg's Metaverse. Maybe he'll hire you as consultants."

"Wasn't he in here once?" Mona said.

Ophelia laughed. "Don't tease them."

"But it's fun," Mona said.

I waited. Prof appeared to be analyzing.

"We're evil women," Ophelia said. She looked at Mona, who nodded while sipping the blue-striped straw.

"I hope you mean 'evil' in the right way," Prof said.

Ophelia's grin sent good vibes. "We make up stories."

"Lots of people do that. It's how boring people get to be interesting," Prof said.

"Touché," Mona said.

"In this case," Ophelia said, "it's a business strategy. If we all just lie any way we want, as soon as a customer cross-checks with another girl, we're found out and the customer leaves in a huff and no tip."

I thought of Mala, Mona's sister. And the lying politicians she ran with.

"So you have lying teams," I said "You all know the details of each other's stories so you can create a virtual reality right here in the Pink Monkey with just your words."

Ophelia smiled.

Mona said, "You wouldn't believe how many guys want to know the details of the private dance that Bill Gates liked best."

"I hear he's divorced," Prof said.

Mona winked. "Must have been my dancing."

"But you're telling us," he said. "Your secret will leak."

"Tommy's a good friend," Mona said. "He helped me a lot. And..."she let the world trail right to her lips on the straw.

I took the cue. "I'll back her up."

"So," Prof said, "if a customer says to his buddy, 'That crazy bitch expects me to believe that she danced for Bill Gates,' you lean over and say, 'She did. It was back in April. He was in town to speak at a cybersecurity conference. He told me how to have security, innovation, and a sustainable environment all at the same time.' Then the guy's eyes light up and he doesn't figure you for a shill."

"And next thing you know," Ophelia said, "he's asking for the Gates' dance."

"Does this work?" Prof asked.

"No one has complained to management yet," Mona said.

"What are you going to do if Gates actually comes in?" Prof asked.

"Tell him," Mona said, "I read your book 'How to avoid a climate disaster.' I was so impressed that I named a dance in your honor. Would you like to experience it?"

I drank some beer. Mona was a genius.

"Brilliant," Prof said.

"So what brings you to the Monkey?" Ophelia asked.

"We needed a place to sit and think," I said. "We have a problem, but lack a plan."

"Guys usually think with the little head in here," she said.

"We're also hiding from some people," I said.

"Can you talk about the problem?" Mona asked. "Or is it one of those top-secret things?"

Her very red lips wrapped around the straw and sucked. I wondered who had invented the straw.

"The first problem is easy," Prof said. "We need a hotel."

"No way," Mona said.

"Hotels are full?" Prof said.

"Maybe. But you guys have friends. Stay at my place," Mona said.

"We couldn't intrude—"

"Tommy Cuda, if I came to your town, where would you want me to stay?"

"In his bed," Prof said.

Mona looked embarrassed for an instant, then she laughed.

"Ha, ha. Dee Dee, don't you think they should stay with me? I work late and sleep during the day. I'll hardly know they're even there."

"I smell a setup," Prof said. "Tommy, we're going to lose this argument."

"He's smart, isn't he?" Mona said.

"I've heard that he's read eighty percent of Wikipedia," I said.

"Eighty-two at last count," Prof said. "But they keep adding material."

The girls were both quiet. Sipping. Then at the same time they said, "You read Wikipedia?"

"I'm a nerd. Guilty as charged."

Mona stood and walked away without a word. Her coconut was still half-full.

"She doesn't like nerds?" Prof said.

"Oh, she does," Ophelia said. "You'll insult her if you don't accept her offer."

"But—"

Ophelia held up her hand. "She'll think her place isn't good enough for you."

"If it's good enough for the lady, it's good enough for me," Prof said. "I can use the Monkey's excellent Wi-Fi to meet high demand. Everything else I can do with a hotspot on my cell phone."

"Ophelia, what does Mona need that we could get for her as a thank you?" I asked. "Something special."

She sipped from her coconut until it gurgled like a kid finishing the last drops of a milkshake. She stood gracefully, pushed her chair in, placed both hands on its back, and leaned over so far her breasts threatened to fall into her coconut. She stared at Prof. Then at me. She straightened slowly.

"Friends," she said. And walked away.

CHAPTER 16

Prof sipped from a coconut drink he had smuggled out of the Monkey. I was halfway through a Stella Artois that the quiet bartender had recommended. We were sitting in my Barracuda on Evan Street, across from a 24-hour grocery store that had once been a member in good standing of a powerful chain, but was now called Generic Groceries.

Mona had returned to the table with a key for her apartment. It was less than a mile from the Monkey, but neither of us was comfortable invading her space while she was still working. So we were trying to do some work of our own while we waited for her to finish her shift.

"Are you sure about the location?" Prof asked.

"Nope. But there's an app on Leni's phone called HappyBox. There is only one entry, and the ID number matches the label on the box I found inside her bed springs."

"So you hypothesize that HappyBox directs Leni on what to do with each package?"

I nodded and drank. "Here's what I think happened. Leni went to Corolla's place. He gave her the box."

Prof shook his head with the twisty straw to the coconut still in his mouth. His was striped blue, like Mona's.

"With a setup like this, he would never handle the goods himself."

I focused across the street on the brightly lit entrance to Generic. To the left of the entrance, two dozen two-foot-square lockers sat in the shadow of escalators that provided access to the second floor. A black and white sign above them read:

AMAZON LOCKERS

"Do you think Leni picked up the package before or after visiting Corolla?"

"After," Prof said. "She would have strict orders to never bring merchandise to his place."

I sipped warming beer.

"The altercation takes place," I said. "Leni rides her bicycle here. The supplier maybe sees Leni pick it up, maybe not. Never sees Corolla. Maybe only sees Leni once. The next pickup uses a different mule."

"And only Leni knows about the HappyBox trick. In fact, maybe only mules know about it. Suppliers and customers are both serviced by Uber-mules who don't know what's in the boxes."

I watched the wall of lockers. No one entered or left the store. After one A.M. Not a popular time to shop.

"Would you design it like that?" I asked.

"For sure. Silo the knowledge. Don't allow anyone to have leverage over your supply chain or customer base."

"Except the mules?"

Prof sipped for a few seconds.

"They get picked up transporting a box. Never even opened it. Only information they could reveal is the location where they picked it up. And the HappyBox app on their phone. Which I'll bet is cloud based and vaporizes itself if the proper codes aren't entered."

"Suppliers and customer don't even know the drop location," I said.

"Or," he said.

I finished the Stella. Maybe it was just the excitement of being back in Chicago, but it sure tasted good.

"Or," I said, "HappyBox controls everything and remembers nothing."

"Exactly," Prof said. "And what it needs to hold during the transaction is carefully encrypted."

"So if a mule talked to the cops?"

"They could shut down the locker system," Prof said.

"But never find Corolla, the suppliers, or the customers. Couldn't the cops set up a sting operation using a mule?"

"They could try," he said. "But Corolla is using students for a reason."

"Regular turnover?"

He nodded. "And they're broke, need drugs, and need money to get through our outrageously priced higher education system."

I faced him. He was slouched low and sipping like we were on a beach in Bali.

"Leni?" I said.

He pursed his lips and tapped the side of his coconut with an index finger.

"She isn't shy about making things happen in whatever way suits her," he said.

"Sorry for the direct question. But is Leni a prostitute?"

"She has the assets and talent. But..." he shook his head. "She'd want control." He laughed. "Maybe she's a pimp."

We both noticed at the same time.

A figure in a black hoodie glided up silently on an electric scooter, stopped in front of the right bank of lockers, and let the scooter handle tilt to the ground. A cell phone appeared. An Amazon box the size of a sleeping cat came out of an aqua backpack and into a locker on the bottom row. Without even a glance around the area, the figure stepped back onto the scooter and continued in the same direction. The entire action took less than 30 seconds.

"You see a face?" Prof asked.

"She never looked up," I said.

"She?"

"Deduction. Aqua fingernail polish matched the aqua backpack."

"Was that Leni?" I asked.

"Too short," Prof said.

"How could you tell?"

"Looked like a little kid on that scooter. Those lockers are eighteen inches square according to Wikipedia. She was barely five feet. Leni is closer to five six."

A persistent buzz, like a contestant pressing a button on a game show, filled the car. I glanced at the dash. It was totally dark and the ignition key was in my pocket.

"Leni's phone," Prof said.

I dug the smartphone out of my pants pocket. The ocean photo on the screen bathed the interior in bluish light.

"Notification from HappyBox," I said.

Prof slid a little lower in the red leather bucket seat. I glanced at the empty beer bottle and considered what my stomach wanted next. The buzzing stopped. We waited. A breeze along the street lofted a red candy wrapper. I'd guess Kit-Kat. My stomach growled.

"Depends on what I assume," Prof said, as if I had asked him a question. "If Leni is playing along with Corolla and behaving the way he wants her to behave, then he thinks everything is copacetic."

"But I have her phone."

He gazed out the windshield at the empty street, or maybe a streetlight, or the moon, or a crack in the side of Generic Groceries.

"You have a phone," he said.

"OK. Maybe Leni has two phones. Why do I have one?"

"To make it possible for you to do something for her."

Now it wasn't technology confusing my life. It was people. I caught myself mid-thought. Maybe it had always been people—the technology was just the messenger that I wanted to shoot.

"Sure be nice if Leni told me what it was," I said.

"She did."

I glanced down at Leni's phone in my hand. It had gone dark. Prof continued staring straight ahead, like a lidar beam pinging the area for motion.

"Her message was 'be me,'" I said.

Prof nodded ever so slowly. "So, Tom, we need to figure out when and how you need to be Leni."

I unlocked the phone and opened HappyBox.

"Maybe now," I said. "HappyBox wants Leni to pick up a package from a locker and deliver it."

"Where's the pick up?" he asked.

"Across the street." Our eyes met. "How many mules do you think Corolla uses?"

Prof pulled out his smartphone and tapped at the calculator.

"Estimate five deliveries per day per mule," he said. "Assume the box that Leni left for us is average. Estimate the street price. Hmm… maybe twenty-five grand per mule per day. Ten mules, a quarter-million dollars a day. Call it a million dollars a week, roughly. Forty or fifty million annual revenue."

"Bazonga," I said.

Prof laughed. "I could be off by a factor of 2 or 3," Prof said. "Or maybe Corolla has a hundred mules in ten major cities and it's a half-billion dollar business."

"Where's the dough?" I asked.

"Excellent question." He popped the handle of his door. The dome light flooded the interior like the sun had risen. I reached up and switched it off.

"Security cameras?" I said.

"No doubt. Remember our aqua-nailed delivery girl, where she came in, how she hid her face. I'm thinking she has this place figured out. Let's imitate her."

I grabbed a shop rag from the trunk and we strolled to the corner, made a legal street crossing, and approached the Amazon lockers on the path of Aqua's electric scooter. The boxes each had a numeric keypad. The HappyBox app indicated A2, the box Aqua had just filled, and provided a four-digit code.

I retraced Aqua's footsteps. At A2 I dropped to one knee, pressed buttons with the tip of my car key, and opened the door with its teeth. Then I tossed the shop rag over Aqua's box and dragged it out. Back in the car we shook the box, but were met with silence. A sealed envelope taped to the bottom of the box was labeled OUT.

"Care to guess?" Prof said.

"The envelope is for someone other than the recipient of the box. Otherwise it would be inside," I said.

Prof pointed at the box.

"A second envelope has already been removed," Prof said.

I speculated. "First mule picks up the box and delivers it to the locker. Takes the first envelope as cash payment for delivery."

"Pure genius," Prof said. "The dealer doesn't ever contact the customer. Sort of like old-school spies leaving a note behind a loose brick in a garden wall."

"Our friend HappyBox wants us to make a delivery."

Prof pressed the box to his ear and twisted his upper body left and right.

"I hear pills rattling. Different contents than the one Leni left for us."

The drive took eight minutes and landed us outside the Natural History Museum staring at an iron rendition of the skeleton of a dinosaur three stories high.

"You sure about this address?" Prof asked.

I parked, let the Hemi idle, and held the phone out for him to read the address in the HappyBox app.

"There's no address on the box," he said. "No name. Nothing but a six-digit code."

"If we drop it at the shipping/receiving door, they won't be able to identify the intended recipient."

"So protocol directs it to an internal dead-letter office," Prof said.

We were thinking along the same lines. The box arrives at an official dead end and sits for weeks, maybe months. There's no return address to send it back to, so it's destroyed. Unless.

"At some point," I said, "a mule walks into the dead letter office and steals the box. So long as he or she—"

"Shey," he said.

I smiled. "Right. So long as shey is smart enough to avoid being caught on video, no one knows where the box went. Or cares."

"Clever set up," Prof said. "Only one thing bothers me."

"Only one?" I laughed.

"Well, two. But I have a hypothesis about the second one. The first one has me stumped."

I figured it would be easy to make this delivery now; the museum had a night box drop off with a silver rotating drum like the post office used, only super-sized.

"How," Prof said, "does the writer of the HappyBox app convince Amazon to play along with these boxes moving in and out of lockers?"

I visualized Generic Grocery. Rows of lockers. The one Aqua had opened.

"There were two banks of lockers," I said.

"Correct. Two pods. Twelve to a pod. Two dozen numbered lockers in the immense Amazon delivery network."

"Do we know that?" I asked.

Prof frowned. "Know what?"

"That all of those lockers are part of the faceless Amazon delivery network."

Prof popped his door handle and stepped into the parking lot, holding the box in my shop rag. He peeled the envelope off the bottom and tossed it to me, then leaned into the car with a big smile.

"No, my friend, we don't."

CHAPTER 17

"I'm glad you came to the club, Tommy. Life is more stable now and I'm saving up money."

"Always nice to have a stash of cash," Prof said.

"Saving for something special?" I asked.

Mona lowered her eyes. Her makeup-less cheeks glowed pink.

"It's just a stupid dream."

"No such thing as a stupid dream," Prof offered.

She glanced at him and back down at the square eggshell-colored tiles of her kitchen floor.

"I love flowers," she said.

"A pretty girl who loves flowers? How unusual," Prof said with a wide smile.

"They're so colorful. And soft. And they always seem like they're smiling at me."

"Doesn't sound stupid so far," I said.

"You'll laugh at me."

"My life," I said, "is not so well organized that I should criticize anyone's dream."

"I had a dream once," Prof said. "I imagined I could run a crypto-exchange out of my house."

Mona's eyes widened. "Is that legal?"

"I'm a look the other way and wink kind of guy," he said.

Mona's bright blue eyes were glued on Prof.

"What happened?" she asked.

"I built it. Didn't turn out the way I planned. But it's working okay."

"Do I want to ask?" I said.

"Only if you know your true desires," he said, and laughed.

"Can you buy crypto for me?" Mona said.

"Oh yes." Pause. "But."

Mona's eyes became wary.

"I hold it for you in my account. You get a little slip of paper indicating a number of shares."

"Like a pawn ticket," I said. "Payable to the bearer."

Prof nodded. "Good analogy."

"And what happens if the pawnshop goes out of business?" Mona asked.

"Your ticket is worth zilch."

I found a beer in the back of Mona's fridge. Shakes of the head told me no one else wanted anything to drink.

"So there is risk," she said.

"As with most things. The bigger risk is the wide swings in the value of crypto."

Mona lifted her hand toward the ceiling.

"Sometimes way up," she said.

"Those are the good times," Prof said.

"How do I buy some?"

"Hand me cash and tell me what flavor you want."

"Then you buy the cryptocurrency in your account?" I said.

"Tommy, Tommy. Did you not study banking? I give the pretty lady a chit for the number of shares of her flavor, redeemable on demand."

"But you don't actually own the shares?"

"Depends on which way I think that flavor is headed."

"There's a word for that," Mona said.

"Shady deal," I said, grinning.

"No, no, um…speculating," she said. "You're speculating with my money."

"Not just yours," Prof said.

"This is legal?" she asked.

"The big boys call it Wall Street. And they have a bunch of rules about what happens when they lose your money. It's not their fault, and there's nothing you can do about it, because you picked the flavor."

"But you're not like Wall Street?" I said.

"You got that right, guitar man. I'm not anything."

"Oh yes you are," Mona said.

Prof's eyes widened. "My reputation precedes me?"

Mona's smile glowed childlike in the kitchen light.

"No silly, you're anonymous. And I bet you don't keep records," she said.

"Just of the ticket numbers," Prof said.

"If it's not a trade secret," I said. "Where's the cash?"

"Safety deposit boxes scattered around the fine state of Illinois."

"There's a catch somewhere," Mona said.

"Several. Want to hear them?"

"Will they give me nightmares? Like you break people's knees and stuff?"

Prof straightened in his chair.

"My dear, do I look like a common street thug?"

Mona shook her head, painting the air with her red hair.

"No. You look like the suave guy who hires them," she said.

"Touché," Prof said. "But my little operation does not require such crude measures."

"You take a percentage upon withdrawal?" I asked.

"More like Visa and Mastercard. I take a little bit from every transaction."

"So I give you money," Mona said. "When you give it back, I get less?"

"That all depends on what happens with your flavor in the crypto market."

"So it's an investment," I said.

"Like a lottery ticket," Mona said.

Prof laughed. "A little. But you get more than one spin of the wheel. Because what goes down, often comes back up."

Mona giggled.

We stared at her.

"I never thought of investment like…you know." She made a circle with the fingers of her right hand, spread her lips, and pumped her arm back and forth.

"Yeah," Prof said. "The girls get all excited when the market is up." He laughed.

"And sad when it's down," she said.

"But there's something else you can do," Prof said.

"Oh, lots of things," she said.

"With the crypto, I mean."

"Oh," she said, and faked an innocent smile.

"Trade them," I said. "As good as cash, but untraceable."

Prof shot me with a finger gun.

"Trade them for what?" Mona asked.

"Any of man's primal needs," Prof said.

Mona's eyes shot back and forth between our faces. Her job at the Monkey put her in close proximity to primal needs.

"Sex and drugs?" she said.

Prof grinned. "You could probably buy rock and roll too if you tried."

"Where do you get your ideas?" I said, rhetorically.

Prof responded without hesitation.

"This one came from Mark Zuckerberg. He once tried to create his own currency. But the Feds didn't like the idea."

"So this is illegal," Mona said flatly.

"It's a gray area," Prof said. "All that I do is give out a paper chit that happens to look a bit like a state of Illinois lottery ticket. It is, as discussed, a pawn ticket to claim your crypto. I am just storing it for you."

"But do you store it in the cryptocurrency that I request?" I said.

"Conceptually yes, but in reality, no. I might store your cash anywhere at all, including gold and silver if I think crypto is going to tank."

"As it often does," I said.

"One must pay careful attention," Prof said with a grin. "And sometimes pull an all-nighter."

"Just like dancing," Mona said.

Prof and I glanced at each other. If he knew what Mona was talking about, it didn't show on his face.

"I feel that I am about to be educated," he said.

The sparkle in Mona's eyes suggested that she enjoyed training foolish boys.

"You saw how the club works. Customers buy colored wrist bands. Special ones with the Pink Monkey logo imprinted on them. The boss changes them often, so no one can cheat by counterfeiting them."

"Guys buy colored rubber bands?" Prof said. "Damn, men will do anything for a naked woman."

"Tommy, would you—"

She didn't have to finish her sentence. I was up and working on another vodka and crazy mango-pineapple-orange drink.

"The TVs show the price of action in the club. Say, two red for a slow dance. You can also use them to buy drinks. Or tip the hostess for a better table."

"Just like cash," I said from the kitchen counter.

Mona smiled. "Almost."

Prof sat and grinned while sipping from his coconut that had been refilled with Mona's special drink.

"When things are slow, suddenly the price of a VIP dance goes down from three green bands to one."

"Big discount," I said.

"Sure is. And the dancers are the ones giving the discount even though the boss makes the pricing decisions."

"Ain't that always the way," Prof said.

Having had experience with Mona, a thought came to mind.

"Mona," I said. "Are you going to tell us that some dancers trade the rubber bands to customers for drugs, then the customers use the bands to buy drinks and dances? So no cash changes hands."

I handed her the fresh drink. She sipped with her full lips that were usually painted bright red, but were pink at the moment.

"Thank you, Tommy. Would you like a red rubber band?"

We all laughed. Once we settled down, Mona continued.

"Some girls have been known to trade bands for drugs. We had a dealer who loved the club. He would come in with lots of drugs in his pockets, and leave happy.

Prof shook his head.

"And," Mona said. "Some girls get a little extracurricular at selling special dances."

"Raising the value of the bands," I said.

Mona diverted her gaze, then met my eyes.

"Sometimes."

"So, Prof," I said, "You have created a kind of private currency."

He shook his head. "Careful what you say, or the Feds will get on my ass. But, yes, it's a form of not really legal tender."

"And just like cash, its value can change," I said.

"The dances?" Mona asked.

I nodded. "Right, the holder can choose to run a special discount. But also, since the ticket is tied to the value of cryptocurrency and its wild swings, it's almost as good as a lottery ticket."

"Better than most of them," Prof said.

"How long have you been doing this?" I asked.

"Since bitcoin came out."

Prof sipped.

Mona drank.

I thought about the ramifications.

"What if crypto crashes and your, um, customers want cash?"

"I hold reserves," he said, "like any good bank."

"You place bets against crypto too," Mona said. "That pay off if it crashes.

Prof toasted Mona with his coconut.

"I also have a policy that no one investor can take out more than their average quarterly earnings per month. So if the worst happens and everyone is wiped out, including yours truly, we should all be able to recover without any dead bodies." He paused and gazed at the liquid in his coconut. "Including mine."

"Scary," Mona said.

"Yeah, life is like that," he said, quietly. And serious.

"Clever," I said.

His smile was sincere. "You expected less from Prof?"

Mona yawned. "Sorry, the dancing adrenaline is wearing off."

"Time for all good children to close their eyes," Prof said. "See you in the morning." He carried his coconut to the sink, rinsed it, and placed it on a pink drainage rack.

"Do you think that's dishwasher safe?" Mona asked.

"A coconut can survive monsoon season. A Kitchen-Aid should be easy."

Prof headed up the stairs.

"It's not a real coconut," I said.

Mona looked at me like I was such a silly boy to not understand her dishwasher joke. Of course she knew it was plastic. Someone had to wash them at the club.

"Tommy, what are you guys really doing in Chicago? I know you didn't come here just to see me dance."

"You're a great dancer."

She blushed again. Usually she wore so much makeup, I couldn't notice.

"Thanks. But you know what I mean."

"Well, I met this girl on the road—"

Mona held up one hand.

"Wait, wait. I've heard this story."

"Not your sister." I smiled. "This just started."

"Why is there always a woman involved?" She sipped her drink and watched my eyes.

"I don't have much data. But I would guess that, statistically, they cause the most trouble."

I hadn't noticed that her kitchen chairs had little blue cushions on the seats until hers came flying at me.

◇

I pushed in the clutch to let the Barracuda roll silently backwards down Mona's driveway and into the street. She was out cold in her bed wrapped in a yellow blanket like a baby burrito. Prof and I were anxious to get to work. I twisted the key to bring the Hemi to life.

"Coffee," Prof stated.

"I know a good place for breakfast," I said, remembering mornings surrounded by the library decor at the Bourgeois Pig. Soon we were seated at a window facing a front yard with a black wrought iron gate protecting it from the sidewalk. A waitress with a tattooed left biceps dropped two coffees, bags of sugar, and a pastel green bowl of individual containers of cream.

It was 8:30 A.M. I had managed five hours of sleep.

"Something bothers me," Prof said.

"Life is like that."

He shook his head, but was smiling.

"That box we delivered last night. Similar to Leni's. But different."

"Same, um, category of product," I said.

"I think so." His eyes roamed around the interior of the restaurant. "Lots of books in here."

"They use the shelved books as decor, but also as thermal insulation."

"Need that shit up here by the north pole." Prof sipped his black coffee and stared into space. "It hit me this morning when I was dreaming about being Charles Atlas. You know, holding the weight of the world on my shoulders. Some unseen person was piling on rocks and making the world heavier and heavier."

"Be interesting to know where the rocks were coming from," I said.

"Dreams don't bother with details. My knees were almost touching the dry riverbed I was standing in when I woke up with a clear question in my mind."

"Wait. If you're holding the world on your shoulders, how can you be standing in a riverbed?"

Prof met my eyes. "Tommy, my man, are you still under the impression that the world makes logical sense?"

"Uh, cause and effect. Force equals mass times acceleration."

"That's the surface of reality," he said.

"That's where I live."

Prof nodded. "You might, but most humans do not."

"Don't leave me in suspense," I said.

The waitress returned with an armload of eggs, bacon, pancakes, and a syrup bottle dangling from her left pinky. The tattoo on her biceps was of an armless female statue. She caught me staring. Before I could pose the question, she said, "The goddess Juno," dropped off the food and disappeared.

"Juno," Prof said. "Daughter of Saturn, sister and wife of Jupiter, mother of Mars, Vulcan, Bellona, and Juventas."

I forked into a stack of pancakes.

"Sister and wife?" I asked.

Prof laughed. "Roman goddesses got around back in the day. Warlike. Eternally youthful."

"Sounds like a Disney superhero," I said.

"Served the same purpose. So, I was carrying the weight of the world on my shoulders and I woke up."

"The box has rocks in it?"

He shook his head while ingesting eggs.

"Doubt it. The one we just delivered was heavier than Leni's."

"And it rattled."

"Too much weight for just tablets," he said.

I bit off a piece of crispy bacon and tried to put one and one together.

"OK, they both contain drugs. But different, because one rattles and the other does not."

He nodded agreement.

The waitress glided up silently on white sneakers with pink trim.

"How's your breakfast?"

"Excellent," I said. "Do you have orange juice?"

"Yeah. In a plastic bottle from a major corporation. It might even have oranges in it."

"I'll try it."

"Do you have a moment to play a game?" Prof asked.

"If it will enhance the buying power of my tip."

I laughed.

Prof said, "I have a mystery box. It contains pills, but it's heavy. So it must contain something else?

She crossed her arms. Her right hand covered Juno.

"What kind of pills?"

"Capsules from Big Pharma with substantial recreational street value."

Her lips danced with each other.

"How big is the box?"

Prof demonstrated with his hands.

"Hmm," she said. "Is there a right answer?"

"We're looking for fresh ideas," he said.

"Okay. Way I see it, wherever there are drugs, there are three other things. But only two will fit in that box."

Prof casually sipped coffee.

"Sex," she said, "not in your box. But wherever there's drugs and sex, you also find…"

We stared at her.

"You're going to make me say it?" she said.

"I am hoping you will," Prof said.

She smiled and winked.

"Okay, smart guy, play dumb. Thinking about heavy objects that could be in a box this big," she mimed Profs demonstration, "that go along with our sex and drugs theme…my first guess is a gun. Or maybe just bullets."

I hadn't considered a weapon. I wondered if Prof had.

Prof nodded, solemnly it seemed to me.

She continued. "In your heavy mysterious box. Wherever there's drugs, there is also…"

She waited again.

"Drug money," I said.

She lifted her right hand off Juno and shot me with her pointed index and middle fingers pressed together to make a double barrel.

"One corporate OJ coming right up. Don't forget that tip guys. My desires are immense and my resources limited."

◇

Prof peeled the top from an individual serving of peanut butter and coated a pancake with the contents.

"Adds protein to balance the carbs," he said. "What's your guess?"

"There are a number of reasons to move guns and ammo. But cash? Whoa, lots of reasons."

"So it's a standard dealer network with a clever level of security to hide the real players."

"No two people in the chain ever see each other," I said.

"Makes it hard for a disgruntled employee, customer, or supplier to drop a dime on the operation."

"Also reduces competition," I said. "No one knows where the customers are."

"Except," he said.

I thought about who knew what about whom.

"The app knows all."

"Its brain will be coated in cybersecurity." Prof paused to eat and think. "Maybe a blockchain thing like crypto. Every transaction encrypted onto the end of a chain."

"I bet HappyBox has a single owner."

"Keeps things simple," he said.

The waitress arrived with a lowball glass full of orange liquid.

"Looks like orange juice," I said.

She met my eyes, her face blank as a mannequin.

"Looks," she said, "can be deceiving." She grinned, flipped her blonde hair with one finger, spun, and departed.

"Beware the goddess Juno," Prof said. "I think she has something to do with fertility." He laughed.

"And war. You mentioned war."

He laughed harder, then stuffed peanut butter coated pancakes into his mouth.

Leni's phone vibrated in my pants pocket, as it had been doing repeatedly since I woke up. It vibrated again. Then a third time. I pulled it out to find three new messages from hohoman25.

"Trouble?" Prof asked.

"Someone wants to talk to Leni on video. Says he has something to show her that is too sensitive to put into a message."

"I bet he does," Prof said, without a hint of humor.

"There are a ton of messages. When will you be back? I miss you. Have you forgotten about me? WTF bitch? When I say login, you better login."

"That last one's probably a politician." He grinned.

"I don't know what to say to hoho-man. What if he has something that Leni actually wants?"

Prof finished his peanut butter pancakes before speaking.

"Two paths," he said. "The human path. We find Leni and have her contact the guy, assuming that she wants to contact the guy."

"Or?"

"We address his security concerns and ask him to upload video of whatever he has to show."

"I bet you know how to handle the security," I said.

"Sure. There are several good options. But…" He reached for his coffee cup just as the waitress returned with a coffee pot in each hand. One had an orange ring around the base. She refilled his cup with high octane.

"But what?" she said.

"We're trying to solve a little computer security problem," I said.

"Ha. There are no little security problems. We're living in Orwell's 1984 without a guidebook."

"If," Prof said," the goddess Juno were dating a guy."

"I don't think she was that dumb," she said.

I tossed in, "Hypothetically."

She placed both pots on the table.

"Does my answer help to address my immense desires?"

Prof and I both laughed and nodded.

"OK, hypothetically," she said, "the goddess is dating a lowly, good-for-nothing male human."

"How might the goddess communicate sensitive personal information to said individual?" Prof asked.

She glanced back and forth between our faces.

"You guys into kinky stuff you want to keep quiet?"

"Not us," I said.

A smile slowly morphed onto her face.

"Of course not," she said. "But you have a friend."

"Correct," I said. "And our friend is about your age and also lives in Chicago."

"Aha! You don't want to know how I would do it. You want to know how she would do it. And maybe she would do it the way I would do it, us being white bitches from the same generation and all."

"That's the gist of it," I said. Leni not being white seemed irrelevant.

"If I wanted dick pics, I'd use a Telegram account that hides my cell phone number. They have a secret messages feature." She hesitated. "Hypothetically."

Prof choked on his coffee.

Her Juno tattoo seemed to be smiling.

"Ready for dessert?" she asked.

"With breakfast?" Prof said.

"Our pies are great. Cherry today. You guys look like you would enjoy cherry."

We agreed. She trotted off to get the pie.

"What do you think, Prof? Will this guy go for a secret message?"

He nodded. "We'll need salacious photos of Leni...to establish trust. Then yeah, he'll go for it."

CHAPTER 18

Prof and I sat in my Barracuda staring at four-foot-high waves rolling up Lakeside Beach. We had the windows down and the radio tuned to KBLU. Albert King was torturing his guitar in subtle ways. I stared at Leni's phone.

"Hoho-man has sent two more messages. One includes the comment: 'You'll want to see this.'"

"I hope it's not his privates," Prof said. "Be a shame to go to all this trouble to see some fat white dude doing the hand jive."

Prof's eyes roamed over the empty sand. "Let's send him a photo."

"Should I caption it?"

"Yeah, with the Telegram address. What's she wearing?"

"Bright green."

"Ooh la la Leni," he said.

"She looks like a Victoria's Secret model."

"You still get those catalogs?" Prof said, laughing.

"Sent."

"Now we wait," Prof said. "And think."

I watched a series of waves roll in. The fourth was the tallest.

"What are we thinking about?" I asked.

Prof counted on his fingers as he spoke. "Where's Leni? Is she okay? What does your Oleace crush want to send you? Why is Leni's boss moving contraband through Amazon lockers?"

"You think it's a dealer network?"

"If it walks like a duck and it talks like a duck."

"It's AI imitating a duck," I said.

Prof's eyes turned toward me. "Point taken."

"Do you think Leni knows?" I asked.

"She had a reason to take that box to St. Louis with her."

A young woman in a white one-piece swimsuit headed toward the beach towing a little boy in black swim trunks emblazoned with light sabers.

"Swimming?" Prof said. "In Lake Michigan?"

"Maybe just here to play in the sand. But some people brave the cold water."

"Does it ever freeze?"

I shook my head. "Too deep, I think."

The woman spread out a blanket with spaceships on it and stretched out on her back. Sunshine sparkled from some kind of gems on her suit. The little guy pulled a pail and a shovel the size of a table spoon out of her carry bag and headed toward the water.

"I'd sure like to talk to Leni," I said. "Find out what 'I'm lost' means."

Prof stared at the hypnotic movement of the water. Or maybe at the kid. Or maybe the white swimsuit. I retrieved the burner phone and pressed redial. The only number I had called so far was my answering service.

A woman's voice said, "Cuda Freelance." I waited for the robot menu selection, but the phone remained silent.

"Hello," I said.

"Hi, thank you for calling Cuda Freelance. I'm Tonya, how may I help you?"

"Hi Tonya, this is Tommy Cuda. I was just calling in to check for messages."

"Hello, Tommy, it's nice to meet you. I took two messages today. Please enter your PIN."

I was surprised that Leni had set up a service with a live human being answering the phone. At least Tonya seemed like a live human being. I entered my six-digit PIN.

"OK, go ahead," I said.

"I'm lost on a mountain, surrounded by natives who are going to throw me into a volcano."

"Is that the entire message?"

"Yes. But there is a second one that came in an hour later from the same number."

"Shoot," I said.

"The sun will set on this day at seven oh four."

I waited.

"That's all," Tonya said.

"Hmm, thanks."

"If that number calls again, should I call you?"

Leni was lost. I needed to find her.

"Sure, anytime. Day or night," I said.

"OK, will do, boss."

The word 'boss' made me uneasy. It engendered responsibility. I thanked her and hung up.

"Long call," Prof said. "Does your assistant, Tonya," he stretched her name out like it had four syllables, "get paid by the hour?"

"They haven't sent a bill yet."

"Anything interesting?"

"Two cryptic messages from Leni an hour apart." I repeated them to Prof, word for word.

His tongue lolled around inside his mouth, pressing his cheek out.

"Volcano?" he said.

"Surrounded by natives."

"Hawaii maybe. But Chicago?"

I pictured a lava-filled volcano in my mind. But it was always in Hawaii or Fiji or Japan.

"Let's work backwards from sunset," he said.

"Sunset changes a little every day. And sets at a different time, depending on where you are on the planet."

Prof pulled out his smartphone.

"Care to guess what time the sun sets tonight in Chicago?" he asked.

"Four minutes past seven."

"So something happens tonight at sunset. Here in Chicago."

The woman in the white swimsuit stood up from the blanket and strolled to the little boy. Prof's gaze followed her.

"Why would she give a precise time?" Prof mused. Then he answered his own question. "A meeting. Where?"

I watched the lake waves repeat, repeat, repeat.

"She's surrounded by natives about to throw her into a volcano."

Prof's eyes returned to the dash of the Barracuda.

"Could be a metaphor. She's captive. Something bad is going to happen at sunset. She's calling for help."

"Why not just say 'help' and give us the address?" I said.

"Because that would lead us into a trap that we might not walk out of."

I recalled the gunfire at Toucan Sam's. This was not a crowd I could predict. I reconsidered. Maybe there was no such crowd.

"Where can we find a volcano in Chicago?" I asked.

Prof worked his phone.

"The AI-injected search engine has found three. Care to guess?"

"A street named Volcano," I said.

He gave me a thumbs up.

"It's a good name for a bar," I said.

"Two for two."

"What about the natives?" I said.

"Gods are angry, sacrifice a virgin. Ancient ritual adored by primitive tribes throughout the world."

The word ancient brought to mind…

"The Natural History Museum. I've never been inside, but they might document tribal behavior."

"The AIs didn't figure that out. They found The Fire Shack on third street. Home of lava-hot eats for fireproof tongues."

◇

The museum was open. We paid the non-member admission fee. Prof consulted a directory sitting under a totem pole.

"Upstairs," he said.

We took the escalator. The walls were covered with artifacts of painted wood, most older than the United States. The past was so different from the present it might as well have been an alien planet. We studied masks carved from trees for men, women, children. Masks for war. Masks for fertility. Sex and violence had been the dominant themes then too.

Prof motioned to our right.

We passed behind a dividing wall into a room with a wide entrance and no doors. In the center of the room was a long glass case that made me think of a coffin for a giant. Spotlights in the ceiling splashed circles onto the case. I started at the near end.

Under the glass a group of hand-painted wooden figures looked like an outdoor judge and jury seated on logs in a forest. A black plaque with silver letters explained that the tribunal was meeting because the volcano god that protected the village had once again begun to belch black smoke into the air. He was angry at the villagers. One of the figurines was sketching in the dirt, dancing, and maybe chanting. The tribunal was listening to what this climber, who had been to the god's mouth, had seen. I wondered what they would have done with a drone and a live video feed.

The second spotlight illuminated villagers attending a beauty pageant with thirteen contestants. All were verified virgins according to the medicine man. This would be an unlucky day for one of them. I glanced at Prof. He was watching pulsing orange lights simulate lava at the top of a six-foot-high volcano.

The next section showed a parade led by children, then adults, then men in wooden armor, and finally one of the girls in a fancy chair carried on the shoulders of eight strong men.

My stomach churned thinking that at some point in the past this had really happened. It wasn't just a scene from a Raider's of the Lost Ark sequel.

I stopped beside Prof.

"Amazing," he said.

"Hard to imagine this was ever standard operating procedure," I said.

"Really? Virgins, volcanos, torture, beheadings, slavery. Any of this still surprise you?"

"Seems barbaric," I said.

"Like Guantanamo? Spies sacrificed by their own country for political gain? Agent Orange? Blind drone attacks on villages full of children? Gerrymandering voting districts to prevent representative government? The NRA lobbying machine for gun manufacturers? What could be more desirable than more and better killing machines in the hands of bigots, alcoholics, and crazy people?"

I waited for more, aware Prof was venting off stress. But he just stared at the virgin suspended in midair by a thread right over the mouth of the throbbing orange lava lights. He moved an arm and pointed without looking.

"Do you see how they did it?"

I studied the group at the top of the mountain. Volcano. Villagers. The chair throne she had been carried on had been fashioned into a catapult with the girl as the projectile. That's why she was in the air on her way to the volcano like a rock thrown at an enemy castle.

"No way," I said.

"Professional historians certainly did research."

"A human catapult?" I was incredulous.

"I'm sure it had an elegant name," Prof said. He arched his hand through the air. "Something like The High Way to Heaven."

I grunted.

"Flight of the gods?" he said.

"How about Angel Wings?" I asked.

"Not bad. Angel Wings for the Chosen Virgin. Everyone likes to be the chosen one."

He laughed a dry, wry sound.

We fell quiet. Footfalls moved past in the corridor of masks on the other side of the wall.

"I've been thinking about Leni's message," Prof said. "What is she really trying to tell us?"

"A safe public place to meet?"

"Maybe. But there are lots of such places. Why this one? Why start with 'I'm lost' in a dream of virgins with death in the offing?"

The virgin hung by the thread, motionless.

"She's trapped," I said.

"Metaphorically at least. Thinks she can't get out or something horrible will happen."

"Lots of bad things have already happened," I said. "Including gunfire at Sam's place."

"Which leaves us with a rendezvous at sunset, no mission objective, and a sparsity of intel on the enemy."

"Sparsity?"

Prof laughed.

We were both deep in silent thought on the way back to Mona's apartment, where we found a note stuck to the fridge with a magnet shaped like a martini glass.

Gone shopping. Working dinner shift at the club. You guys have fun tonight. <3 Mona

"Prof, you ever had dinner at a strip club?"

"Every Thursday at the Hoedown." He didn't laugh. My expression communicated the question. "Full name, The Go Down Hoedown parlor and dance hall. Little joint next to an auto parts store in a strip mall. Great tacos. Thursday is all you can eat. I don't really go every week. But once a month at least."

"Taco Thursday at a strip club?"

This time he laughed. "Plenty of tacos at the Hoedown."

"You've been quiet," I said.

He nodded slowly. "Can't stop thinking about humans catapulting humans into a fiery death pit." He paused and stared at Mona's note. "We're still doing the same thing. Only now it's a ghetto instead of a volcano." His eyes moved from the note to me. "Which leads us back to Leni."

"Any guesses?"

Prof shrugged, exposing the slenderness of his upper body hiding inside a white dress shirt with the top three button open.

"Don't have to guess much. The reality is obvious."

"College girl crushes on professor," I said.

He nodded. "That's step one."

"Professor gets her involved in some sketchy business."

"Step three," he said. "Step two is the romance. They become intimate. She falls into a mental state that she calls love. And…"

"They live happily ever after," I said.

He laughed. "You know that ain't true even in your honky privileged world. Maybe especially not true, you people have options."

"I was being optimistic," I said.

"In step three he establishes dominance. Uses her desire to control her."

I thought of Leni's torn clothing while dealing cards at the rest stop.

"And when that doesn't work, he abuses her physically," I said.

Prof opened the fridge, removed a green bottle of sparkling water, and closed it.

"Crime statistics would back you up," he said.

He poured some water into a glass, glanced at me. I nodded. He poured a second glass.

"So Leni's trapped," I said.

"Let me count the ways. She's emotionally involved, wants this guy to be Mr. Right. Fogs her thinking. Case in point, she ran away without a plan. Maybe not even wanting to leave, but needing to protect herself in the moment."

"Maybe she wanted to see if he cared enough to chase her," I said.

"That's been tried before."

"Or maybe part of her truly wants to get away."

"Part of most people wants to escape their present circumstances," he said. "Only natural."

"And sometimes that part wins?"

Prof smiled. "Witness the random cruising of Mr. Tommy Cuda."

When he stopped laughing I continued.

"Next reason?"

"The nature of the delivery business scares her."

"Thus, the stolen box?"

"Might not be stolen," he said. "We don't know when it was supposed to be delivered."

"So we check HappyBox for a code number. Maybe Leni ran before she could deliver it."

"But."

"Hmm. But she left it behind," I said.

"Correct."

"Not an accident. She meant for us to find it."

"Correct again," he said. "It was well hidden. Only someone actively looking would have ever found it."

He sipped his water.

"And Leni wanted us to find it because…" I said.

"You have her phone. Therefore, you would find HappyBox. Therefore, you would search her room, open the box, and learn what was inside."

"Why?"

"So you can tell her."

That was a long train of causality. Why make life so complicated?

"Plausible deniability," I said.

"Yep. She's worried what her boyfriend is up to and wants to know."

"This way she can deny ever opening a package."

Prof placed his empty glass in the stainless steel sink with a soft clunk.

"Is this the reason for secret meeting?" I asked. "So we can tell her what we found?"

He turned around, leaned against the counter and crossed his arms.

"Not we. You," he said.

CHAPTER 19

Prof and I decided to prepare for the night ahead by napping. When I woke up, the Telegram app showed six new messages from Hohoman25 to the new account I had created on Leni's phone. All six were one-minute videos. I turned the audio all the way down since Prof was asleep upstairs, and watched them in order.

Leni's smiling face. Her lips shaping hello. Then the image swirling: ceiling, edge of table, black refrigerator. A body flashed past. Still image of the ceiling for many seconds. I guessed.

Leni answered an Oleace call. Got interrupted.

Movement reflected in the shiny door of the fridge. I leaned closer to the phone.

Leni on her back on the kitchen table, fists flailing but not connecting. A man's left hand around her throat, right one smacking her face with an flat palm. Her mouth was open. I needed to check the audio ASAP.

I hesitated.

Would Leni want anyone to see this?

I tapped Pause.

The man's hand froze in midair.

'Be me.'

How could this recording exist? I speculated. Leni and Corolla are having dinner at his place. Hohoman25 calls. Leni answers, intending to tell the caller that she's busy, but talking to him briefly so he will call back later. Corolla tells her to put the phone away. She is slow, he is impatient, he grabs for the phone. They struggle. The phone lands on the floor.

Meanwhile, at the other end…

Hohoman25 places a video call, anticipating a hot chat with Sally. He is recording the session so he can watch it again later. When the phone hits the floor, he keeps recording, wondering what is going on.

I put the phone into my jacket hanging in the hall closet. What was going on was rape. Assault. Domestic abuse. How else would you describe being held down and smacked around?

Fun?

Prof plodded down the carpeted stairs in his bare feet while slipping a red shirt over his head.

"What's next?" he asked.

"Dinner, I said. "And a movie we have to see."

◇

We arrived at the Natural History Museum 45 minutes early and stashed my car deep in an underground lot. We made our way to the volcano room that made me wonder what was 'natural' about this history.

"Ideas?" I asked.

"Kill the lawyers," Prof said, laughing. "What would Shakespeare do next?"

"Have everyone die," I said.

He nodded. "Let's split up. Leni's guy doesn't know me on sight. I'll sit on that bench," he pointed to a polished silver bench with curved arms near the elevators, "in plain sight. You hide behind the volcano and keep one eye on me and the other on anyone that approaches the bench."

I gave him a thumbs up.

He turned and spoke toward the volcano.

"You ever wonder if a belief is like a virus that infects brains? Passes from one to another, generation to generation, until enough brains become immune that it dies out?"

"No. But sounds logical when you say it."

"We need hand signals. I'll touch one ear if Leni is alone. And my chin if she has company."

"One if by land, two if by sea."

He chuckled. "If I stand up, he brought an army."

"In which case, we disappear?"

He looked around the room. Stepped into the hallway and looked some more. "How? Any emergency exit will set off alarms and pinpoint our location."

I recalled the gunshots at Toucan Sam's. Being found was a bad plan. Then I recalled visiting a clothing boutique called GET OVER IT.

"Is the museum gift shop still open?" I said.

It was. I scored a gray hoodie several sizes too large with a dinosaur skeleton printed across the back in black, sunglasses with fake tortoise frames modeled after a 600-year-old sea turtle shell, and an adjustable black baseball cap whose bill had plastic teeth along the edge shaped after a flying reptile. Prof shook his head at me when he wasn't outright laughing.

"You look like an adolescent who hasn't outgrown his dinosaur phase."

"Might work," I said.

"That night at Sam's, how good a look did he get at you?"

"A couple of us were standing nearby, but he was focused on Leni. I don't know if he even noticed me."

Prof pushed the UP button for the elevator.

"Maybe not. The guy was likely armed. White guys tend to feel superior because of the bubble they grow up in. Leads to overconfidence. Plus, he had backup outside. Everyone heard shots. Knew he had backup. And something else."

"Maybe he was high," I said.

"Yeah, some people function incredibly well on weird combinations, like cocaine and vodka. Ask any rock star. But I was thinking of Leni. When a woman is involved, men get stupid. Part of evolutionary design."

We returned to the volcano room. Prof headed for the bench. I removed the tags from my new clothes and became DinoBoy. I settled into a spot where I could see Prof with my head lowered and eyes peeking over the top of the sunglasses.

Waiting requires patience.

Not my strong suit. To me, life is most like a series of quarter-mile drag races. First do this. Then that. Only then move onto a third thing. Some people claimed that attention spans were growing shorter from social media. To me, they've always been short. From three-minute 45 rpm records to comic books and the 13 or so seconds a Hemi requires to cover a drag strip.

Prof shifted his body position but remained seated with one hand in his lap and the other on the arm of the bench. I passed the time watching Hohoman25's video clips of Leni, hoping to notice a detail I had missed. Check on Prof. Watch a little video. Freeze frame. Scroll through a frame at a time. Repeat.

I grew angry watching Leni's distressed face flop back and forth on the table. A man's features flashed onscreen twice near the end. I hoped that and DNA would be enough.

But only if she reported the crime. And testified.

I felt cold as the thought if she were still alive to testify passed through my head.

Prof's left hand rose slowly and scratched his right ear. Then he held up a wait signal with his right hand.

Leni came into view and approached Prof's bench. She ignored him, walked straight toward the volcano room, and entered from the end where the villagers were gathered with the maidens. She stopped and looked around.

I barely breathed, watched Prof, listened for footsteps.

All quiet.

Leni drifted along the opposite side of the display until she stood directly opposite me. Her lips moved, but I couldn't hear the words. I shuffled forward until my hips pressed against the display.

Her eyes moved from the volcano to the flying figure.

She whispered, "Turbo-bronze metallic."

I said, "Barracuda."

A smile formed on her pale lips.

"Thanks for coming, Tommy."

"I have a message for you from Hohoman twenty-five." I passed her phone across the boiling lava.

By the end of the first video her wet eyes reflected orange lava light. By the end of the last clip, tear trails glistened on her brown cheeks. She handed the phone back.

"Don't you want it?" I asked.

She shook her head. "There's too much there I don't want any one to know." She looked up into my sunglasses. "Especially him."

I pocketed the phone. It vibrated with an incoming message that I ignored.

"I'm lost inside his world," she said. "If I leave him, he says he'll have me thrown out of school."

"Could he make that happen?"

"The golden boy bringing in research grants, giving magazine interviews, publishing academic papers? Sure."

"But you haven't done anything wrong."

Leni stared at me and double-blinked her eyes a couple of times.

"Since when does the truth matter? How do I defend myself against his accusations? Besides, he doesn't have to get me thrown out, just create enough doubt that my scholarship doesn't renew."

"You mean like an off-the-record side conversation with the scholarship committee?"

"See why I'm stuck?"

"But he—"

"I know what he did. And you saw how he did it."

"Have him arrested."

"Those videos show two people having rough sex. Some girls like it that way. Many more don't, but they accept it." She closed her eyes. "We've been dating for five months."

I opened my mouth to speak but caught myself.

She spoke to the volcano. "When emotions are just right, it feels nice to believe a man wants you so badly that he can't control himself."

I bit my tongue so I wouldn't offer advice.

"Mutual desire. Passion. An unexplainable supersonic connection." She paused. "Sex is violent and uncontrolled at its core. It's easy for things to get out of hand."

I remembered Prof's comment and said, "Evolution demands consummation of desire."

"Pfft. More like men want unfettered access. Did you know that a woman couldn't be legally raped by her husband until 1993? You marry it, and it's yours whenever you want it."

I hadn't known. I wondered what happened in 1993.

"So, the courts can't help?" I said.

"How? Take away his job. Throw him in jail. Where does that leave me? No college and swimming in debt to lawyers."

"A non-profit might take your case."

"Maybe," she said. "Then what? I write a book about my experience and get death threats for the rest of my life?" She reached out and poked the virgin doll with a fingertip. It swung over the lava like Edgar Allen Poe's pendulum. "Remember Monica Lewinsky? All she did was give a guy she liked a blow job. And society totally messes up her life."

"OK, no cops." I paused. "I'm sending messages for Sally. But the natives are getting restless."

"I'll send you something to keep them happy while I'm away on… um…vacation." She hesitated before softly saying, "Tommy, it took me years to build that list of fans. Please don't lose them."

"I'll be the best Sally I can," I said. "New subject. When you deliver a box, remind me how you get paid?"

"Envelope taped to the bottom of the box."

"Where do you pick up the packages?"

"Residential address. Usually from inside a mailbox. Or sitting on a porch or behind a bush. The app always knows."

"No one hands it to you?"

"Never."

Her tears were dry. She had never even reached up to wipe them away. Sagging eyes suggested that she hadn't slept since we listened to DragonZone in the alley. Her hair that had been so impeccably straight at Toucan Sam's was a tangled mess.

"So the pick up location isn't the sender?"

She shook her head. "I doubt it. Crazy places. A park garbage can. Under a bench. Behind a tree on the street."

"That HappyBox app," I said.

She nodded. "It knows everything. Uses some kind fancy encryption and codes. Nothing is saved on my phone."

"You sure?"

"Nope. But after a delivery, everything goes poof."

Her eyes lifted to mine but she didn't speak.

I looked back over my sunglasses.

"I have a feeling," I said, "that someone named Leni has been writing down addresses and codes on paper where the app can't reach them."

Her lips twitched toward a smile.

"Now why would I do a thing like that?"

"Because you're smart and your relationship had speed bumps long before that video was recorded."

She shrugged one shoulder under a too large gray T-shirt. "I don't know if the info will help. I've never seen anyone, so I can't identify anyone."

But maybe her data could.

"Does anyone know you have it?"

Cheek muscles tensed under her bronze skin.

"I might have alluded to it during a fight."

Prof was no longer at the bench.

I said, "How did you get to the museum?"

"A rented e-scooter. I wasn't followed." She hesitated. "He doesn't care what I do so long as I come when he calls. Most of the time I'm in class, studying in the library, or out delivering. Not an exciting life."

"Or telling fortunes." I smiled and tapped my pocket. "Or on your smartphone."

She finally smiled. "Oh yeah. Playtime."

"Busy girl."

"Show me a college student who isn't busy and I'll show you one who is flunking out." Her eyes danced to the empty bench. "Did you find it?"

"The bedsprings were squeaking."

"Hmm, what was going on on that bed?" She laughed lightly then instantly became serious. "What was in it?"

"You don't know?"

"I'm like the Amazon driver. I move things. I'm not responsible for the contents." She paused. "That's what Corolla told me to say if cops ever stop me."

"I found a box. Prof and I peeked inside. You want to know what we found?"

Leni sent the virgin swinging again with a tap of her finger.

"Let's get out of here," she said. "Sacrificial virgin patriarchal societies give me the creeps."

We caught up with Prof returning to his bench. He had made a sweep of the front of the museum and checked in the restroom. The coast was clear. The three of us went to my car.

Leni leaned against the front fender and stared up at Orion. We waited for 5 minutes. She didn't seem able to make up her mind.

"Come with me," Prof said.

"If I hide, he'll look for me. Or he'll send his gangster friends. I'm better off delivering boxes and going to summer school."

Prof and I exchanged glances. I shrugged. He shrugged. No one proposed a solution.

"Tommy, let me borrow my phone," Leni said.

She sat on my fender and took selfies, unbuttoned her shirt, tapped out messages, and cooed sweet nothings at the phone. In the middle of sending a message she turned to me.

"I had better know what was in that box."

"We're not certain," Prof said.

She continued taking selfies. "Will it stop me?"

Prof glanced at me.

"Depends on your goal," I said.

"Psychiatrist."

"You want to shrink heads?" Prof said, apparently surprised.

Leni shifted her head while smiling and taking selfies.

"Yes. So I need to excel in pre-med. And…" her flash flared, "have the right sponsors."

Her behavior made sense.

"Powder," I said. "Could be lots of things."

Leni lowered the camera and looked at us.

"I'm a pusher?"

"More like a mule," Prof said. "You move product from place to place, but don't contact either the supplier or the buyer."

"Or the big money," she said.

"There's a little wrinkle," Prof said.

"Ain't nothing little around Corolla," she said.

"The second box—"

"What second box?" She glared at me.

"Your HappyBox app showed us where to deliver the box you hid at Prof's place," I said.

"Good. I'm in big trouble if it disappears."

"We staked out the lockers. Girl on a scooter arrived and dropped off another box."

"You had my phone," she said. "The app thought I was there and gave you the job, just like Uber." Her eyes moved from Prof standing near the trunk to me sitting on the curb in the next parking space. "And?"

"Didn't open it," Prof said.

Her eyes widened. "You had it in your hands and you didn't open it?"

"Didn't have the materiel to reseal it," he said. "We worried about delaying the delivery."

She winked at me. "But you have a guess."

"I always have a guess," Prof said. "Based on weight, size, and what we might call context, highest probability is pills and cash."

Leni froze for a microsecond, her eyes wide.

"Of course," she said.

The headlights of a turning car swept over the three of us. The lights headed our way.

"Cadillac," I said.

Leni tossed her phone into the air. I caught it with two hands.

"Do you want to go back to St. Louis?" Prof said.

"Depends on the cost," she said.

The Caddy stopped sideways behind the Barracuda, its passenger door about a foot from where Prof stood with both hands in his pockets. I recalled our conversation about handguns and slipped my right hand into my jacket pocket as I put Leni's phone into my jeans. I hoped for a casual conversation.

The driver's door opened and a guy I barely recognized stepped out. The rumpled, sleep deprived, frantic professor who confronted Leni at Toucan Sam's was now a fresh haircut, three-piece suit dude wearing the Cadillac like a comfortable afterthought. I knew of two things that could transform a human so quickly: really good news, and drugs.

He stepped out, placed his forearms on the roof of the Cadillac, and clasped his hands, apparently confident that the car was so clean it wouldn't soil his suit.

"Hello, Lenore."

"Hello, Markus."

Leni glared at Markus.

Markus's eyes hovered on Leni.

"Are you going to introduce me to your friends?"

Before she could respond, Prof said, "Carl Roberts Longfellow the third. Friends since kindergarten."

Markus grinned. "Doctor Markus Corolla."

"Tommy Cuda. Freelance consultant," I said. "I've known Lenore all the way back to the middle of last week."

His face showed no amusement. No threat. No emotion. But his eyes channeled a wild tiger. He nodded once.

"Gentlemen, the pleasure is mine." To Leni he said, "Are you finished here?"

Prof adjusted his footing without moving his body.

"A Poor Hungry Doctor," I said, "or a Money Doctor?"

Markus laughed. "A poor hungry one I'm afraid. Psychology. I help people change their minds."

"Isn't that the purpose of education?" Prof said.

Markus laughed like we were stand-up comics.

"You can lead a horse to water," he said, "but you can't make him drink." We waited. He went on. "The context in which new information is presented is critical to success."

"Show, don't tell?" Prof said.

Markus smiled. He reminded me of Batman villains. All of them.

"Drug rehab," Leni said. "Among the college-age generation. Markus is a world expert."

"Let's not exaggerate," he said, while implying with his demeanor that she wasn't exaggerating.

"The University of Chicago fast-tracked tenure to keep you," Leni said.

Markus's face remained calm. "Great universities recognize a golden goose."

"Chasing a Nobel Prize?" Prof asked. "U of Chicago has had a bunch."

His hands still clasped on the Cadillac's roof, Markus's eyes floated to Prof.

"I seek to help people. Especially young people who are destroying their lives with chemicals in a misguided attempt to find happiness."

"Tough job," Prof said. "Kids aren't much for listening to reason."

"You are well informed," Markus said. "That's why my methods eschew talk therapy. We connect at a more primal level."

"Doctor Corolla," I said.

He lifted a hand. "Markus, please. We're all friends here."

That was a twist. "Markus, could I ask a somewhat indelicate question?"

He smiled like he didn't mean it, but nodded.

"How is it that a famous faculty member at a prestigious university is present in St. Louis when a gang shoots up a local bar?"

His expression didn't change. Even his Cadillac-blue eyes were empty.

"Drugs," he said. "The pharmaceuticals that permeate American culture from the very bottom to the rarefied atmosphere of the most elevated board room. My work puts me in direct contact with individuals from every race, religion, and walk of life. Including, perhaps even especially, gang members."

"So you were working?" Prof asked.

"I am always working."

I wondered if he thought he had been working when that video with Leni was recorded.

"How about now?" I asked.

He shrugged. "Now, I am fetching the lady to go out for dinner."

I remained seated on the curb with my hand in the pocket of my jacket, trying to be ready for whatever was coming.

"Thanks for touring the museum with me, guys," Leni said. She took three steps towards the Cadillac, stopped, and turned to face me. Her voice was calm, but both of her fists were clenched so tight that her knuckles were bright dots.

"Thanks for your help, Tommy. I bet you can find a way to save that girl before she lands in the volcano."

She spun on a heel, headed to the car, waved to Prof, slid onto the creamy leather bucket seat, and was gone.

Prof removed his hands from his pockets.

"Would you have shot him?" I asked.

"I am not in a hurry to ruin the lush life I've created through ingenuity because whitey has his eyes on a mulatto girl. On the other hand, friendship is sacred, and I will protect Leni as necessary."

I stood up. My legs shook, maybe from squatting on the low curb.

"Any ideas?" I asked

Prof headed for the passenger's seat of my Barracuda.

"Follow the money," he said. "It's always about the money."

CHAPTER 20

Prof and I locked ourselves in the Barracuda. He contemplated while I flipped through the photos and videos Leni had made sitting on my fender. She smiled, brooded, pouted, kissed, and whispered phrases lifted from steamy romance novels.

"Who does Leni work for?" Prof asked.

"Oleace," I said. I spelled it for him.

"Ah," he said.

"Ah?"

"Oleace is a species of fragrant flowers. Sort of like the name rose."

"And its purpose is?"

"Make money by connecting exhibitionists with voyeurs."

"Live porn?" I summarized.

"All of that," Prof said. "But so much more. A pay-to-play social network. No matter what game you want to play, someone, somewhere in the world, is happy to play it with you."

"At the right price."

"There is no free lunch," he said.

"So if a guy just wants to talk to a pretty girl?"

"Show me such a guy," he said.

"Loud, dish-tossing breakup. Loses his woman. Pickup truck gets repo'd. Needs a woman to console him, reassure him, shoulder to cry on. Manhood restored."

"Dude needs a therapist," Prof said.

"So Leni's an amateur headshrinker?"

"Might be where she got the idea to become a psychiatrist," he said.

"That means her income is delivering boxes and comforting guys?"

"They're called models. Or sometimes cam girls. Neither is entirely accurate."

"What would you call them?" I asked.

"Often." He laughed. "Hmm, anonymous virtual prostitutes having virtual sexual relations with anonymous guys and gals they meet in a virtual environment on the Internet."

"A Silicon Valley startup attempting to disrupt sex?" I said.

"Teledildonics."

"Sounds like something developed by NASA."

Prof grinned. "Probably was. A computer in one place reaches through the Internet and controls a robot in another place."

"The name suggests—"

"Dildo." Prof leaned forward and stared through the windshield at the Natural History Museum entrance.

"You have an idea?" I asked.

"There's one bouncing around trying to understand why Leni isn't running home to mom. She started to, but changed her mind."

I waited while his idea bounced.

"Something we haven't considered," he mused.

"We have drugs and money moving in opposite directions. The drugs have to come from somewhere, and the money has to end up somewhere."

"True. You should go private-eye what all that money is doing. And for whom. But," he paused, "there's something else that could be happening here. It would trump everything."

When the world didn't make sense, it usually meant…

"The government's involved," I said. "Markus is a DEA agent. And we're about to mess up a multi-million-dollar sting operation."

Prof turned to me. "That's a hell of a good idea, Thomas. But I think there's a simpler explanation."

"Occam's razor, right? The simpler explanation is usually the correct one."

He nodded. "Nature is efficient. Likes things simple. And this is the simplest of all, though it defies all logic." Prof peered out his window at the sky. "Tommy, you ever look at a star a million light years away and try to comprehend that what we are seeing happened a million years ago? And that the star might not even be there anymore?"

"I once had to write an essay about how the stars made me feel. I titled it Minuscule."

"Cool. A teacher trying to make teenagers contemplate the unlikely reality of their own existence. What did you write?"

"Algebra."

Prof laughed. "Staring into the abyss of the cosmos, you wrote math?"

"I wrote that human's understanding of the Universe was just a model based on available data. Each of us is simply the outcome of all the data we have acquired from what has happened to us." I stared into space remembering how hard I had thought about this essay as a high school senior. "So I wrote the equation: I sub t equals f of x, y, and z, where t equals NOW."

"Which means?"

"Me, the I of NOW, depends on where I am standing in the Universe at any given moment. People in Australia aren't seeing the stars right now because light from the sun blocks them out. But the stars are still there. An alien close to one of the other stars would see our sun as it was a million years ago. You and I never see the sun as it truly is. We see it eight and a half minutes in the past."

"Meaning no two people have exactly the same experience," he said. "Every 'I' is unique."

"And my 'I' changes constantly as new data arrives."

"Data is why you're driving Route 66 isn't it? It's not about getting your kicks."

That surprised me. "Did I mention Route 66?"

"No. But you're driving from Chicago to St. Louis in a car that's old enough to be in a museum. And you're a blues player. I bet you know a couple versions of that song. And you're a romantic, helping the stray kittens you meet on the road. I added it up."

"Leni is right about you, Prof. You're smart. Way beyond Wikipedia."

"A liability I am trying to overcome." He laughed softly.

"Sorry. We got off track. You had an idea about Leni?"

He nodded. "I propose that she does not have the slightest idea what she's doing, because she's in love."

I contemplated the dark spots on the moon and the collision of celestial bodies that had caused them.

"Student-teacher hero worship?"

"Shared interest in psychology fueled by physical proximity in a classroom."

"What about Markus?"

"White-privilege college boy. Golden goose of the university. Works with people who have troubles."

"Manipulation?"

"A definite maybe. A guy like that manipulates the entire world on a daily basis. But, of course, it's for our own good." Prof's laugh had sinister undertones.

"Cynical," I said.

"Skeptical. Our Markus has secrets."

"Maybe he really likes Leni," I said. "He's what, in his thirties? She's super attractive."

"Or maybe he's accustomed to getting what he wants."

◇

Prof sank into silence on the way to Mona's place. I shifted at low rpm and eased the Hemi along like we were a Prius trying to break 50 miles per gallon. The look in Leni's eyes at the museum haunted me. The rape video filled my head. A jury of twelve peers made me wonder who the peers would be. Proving lack of consent loomed large as I recalled Leni taking photos of her cleavage in a parking lot. And me about to send those photos to strangers on the Internet.

Then images of blue Pacific waves arrived to ask how I was going to get closer to it. Becky's face playing the heroine in a summer play in the small Ohio town where I had grown up, insulated from the problems of the real world, seeped in. I imagined my buddy Rod working late in his garage, still trying to beat me in a drag race, as he had done since we both got our first car.

Prof's voice shook me out of my reverie.

"We have a problem."

"Only one?" I said.

"I've been attempting to understand Leni's behavior."

"She's a woman. Is that possible?"

We both laughed, but without conviction.

"I've known Leni for years," he said. "We went to the same schools. Something is off."

"Being raped could do that."

"She should want to stay away from him."

"She ran away," I said.

"And then ran back. At first I thought she was preventing conflict. Now I think that as soon as she saw him in Sam's place, part of her wanted to go back. This will sound like an unfounded mental leap, but I think she's a prisoner."

"Metaphorically? Like a prisoner of love?"

"Maybe." He was quiet for a few seconds. "Look from inside her life. Delivering packages. Working Oleace online. Financially unstable. A good medical school. Then a long, expensive specialization. How to get in? What better than support from the Young Turk of the psycho-scene himself?"

I pulled away from a traffic light and the Tesla beside me pulled ahead. I instinctively glanced at the tachometer, then let it go.

"So she's trapped by her desires?"

"Maybe," he said. "We know he abuses her physically. Ever hear of Stockholm Syndrome?"

"In name only."

"A victim starts feeling the warm fuzzies for her captors. Happened back in the twentieth century. Bank robbery in Stockholm. Hostage situation."

The Tesla moved into my lane. I made the mental effort to ignore it.

"Leni isn't asking us to do anything," I said. "Should we intrude on her life?" Then I remembered her parting comment about saving the volcano girl.

"It depends," Prof said. "What did she really want when she gave you her phone?"

I recalled the bright headlights of the Cadillac parked behind me in Prof's driveway. Blocking me in. And the tuner car behind him, preventing escape.

"Leni looked at me and said 'be me.' Then told me a six digit number, got out, and left her smartphone on the passenger's seat. I figured she meant: be me online."

"She could have meant, put yourself in my place. Figure out what to do. Save me."

"But we just met a few days ago."

"True. But you were the only other person in the car."

"She could have sent a message to her old friend Prof." I grinned.

"Also true. Maybe she admires your special talents. Or maybe she thinks a white guy has an advantage in Markus's world. Maybe she's too proud to ask me and impinge on my life. Or maybe she just likes you."

I stopped on the street in front of Mona's townhouse. The windows were all dark. I shut the engine off.

"OK," I said. "Let's assume that Leni wants me or us to 'be her.' What should we do?"

"Apply the Golden Rules," he said.

"Rules plural?"

"For sure. There have always been two," he said.

"Do unto others as you would have them do unto you."

"If you were Leni, what would you want us to do?" Prof said.

"Get me away from Markus without destroying my future."

"Bingo Boingo. Know how we do that?" he said.

"Nope."

"Kidnap her."

The sound of screeching insects and far away traffic resonated inside the car. I ran a series of possible actions through my head, including Jake and his team providing a distraction.

"Doesn't work long term," I said.

"I've been working on that. So far my ideas have multiple failure modes. Markus holds too many cards."

We sat in the car and didn't speak for several minutes, cogitating.

Without warning, I said, "What's the other one?"

Prof glanced at me quizzically, then recalled the context.

"Shey with the gold, rules."

◇

We went inside to a rising sun. Mona was out. Made me wonder if exotic dancers ate breakfast together after a long night shift the way my bands did, staying up for hours eating pancakes and smoking, when we all desperately needed sleep. Prof went upstairs, confident his subconscious would find a solution while the rest of him dozed.

I sat on the couch and popped the top on a cold beer. I reviewed the photos Leni had taken in the parking lot. Dozens of selfies with facial expressions from pouting all the way to 'faster faster, I'm about to orgasm.' Eye rolls. Shy smiles. Parted lips. Licking lips. Tongue out. Tongue in cheek. Shots from neck to navel. Bare breast. Erect nipple. Enough angles for a sculptor to reconstruct her.

Videos repeated the photo content but with narration. In each she had breathlessly spoken the target's handle so I knew where to send it.

@Venuslover

@Maximum69

@somelikeitrough

@hot4u451

I sent the videos first, waiting for each file to upload. Then I guessed.

The more revealing photos went to the accounts with the longest message threads—one going back a full six months. I reused the photos to cover all of the accounts. I made up messages that Sally might send. To @MonsterDong, who had written:

Sally, Sally, don't leave me. I need you more than yesterday.

Which sounded vaguely like a Paul McCartney song. Sally wrote back:

Love is such an easy game to play.

@MoonDog wrote:

Cha-cha-cha changes happening in me kitten. Bring your pussy here.

What would Sally respond?

The only constant is change. Kitty can be seen on my premium page 24/7.

I realized I was being a ghostwriter. Maybe lots of cam girls used one.

A message arrived from @allhandsondeck.

Sally, my sweetness, where can we meet? I will fly to you today.

Not a good idea. Sally wrote back:

Against the rules bad boy. I will get fired and you will have to support me AND your wife.

It struck me that colleges could use Oleace to teach creative writing. Or improv comedy. Or operate a short story contest where each team member writes one sentence before passing the story to the next person.

I felt exposed revealing parts of myself to strangers. No, not me. Leni. Not even Leni. Sally, a completely fictional character from a novel named Oleace.

I reverse-scrolled through Sally's posts. Read in isolation, one after the other, they conjured a fever dream of longing from the couch in Freud's office.

Another message arrived. How did Leni keep up with this stuff while studying?

Sally! Did you watch the video. I'm worried. What is going on? How can I help? When will you be back?

@hohoman25 was asking a very good question.

Not having an answer, I stripped, stretched out on the couch, and fell asleep before I could count a dozen Barracudas doing the quarter mile against Rod's Corvette.

CHAPTER 21

A loud truck ruined a nice dream about playing a guitar solo at a Woodstock Reunion Festival in an open field filled with thousands of fans while a blonde girl in the front row waved peach-colored panties over her head.

The HVAC system ceased blowing.

In the ensuing quiet, tapping above me indicated Prof was up and tending to his business empire. I arched my back and swung my bare feet to the floor while encouraging my brain to plan the day. And the week. And find a way to get back on the road.

Or not.

I was on the road to have new experiences and meet interesting people. The road was delivering.

I got dressed and folded the blanket back into its spot in the hall closet. A closed bedroom door suggested that Mona had come home after I fell asleep. For a moment I wondered what she wore to bed, which prompted the memory of her twin sister's body pressed against mine in a hotel named W. Only weeks had passed since that night. Mona was doing well. Her sister was right where she should be.

I crept up carpeted stairs and knocked softly with one knuckle. The typing stopped and the door swung inward. Prof stood there in black jeans and nothing else, his lean muscle under taut dark skin reminding me of Bruce Lee before a match.

"Morning, Prof. You up for breakfast?"

"Got a lot of work to do. This traveling is playing hell with my daily routine."

"Would ruin mine too," I said, "if I had one. How about we go talk to your goddess Juno friend?"

He grinned. "My interest was obvious?"

"The table was shaking from the strength of the vibe. I suspect she got the message."

"I don't even live in Chicago," he said.

I smiled. "Yet."

He laughed. "Men have chased skirts to the far ends of the Earth, haven't they?"

"And founded great civilizations." I recalled the display. "And ended the practice of throwing virgins into volcanos."

"Meaning I should go to breakfast just in case a certain waitress is working and just in case she likes tall, dark, skinny guys from Missouri, who are leaving in a few days."

"That's one way to look at it."

He squinted an eye at me.

"It's also good for your mental health," I said. "Nature has placed an opportunity in your path. This opportunity is not well defined. But if you go to breakfast, you hold the door open for more opportunity to flow in."

"I'll be down in a minute," he said, and closed the door.

I sat on the couch and checked messages. Most accounts that received a photo sent a positive response. A few sent insults. One complained: What good is a whore that ain't available?

I called my service.

"Cuda Freelance," Tina cooed.

"Hi Tina," I whispered, so as not to wake Mona. "Got anything interesting?"

"Oh," Tina whispered back, "a call was recorded at three A.M. Do you want me to play it now?"

"I'll listen later."

"The computer shows it as four point seven seconds," she whispered.

"Thanks. Talk later."

We hung up.

Cuda Freelance having a live person was professional. But trusting Tina with sensitive information would have to wait until I knew her better. I dialed in and played the message.

"Stay away from Lenore." Click.

I played it again. No background sounds. No preamble. Not a deep and confident voice like Markus. More soda pop commercial.

Prof descended the stairs and headed for the door. I followed him out. He caught my eye across the roof of the Barracuda.

"What happened? You look like we're going to your dog's funeral."

"Got a message through my service. Processed voice. Told me to stay away from Lenore."

"Lenore, not Leni?"

"Makes you wonder, doesn't it?"

"Yeah," he said. "Makes me wonder what's for breakfast. I've been working for hours fueled by stale animal crackers I found in a drawer below Mona's silverware."

"She doesn't keep much food in the house."

He shrugged and slipped into the car.

"When you work at restaurant, you got your own chef. Why have food at home?"

"I doubt Mona is home alone often," I said.

Prof nodded. "With her beauty and that club, she probably has dates lined up for the next 100 days."

I coasted backwards into the street, then fired up the Hemi as quietly as possible.

"You'd think there would be some leftovers."

Prof said, "Mona doesn't strike me as a leftovers girl. She gets fresh every time."

I headed toward the Pig. In about a mile, I smelled something odd. Burning. Maybe a brake problem. Or an electrical short. My friend Chin had done a lot of work restoring the interior. I sure didn't need another fire.

"What's that smell?" Prof said.

I glanced in the rearview mirror. A cloud of blue smoke was following us like a contrail. I pulled over fast so we could jump out. A quick look through the grill didn't reveal anything. I released the hood and lifted it slowly, not wanting to give oxygen to burning fuel.

No smoke under the hood.

Surrounded by billowing blue smoke we dropped to our knees and discovered a long gray rectangle stuck to the side of my fuel tank.

◇

"You can buy these at Walmart," Prof said. "It's a colored flare for gender reveal parties."

"It's a boy," I said.

He brushed road grit off his knees.

"A boy letting you know he can booby trap your car."

"Stay away from Lenore?" I said.

"Far away. Leni has her own place. Her bicycle. Multiple jobs. So Markus showing up at the museum means he's keeping a careful eye on her."

"Because…"

"He doesn't want cops. Cops would throw a Pink Monkey wrench into his life."

I laughed lightly, releasing tension.

"Or," I said, "he loves her and believes abuse is part of good relationship."

"Or she knows a secret."

"All of the above?" I asked.

"Possibly."

The blue smoke bomb expended itself and fizzled to white before stopping altogether. I removed the tape, the still hot box, and a smaller box inside.

"Motion sensor," I said. "A guy could install this in about five seconds."

"Or a girl. Drops her purse, gets down on her knees to pick it up. Slaps that onto the tank. Had it been a bomb, we'd be going to a funeral."

"We should be careful," I said.

"Well, Cuda, I was being careful," Prof said.

"Still hungry?"

"You bet. Could be my last meal." He was laughing as he buckled himself in.

The trip to the Pig was uneventful. We even got the parking space across the street from the front door.

"You have a deal with the city to make this your personal spot?" Prof asked.

"Next year they give me the key to the city."

"I bet they have a crime-fighting award for private dicks," he said.

"Not eligible. I'm a freelance consultant."

"Funny business is our specialty," he said.

We headed straight for the grandeur of the oak door with a fleur-de-lis etched into the glass. As we reached the steps, something blue streaked past us and into the restaurant.

"It's a train. It's a plane."

"It's a speeding waitress late for her shift," Prof said.

"Was that the goddess?"

Prof sniffed the air. "Almost certainly."

"The nose knows?" I said.

Prof nodded. "One of the most important senses in the mating ritual. Pheromones precede all other moans."

"Prof, you ever think maybe you read too much?"

"It adds up."

"Ever forget anything?"

Prof looked thoughtful for a few seconds.

"Not that I can recall," he said, laughing and yanking the handle of the ultra-wide door.

Our table was available so we didn't wait for the hostess. The goddess arrived wearing a tight top the color of copper with long sleeves that covered her tattoos. Her earrings were huge black hoops made of carbon fiber. She poured two coffees.

"You guys come back to ask me more questions? I could use the money."

"We'll think of some," Prof said.

Her smile combined gleaming teeth with fire engine lipstick.

"Menus, or same as yesterday?"

We agreed on same.

"You remember what every customer had yesterday?" I asked.

"I have a trick." She spun and walked away.

We both watched the swaying black skirt that seemed like part of a loosely defined uniform.

"A trick?" I said.

"Must be a good trick given how busy this place is," Prof said. "There are almost as many people in here as books."

"Photographic memory?"

"As rare as those people who can multiply huge numbers in their head."

She came back with my orange juice.

"Breakfast will be a few minutes. The kitchen is mad at me for being late." She tilted her head. A black hoop tapped her shoulder. "Sorry. What's the question?"

I cast my mind for something clever.

Prof spoke up. "It's kind of personal."

"Wouldn't be fun otherwise," she said.

"Well," Prof said. "We've been calling you the goddess because we never introduced ourselves.

"Tommy and Prof," she said.

I thought back. "You have guess names trick?"

"Yep. And if you had been paying attention, you would have noticed that I signed my name like John Hancock did on the Constitution. You ever wonder about his name? John Hand Cock?" She laughed.

"I was distracted by your tattoo," I said.

She smiled. "Nice try. Chianti. Spelled like the wine but pronounced with a soft shh…like you're telling me to keep a secret." She laughed again. "That's how my mother described my name to other mothers when I was little. But it confused people too much, I spell it with an S now."

"A pleasure to meet you, Shianti," Prof said.

"Are you going to reveal your trick?" I asked.

"Is that today's hundred-dollar question?"

"No, no. I'm sure Prof has a better one."

"I'll give you a hint," she said. Moving her eyes, she added, "You called him Prof."

"But I rarely call him Tommy," Prof said.

"True. But Tommy has a history with the Pig."

Of course I did. A waitress studying criminology.

"You're a college student?"

She pulled the skin below her eyes down with a thumb and index fingers.

"Does it show?"

"Drama major," Prof said.

"Close, no cigar," she said.

"English. You want to be a writer," I guessed.

"Also close. Still no stogy."

Writing plus drama would equal…

"Filmmaking?" I said.

She pointed a finger pistol at me. "Bang." She disappeared into the kitchen.

Prof stared at me.

"Yeah. Met a waitress studying criminology. She helped me out with a project."

Prof smiled. "A project? I've never heard it called a project before?"

"Things didn't go that direction," I said.

"And now you're wondering what life would be like if they had?"

"Robert Frost has always had me wondering about the path not taken."

"Hard not to wonder about the past. But we have an immediate challenge." He paused. "More than one."

Shianti returned with a duplicate of yesterday's breakfast. She knew which parts were for Prof and which were for me.

"Good trick," I said. "Have you written a book about your memory system? You'll be rich."

She grinned. "It's not that complicated. But if I reveal all, you must swear to keep silent. My customers think I'm a genius, getting their order right day after day. Wouldn't want to smudge my image."

"I'll swear," Prof said. "If you don't tell us, we are going to spend many sleepless nights trying to figure it out."

"There are better ways to spend sleepless nights," she said. "Here's a hint. Guess where we store the checks after you pay them?" She moved to the next table to take the order from a guy wearing a three-piece suit with no tie.

"Hmm," I said.

"If she has yesterday's check, she can duplicate the order."

"Digital cash register," I said.

"Indexed by time and table number," Prof said. "Voila." He started eating. "What should we ask the goddess today?"

"What's our objective?"

"Save Leni. Fall in love with Shianti. Take her home to meet the family. Get married. Make babies. Live happily ever after."

"You read romance novels?"

"Of course. They are filled with the deep truths of the human spirit." His eyes said he was serious.

"Such as?"

"Like how romance novels are pure fantasy." He laughed.

"What question helps Leni?"

Shianti returned to freshen coffee. Her eyes moved between our faces like Poe's pendulum.

"Well?"

"It's delicate," Prof said. "But we have good reason for asking."

"A friend in need, no doubt."

Prof cleared his throat and leaned toward the salt and pepper shakers at the center of the table.

I leaned in.

Shianti bent forward at the waist until the three of us formed a tight huddle.

"What would you do," Prof whispered, "if you were raped?"

Shianti's long lashes blinked repeatedly over pale blue eyes.

I held my breath.

"Do I know the guy?" she asked.

"Yes."

"Are we married?"

Prof shook his head.

"Dating?"

"For five months."

Her painted lips rolled inward and held tight. I took a quiet, shallow breath.

Shianti leaned in closer and lowered her voice.

"I'd buy a gun," she said. Then she straightened and walked away.

CHAPTER 22

Our eyes met across the table. Prof's black eyes showed no surprise.

"A gun?"

"Not my first guess," he said.

We ate in silence. I thought about what Shianti might do with her new gun. I wondered what Leni's first move had been before she visited the clinic and landed at a roadside rest stop. I pressed my left elbow against the burner cellphone Prof had loaned me, snug in my jacket pocket. I did the same on the right. The five-shot revolver Prof had insisted I carry pressed back. I recalled him casually reaching into a kitchen drawer and handing it to me, clean, loaded, ready to go to work.

"Prof," I said. "You loaned me…" I made the same gesture Shianti had made.

He nodded.

"How many toys do you keep in that drawer?"

He finished chewing. Drank some coffee.

"They come and go. I don't keep careful records."

Of course not.

"Do you think Leni might have the same idea as Shianti?"

His forkful of pancakes reversed in mid-air and lowered back to his plate.

"I didn't check the drawer."

"So our friend might be armed and dangerous?" I said.

"She's an only child. It's best not to push her around." He contemplated for a few moments. "And she's been known to act on what the cards tell her."

The thought of Leni setting Markus up for a bullet seemed improbable and inevitable at the same time. Could 'I'm lost' have been referring to her future?

Shianti returned with a coffeepot in each hand and refilled our cups.

"All good, guys?"

"Food is great," I said. "But that, uh, accessory, you mentioned."

Her eyes danced above a tiny smile. "To ensure that it didn't happen again. Men think, 'hey, we did it before', so the gates are open and they can have all they want."

"Not retribution?" Prof asked.

"Hell no. I'm not going to sacrifice my one life for some loser to be six feet under. What good is revenge if it leaves me rotting in prison without a hard dick in sight?" She laughed, then turned poker face. "Some prick violates me, I don't want him dead. I want him to suffer." She smiled and added, "You guys sure come up with the questions." She walked away.

"She's got a cool head," I said.

"Not like Leni," Prof replied, somewhat wistfully.

We returned to eating.

Leni having a gun would raise the stakes if things got heated with Markus again. I stalled mid-thought. I was interfering with other people's lives. What was I even doing back in Chicago?

The cosmos replied: Having an adventure.

"Ideas?" I asked.

"Lots," Prof said. "None with a happy ending."

"Hard to come by outside Hollywood."

Prof buttered his last piece of toast. Then smeared it with purple jelly from a single-serve container.

"This Markus dude," he said. "Big man on campus. High profile job. Nice wheels. Why risk all that to rape a coed? It can only lead to trouble."

"You're being logical. Cost benefit analysis. If everyone did that, Trump could never 'grab 'em by the pussy.'"

Prof smiled. "Some quotes stick with you, don't they?"

"Especially the profound ones that reveal deep truths about the nature of man."

We both laughed, knowing that quote revealed plenty, and not just about the guy who said it.

Prof bit into his newly coated toast and chased it with coffee.

"So," he said. "I'm trying to live in the now. Things are good. We found Leni. We've met Markus. Everyone is healthy."

"You saw the video. What do you think is going on?"

"Couple has a fight over smartphone interruptions. He feels he isn't getting enough attention. You and I know why Leni answered that phone—she's trying to keep cash coming in. We do not know if Markus knows why she answered that phone." He paused in thought. "I think he doesn't know about Oleace. Which is a good trick on Leni's part. So he gets pissed off. Grabs the phone, tosses it. But it was on a video call so it keeps broadcasting. The guy at the other end was recording Leni. He keeps recording."

I sipped orange juice. Prof continued.

"Markus makes the primal move to establish dominance: he hits her. Tries to tear off her shirt. This time—I imagine there were others —this time Leni's no really means no. But Markus doesn't stop. We don't know exactly how it ended once they move out of the frame."

"Leni grabs her phone," I said. "Escapes, reports the rape as a Jane Doe. Next thing, I meet her at a highway rest stop where she's trying to raise bus fare by telling fortunes."

"How did she get to the rest stop?"

I shrugged. "She asked me if I was one of those ass-or-gas guys when I gave her a ride."

"OK, assume she hitchhiked. The negotiation ended with her being dropped at the rest stop."

"Which leaves us where?" I said.

"Confused. But not hungry." He smiled.

"Inaction feels like the wrong path. Leni met us at the museum for some important reason."

"Call for help?" Prof said.

"She could have left that message with my service."

We both finished our coffee.

"Maybe," Prof said, "she wanted Markus to know that we are close and paying attention in an effort to intimidate him."

"Which is why he warned us to stay away."

Shianti arrived table side.

"Anything else guys?"

"Do you have donuts to go?" I asked.

Shake of the head. "Nope. But we have an amazing new muffin with twirled caramel and chocolate chips."

Prof nodded.

"How about a half dozen to go?" I said.

She smiled. "You guys are all in, aren't you?"

"I'm going to see a friend and need a peace offering. Better add three large coffees."

"I'll give you our to-go pot. You'll like it."

"As the goddess wishes," I said.

She returned in a couple of minutes with a brown grocery bag with twine handles.

"Your offering," she said.

"I have a question," Prof said.

Shianti tilted her head. Her golden curls flopped onto her copper shirt like roiling water down a river. She gazed directly at him.

"Does your boss have a rule about not dating customers?"

She tilted her head slowly to the other side.

"No one has ever bothered to ask me that. But, in fact, he does. He thinks that the ratio between the business it would bring in versus the amount it would drive away would not be in his favor."

Prof nodded slightly, possibly agreeing with the boss's assessment.

"Wouldn't want you to get fired," he said.

She shrugged. "It's not that great of job. Plus," she grinned and rolled her eyes to one side, "I'm not so good with rules. And," she turned over the receipt lying on the table. "You guys like to ask questions. I can be a participant in your survey." She handed the paper to Prof, winked at me, and walked away with my cash.

I considered for a moment, then said, "Prof, how do you think Shianti would make the guy suffer?"

◇

I pulled to the curb in front of Water Tower Place on North Michigan Avenue. An eight-story shopping mall inside claimed to have over one hundred stores. Prof eased the passenger door open.

"Gonna go see what's hip in Chicago," he said, before stepping out and swinging the door closed.

I drove across town and parked in the lot of a church with a copper dome oxidized to mint green. There were two other cars, both hybrids. I started walking, then backtracked to the church and up stone steps worn to curves by thousands and thousands of worshippers. The ten-foot-tall wooden doors were unlocked. The massive interior was lit by afternoon sunlight filtering through multi-colored stained-glass windows. My footfalls echoed like rifle shots in a canyon.

I saw no one.

I found what I was looking for ten steps in: a four-inch pipe standing upright with a slotted brass plate across the top.

DONATIONS WELCOME

I folded a twenty and tapped it through the slot—a thank you for a parking place that would prevent my Barracuda from being seen at the building I was about to visit. My car was old. Unusual. It stood out in a crowd.

I didn't want to be remembered.

Shianti's satchel dangled from my right hand as the spaciousness of the architecture soaked into my bones. Places of worship projected a special aura. Not nature. Not civilization. Billions of lightyears of cosmic distances hovered in the air. And asked questions.

Where is Leni?

What is she planning?

At my current pace, it could take a year to reach the Pacific Ocean. I'd be thirty.

So?

What else was I going to do? Go back to working on cars in a Walmart garage? Join a traveling blues band? Start a real consulting company? Get an official private-eye license?

I turned and walked out.

Many questions. I had an idea where to find the answer to one of them.

The walk to the faded building was about a quarter mile. I smiled. The length of a drag strip. I figured Shianti's to-go pot would keep the coffee hot. I entered through a door with no glass and walked up the stairs. The third story hallway hadn't changed in the weeks since I'd last seen it. Yet, it felt like a memory from the distant past. Maybe time wasn't about seconds. Maybe it was about how many new events per hour happened to your brain.

The office door was standing eight inches ajar, just as it had been the first time I approached it. I tapped on the frosted glass in the top half.

"Go away," a male voice said.

Detective Braden's attitude hadn't changed.

I hung the bag from my left index finger and placed my arm through the opening, letting the aroma of fresh coffee and Shianti's muffins attack the occupant's nose.

"If that's food, get in here."

I elbowed the door open; closed it behind me. Braden was wearing his ever-present frown.

"Well, well, well. If it isn't Mr. Cuda. I thought you were going west to surf?"

"Got waylaid," I said.

"Another woman, no doubt."

He motioned for me to take the interrogation chair in front his tired wooden desk. His green blinds were closed, but plenty of light seeped between them, backlighting him into a near silhouette. I placed the bag on his desk.

"How did you know?"

"Statistics," he said. "What'd you bring?"

I placed the disposable coffee pot and two recyclable cups on a desk with enough cup stains for them to be a design element. As he poured two cups of coffee, I put a muffin on a napkin and slid it across his desk.

"Specialty of the house. Caramel and chocolate chip."

"What do they call it, a sweet heart attack? How many did you bring?"

"Six."

"OK, you can have one." He sipped the coffee. "Good stuff. So, tell me about this new woman."

"College student. Professor boyfriend. Date rape. Part of the encounter is on video."

He bit into a muffin the size of a baseball and chewed.

I waited, knowing he would speak when he was ready for more information.

He licked his lips. Sipped coffee.

"Good stuff. She going to press charges?"

"No. She doesn't think it will do anything except expose her personal life."

"Which she wants to keep personal?"

I nodded.

"Most people do. Privacy is a prerequisite for freedom." He took another bite of the muffin and brushed crumbs off his blue tie.

I ate my muffin. I wasn't hungry, but it was delicious and I didn't want him to eat alone, although Braden wasn't one to care.

"Not much I can do officially if she won't press charges. Tell me about this recording?" He poured himself more coffee.

I put Leni's smartphone on his desk and leaned it against the half-empty coffee pot, then started the video.

Braden stopped eating. His right arm rested on his desk with his right hand wrapped around the to-go cup. He didn't move. He just watched.

"Again," he said.

I tapped play. We watched to the end.

He moved muffin to mouth with his left hand.

"Easy to ID the location and the girl. A little bit harder with the guy. No tattoos, birthmarks. Only a profile of the face."

"We know who it is," I said.

He laughed. "You know who she claims it is." He sipped.

"There's a rape kit."

"She won't press charges, but there's a kit?"

"She went to campus services. Didn't name names. They did a Jane Doe kit."

"Good start."

I had used the unlock code for Leni's phone often enough to have it memorized. So I gave it to him.

"You come in here with your heart attack muffins thinking you can talk me into having that kit processed to see what the DNA says. You want to know if it will hold up in court."

I nodded while drinking.

"And," I said, "I hate to even think this. But in the case of an existing relationship…"

"You think the little lady might be lying to get revenge on a guy she thinks isn't treating her right."

"Crossed my mind." I hesitated. "I don't know her very well."

"I can have the kit processed with a phone call. After I do, what do we know?"

"Who done it," I said.

He shook his head. "Only if we can obtain a DNA sample to match. Otherwise we only know that we have an identifiable sample."

"What if I get a glass or a toothbrush?"

"We need something that will survive a trial."

"She doesn't want to go to court."

"It's how our judicial system works. Innocent until proven guilty beyond a reasonable doubt. There have been some high-profile guilty verdicts. Bill Cosby. Donald Trump. That comedian who liked to jerk-off in front of women. Cosby did prison time."

I chewed the sweet blob of muffin in my mouth.

"You're suggesting she put herself on trial right along with him?"

"I'm not suggesting anything. Crime and punishment is a complicated landscape. Just ask Dostoevsky. Took him twelve hundred pages to explain it." He broke a chunk from his muffin. "I'm saying that you need an objective." He popped the chunk into his mouth and met my eyes. "Confirming the identity of the rapist would be a good first step. In my professional experience, women lie as a life strategy." He sipped coffee before adding, "statistically."

"You really think women lie regularly?"

My detective friend chewed slowly, swallowed, and washed it down with a long pull on his coffee cup.

"Mr. Cuda, I'm a detective. I'm not paid to think, or present a case, or reach a conclusion. That's up to the DA, a duly elected official representative of the people. I, as a lowly detective, am paid to collect evidence."

I nodded and smiled. "And the evidence would suggest that not only do the women you have experienced through our criminal justice system lie regularly, they are good at it."

"Practice makes perfect." He fumbled another chunk of muffin off with his left hand. "I am confident that you brought this fine cuisine here to ask a favor. Now that we both understand the situation, what is it?"

"Well, um, the first one…"

CHAPTER 23

I left the muffins with Braden, stopped in the quiet of the church to contemplate what that Jane Doe test kit might reveal, and tried to predict how the result might change things. Realized that my foundation of objective knowledge was shaky, and I was getting no closer to the Pacific with each passing day. I also wasn't earning money. Although I wasn't spending much either, due to the kindness of new friends.

I drove Lakeside, left my brothel creepers and socks in the car, and walked along the beach barefoot. I marveled at how standing in the sand alone, staring over the indigo waters of Lake Michigan on a dark night, felt isolated and desolate. But rotating 180 degrees found me staring into a city of two and a half million humans. Paupers to billionaires. Men, women, and children of every shape, form, and color. Doing what?

Living Tommy. They're living.

And what am I doing?

Wandering, Tommy. Exploring.

Which is a form of living. Continuous change. The thrill of novelty. The magnetic draw of the unknown. No responsibilities.

Then why am I so worried about Leni? I barely know her.

So?

You do know her. And you know bad things have happened.

So?

You might be able to help. Spread the love, Tommy.

I drove back to Mona's and pulled into her one car garage. The only thing in it was a full-size pink bicycle that said Barbie on the down tube. The tires weren't flat. I imagined Mona riding it to a coffee shop, attracting attention.

Mona might be home and sleeping, so I lowered the garage door carefully by hand, entered the house, and removed my shoes even though creepers were supposed to be quiet.

No one in the kitchen.

I made my way up the carpeted stairs and stopped at Prof's room. His door was five inches ajar. No keyboard sounds. I was about to move on when a beep stopped me. A single beep, like a microwave saying the food was ready.

I eased the door open with two fingers. It creaked most of the way. The bed was made. The place looked like a fresh hotel room that I had just checked into.

Another beep.

I located the source in the top drawer of the nightstand between the bed and the one window in the room, currently covered by forest green curtains. I moved the laptop from the drawer to the top of the nightstand and sat on the single bed. The box springs groaned, reminding me of Leni's bed back at Prof's place, and the hidden box inside.

I opened the laptop. It didn't ask for a password. Odd, considering Prof's extensive knowledge of computing. A message window appeared in the center of an otherwise blank screen.

I have been detained by our friend in the blue car. He lost Leni again, believes we are to blame. I am attempting to disabuse him of this notion, but the man has a bad attitude. See folder named LeniWorld. — P.

I reread the message twice. Leni was AWOL. Markus had detained Prof. Markus had a bad attitude. Prof was armed. I took a photo of Prof's message with Leni's smartphone and closed the window. The screen wasn't blank. It was a black desktop with a single folder named LeniWorld that had been hiding behind the message.

It occurred to me that Prof's recent tapping hadn't been work. It had been research. He had accessed this laptop from his phone to tell me about it. I found two folders inside LeniWorld: Markus and Lenore. I started with Lenore.

High school photos of Leni with short hair barely covering her ears. Leni cheerleading in a purple and white outfit. Pompoms in the same two colors. Leni in a drama group doing Medea. Leni playing field hockey in a purple shirt.

A set of photos had Oleace in the file name. Leni in red lingerie, white, mint green. Fishnet stockings. Short skirts. Then a list of addresses: one in St. Louis, two in Chicago. Photo of Leni standing near Markus at an outdoor event where he was cutting a white ribbon with two-foot-long scissors. Unclear if they were a couple or she was part of the audience. Her admiring expression suggested something was going on. Leni telling fortunes from a booth at a fundraiser. I wondered how long she had been using tarot cards. The one I had drawn at the rest stop felt brand new.

I opened the second folder.

PDF files. The first was a technical paper.

The Short-Term Effects of Nature Intervention on Opioid Addiction.

The abstract claimed a 50% success rate after 6 months from a 30-day immersion program. It focused on survival skills and isolated the individual from both urban settings and modern communication technology.

I recalled tossing my smartphone out the window of a rolling Barracuda, and the sense of freedom I still had from it. Almost a month ago. A lot had happened since that day.

I scanned the paper for details—methods, number of participants—wondering what being isolated in a tent in a forest for a month would do to my brain. Or the mind of an addict.

Made me wonder.

Were we all addicted to something? Beliefs. Substances. Lifestyle. Recognition. Pets. Whatever it was that got us out of bed in the morning. Was addiction part of the human condition, some just healthier than others?

Maybe not.

Maybe they all took a toll. Society was just accustomed to paying the price—so they accepted the cost as normal.

What would be normal in a forest?

I worked my way through the technical papers. They all related to narcotic addiction and how to address it. One was titled:

Living with Addiction—Abstinence: Not the only Option.

I'd bet Markus had taken heat on that one.

The obvious conclusion was that Markus, as the lead author on every paper, was famous for good reason. He was performing modern scientific research that was proving what the Chinese ancients and Walt Whitman and John Muir had all preached: Humans separate themselves from nature at serious peril to their mental health.

I scanned two more papers but couldn't find a source of funding for the projects. Research required experiments and employees. Something as complicated as shepherding drug-addicted college kids into the wild required money.

Big Pharma came to mind.

They like monopolies. They don't like competition from the street and they sure don't like customers dying from overdose. Too many deaths awakens government regulations that screws with their primary business of pushing pills through MDs.

A footnote caught my eye.

The authors gratefully acknowledge partial funding for this project provided by Nature Incognito.

Prof's loaner burner phone buzzed. No one had the number except Prof.

"Hello."

"Where is he?"

A woman's voice. Vaguely familiar. Not Leni.

"Who are we talking about?" I said.

"Don't B.S. me, Tommy."

"Shianti?"

"Of course. How many dinner dates does Carl have in one night? He promised to meet me. But told me that if he didn't show up, I should call you at this number."

"Prof got…um…tied up in a complex project we're working on."

"It had better be important. He didn't even text. Just let me sit here waiting."

"I'm sure he did everything he could."

"Is this some kind of stupid game you guys play on strangers?"

I stared at the laptop wondering what else it could tell me.

"No, Shianti. I know Prof wanted to see you. I dropped him at the Water Tower mall so he could shop for new clothes."

"He doesn't need clothes to impress me. He just needs to show up."

"Shianti, he's—"

"Don't make excuses…wait. Is he okay?"

"I don't know for sure. He left me a message. But I haven't been able to reach him."

"Oh my god! This happens to me all the time."

All the time?

"What happens, Shianti?"

"Whenever I find an interesting guy, something happens to him. Something that has nothing to do with me. But it messes up my opportunity." She paused and took a breath. "Tell me he's okay."

"I think so. I'm back at the place we're staying." I scanned the pristine room. It looked as if Prof had never been there. "He hasn't been here all day." An idea swept across my mind. "What did you say you were studying in college?"

"Tommy, I'm sitting alone at a table for two in a fancy restaurant. The waiter keeps staring at me like he thinks I'm an escort girl. Can you get here fast?"

"Ask him for a list of their imported beer. And tell him your boyfriend is running late."

◇

I pulled up in front of the London House as the valet was holding open the driver's door of a candy apple red Corvette for a woman in a white dress who had more curves than the car. She was alone. The valet and I watched the Corvette pull into traffic. He waved me forward. After I stepped out, he leaned in until his head was even with the steering wheel.

"Man, they don't make them like this anymore," he said. "My Uncle Murray had a muscle car that smoked so many tires he had to cut back on his drinking to pay for them."

"Automotive technology has come a long way."

"But here you are still driving a horse and buggy. Why don't you trade to modern?"

"They don't make them like they used to."

He nodded as he straightened.

"You see that Corvette? Nice car. But the charisma is lacking with a mid-engine."

"True. But it's fast."

He agreed with his eyes.

"How long will you be, sir?"

"Just here for dinner."

He glanced at my dark blue sport coat that had come from the Get Over It boutique, the white shirt I borrowed from Prof's room (cuffs turned up because Prof was so tall), and the gold tie I had found in Mona's dresser that probably wasn't hers. It all went together reasonably well with my best black jeans and black boots that I had quickly shined with a damp paper towel. He handed me a claim check.

"We get quite a few vintage cars here. I must say, the color is unusual."

Under layers of road dust, the color looked like tilled soil.

"Glistens pretty well after a wash and wax. Turbo bronze metallic."

"Turbo way back then, a vehicle ahead of its time. Would you like me to have it washed for you while you dine? The guys aren't busy. They'll do a good job. The hotel adds it to your dinner check."

Shianti deserved a clean car.

"I would greatly appreciate that," I said.

"The red leather looks recent. Anything for the interior?"

I shook my head.

He hopped in behind the wheel and eased the car away like he was taking a driving test.

I found the restaurant on the top floor and started to tell a hostess with dark eyes, gold eyeshadow, and a perfectly spherical Afro even bigger than Naomi's that I was meeting someone, but she cut me off.

"Shianti will be glad to see you. That girl seems mighty nervous. Is this your first date?" She smiled. "Not to pry. We get a lot of first dates, with dating apps and all. People think of a place to impress and the London House comes to mind. As our website says, 'Best Rooftop Bar in Chicago.'"

I opened my mouth to tell her I was pinch-hitting but decided it was too complicated, irrelevant, and not in line with the story Shianti had told her.

Her Afro shifted to and fro as she examined me. We started walking.

"Are you a—," she began.

"Musician. How could you tell?"

She smiled brightly.

"You want the truth? Musicians dress funny. It's like they were choosing their outfit and a really interesting song came on, so they stopped paying attention."

I slowed. She took two more steps, realized I was gone, stopped, and waited.

When I reached her I asked softly, "What would you change?"

"If we had time, everything. But a different tie would be a major improvement." She turned toward the side of the room and wiggled a finger for me to follow.

"You need integration. Since we require ties, and most guys under thirty don't even own one, we have a loaner collection." She led me through a swinging door into a room that contained plates, silverware, and an armoire filled with men's clothing.

"This," she said. She held a tie over mine. It had narrow diagonal stripes of midnight blue over a rich gold that made my tie look yellow.

"It's great. Can I borrow it?"

"Yes, indeed. And if your check is large enough, you can keep it. You'll need it again."

She peeled off my tie and handed it to me. In a few seconds she had a perfect Windsor knot in place. Her perfume carried me to a tropical beach as she fastened the top button of my shirt behind the knot.

"You've done this before," I said, folding Mona's tie into the pocket of my jacket.

"You'd be amazed at how many customers would be back here for half an hour trying to get a knot right if I didn't do it for them." She led the way out and stopped as we approached Shianti's table. She leaned closer and whispered, "You've got a bombshell there, be careful trying to defuse her." She laughed as she walked away, leaving me to travel the last few yards alone.

Shianti's off-white dress was shimmering more than the Corvette driver's. It revealed long, tanned legs ending in wraparound gold straps of gold shoes. A matching gold clutch was lying on its side near a glass of red wine. The table was set for two. A menu lay in front of the empty chair. I'd bet on a beer list.

"Hello."

Shianti turned. Her face was statue smooth. Sky blue eyeshadow accented deep set shining blue eyes. Our Bourgeois Pig waitress had transformed onto a Hollywood red carpet.

She eased her chair back and started to stand.

"That's okay, don't—"

But she was up and wrapping both arms around me like I was returning from war. I hugged her gently.

She said nothing.

After a few seconds she released me and sat back down. I sat across from her. Her wavy blonde hair cascaded over bare shoulders. The goddess on her biceps stared at me boldly.

"Thanks for coming, Tommy. I thought for sure Carl had stood me up and here I am all decked out and guys are sending drinks from the bar and asking if I'm alone, do I want company, am I staying at the hotel? The management thinks I'm a professional trying to work their restaurant." She sipped her wine. "Now they all know that I was waiting for a cute guy who finally showed up."

"Welcome to London House, sir. Can I get you anything?" a deep male voice intoned.

I glanced at the list on the table.

"Heineken dark, please. And dinner menus. I'm afraid I was detained and the lady is ravenous."

His eyes danced to Shianti, held an extra beat, then flashed back to me.

"We have an excellent brie, fruit, and nuts appetizer if you would like something quickly."

Shianti gave me an almost invisible nod that didn't even move her hair.

"Yes, please. And water with gas for the table, if you would."

He bowed, took a full step backwards, spun and walked away with deliberate steps.

"Prof, I mean Carl," I said, "went to see, um…a professor at the university this afternoon."

"And that's more important than me?"

I shook my head. "No. It got out of hand."

She squinted disbelief and reached for the stem of her wine glass.

"I'm listening. I don't want to assume, so I'll ask. Is Carl buying us dinner?"

I grinned. "Oh yeah. He'll be happy to do that."

She smiled for the first time since my arrival. How much would Prof want me to tell a waitress from the Pig who wanted to make films?

"Shianti, there's something going on. We don't really know—"

She cut me off with her free hand while drinking wine.

"Let me guess," she said. "Someone got raped. Or claims she was. You and Carl know the girl. This is a crime. But it's a delicate situation. Hard to report. Hard to get justice. Many people, including women, don't grok what a big deal it is to be forced to let someone use your body. There are no clear answers. Maybe there's more than one side to the story." She placed her glass on the white tablecloth and met my eyes. "And you guys have no idea what to do."

"Good summary," I said.

An extravagant cheese plate arrived with a foam-topped glass of dark beer. Condensation formed rivulets down the side.

"But," she said, picking an almond off the plate. "Carl…um…Prof got his butt in a grinder and missed out on the date of his lifetime."

Of this I had no doubt.

I nodded agreement and sipped my beer. It was cool and smooth and one of the best beers I had ever tasted.

"Now what?" she said.

"We have a nice dinner after I tell you how amazing you look and how distraught Prof will be when he finds out what he missed. Then you'll have to decide."

Shianti placed the almond carefully between her teeth, then wrapped her lips around it as if it were a tasty morsel of the world's sweetest chocolate. She didn't seem to be aware that she was generating enough sexual energy for an entire cruise ship.

"Decide what?"

"Are you in or out?" I sipped my beer.

The waiter returned. Shianti ordered grilled trout. I went with a steak and some special wedge fries, the closest I could get to a cheeseburger. After he departed she stared into her wine glass and twirled the stem.

"How dangerous is it?"

"Unknown. However, Prof gave me a burner phone and a handgun that I doubt has a registration."

Shianti rolled a single nut across the cheese plate, back and forth under her index finger. Her fingernail was the color of a ripe mango.

"How well do you know Prof?" she asked.

"As well as you can know anyone in three days. Outside of a war zone."

She ate the nut. Teeth first. Puckered lips to surround it. Slow motion chewing.

"So you're in no man's land too?"

I shrugged. I was, but didn't feel like it. I felt like I had known Leni and Prof since childhood. Maybe something about shared strife. The psychologists would have to figure it out for me someday.

"I want to be a private investigator. I'm not one now. I need training and a license. So now I'm a freelance business consultant. Any business you want to hire me to dive into." I paused. Then, "At the risk of boring you, I felt trapped after college. You know, like, is this all there is to life? Is this what I've worked for? So now I'm on an extended vacation, following Route 66, the mother road, all the way to the Pacific Ocean."

"Getting your kicks?"

"Mostly meeting nice people in challenging situations. Occasionally, I get a paying job."

She spread cheese and honey onto a cracker the size of a Rolex.

"And you've been hired for this case…er…consultation?"

"Not in so many words. Prof offered a place to stay and the…tools that I mentioned. Leni gave me an online media job."

She licked honey from her lips without disturbing her lipstick.

"This Leni person's rape," she said. "Recent?"

"A few days ago."

She nodded slowly. The curls kept up.

"She said, he said," she said.

I considered. "Hmm…are you in?"

She laughed. The sound was pure and simple.

"Only on a need-to-know basis, huh?

Our waiter arrived with a wheeled, silver cart. He served Shianti's trout on a plate the size of a flying saucer, offered pepper. She declined. He gave me a steak still sizzling on a metal pan, offered pepper. I accepted.

"Bon appétit," he said, and pushed his cart away.

"Amazing place," she said.

"Prof can be an amazing guy."

She looked at me with a blank expression.

I smiled.

"OK,OK. I'm in. The curiosity is killing me."

"There's a recording."

Her knife stopped moving. She leaned in until her lips hovered over the brie.

She whispered, "No shit?"

"Leni's smartphone got tossed during a fight. It recorded some action."

She didn't move. "And?"

"Grabbing, slapping, rough penetration. He claims she likes it that way."

Shianti sat up straight.

"Misogynistic prick," she said, not whispering.

"Leni agrees."

Shianti tasted her trout.

"You know Stravinsky?" she asked.

"Was he a guitar player?" I smiled.

"Ha. I'm thinking about The Rite of Spring."

"Primal dance. Big stir at its premier," I said.

A smile slowly lifted her cheeks.

"Yeah, first time I saw it I was breathing hard by the end. Made my date take me straight home."

"Lucky guy," I said.

She squinted at me. "You're a private eye?"

"Sorry, bad assumption. Lucky date."

"I'm messing with you. So, Prof didn't show up. I'm in. What in holy hell is going on with you guys?"

"Here's the Reader's Digest version. Our friend was raped. Ran away. This guy Markus chased her. Caught her. She came back to Chicago with him. Prof and I met her in secret. She wants to get away again. Prof went shopping, but has now been detained, i.e. kidnapped. I think by Markus, because Prof says that Leni is gone again. I haven't heard a word from her, so I have no idea where she might be at the moment."

"All that in three days?"

I nodded and drank the excellent beer.

"What's your next step?" she said.

"Enjoy dinner with you."

She smiled and might have blushed. "Maybe you can take me to see Stravinsky some day. But for now, tell me what Tommy, master investigator, does next."

"Interrogate you for helpful information. When a problem appears unsolvable, new data is the best hope."

"I'm a film student and a waitress. What can I tell you?"

"You're also an attractive woman who has life experience with the male animal. And you live in Chicago." I paused, seeking a place to begin. "Do you ever order from Amazon?"

"Do you mean the trillion-dollar monster that destroyed main street USA? The monolith that has driven more companies out of business than Sam Walton? The target of repeated unionization efforts. That Amazon?"

"I hear they sell books," I said.

"For sure. Amazon has shuttered more bookstores than government censorship raids." She sliced her trout and guided a piece carefully past her painted lips. "Yes, I buy from them. Sometimes they are the only game in town."

"Ever use an Amazon locker?"

She nodded. "I'm at work when they deliver. Packages get stolen. The lockers are easy and I can pick up anytime. At the Post Office I have to stop during business hours because the deliveries are always bigger than my tiny P.O. Box."

"A woman of experience."

"When you're working your way through college, you need two things: cheap, because you have limited funds, and convenient, because you have limited time. Jeff Bezos understands my needs." She smiled.

"If Jeff sees that smile, he'll be posting more dick pics that will get him in hot water."

She laughed with one hand over her mouth. "You say things in the strangest ways, Tommy."

"Just trying to entertain you, and control my inner Stravinsky."

"You're a good juggler. Ask me something."

"Every use an app called HappyBox?"

She shook her head and laughed with her lips closed.

"Sounds like something this girl should try."

"No, no. It's a delivery app. How about a website named Oleace?"

She tilted her face down and lifted her eyes to meet mine.

"When you said in or out," she said, "you meant all the way in, didn't you?"

I choked. "Sorry, didn't mean to pry into your personal life. That site is…uh…involved."

"Involved, but not committed," she said, and started laughing.

"I'm missing something," I said. "Not unusual for me."

She held up a hand for me to wait while she regained her composure.

"My grandpa's joke. Took me a long time to realize what he was trying to teach me and how often it would be relevant." She forked rice onto a piece of trout and slid it into her mouth like sushi.

I drank beer and waited.

She waited.

I waited.

She won.

"OK, OK. What's the joke?" I said.

"In a bacon and eggs breakfast, what's the difference between the chicken and the pig?"

I could guess. But I wanted to hear her tell it.

"I can read it in your eyes," she said. "Correct. The chicken is involved, but the pig is committed."

"Moral of the story," I said. "In any situation, be sure you know if you are the chicken or the pig."

Her curls flowed with her nod.

"Or," she said. "If you're the egg."

"I like your grandpa," I said.

"He's a great guy. Knows hundreds of jokes. At the time, I thought he was just entertaining me."

"And now?"

"Each year, I understand more jokes."

"The moral to the stories?"

She shook her head slowly. "I don't know if they have morals, or warnings."

"So, you've heard of Oleace?"

"Oh yes. Heard of it. Used it. Have friends who use it. Friends who work there. It might be the biggest operation of its kind in the world. Popular on college campuses. All that steamy video streaming probably accounts for a third of Internet traffic." She laughed. "I don't know that, it's just a rumor I heard. But think about the marketing pitch to horny guys. 'Girls from every country in the world are waiting to undress for you.' If that's not the essence of social media, I don't know what is." She sliced and ate. Her eyes glistened. "Did they meet on Oleace?"

"No," I said. "University classroom."

"Real life encounters are more complicated."

"As they have been for millennia." I finished my beer.

"True, but they've only been competing with Oleace for what, the last five or ten? You ever hear of the sex robots the geeks in Silicon Valley are working on? Life-sized Barbies that talk and moan and have anatomically correct orifices?"

"Only in locker room chatter."

"It's a hot topic in my Modern Psychology class. Filmmaking is all about psychology. Want to hear some statistics?"

I looked around for the waiter. Gestured, he nodded.

"Math isn't my strong suit," I said.

"Not important. Let's say we randomly select ten thousand undergraduate males. We show them a video of a sex robot being designed, assembled, programmed."

"Like watching that show How Things Work? Except it's a sex machine."

"Oh, the designers never call them machines. But yes, that's what I mean. Then we let the ten thousand college-boys spend a night alone with the robot. In the morning, the boys are made an offer. One, you can keep the robot for the remainder of your degree program, but you are not allowed to have sex with real women. Or, you receive the purchase price of twenty thousand US dollars in cash. Now you can date women, but you cannot use a robot until everyone in the study matriculates. What percentage of perfectly healthy, college-aged men, in their sexual prime, chose the robot?"

"You could make a documentary about this study. Maybe win an award. Whichever decision, it only holds until all members graduate. What if some drop out of college?"

"Dropping out removes them from the study. After graduation, you can return the robot, or buy it out for the residual value. Sort of like an auto lease. And yes, the robots are insured." She smiled. "In case someone elopes with one."

I finished the of my steak while trying to inhabit the mind of my nineteen-year-old self.

"Is this some sort of game theory thing? An inferior sure thing versus a superior maybe?"

A devilish grin under sweetheart eyes answered me.

"Inferior is in the eye of the beholder," she said. "Imagine a sparkling conversationalist who can talk baseball scores, and odds, and fantasy teams all afternoon with a smile and give you a great blow job at bedtime. No blind dates. No rejection. No risky financial investments."

"You've been studying this."

"It was on the final exam." She twirled a curl around her right index finger. "So…what's your assessment as a private eye?"

"Fifty-fifty."

"A nice safe guess," she said.

"Balanced," I said. "If half choose the robot, taking them out of the real-girl game, then the odds get better and better for the guys who take the money. Twenty grand is two hundred college dates at hundred bucks a pop. A surplus of available women waiting for a date is adolescent heaven. So supply and demand would find an equilibrium."

She placed her fork on her plate and folded her hands in her lap.

"Do you really think ten thousand testosterone fueled boys could figure out your game theory analysis and want to be in the supply-demand curve you predict?"

"It's just a guess. I haven't seen the robot." I laughed.

"Good point. The quality of the robot is a key component driving the decision. Thus, the test drive." She tilted her head. "Ready?"

I swallowed. "I feel like I'm on a game show about to win or lose a prize."

"Ninety-two percent chose the robot."

"Must be some robot," I said.

She sipped her red wine. Then she sipped sparkling water.

"Says something about the male psyche," she said. "And priorities. But I'm not sure what."

"I wonder how it will all work out."

"We'll know in a few years. The robot company is providing a thousand version four-point-oh robots to continue the study. They have nine thousand applicants to choose from."

"I thought this was a mental exercise." I stared down at the street. A green Jeep with a five-point military star cruised through an intersection. "Are they really going to do this?"

"It's a study right here in the University of Chicago's psychology department. They are still taking applications." She laughed. "Next year they plan to design a study for women."

Her face was calm. Expressionless.

"You applied, didn't you?" I said.

She grinned that devilish look again.

"How often does one get the opportunity to contribute directly to the advancement of science?"

The waiter arrived with a dessert cart. I immediately wanted to eat the whole cart.

"Crème Brûlée please," Shianti said.

He placed the creamy concoction in front of her, lit a tiny blow torch, handed it to her, and waited while she caramelized her own sugar topping.

He turned to me.

I considered having the same so we could discuss it, but the layered chocolate cake chanted my name. The waiter handed me a silver canister that was frigid against my palm. It emitted a steady stream of fluffy whipped cream. I drew a heart on my cake and winked at Shianti.

She laughed at me.

"Why?" I said, picking up my dessert fork and deciding where to attack the cake.

"Why do I want to be part of science?"

"Why do you want a sex robot?" I smiled.

"Women have had robots for decades. Some boyfriends are really just sex robots. Some husbands too. I stick with things that vibrate in just the right way. To my mind, a robot is a larger version of a vibrator that can hold me and whisper sweet words in my ear at the right time."

"I bet we could get your smartphone to do some whispering," I said.

She gave me a look that suggested she had thought of this long ago.

"Why is the psychology department interested?" I asked.

She spooned creamy dessert onto her tongue and closed her eyes. Her face transformed into the essence of bliss.

"Two reasons. Someone will fund it. Sex always shakes the money tree. And the lead investigator is kind of famous. He is proposing that reducing sexual angst during the high-pressure college years—" she stopped. Her eyes drifted. "Ever read Bertrand Russell? The math guy. He postulated that, given our current life expectancy, humans should have three marriages, not one. The first, right after high school to provide sexual release during the study years, should remain childless. The second, once you are established in your profession, to produce children. And the third to provide companionship in your old age, should you make it that far."

"Lots of people sort of do it that way," I said.

She nodded agreement.

"But with tremendous emotional pain," I said. "Because they think each one is until death do us part."

"Breaking up is hard to do."

"So the robots replace Russell's first marriage?"

"Yes." She sucked custard off her spoon.

"This is healthier for students?" I asked.

She scooped carefully for the last bit of brûlée. I was only halfway through my chocolate mound.

"The hotshot researcher claims there is a causal chain: sexual problems lead to drug abuse lead to overdose and suicide."

"Therefore," I said, "eliminate the sexual problems and the drugs and deaths disappear."

"All for the price of a silly little robot with a computer chip for a brain."

My breath caught mid-thought.

"Wait. Who is this researcher?"

"Had to memorize his name for the test," she said, "Guy name Corolla."

CHAPTER 24

I considered robot sex while nursing my beer. Better or worse than masturbation? Better or worse than hooking up with a random party goer? Than a bacchanal fueled by pills, smoke, and alcohol? Than the world's oldest profession?

"Would you try one?" I asked.

"Do you mean 'Do I own a vibrator?' Of course. All the smart girls have a collection. Look." She dug around in her shiny gold purse and produced a black tube with a protruding red stick. She twisted the bottom and it started humming. "The company is called Magic Wand."

"Gives new meaning to Harry Potter," I said.

Shianti laughed softly and turned off the mini-vibrator.

"Girls," she said, "have needs. Guys just don't know how to fulfill them."

"Seems like a failure of evolution."

She shook her golden curls.

"Oh no, it's perfect. Keeps everyone on edge and ready. The exploding population of the planet is living proof."

I almost mentioned that the birth rate in the U.S. was hovering below the replacement rate and Japan had a population problem, but stopped myself. I met her eyes and tried to appear serious.

"Do you go through a lot of batteries?"

She didn't even blink. "It's rechargeable."

The waiter appeared.

Shianti ordered herbal tea. I ordered coffee. I ate some cake covered with whipped cream.

"Ever hear of Nature Incognito?" I asked.

"Who could avoid them?" She reached for her wine. "They're more prevalent than the Campus Crusade for Christ do-gooders who get in your face while you're running to an exam."

"Thoughtless."

She smiled, her lipstick still perfect. "The Incognito people are out to save the world from drugs. Flyers everywhere. Bright yellow carrying a subliminal message: Don't be a coward, face your addiction."

"As an aside," I said, "shouldn't the word 'coward' mean moving in the direction of a cow?"

She raised a hand to her mouth and almost spit out her wine.

"What planet are you from?"

"Ohio," I said.

She shook her head and dabbed at the corners of her lips with the snow-white napkin that had been on her lap. Uncovering her legs. Which I noticed. Which she noticed me noticing.

"Yellow hoodies too. Their motto across the back. 'Nature is the way.'"

"Nature has a lot going for it," I said.

"If you can find it. When was the last time you experienced a natural event?"

"A few hours ago. I was standing barefoot in the sand staring out at a watery horizon that seemed to stretch to Mars."

"Wow, that's kind of romantic. What were you doing besides staring?"

"Remembering a young mother watch her son play with a tiny plastic shovel. And thinking about the current situation."

"Evolution in action. Why do you care about Nature Incognito?" She tilted her head. "You have a problem we should talk about?"

"On our first date?" I said, laughing. It finally hit me that maybe this entire evening was a setup. Prof playing matchmaker. Maybe Markus wasn't holding him at gunpoint.

Would Prof do that?

Yeah, he might. But what if he hadn't?

"They fund a lot of research," I said. "I've been reading the results of their intervention methods."

Shianti spun her glass on the tablecloth by rotating the stem.

"Don't take this wrong. But you don't seem like a research report kind of guy."

"I'm private-eying on a person of interest."

The magically appearing waiter delivered tea and coffee.

"Will there be anything else?" he said.

"Are you hiding a fork in your pocket?" Shianti said.

The waiter blushed.

"I'd like to help my beer-swigging friend finish his cake."

The waiter held up a finger for us to wait. He returned in less than a minute with a fresh slice of cake, a dessert fork, and his chilled silver canister.

"On the house," he said. "The manager feels we should have been more attentive to you while you were waiting alone."

Shianti winked. "Please thank the manager for me." She slathered the cake in whipped cream and handed the canister back.

"Brrr," she said.

The waiter smiled, bowed, and went away.

"You have to help me," she said.

"Too much cake?"

"Yes. And too many problems that require a private-eye." She forked through the whipped cream to the cake and brought it to her mouth. "You know, you never think about hiring a private eye until you meet one."

"Business consultant," I said. "Why could you possibly need a private investigator?" I asked. "If that's not too direct."

Her eyes smiled. "I don't. I'm messing with you. Why do you care about the Nature people?"

"I'm following the money."

She forked cake and whipped cream past her painted red lips without touching them.

"What money?"

"Two kinds so far. Doing research costs big bucks. Corolla publishes a truckload of technical articles. Requires test subjects, drugs, data analysis, computer equipment. Not to mention paying the principal investigator."

More cake. Tea. "Number two?" she asked.

"Amazon boxes that contain cash. I think. Maybe."

Shianti twirled her fork in the whipped cream and licked it off, seemingly unaware of the erotic energy she was transmitting.

"You can't buy cash from Amazon," she said.

"I know. So what's going on?"

She frowned. Pouted. Sat motionless. Then, "You think someone is using Amazon lockers for nefarious purposes?"

"I do. But I don't know who, how, or why."

"Good job. You've almost cracked this case."

I sipped delicious coffee, ate cake, and watched Shianti. Her eyes roamed the room but didn't settle on anything.

"Do you know where Nature Incognito is located?" I asked.

She nodded while chewing.

"They make it easy for a sleep deprived, strung out, addict to find. Leased a building right across the street from the campus art center. I figure they located where the demand was highest."

"Artists?"

Her curls bobbed agreement. "You probably know that creative types don't have as many dopamine receptors as normal people. I think it frees their minds to do weird things. And cool weird things are what society calls creative."

"Whoa, back up. Dopamine receptors?"

"Yep. No point in pumping out dopamine if you don't have receptors to make you feel good."

"You're saying creative people are genetically pre-determined?"

"For the most part," she said.

"Incognito puts their offices near the art building because more artists use drugs, ergo, more artists require intervention therapy?"

"Sound business strategy." She placed her fork on the plate beside her remaining cake. "The cake wins. But, wow, does it taste good."

"How are your dopamine receptors?"

She grinned. "I think they're full." She reached for her purse, pulled out her phone, checked the time, then withdrew a slender wallet the color of eggshells.

"Prof's buying," I said.

"He's not even here. We can't let him treat."

"He'll be insulted if we don't. He's letting me crash at his house in Missouri. The only thing he lets me pay for is gasoline. He says it's punishment for driving a guzzler."

"Will he really be upset?"

Her eyes were wide, and beautiful, and wet, and I almost forgot the question. I drummed my fingers on the table.

"You know. I've never seen Prof upset. I don't know what he'll do."

Her frowning pout returned.

"It's not fair," she said. "He needs to be here so I can argue with him."

Two puzzle pieces clicked together.

"Do you think Incognito is closed by now?"

Her curls flew from side to side.

"No way. Nighttime is prime time for them. They're open 24 hours a day, 7 days a week, including holidays, holy days, and during a total eclipse of the sun. They claim 'Here when you need us' on their T-shirts."

"Let's go visit? Cuda Consulting will buy you dinner as a thank you. If Prof insists, he can reimburse the company."

She frowned a moment longer, then slid her wallet back into her gold purse.

The waiter arrived.

He and Shianti showed surprised as I placed four pictures of Ben Franklin on the check.

"Could I trouble you for some twenties?" I asked.

He nodded and dashed off.

"Cash?" she said, wide-eyed. "No cell phone. Ancient chariot. You're a time traveler from the past. I thought they always came from the future."

I leaned back in the chair and met the gaze of this amazing woman I had been lucky to meet.

"No time traveling. Things from the past have solidity that ephemeral bits and bytes lack. I'm on the road to find more."

◇

We parked in the lot for the performing arts building. Shianti was right. I could throw a rock from the front door and break a window in the Nature Incognito office. We walked against a red light across a grassy boulevard and four lanes empty of traffic. A series of brightly colored posters in the windows of Incognito showed waterfalls and canyons.

"Was a massage parlor," she said.

"And before that?"

"Dental office. On-campus services put her out of business."

"Looks like a travel agency now," I said.

Her white dress sparkled from green to amber to red. Still no traffic.

"It sort of is." She giggled and took my hand in hers. Warm and soft registered in my head. "So. What's our strategy? Are we a couple? Does one of us have a problem? Or do we have a joint problem?" She laughed. "No pun intended. Or maybe we have a friend with an addiction and we're trying to save her."

"We could be journalists."

She waved her hand down her body.

"Dressed like this?"

"Point taken. And why would we be visiting late in the evening dressed for a country club gala?"

"And sober. Well, mostly sober." She smiled.

One car cruised past behind us. Standing across from a college campus late on a summer night felt desolate. Like we were in some kind of urban desert.

I said, "I've heard it's best to stay close to the truth when lying."

"OK, we're on a hot first date. Set up by a mutual friend. We've been eating and drinking at a fine restaurant."

"But our friend is missing," I said. "And we hope he or she has checked in for treatment."

"Which, she or he?"

"Let's use a girl who is going through a personal relationship crisis. We're concerned about an overdose."

"Do we name names?" she said.

"We're Bob and Alice," I said.

She smiled. "Which one of us is Bob?"

"Ha ha. Spies in mystery novels use Bob and Alice."

"Mystery novels, fast car, clandestine private eye. Do I have that straight?"

"And accidental date with a goddess." I couldn't tell if she blushed or the traffic light behind me had turned red.

"OK, Bob," she said, "here we go." She led the way to the door. I reached for the silver handle and opened if for her. An electronic version of wind chimes announced our arrival.

The waiting area was bathed in low yellow light from two table lamps. A counter to the left held a machine for paying electronically. An aisle leading toward the back split the building in half. The rooms on the right had blinds inside the half windows in the doors. Typical dentist office. Treatment rooms on the right. Administrative offices on the left.

The shoe fit.

Or the rooms on the right could be used for candlelit massage spaces. I imagined a few people waiting, sipping cucumber water. Reading Vogue. Or Kahlil Gibran. The delicate sounds of a plucked zither wafting down from hidden speakers in the ceiling.

This room had no music.

It did have magazines positioned carefully in a curved row across a shiny silver coffee table. All of the covers showed more of what was in the window.

No psychology mags. No self-help. No news sources.

No one at the counter.

An old-school silver bell sat beside the credit card reader waiting for someone to tap its button. I headed for the bell. Shianti sat down on an olive-green sofa and picked up a magazine showing a young woman strapped to a yellow hang glider about to step off a cliff.

Two stacks of boxes sat against the wall behind the counter. The side had been labeled:

FOOD SUPPLIES

by someone with a red sharpie.

Between the boxes a person sat cross-legged wearing a fat set of black headphone cans, barefoot beside a pair of white Nike's that looked three sizes too large. I could see disheveled brown hair under the phones, but no face. Shey was reading a comic book. A black and white comic book. I tried to recall the last time I had seen a comic book. Frat party. A girl who loved Japanese manga. I wasn't certain I had ever seen one in black and white.

I cleared my throat.

No reaction.

I tapped the knob on the top of the bell. It clunked like it had a sock stuffed inside.

No reaction.

Must be the headphones.

I knocked on the counter with two knuckles. Nothing. I glanced over my shoulder. Shianti was staring at me quizzically. I tried the clunking bell louder.

"Excuse me," I said.

I stepped around the counter and stopped with my boots beside the Nikes.

The figure leapt back and stared at me. Based on sparse facial growth, he could still be in high school. But he might also be a late bloomer in his third year of college.

He reached up and peeled off the headphones.

"Man, you scared the crap out of me sneaking up like that. Why didn't you ring the bell?"

"I did. Twice. Knocked on the counter. Said 'Excuse me'. Must be a good book."

He looked down at the dog-eared comic in his hands.

"Yeah, these are amazing. So much better than the modern shit."

I could relate. "You really read on paper?"

"Always. These are the originals. A friend of mine collects them from all over the world. I'm working through the entire set from the very first issue to its death."

"Been a long time since black and white comics were a thing, hasn't it?"

"Decades." He handed me the book. "Check this out. Can you imagine this all started with one guy in New York City drawing and printing these himself? The dude is super talented."

I read for a page. Then two. Then three.

"Ninja turtles?"

"Yep. Before TV. Before movies. Before Disney turned them into a joke. Before all that happened, the teenage mutant ninja turtles were that little comic book. I hope the guy got super rich."

"Me too," I said, handing the book back.

He stood up in one motion. Five ten-ish and yoga instructor lean inside a yellow Incognito T-shirt whose sleeves had been cut off.

"I don't usually get action until after the bars close. Or dawn. Something about sunshine seems to affect people."

I nodded. "Yeah, midnight is when the wolves howl. Rarely a time for constraint."

"Did you really ring the bell?"

"Twice. But there's a mouse inside."

He frowned, stepped over to the counter, and slapped the bell with his palm. It clunked. He shook his head.

"Clarence thinks it's funny to stuff cigarette butts inside." He turned the device upside down, unscrewed the bell and dumped the contents into a small wastebasket beneath the counter. "So how can I help you?" He noticed Shianti. "Hi, my name is Roger. Sorry to keep you waiting."

Shianti flipped curls with one hand and switched the crossing of her legs, not bothering to pull her dress down.

"No problem, we thought this place was empty, which would be totally weird with an unlocked door."

"That door is always unlocked. And there's at least one person here to talk to all the time. We specialize in nature therapy. But we've had more than one potential suicide walk in on their way to a tall building."

"You must have a lot of training," she said from the couch.

He shrugged, tensing the sinewy muscles in his neck.

"I'm a psych major, so I've had more than most. But Natnito, that's what we call this place, has an internal training program you have to pass before you can work here."

No one spoke.

Roger looked from me to Shianti and back.

"I have a friend," I said.

"We all do," he said. His eyes drifted to Shianti. "She looks fine to me. Do you want me to take vital signs? That's where we start to find out what's really going on."

"Not this friend," I said. "We were out having dinner and our conversation turned to helping our mutual friend. So we stopped by to find out if, uh, the Natnito experience might be right for her."

"Depends."

"On?" I said.

"If she's right for the program. Natnito is incredibly selective. Is the addict physically fit? Is the substance something we deal with? We can't address all addictions."

"Appears to be commercially available pills. That's mostly a guess. First we have to find her."

"Ah," he began and then stopped. He glanced at Shianti. She noticed and smiled. "We don't chase runaways."

"We'll take care of that. We're here to learn about options. How, exactly, does the Nature Incognito program work?"

Roger reassembled the bell, placed it on the counter, and tapped. It dinged harshly.

"You can pay to play or join a research project. If you qualify for a project, you go on the trip for free. Food and lodging included."

"Hard to argue with free," Shianti said from her perch on the couch.

"The trips are really great. The staff keeps you so busy and tired and well fed that you barely have time to miss getting high."

I glanced at Shianti and she shook her head ever so slightly, discouraging me from asking if he was speaking from experience.

"Any research projects starting soon?"

He nodded. "This weekend. But we just filled the last slot."

"How do research and rehab go together?" I asked.

While Roger talked about how new procedures had to be tested in the field and required a control group and large sample sizes to be statistically valid, I looked the place over.

Not much under the counter except for a pair of closed drawers. The FOOD SUPPLY boxes were all taped shut. I mentally compared them to the boxes in the lockers. Seemed to me one box would fill one locker. I stepped sideways and patted the top box. Full. I picked it up, maybe twenty pounds.

"Those are for the project," Roger said.

I let the box rotate 90 degrees onto its side and snuck a look at the bottom.

"Be careful," Roger said, "those have to stay sealed."

The first layer of cardboard was missing where something the shape of an envelope had been torn off. I heard Roger say "Doctor Corolla" and paid closer attention.

Shianti had magnetized Roger. He was now standing right beside her. Roger talked about the value of original research to find a way to heal people who had been 'misdirected' by substance abuse. He ran down a list of famous pop stars—Bieber, Bowie, Brittany, Clapton— who had fought their demons to get clean.

The doors to the massage rooms suggested something simple inside. Probably 8 by 10 foot room, massage table, sink in the corner. Modest sound system to pipe in nature sounds and meditative music. Maybe carpeted to keep the room quiet.

At eye level a dark bronze ornament decorated the door of all four rooms. Maybe eye candy, but they resembled deadbolts. Which would make perfect sense if they were on the inside of the door to prevent someone accidentally walking in during a massage. On the outside, they probably didn't even meet fire code.

The bolt on the first three rooms was swung left. But on the fourth, it had clearly been engaged. If anyone was in that room, they'd have to break the door down to get out.

"Besides this reception area," I said. "What's the rest of this place used for?"

"The usual," he said, still staring at Shianti. "Offices for interviews. Computers for record keeping. The rooms on the right are mini-hotel rooms. Many clients, well most, need a way to get off the street before they can begin to heal. We provide these on a short-term basis. But they're enough to kickstart recovery."

"For a fee?" I asked.

"Yes, for sure. We must generate income to remain a going concern."

"I bet that line is in the brochure."

Roger nodded. "Sure is. And one of the top ten we had to memorize to become a team member."

Shianti stood and wiggled her hips while pulling her dress down.

Roger held up a finger for me wait, grabbed his Nikes, and disappeared down the hallway.

I gestured for Shianti to come closer.

"Can you distract this guy while I search the place?"

She tilted her head and gazed into my eyes.

"Do I have boobs and a little white dress? Of course I can distract him. When you hear me giggle," she demonstrated, "you've got thirty seconds left."

When Roger returned, he was wearing his shoes, holding a ring of keys, and smelling of drugstore cologne. Shianti hooked an arm around his elbow.

"I'm Alice. You know, like the girl with the magic looking glass. Show me how this place works. Bob will wait here and watch the door. He gets bored with details, don't you, Bob?"

I nodded slowly, almost slipping through the looking glass right behind Roger.

"If anyone comes in," Roger said, "ring the bell a couple of times."

I strolled to the table, grabbed the top magazine and slouched onto the couch.

"Will do."

Roger fumbled the keys but eventually opened the door to the first office. I heard him say, "This room is the heart of the operation," as the door clicked shut behind them.

CHAPTER 25

I placed the magazine open on the table, made a beeline for the food supply boxes, removed the top three, and flipped the bottom box upside down. It was sealed with clear tape. I went to the counter. Drawers. A dozen capped ballpoint pens. A notebook for signing in: name, date, phone number. I took photos of two pages at a time for the previous two months using Leni's phone. I grabbed a pen and poked holes in the tape until I could tear it and flip open the four flaps.

Smaller boxes. Maybe identical to Leni's box.

I paused for one breath to listen for a giggle. Murmuring voices filtered through the wall. I opened the bottom of a smaller box.

Energy bars promising a full day of protein requirement. I grabbed the next box and shook it. And the next. Eight small boxes to each large box.

The sixth box rattled.

I opened it fast. Found a bottle of 200 caplets packed beside some energy bars. I took photos and repacked as best I could. Then I stacked the three untouched boxes on top of the one I had just molested.

I listened again.

The deadbolt rattled in the back of my mind.

I pulled off my boots, left them beside the couch, and hustled down the tiled hallway in stocking feet. I pressed my ear against the fourth door.

HVAC hum.

No giggles.

I pulled the sleeve of my borrowed shirt over my hand, suddenly aware that leaving fingerprints behind was a bad idea. The bolt slid easily. I rotated the doorknob with my shirt-covered fingers and eased the door inward. The room was lit by a pink nightlight stuck into an AC socket on the near wall. No massage table. No paintings. A woven mat on the floor occupied by a figure in a brown sleeping bag whose face was turned away from me. I was reminded of a homeless person under a bridge. Black shoes with gray laces stood at the end of the mat. I stepped inside, keeping the door open so I could hear Shianti giggle. Light from the hallway revealed gray walls, dark walnut floor.

The shoulders shifted.

I leaned forward and recognized Prof's profile at the same moment that I heard Shianti giggle from across the hall.

"Prof, it's Tommy." No reaction.

I shook his shoulder. No reaction.

"Prof, I'll be back with help."

I pulled the door closed on my way out, fumbled for a few seconds with the deadbolt, and hustled to the couch. As I spun and sat down, I grabbed the magazine and lifted it up to cover my face. Shianti's heels clicked on the tiles of the hallway. She was carrying a yellow Nature Incognito bag with a logo: a human profile on one side and a leafless tree on the other. Her bag bulged against her bare leg.

I realized I was holding the magazine upside down, so I closed it and flipped it onto the table.

Roger was two steps behind Shianti, his eyes on her.

"You look comfortable, Bob," Shianti said. "I hope I didn't take too long. Roger knows a lot about the program."

"I've been to several," he said. "Natnito does a great job of helping people make their lives work without drugs."

Shianti held up her bag. "And they have scientific studies to prove it."

I slipped my boots on. "Glad we stopped by. Sorry to interrupt your reading."

Roger smiled. "These are great comic books. Shianti, I bet you would like them."

"Like what?" she said.

"Teenage Mutant Ninja Turtles."

"I wore a Mutant costume for Halloween one year as a kid. Are they still around?"

"Roger is reading the originals," I said.

"Fascinating," she said. "I thought Disney studios just made them up. Like Mickey Mouse and Tinker bell."

"Disney didn't invent Tinker Bell," Roger said. "They adapted the character from a play."

"Really?" she said.

Roger nodded with a huge smile.

Shianti held out her hand to shake goodbye. I could tell Roger was surprised. Maybe a little something else had gone on inside the office.

"Thank you for the tour, Roger," she said. "You're doing great work."

"Thanks. We depend on donations from concerned citizens." His eyes leaked the question in his head: Would he ever see Shianti again?

She smiled, and didn't answer it.

The door triggered a chime again on our way out. Neither of us spoke until we were across the boulevard.

"Something is rotten in Denmark," Shianti said.

I waited for more.

"Roger got anxious talking about their funding. Not like he knows they're doing something illegal—more like something magical is happening, but he doesn't know what it is. And he's afraid to ask questions and appear foolish."

"So he plays along and pretends to understand?"

"That's how most people live."

"Fake it 'till you make it," I said. "That's what social media is about. Pretend you are something. See how people react. Live in a virtual reality bubble. Forget real life, it's slow and messy. I wonder what goddess Juno would say about that?"

She glanced down at her arm. "Nothing. They didn't have to deal with the Internet." She slowed a bit. "Funny how none of those super powerful gods knew the Internet was going to happen."

We approached my Barracuda, alone in an empty lot amid splashes of lamplight.

"We have a new problem," I said.

"Already?" She lifted her yellow Natnito bag. "We haven't even examined the booty from our heist yet."

I pulled a bottle out of my pocket and shook it so she could hear the caplets rattle.

Her eyes opened wider. "Where did you get those?"

"From the bottom of a food supplies box."

"What is it?"

We reached my car. I opened the door for her, held her bag, then handed it back to her.

"It looks like a prescription pain reliever. But I have reason to be suspicious."

I closed her door, walked around the trunk, and slid in beside her.

A small white SUV with roof lights cruised into the parking lot blinking a lot of amber. I waved to the security guard behind the wheel. He didn't smile. But he didn't stop. Although his eyes lingered on Shianti.

"You're a private eye," she said. "Of course you're suspicious." She laughed. "By the way, thanks for the acting job. I haven't played a cocktease since high school."

"Poor Roger."

"Over matched for sure." She laughed.

She was right, this could be fun. Except for the looming downsides.

"Remember I told you that Prof got seriously detained?"

"Oh, I haven't forgotten. I'm mad as a hatter working double shifts."

"Did you notice the room on the right side of the hallway?"

"Sure. The place still looks like a spa. Which is nice. I like massages." She smiled at me. I'd swear her eyes twinkled under the streetlamps.

Focus Tommy.

"Those rooms have a strange feature. There's a deadbolt to secure the door."

"Yeah. Nice polished bronze." She frowned.

"Right. On the outside. The fourth room was locked."

She twisted her body on the red leather seat to face me.

"No freaking way!"

I nodded solemnly. "Out cold on a woven mat. Or drugged. I tried to wake him up."

"Why would Nature Incognito—" She froze. "Does he? I mean, would he? Uh, maybe?"

"Prof has an abuse problem and decides to check himself in without telling me?"

She nodded. Somehow, her curls were as fresh as when I walked into the London House.

"I've been staying with him for a couple of days," I said. "He works most nights."

"As a college student holding down a job, I know the feeling. Drugs help. But why check yourself into rehab when you have a date with the hottest waitress at the Pig?" She gave me a radiant smile.

"Foolish," I said. "Unless he found a way to find out more about our…friend. Or he got bad drugs. He's an awfully smart guy though. Or—" I stopped short. Even contemplating the thought made me anxious.

"What? Tell me, tell me."

"Somebody slipped him a roofie," I said.

She laughed. "I was all ready and they beat me to it," she said, with a perfectly straight face.

I shook my head. "Thanks for the tension relief. But if someone gave Prof a date-rape drug and grabbed him against his will, we need to know why. I dropped him off to go shopping."

"Prof went shopping?"

"He wanted to look sharp for you tonight."

"Oh," she said softly.

"But now I'm wondering if he had a plan and was going after Leni by himself." I hesitated. "In an effort to protect me."

"And setting you up with a hot babe."

I smiled and watched her eyes. "The hottest."

She blushed a little and said, "Now that we have that established, what are we going to do about Prof? We can't just leave him in there unconscious."

I tapped the wheel with my index finger just to be doing something while thinking. "If you sweet-talk Roger while I spring Prof. And Roger calls someone within an hour. Where are we at that point?"

"My place," she said.

I shook my head. "Too dangerous. Whatever is going on already involves a rape and a kidnapping. It's unsafe and unpredictable."

"Just like life," she said. "Stay tonight. You can find a new hideout in the morning." She stared into me with an immobilization ray. "Really. I want to help. My life has been more exciting in the past twelve hours than in the last twelve months combined. This…situation you're working on has depth and human interest. It's important. It's fun to be a part of it."

"You have an unusual definition of fun," I said.

The ray continued for a few seconds, then she burst out laughing.

"I meant—"

She held up a hand to stop me and said, "Here's what we're going to do."

◇

Shianti's plan had only a few steps, but critical timing. To kick it off, I parked the Barracuda in the darkest spot of the art building parking lot, facing the front window of Nature Incognito. Shianti insisted that Roger would be much more comfortable if he could see the front door to the office he was supposed to be watching.

"You sure you're okay with a manual?"

"H pattern," she said. "Push clutch. Move little stick. Ease clutch out. Stomp on gas. Vroom." She smiled. "Don't worry. My brother raced sports cars in a club. I secretly learned to drive so I could joy ride when he was out of town. I don't think he ever figured it out."

"This has a lot more power."

She grinned. "A stick is a stick. And bigger is better."

We shook hands for luck. I stepped out of the car. She positioned herself behind the wheel by crossing over the shifter, butt first. She grabbed the adjuster and glided the seat all the way back.

"You'll never reach the clutch from back there," I said through the open driver's door.

"Tommy, driving is the second thing I'm going to do, remember?"

For a moment I envied Roger. Then I set off for Nature Incognito. The electronics tinkled as I entered. This time Roger popped up from his reading position like a jack-in-the-box. It took him a moment to recognize me. His brow scrunched.

"Forget something?"

The door swooshed closed behind me. I walked up to the counter.

"Alice asked me to do her a favor."

"Oh no," he said with a knowing smile. "She does have a problem."

I toyed with the bell with my left hand, but didn't ring it.

"Some might call this an opportunity."

His black and white comic book dangled from his left hand. He didn't say anything, but his eyes were searching for understanding.

"Like I said. Alice asked me to do her a favor."

"I bet she wants to score a hit from our reserves. I mentioned them to her. Sometimes drugs are the best initial treatment. So, you know, you can get to the next step. I thought her eyes looked a little funny."

I shook my head. "No. She asked me to cover for you behind the counter."

"What? Why would—"

"She's waiting for you." I gestured over my shoulder with my left thumb like I was hitching a ride. "In my car. It's parked in the art school lot."

"She's—" he began, but stopped.

"Said she wants to talk to you alone. Can you show me what to do if someone comes in?"

He wagged his head as if he were just waking up from a sound sleep.

"Uh, sure. The form and pens are in this drawer. Tell them to fill out an application. If they're too high to write legibly, take them into the back office and interview them. Fill the form out yourself. Have them sign and date it. If they're really incoherent, start the tape recorder."

Roger sat on the floor to put his big Nikes on. I circled the counter and opened the drawers to find the forms and pens that I already knew were there. I took one out and pretended to read it. Roger tied his sneakers. My mind wondered to the perennial question: Are sneakers or brothel creepers the quieter shoe?

"Thanks, Bob. I won't be long." He paused, his entire body frozen in place. "Actually, I have no idea how long…"

"I'm not going anywhere," I said. "Alice has my car keys."

Roger smiled, probably wondering why I would trust a flaky blonde with my keys. He stopped at the door.

"Isn't Alice your, uh…you came in together."

"Not at all. We have a mutual friend."

He became relaxed and energized in the same moment.

"Good, good," he said, apparently to himself, and walked out the door as the chime did its Tinker Bell imitation.

I sat in Roger's spot on the floor and read the cover of a comic book while counting seconds. Four turtles with masks living in the sewers of New York City. I debated whether they resembled Zorro or the Lone Ranger. Decided they'd be a big draw as a tag team of mutant wrestlers.

100.

Roger would be with Alice by now. I walked over and opened the front door a few inches. Distant traffic. No car horn. No revving Hemi. I closed the door and, without thinking too hard, turned the small knob to lock it. If Roger came back early, it would slow him down. I hustled to the interview room in back. It should have…

Chairs. Four chrome-legged plastic yellow ones around a white round table. Friendly. Intimate. In the next office bookshelves covered the walls and boxes covered the shelves. All nicely labeled. Camping gear. Consumables. The last office, where Roger had taken Alice, had an office desk with a black computer sitting on it and a five-wheel executive chair.

I grabbed the chair and rolled it toward the massage room while worrying about security cameras. Decided no, too many privacy concerns. And Roger had told me to start the tape recorder for an interview, so maybe Nature Incognito didn't want a continuous record of what went on inside.

I threw the deadbolt and pushed the chair into the room. Nothing had changed. I unzipped the sleeping bag while calling Prof's name; no response. I lowered the chair as far as possible, got my arms under Prof's shoulders, and stood. Then I fumbled us toward the chair and managed to get him seated.

I walked backwards, pulling the chair behind me and letting his feet drag on the floor. The hallway ended in a T. The restroom and red EXIT light were to my right. When I hit the crossbar of the door with my butt, the bar depressed, the door flung open. No alarm sounded. Prof and I were in a gravel alley lined with garbage cans along one side.

I jammed the door open with the chair with Prof still in it.

"Sorry, Prof," I said, as I lifted him to the gravel and propped him against the concrete block wall of the building as gently as possible.

"I'm going back to get your shoes."

I returned the chair back to the office, grabbed Prof's shoes, locked the massage room from the outside, and ran back to Prof.

"Wait here," I whispered in his ear. "I'll be back in a few minutes."

I picked up the gravel bits on the floor that had been left by the chair's wheels. Markus would figure out what happened as soon as Roger described my car. But any head start would help. When I reached the reception area, I opened a comic book to the middle and placed it face down beside Roger's sitting spot. Then I stood at the front door and held it ajar.

Listening.

It felt like an hour ticked past before my Hemi started up. I closed the door, sat on the floor, and actually read the comic book. Roger came through the front door about a minute later, eyes glassy, grinning.

"No one came in," I said.

Roger blinked several times and tried to focus on my face, without much success.

"Thanks," he said. "Thanks a lot."

I helped him sit down on the floor and placed a comic book in his hand. He stared at it, but didn't seem to be reading.

I let myself out the front door, walked causally past the windows full of nature photography, ran half a block to the entrance to the alley, and up the alley toward Prof. The Barracuda was there idling when I arrived. Together Shianti and I lifted Prof and wrestled him into the passenger's seat. I tossed his shoes in the back. Shianti crawled between the seats and sat behind Prof.

I eased the clutch out and crept down the alley.

Shianti reached forward for Prof's wrist.

"Sixty-five," she said.

"They're going to find out," I said.

She giggled. If the devil could giggle, that's what he'd sound like.

She said, "Not from Roger they won't."

CHAPTER 26

We were halfway to Mona's place when Shianti again insisted on using her apartment.

"That's not a good idea," I said.

"You don't think my place is good enough?"

"Shianti, I live out of an antique car. Anyplace is good enough. That's not the issue."

"But they know about Mona. You told me about the smoke bomb. No one knows who I am or where to find me."

I stopped for a traffic light. Prof snored softly with his head against the passenger window.

"Let's keep it that way," I said. "Things are getting weirder."

"And exciting," she said. "Think of what we're learning here."

The light turned green. I eased away.

"Yeah, we learned that we don't know what's going on." I gestured with my head. "We still don't know what happened to Prof."

"Someone from our short list slipped him a roofie," she said.

"And dragged him to Incognito?"

"Where better to hide a drugged person than a rehab facility? Anyone could have dropped him off. Look, my friend blacked out at a party. Can you take care of him?"

"Convenient," I said.

"Smart. Turn left here."

I turned.

"Drive towards the Pig," she said. "I'm within walking distance. Walking is convenient and healthy and I get to see the city close up every day. Kids. Dogs. Buildings. Candy wrappers drifting along the curb."

"Not something most people think about."

She met my eyes in the rearview mirror. Twirled a finger in her hair.

"Got it. You're not most people."

"There's those private-eye powers of observation at work," she said, with a wink of long eyelashes.

"I feel bad imposing on you."

"Where are you staying now?"

I laughed. "I'm imposing on a friend."

"So. We're friends. Impose on me."

We rumbled along at the speed limit.

"We've only just met."

"But we've been through so much together."

I didn't argue. "And we both like chocolate cake."

"There you go," she said.

"We can't go to your place."

"There are a lot of guys who'd jump at this."

"Shianti, it's not safe. This car is so recognizable I might as well be wearing a GPS tracker."

She leaned far forward and patted the dashboard. "We'll hide it."

"Not easy."

"Wait 'til you see my apartment."

I imagined living in Chicago and going to film school on a waitress's income.

Shianti pointed. "The peach one."

I followed her finger to a row of renovated townhouses, each with a one car garage.

"You have a rich roommate?"

"Nope."

We were not in a starving student zip code. I pulled across the sidewalk into the driveway and stopped with the headlights throwing white saucers on the garage door.

"You won the lottery?"

"I wish. Wait here."

She took a look at Prof, then worked her way out of the driver's door while I leaned forward. She disappeared through the main entrance.

"Hey, Prof. You awake?" I said.

Nothing.

The garage door in front of me rumbled up. The tail reflectors of a metallic gold Cadillac Coupe with a black tail fin glowed at me.

My first thought: OMG, Shianti, someone parked in your garage.

She waved at me to get out of the way. I backed onto the street, she drove out, and waved at me to go. I pulled into the cleanest garage I had ever seen and killed the engine. It was empty except for a pink bicycle hanging upside down along the front. The garage door closed behind me.

Shortly, Shianti came in through a side door and opened the passenger door of the Barracuda.

"We can use my car to move around. No one knows it. Or me."

"Great plan. I'm just super uncomfortable putting you into an unknown situation."

"Oh, Mister Cuda. Life isn't about being comfortable."

Her legs drew my eyes. I cleared my throat.

"Step one, we move Prof into your apartment," I said.

"He's sleeping fine. Maybe we leave him rest here so we don't injure him dragging him around."

"OK. What's step two?"

She held up the yellow bag she had filled at Incognito.

"Examine the booty."

"Won't they miss it?" I said.

"Sure. Eventually. Then they'll try to figure out who took it home and didn't bring it back." She paused. "Or."

"Or we put it back before anyone knows it's gone."

"There's that private-eye mind again. That's why I made a date with Roger."

"A date?"

"Well, more like a strategic rendezvous. I distract him while you put the booty back."

"After we read it."

"And photograph it. Like in the spy movies."

"Doesn't someone die in those movies?" I said.

Her curls swayed as she shook her head.

"Wherever did you get such a cheery disposition? Come on, let me show you the hideout." She eased the passenger door shut while I held onto Prof, then eased his head back into sleeping position.

I followed her through the side door into a foyer, past a kitchen table of white marble, up stairs covered in carpet the color of eggshells, down a hallway and into a bedroom bigger than a two-car garage. The headboard was carved mahogany and the quilt twinkled like it had diamonds in it. It didn't, the reflection was from silver thread, but the effect on the midnight blue quilt suggested a moonlit night on the open sea.

Shianti tossed the yellow booty bag on the bed and turned her back to me. She lifted her hair with two hands, revealing the gentle curves of her neck, and a small, round tattoo at its base.

"Help me with this."

Using both hands, I found the microscopic white zipper and eased it down to her waist.

"Thanks."

She pushed the dress off her shoulders, wiggled her hips, and dropped it around her high heels. Then she peeled off the heels and strolled to the closet wearing a white bra and panties with just a hint of lace.

I sent commands to my eyes to avert, but they ignored me.

She slid a mirrored door to the right, revealing a closet stuffed tighter than a sale rack.

"Something comfy," she said. Her left hand came up behind her and unsnapped the bra in a quick motion that would have taken me half a minute and two hands to achieve. She tossed a dark blue hoodie over her head that reached to mid-thigh and slipped into blue jeans that were baggy and full of holes.

Feeling useless, I retrieved her dress and shoes from the floor and carried them to her.

"Thanks, the shoes go into that cubby, and the dress hangs up there." She pointed.

I put her things away.

She fluffed her hair with two hands. "Feels good to be out of the torture shoes." She wiggled her toes. "Homo sapiens were meant to be barefoot."

"I think we're born that way."

"Cute."

"Why do you wear them?" I asked.

"Makes me taller. Feels powerful. Shapes the leg muscles. Attracts men when I walk. Makes other women jealous because they don't have them, or can't wear them, or hate them. All the standard reasons that humans do most things. You ready to get to work?"

"Just thinking about paperwork makes me thirsty."

"Hydration is critical to carbon-based life forms. Light or dark?"

"Whatever you'd like gone," I said.

She led me down the stairs. At the bottom she stopped quick and spun around to face me.

"Aren't you going to ask?" she said.

"I was waiting for the right moment."

"Now is good."

"You work as a waitress at the Pig. Yet—" I gestured at the room.

"I have a superfast car, a beautiful apartment, and a dream closet."

"Yes."

"Doesn't add up in your private-eye head, does it?"

"Not yet."

"Explore the options while I open some wine and find you a beer." She headed for the kitchen.

I followed and spoke to her back. "You come from a rich family. But then why work at the Pig when you could be making films?"

Shianti chose a bottle and attacked it with a device that looked like a staple gun.

"Doing good so far," she said.

"Option two. You have a sugar daddy. But why would he want you working as a waitress?"

She poured her wine into a crystal glass with a stem tinted aqua. "Go on."

"Three. None of this stuff is yours, but for some reason you get to use it. Maybe you have a generous roommate who wears the same size dresses as you."

She sipped. "I know. I'm supposed to wait for it to breathe. It can breathe in my stomach. Any more guesses?"

"Rich boyfriend from Chicago. But he attends…hmm…Yale. So you get the place while he's at school."

"That's clever. Maybe I can use that in the future."

"Am I close?"

She sipped, pulled the refrigerator door open with her bare toe, grabbed a bottle without even looking, and handed it to me.

"Does it matter?" she asked.

"Option five. This is paid for by Mafia money. You work at the Pig to have clean cash for spending money."

"Tsk. You think I could be so evil?"

"You're human," I said, smiling.

"You really want to know?"

"Only if you want to tell me."

"I have an uncle who hit it big in Silicon Valley conning someone out of something. He bought this place. I pay utilities and taxes. An investment for him and a great place to live for me."

"But?" I said.

"You heard me think that, didn't you?" She laughed and drank. "My Dad gave me a debit card and a monthly allowance."

"Ah," I said. "And he sees the monthly statement of where you spend his money."

"He has strict rules," she said.

"And they don't include the dream closet?"

She tapped her biceps.

"He's not a Juno fan?" I said.

"Hates tattoos. Thinks they make women look cheap. He'll go ballistic when he finds out. I'm trying to prevent that until after graduation."

"Good luck," I said.

"So long as he doesn't come into the Pig."

"I bet you have a spare shirt at work."

"Good idea. I know exactly the one."

"Black. Long sleeve. Loose fit so it can go on fast over anything. But high quality so he doesn't think you're cheap."

She wagged her index finger at me. Then she placed her half-empty glass on the counter and poured the contents of the yellow shoulder bag onto the center of her white dining table. Brochures. Forms. Files with little metal strips for hanging inside a drawer, a sheet of yellow 'I donated' stickers, and two yellow T-shirts with the Nature Incognito tree-face logo over the left breast.

"Roger gave you files?" I asked.

"'Gave' isn't quite accurate." She sorted the booty into stacks along the far edge of the round table. "Roger had his eyes closed."

"Why would Roger close his eyes if he could be looking at you in that twinkling dress?"

Her little smirk told me how easily she manipulated men. Probably starting with her father. I should be cautious, but she was just so friendly.

Shianti handed me a stack of standard 8 1/2 by 11 inch black and white forms. I scanned the titles.

DONATION

WEEKEND WARRIOR APPLICATION

TWO-WHEEL INTENSIVE

OVERNIGHT 24-HOUR CLEANSE

BECOME A VOLUNTEER

I read the DONATION form. It asked for personal details but also had an anonymous box to check. Form of payment included bitcoin and cash. Plenty of space for the amount, just in case you needed a lot of zeroes. The other forms could have been generic examples downloaded from the Internet to collect personal, confidential, medical history including drug usage and duration of addiction. Not unusual. I read the VOLUNTEER form last. It emphasized the ability to keep secrets.

Shianti shuffled papers. Handed me a stack.

"These make the rehab experience look like a trip to Bali," she said. "But you get to be the gardener and the fire builder rather than lying on a hammock all day holding a coconut."

"Do they drink rum in Bali?"

"Ha! One can find certain vices anywhere in the world. Rum is one of them. The British Navy made sure of that. Did you know that British sailors had a daily rum ration?"

"That'll maintain morale."

"Works for most people, most of the time," she said, reaching for her wine.

"What do you think of Natnito's marketing?"

Shianti shrugged. "I've seen worse from bigger companies. Did you ever see the Hewlett-Packard Enterprise logo? We studied it in marketing class. Are you ready? After spending untold sums on marketing companies they came up with—" She paused to sip. "A green rectangle. Looks like the border of U.S. currency. I mean, they might as well just say 'give us your money.' A green rectangle. Holy hullabaloo, how do things like that happen?"

"Nobody in a position of power at the company with both guts and talent would be my guess."

"Ooh…good one, Tommy."

"Are you really going to wear a Natnito shirt?"

"For sure. Feel how soft they are. Like that old TV commercial where the dweeby guy squeezes the toilet paper." She stroked the folded shirt gently across her cheek.

Three files remained. She sipped. I drank.

"Why these three?" I asked.

"I didn't have room for more."

I leaned in to read the labels.

ACCOUNTING

STRATEGIC PLANNING

HR

"You stole the Human Resources files?"

She swigged the last of her wine. "Borrowed." She smacked her lips. "Definitely borrowed."

"Where should we start?" I asked.

"More wine."

I hopped up and refilled her glass. I had a couple of fingers of beer left, but I got another bottle anyway. Shianti trotted off in the direction of the garage. I opened the folder marked ACCOUNTING. Receipts from hotels, sporting goods stores, grocery stores, clothing stores. Everything needed to take a group camping.

Drugstore.

I stared at the receipt, thinking about the caplets in the Amazon box. Maybe those pills were a medical treatment prescribed by a doctor. But why retain paper receipts? Because they are following government regulations. Certainly the rehab program had been approved by som organization.

Hadn't it?

Shianti padded back into the room.

"I, uh, stimulated Prof a little and got no reaction."

"Must have been a powerful drug," I said.

She grinned. "Thanks." She unfolded a yellow shirt and spread it out on the table face down. Then she peeled off the hoodie and hung it on the back of her chair. Her white bra was still upstairs in the bedroom.

I shifted my eyes to her Juno tattoo.

She slipped the T-shirt over her head. It was several sizes too large, but she looked pixie cute the way girls do when wearing their boyfriend's clothes. She glanced at the document I was reading.

"Find anything interesting?"

"You," I said, partly because I thought she wanted me to notice, and partly because, well, she was interesting.

"Well, duh?" she said, and laughed.

I handed her the receipt from a pharmacy.

She said, "Hmm."

"Copies of prescriptions for pharmaceuticals that would liven up any frat party."

"Speaking from experience?"

"A little," I said.

"Conclusion?"

"Nature Incognito dispenses narcotics as part of their program."

"I've heard of methadone treatment. Something like that?"

"But I thought the pitch was to disappear into nature and find the natural Rocky Mountain high that John Denver sang about."

Shianti reached for her wine glass.

"Probably the thin air." She grinned. "Well, that's the marketing pitch. You know the difference between marketing people and sales people, don't you?"

"I missed that class."

"Ready?" She sipped. Waited. "Marketing people know they are lying." She laughed. "Anything else of interest?"

"I don't know if this is interesting. But it's tingling my private-eye intuition."

"You ever notice that private investigator, P.I. spells Pi, the ratio of the circumference of a circle to its diameter, which is an irrational number with no end."

"You study math?" I asked.

"Nope. That's from primary school. Spooks me. Why should that simple ratio be this weird, infinite, undefined thing? You can calculate it to any precision you want, but it can never be known exactly." She sipped red wine.

"You're suggesting that intuition is like pi?"

"I mean like, at some level of detail, everything is unknown."

"Spooky is right," I said.

"Tell me about your spooky insight."

"Let me ask you a question. In the twenty-first century, what percentage of donations to Natnito would be credit versus cash?"

Her lips rolled inward as her mental gears spun.

"Depends on how they solicit. If they stand on a sidewalk with a bucket, most would be cash. Incognito volunteers are visible on campus to the point of annoying."

"Maybe that's why so many donations are flagged as cash and anonymous," I said. "Maybe a large cash inflow isn't unusual for a non-profit."

Shianti sat down in the chair across from me. Motion under her new shirt brought back images a bra being unsnapped with one hand.

"Tommy is following the money. Cash is collected. Then what?"

"It goes into a bank account that pays for building leases, utilities, supplies like tents and sleeping bags."

"You mentioned research. That consumes beaucoup dollars."

I dug through papers looking for references to research projects. Found none. But I did find a reference to a payroll company. And a list of names who were receiving checks. Paging backwards in time produced W-2 forms for a handful of permanent employees and 1099s for several people with Ph.D. after their name. One of which was Markus Corolla.

"Explain this," I said, holding up Markus's 1099 form.

"Easy. He's the principal investigator on research projects. Has to do the hard parts, including getting the results published."

"Hundreds of thousands of dollars?"

"He's paid for being smart, not putting in long, sweaty hours like the poor little waitress at the Bourgeois Pig."

I laughed.

"What's funny?" she said.

"A beautiful college student living in this townhouse, driving a luxury sedan, while obtaining a filmmaking degree from a prestigious university being referred to as 'poor.'"

Shianti pouted. Then stood and shuffled her bare feet across tile that was probably real stone. She punched me on the arm.

"OK, you're right. I must maintain perspective. But lots of people don't make that much money in a decade. Before taxes."

I massaged my arm. "You pack quite a punch."

"Oh, stop it. That punch couldn't disable a flea. What do you think the money means? Famous smart guy gets research grants from non-profit and publishes landmark papers. Not going to grab attention away from puppy videos."

I studied the document. Just a way to report income to the government. Clean. Legal. Maybe Markus was even working cheap for Nature Incognito to help move science forward and help people who needed help. A pretty explanation, but the guy I met didn't fit it.

"Something bothers me," I said.

She patted my punched arm. "Keep it in mind. Maybe it will lead somewhere." She went back to the wine bottle and was about to refill her glass, but corked the bottle instead.

"Your turn," she said.

"May I borrow a pen and paper?"

She reached into a drawer beside the stove and give me a pad with Grocery List pre-printed across the top and a pen missing its cap.

"Going to write me a love letter?" She batted her eyelashes.

I smiled. Flirting seemed to be built into her DNA.

"Need to leave a note for Prof in case he wakes up while we're sleeping."

She met my eyes and held them for five seconds.

"Turn right at the top of the stairs. Spare bedroom is all ready to go. My girlfriends crash there. Also, a futon in the den downstairs, or couch surf in the living room. It's real comfy. I like to fall asleep while watching movies."

"The directors wouldn't be happy to hear that," I said.

"They should be proud. I demonstrate that their work is serving a useful purpose to society."

"I'll direct Prof to the spare room. No, wait. He probably shouldn't be on stairs by himself."

"Couch," she said. "Easy to find. Just flop and drag the afghan over you. Voila, instant slumberland."

I gave her a thumbs up while adding bullet points for Prof.

- You were drugged (we think)
- The goddess insisted we stay at her place
- Comfort is available on the couch in the living room
- Shianti is upstairs to the left in the master bedroom
- I am upstairs to the right in the guest bedroom

"Remind him that he owes me dinner," she said.

- Remember that you owe Shianti dinner!

When I reached my car, I slid into the driver's seat and left the door open. Prof had slouched down slightly, but looked about as comfortable as a tall guy sleeping in a car could look. His breathing was steady. I took his pulse and respiration rate. Then I took mine. We both seemed normal.

I folded the 'grocery list' and placed it on his lap.

Gently, I said, "Prof, it's Tommy. Can you hear me?"

I sipped my beer and tried to guess why anyone would drug and kidnap Prof. To Nature Incognito of all places. Trying to get him out of the—

I froze. Blinked.

Prof found Markus. They talked. Could Prof have a habit and Markus was actually trying to help him? And I had monkey-wrenched the plan?

Maybe.

But Prof was super smart. He had found a way to reach me via his laptop.

My answering service.

I called in on the burner phone. Played the first message.

Lots of people noise. Whispering.

"Tommy. I saw Leni in a boutique. I'm going to make contact."

Eight hours ago.

Another message. More whispering. Not Prof.

"He made me do it, Tommy."

Click off.

Maybe Leni. Probably Leni. Do what?

I imagined being alone and stalked by an abuser with the resources of Markus Corolla. What would I do if I were Leni?

Run!

She had tried that.

Cops?

Useful as a last resort. But Leni…I remembered her Oleace job. I switched on her phone.

Prof made snorting sounds beside me, then fell silent.

I turned off the dome light, left the driver's door open, and went back inside. Shianti wasn't around. Her kitchen clock, white with gold numerals, indicated midnight had slipped by twenty minutes ago. I wondered briefly how Mona was doing. Likely at the club. Likely surrounded by men fantasizing that they were in her league. I called her home number from the burner and left a message that we wouldn't be back tonight, but not to worry, everything was fine.

Which it wasn't.

Prof was in an unknown state. Leni was missing. Markus had threatened us. Native Incognito's books connected big dollars—by my Walmart mechanic standards—to the well-known yet mysterious Markus.

I thumbed through dozens of messages from Leni's admiring fans while sipping beer at the kitchen table. I saved time by sending the same reply to all members, occasionally customizing for those who sent a long message. One stood out.

"The video?"

From the person who had sent the attack video. What had interrupted their private conversation? Did she do personal visits? Could he come visit?

I had no idea how to reply, so I didn't. I would have to deal with it eventually. Or maybe Leni would when she returned. Or we found her.

I watched the rape video again. This time I noticed a hand flash into view from the self-facing camera. I replayed it. First he hit her, then he grabbed the phone. If this was foreplay, it was news to me.

You're not exactly experienced, Thomas.

I reserved judgement. Bottom line, Leni was trapped and part of her wanted out. I needed to talk to her. I thought about Prof snoozing in my car and wondered why I wasn't cruising down Route 66. Didn't hear a good answer.

I switched my attention to the top article on the stack of scientific papers. M. Corolla was the first author. I paged through, glancing at graphs and tables and percentages. If I understood it right, sports on the water (paddling kayaks, a game called Animal Ball) were more successful at breaking addiction than sports on land. At least the two that had been tested: soccer and volleyball. The test had been two weeks long with a follow-up at 60 and 90 days.

I was no statistician.

I considered trying to read the rest of the stack but put it off until morning. It had been a long, crazy day. I left the kitchen light on in case Prof woke up and wandered into an apartment he had never seen. I headed upstairs. Near the top, two stairs squeaked, reminding me of the Japanese art of installing walkways around homes that made noise to announce intruders. Sort of a medieval watchdog without the vet bills.

I heard my name being called.

I turned left toward Shianti's room and pressed my ear to the door.

"Tommy, is that you?"

A fair question for a woman who lived alone.

"Tommy passed out drunk. I'm a vampire making my rounds."

She giggled. "Come in for minute."

I opened the door and stepped into the palatial space illuminated by an electric candle flickering inside of a glass tube.

"How's Prof?" she said from beneath the midnight blue starry-starry night quilt pulled up to her chin.

"Making snoring noises."

Her face was surrounded by curls spread out on a white satin pillow, like a golden halo on an angel. Her eyes held on me.

I asked, "Why are you so confident that Roger won't spill the beans?"

"Because I made him promise not to tell anyone we were there if he ever wants to spill something other than beans." She smiled in the flickering light.

"What did—" I stopped myself. "Sweet dreams, Shianti."

"Thanks." She repositioned her body beneath the quilt, making me wonder what a transparent blanket would be like.

"Tommy?"

I walked to the side of the bed and squatted so our eyes would be at the same level. Her face was childlike without makeup. She had a tiny pimple on the left side of her forehead. She had been crying. Maybe.

"What happened?" I asked.

"Nothing."

Hmm. No meant no. But nothing rarely meant nothing. I sat down cross-legged on the floor.

"Want to talk?" I asked.

"What about?"

I shrugged. "Anything to help us wind down so we can sleep and be ready for tomorrow."

"That's what I'm worried about."

"You seem more action-hero type," I said. "They never worry."

"That's what worries me."

I tried to assemble her words into a logical structure.

"It worries you that you're an action-hero?"

"Yep."

I stayed quiet. She rolled toward me and stared at the fake flame wagging inside the tube.

"It's okay during the day," she said. "Then I can do stuff. Keep things moving. Make progress. But at night…" She fell silent with her lips slightly parted.

"At night the demons of doubt come out to dance," I said.

She almost smiled. "Yeah."

"Your subconscious wants in the game too," I said.

"Feels…"

I waited. And waited.

"Scary," she said. "Like I'm being sucked into a black hole and no one will ever see me again."

"Sounds scary," I said.

"I hate being in this apartment all alone. I feel like I'm being attacked from all sides."

"Ever been attacked?"

"I don't talk about it."

"OK," I said. I waited some more.

"Hold me. Come under here and hold me."

I waited to give her time.

"But," she said. "I sleep nude. Can you hold me without having lascivious boy thoughts?"

I spoke softly in the dark room.

"Shianti, you're beautiful. A goddess. You're smart. Last I checked, I was a healthy adult male."

"So evolution is going to give you lurid thoughts?"

"Very high probability."

"Can you have these thoughts and not act on them?"

"By exercising a stupendous amount of self-control and will power —yes, I think maybe I can."

"Then take your clothes off and get in here."

I placed my two borrowed phones beside the candle and stacked my clothes on the floor next to the nightstand.

"Should I blow out the candle?"

She giggled, punched my arm, and lifted the corner of the blanket. I slipped in beside her and our limbs entangled.

She sighed. "Thanks, Tommy. Have lovely, lascivious dreams."

An attractive woman in close proximity puts various systems in the male body into overdrive. I tried to push in the clutch and downshift as her breathing told me she was drifting into slumberland. In a few minutes, the light of the candle became a gray mist as I faded toward that dream.

CHAPTER 27

A noise snapped me to consciousness. I was in Shianti's king-size bed in her king-size bedroom, her face resting on my shoulder. A curl of golden hair tickled my left eyelash each time I blinked. The candle shadow-danced the room.

The noise coalesced into a smartphone vibrating on the nightstand. I reached for it with my free arm while trying not to disturb Shianti, brought it to a half-open eye, and squinted at red and green buttons. A train of: who is calling Leni? can it be Oleace? I can't speak now? ended with a decision to wing it.

I tapped Answer.

Audio squawked out of the earpiece. I lowered the volume drastically and pressed the phone to my ear.

Shianti didn't budge.

"No, I don't want to. I told you before I don't want to. I'm fine now. I want to stay in school. I can't miss two more weeks of classes."

Leni's voice. Shouting.

"Attend online classes between treatments."

Maybe Markus. Probably Markus.

"I am not letting anyone experiment on my body."

"Leni, Leni. We're not talking about anything you haven't done before."

Drugs or something else?

"When I gave you that new phone, you promised not to get addicted again. And now you pull it out during our conversation."

"I caught myself and put it back in my purse."

She didn't say she left a live call going.

"That's why you need a two-week session. To create new habits."

Long pause.

"You want to control me."

"Someone needs to."

Yes, Markus for sure.

"But it shouldn't be me. You should control yourself."

"Oh yeah. And you have to approve my every move."

"Of course."

Leni's breathing was audible in the quiet.

Then Markus's voice. "I do not want a woman near me who cannot be trusted. No flakey chicks where I don't know what she's going to do or say at any moment."

"You're suffocating me!"

"I'm freeing you from stupidity."

More silence.

"Leni, if you're going to live in my world, there are…complexities that must not be disturbed."

"And I disturb them?"

Shianti's quiet breathing filled my other ear. She still hadn't moved.

"You can't run away, talk to strangers and…not do your job just because you won't put your damn phone down."

"You hit me."

"Violence makes some people pay attention."

"And I'm one?"

Pause. No background sounds. I imagined them face to face across the kitchen table I had seen in the video, Leni's purse sitting on it with the new phone inside broadcasting.

"You're paying attention now."

"Which means your bullying is working, so that makes it OK?"

"All's fair."

"This isn't love or war."

"Then what is it?"

A glass touched down on a hard surface. Leni's breath came in short gasps.

I had an idea what it was. A combustible mixture of hero-worship, boy-girl attraction, money, and Leni's ambition to change her life's path by finishing college by whatever means necessary.

"Life," Leni said.

Long sigh from Markus. "Where does that leave us?"

"Trying to make things work without you suffocating me."

Glasses tapped the table.

I wondered what they were drinking. And why have this conversation in the middle of the night? I answered my own question. Because people got tired and alcohol loosened lips and they had arguments that should have waited until morning.

"OK, Leni. Forget two weeks. Do a three-day weekend retreat starting tomorrow. See if that will get us to a place we both find acceptable."

Was that the sound of a blown kiss?

Chair legs scraped tile. Footfalls moved away from the phone.

When I hadn't heard anything new for a full minute I ended the call and placed the phone back on the nightstand beside the flickering electric candle. Shianti's face was peaceful. Her breathing steady. Her body soft and warm against mine. She would have no trouble extracting information about the weekend retreat from Roger. I tried to fall back to sleep as images of Roger and Shianti in the bucket seats of my Barracuda intruded.

◇

Prof was sitting at the kitchen table starting out the window when I plodded down the stairs barefoot in jeans and yesterday's T-shirt. Sunlight had invaded the living room. The afghan was positioned perfectly over the back of the sofa. He was dressed in the clothes he had been wearing last night, yet they barely looked wrinkled.

"How was your nap?" I asked.

"Longer than planned," he said. "How was your date?"

I poured a half-glass of orange juice. "Did you set me up?"

"Didn't you feel her vibe at lunch?" he asked.

"Sure. Thought it was for you."

"Age-old tactic. Get to the real target through the friend."

"Is that what she was doing?"

He shook his head. "She was reacting to the stimulus of the moment. I read between the lines."

"She's an interesting lady."

"Sure is. Look at this place. Must have an income from somewhere besides the Pig. Unless she owns the place."

"Or a rich uncle."

"That'll work," he said. "I got news, want to sit down?"

"Stiff from a new bed. I'll stand."

He laughed. "Stiff? That's funny." He laid out articles in a row like playing cards. "What we have here are research reports published in journals like Pharmacotherapy and Current Drug Therapy. They seem legit based on the editor and board member credentials. Maybe not top tier."

"It's morning. Keep it simple."

He grinned and pointed. "Top row, Markus C. is first author and principal investigator."

"He calls the shots and reports the results."

"Right." He waved his hand across the table. "The rest of these, principal investigator, but not first author."

"Who is?"

"There are two. One at the University of Notre Dame, the other at the University of Wisconsin at Madison."

"Well-known schools," I said.

"Yes. But not Harvard and Yale."

"That mean something?"

Prof shrugged. "I can speculate."

"Better you than me," I said.

"I think," he tapped the second row of articles, "our man Markus is balancing a quantity versus quality calculus."

I sipped, marveling at how great cold orange juice could taste in the morning.

"You mean Markus is gaming the science system?"

"They all do," Prof said. "Publish or perish is real. This represents his particular strategy."

"Your smiling eyes tell me you have an idea."

"Imagine if you will, that the average research grant provides X dollars in funding. Depending on the type of study, some portion, let's say Y percent, goes to the principal investigator to pay for his time."

There were the letters PI again: Principal Investigator.

"Two ways to play," I said. "A really big grant with a large chunk of dough for the PI because the grant is going to run for months and months." I paused. "Or smaller grants but more of them. Less pay for each grant, but more paydays."

"Precisely," he said. "And somewhere in there hides?"

"The peak of the profit curve. A game of grants to generate new information while also making money for the PI."

"On top of a university salary and the quest for the magic of lifetime employment through tenure."

I said. "Like any good game, there are multiple ways to score points. It's not just about the dollars."

"You are wise beyond your years, my friend."

I shrugged. "Pretty much like playing Mortal Combat."

"Or life in general," he said.

Leni's voice saying life echoed in my inner ear.

I said, "Same old, same old?"

"Yes and no. With two exceptions, both for small amounts for meta-studies of previously published research, all of these articles were published about research projects funded by a single source."

I refilled my orange juice. "Give me one guess. Nature Incognito."

"You cheated," Prof said. "Since you're so smart, what did you notice about the co-author?"

I thought hard but came up blank and shrugged.

"This guy from Wisconsin, the land of cheese, is on every paper. Dr. Ilya Kartovska."

"You want an OJ?"

"No thanks. I checked out Ilya. Care to guess his specialty?"

I sat down across from Prof. "I figured everyone on the paper was a psychologist."

Prof shook his head. "Chemist."

"Do you know why Markus needs a chemist on a rehab paper?"

"Not yet. But when I woke up, I had a message from Jake."

"Something wrong back home?" I asked. "Naomi okay?"

"Had a message from her too. She enjoyed your, uh, workout." He smiled.

"I felt awfully clumsy helping her."

"You get the hang of it after a while. She's a very capable woman. But back to Jake. I didn't tell you, so you would have plausible deniability if things got crazy."

"But you're going to tell me now?"

"Have to," he said. "This is a surprise to me, which I hate because it means that I'm not keeping up. And this info puts us into a new ball game. Maybe even the major leagues."

"I am now officially worried."

"First, background. You will recall the box you found hidden in Leni's bed at my place. A visual inspection suggests certain substances. But a visual doesn't reveal much. Anything can be made to look like anything. So I stole some."

I nodded, drank OJ. "And you passed it to Jake for, um, analysis."

"Precisely."

"The results surprised you?"

"In retrospect," he said, "I should have predicted this. But the presentation was very convincing."

"Go on."

"Fentanyl."

"It was laced with fentanyl?"

"High quality."

"We conclude," I said, "the stuff was created in an illegal lab that is importing Chinese fentanyl and mixing it with substances from Big Pharma."

"That's one explanation," he said.

"Which requires modern equipment. And someone with expertise."

Prof nodded and tapped an article. "A chemist."

I sat back and stared out the window at a blue sunlit sky.

"You're suggesting the Amazon box under Leni's bed is connected to the guy who wrote these articles?"

"Stranger things have happened," he said. "Remember Fair Game? A journalist criticizes U.S. foreign policy; his CIA wife is outed. Chief of staff to the Vice President of the United States gets convicted and pardoned.”

“Speaking of strange, Shianti and I visited Nature Incognito. I found boxes labeled Supplies.”

“And you got nosy.”

“Natural curiosity of the private eye. Most contained packaged food. One of them had Amazon boxes.”

“Did they rattle?”

I nodded. “It’s a rehab program.”

“And customers need a fix,” he said.

I gestured towards the articles on the table.

“They all use a phased regimen. Cold turkey is only one option.”

Prof put his chin in his upright hands. “Cold turkey is a weird phrase. I’ll have to look up its origin. But I agree.”

My burner phone emitted an electronic sizzle that reminded me of a burger on a hot grill.

“Excuse me a second.” I lifted the phone. “Hello.”

“Kelsey, your lazy butt isn’t sleeping? Color me surprised. Report is on my desk. Bring scones and coffee.”

“What kind of human makes a call at seven eighteen A.M. on a weekend?” Prof asked.

“Cop.”

Prof grinned.

“I gotta run an errand,” I said. “But Leni is going on a retreat this weekend. Shianti thinks she can get details from Roger.”

“I’ll handle it,” Prof said.

“One problem. My car has been ID’ed by the Markus group.”

“That smoke bomb convinced me,” he said.

“It’s hiding in the garage.”

“I saw something,” he said, and held up a finger for me to wait. He headed out to the garage.

I went upstairs and poked my nose into the master bedroom. Shianti was lying on her side facing the blind-covered window, hugging my pillow with both arms. No way was I going to wake her up and ask to use her car. Besides, she and Prof needed it to go see Roger. I eased the door closed and went back downstairs.

Prof was rolling the pink Barbie bicycle down the hallway.

"Your chariot, sir," he said. Part of the lower frame was the size of my wrist. "This was upside down and plugged in."

I squeezed the tires to test pressure, adjusted the seat up, and straddled the e-bike.

"Can you handle all that power?" Prof asked, grinning.

"I'll try to avoid a speeding ticket."

Prof's face turned serious. "Stay off the radar."

"Agreed. This is no time for cops."

"Rarely is." He gestured toward the bicycle. "The blue LED means it's fully charged."

I rotated my wrist and made motorcycle noises.

Prof shook his head.

I got dressed and put on my creepers, figuring them for good bicycle shoes. Jacket, wallet, two cell phones, and I headed for the Bourgeois Pig.

◇

Chicago traffic looked a whole lot different from the skinny seat of a bicycle, even though I sort of had my own lane. When a red light stopped traffic, I kept riding between the curb on my right, and the stopped cars on my left up. It was fun not stopping so often. Maybe this was why Leni delivered boxes on her bicycle: fun, efficient, and cheap.

Loaded with a mini-pot of coffee and six scones in three flavors, I cruised toward Braden's office, parked behind the church, and found his door ajar. I lifted my free hand to knock.

"C'mon in, Kelsey. I can smell you."

Braden was wearing the same jacket. Fresh shirt. Maroon tie with fine gold thread.

"You always work on Saturdays?" I asked.

"I always work," he said. "I'm only home on weekends that don't have a red-hot finding ready to break open a case. Used to be half of them. Now it's barely once a month."

I unpacked my bag and poured two coffees. Braden waited, selected a maple scone, and tasted it. Then he tested the coffee.

"Where'd you get that Jane Doe code you gave me?" he asked.

This was delicate. I had to protect Leni. She was my client—sort of.

"From Jane Doe."

"You've met her? Face to face? None of this virtual gobbledygook?"

"Multiple times."

"How old would you say she is?"

I shrugged. "Early twenties."

"Not a minor?"

I shook my head. I hadn't seen ID, but was confident that Leni was over 18. Well, somewhat confident. Looks were tricky. Especially with makeup.

"College student," I said. "End of her second year."

Braden chewed a scone. "Those were great times. I learned a lot in college." He actually smiled. "Even went to some classes."

We ate and drank. The sunbeam on his desk shrank a bit.

"Interpreting DNA tests is a tricky business," he said. "Snips of this and that. Matches. Mis-matches. But done right, they're reliable."

"So whatever you tell me I should consider reliable?"

"Let's just say, admissible in court."

That was plenty reliable for me.

"Please don't tell me they found nothing."

Braden held up a hand and swallowed.

"Great scones," he said. "They found plenty. Jane definitely had unprotected sex with someone within the time frame she claimed on the report."

"So you can nail this guy?"

He blew across the top of the coffee in his paper cup.

"Maybe I can find him if we start scanning DNA databases. There are only a few big ones, and they mostly cooperate with authorities if we do all the paperwork."

"But you don't have paperwork."

"I don't even have a woman filing a complaint. I've got a fly-by-night wannabe private dick playing in my sandbox." He hesitated.

"Again." He stared at me, then smiled, then frowned. He said, "Prepare yourself."

I was already sitting down, so I put my coffee on the desk and placed my cranberry scone beside it. I folded my hands on my lap and met his eyes.

"Ready."

He took a long inhale and let it out slowly.

"I see a lot of shitty crimes in my job. People treat each other worse than they treat dogs. Or cats even. It gets to me once in a while."

I resisted the urge to imagine the worst things I could think of. But they came crashing in anyway: serial rapist, AIDS, gang rape.

Braden sipped his coffee. "There's no way to sugarcoat this, so I'm just going to say it."

"Is it better if I don't know?" I asked.

His head wagged slightly. "You have to know. Until you know, we can't figure out what we're going to do about it."

"She and I just met."

He stared at me. "Another hitchhiker?"

"Fortune teller. Uses tarot cards."

"Which one did you draw?" he asked.

"The Magician."

He nodded and drank some coffee.

"Good, you're going to need it." He pushed the last bite of his first scone into his mouth, chewed, and swallowed. "The guy who did Jane. No doubt in the data. No errors. I leaned on the lab boys hard. That guy, way, way behind a scientific reasonable doubt, is her father."

CHAPTER 28

My appetite disappeared. Detective Braden was seldom wrong, so I didn't go down that path. I thanked him. He told me to keep in close touch. Then told me again with a look in his eye I didn't want to test.

I left the door ajar on my way out.

I pedaled away from Braden's office with no destination, my head spinning faster than the bicycle's wheels. I goosed up the electric assist.

What is Leni doing?

What is her father doing?

A horn blared. I jerked my eyes up and realized I was about to ride through a red light. I squealed to a stop, fishtailing the rear wheel.

I needed to think but had no idea where to begin, so I stepped off the bike and walked it onto the sidewalk. I leaned it against a gray building with a corner stone dated 1938, then sat on the sidewalk and stared at distant clouds forming over Lake Michigan.

Leni said, "I'm lost."

Prof said, "Fentanyl."

The lockers. How could Markus get into Amazon lockers?

I studied the picture of the two racks I had taken with Leni's phone. Sixteen lockers. The schoolgirl on her scooter going in and out.

I had my destination.

I retrieved my coffee cup from a side bag, chugged it, and set off. It was not quite 9 A.M. when I sat down across from the 24-hour

Generic supermarket beneath a shade tree. A steady stream of shoppers flowed in and out.

No one touched a locker.

I called my service on Prof's burner phone. Tina told me there were no new messages. I wondered if she was an AI bot, then wondered how I would be able to tell. I decided sitting here was a fool's errand. Lacking a better idea, I headed toward Shianti's townhouse. As I was passing through a traffic light a few minutes later, a truck the color of wet concrete sporting the smiling Amazon logo passed going in the opposite direction.

I stopped at the curb and dismounted to wait for the WALK signal. The Amazon truck grew smaller as seconds ticked away. The instant the light changed, I walked the bike across to the opposite curb, mounted, pushed the electric assist to maximum, waited for the green light, then rode as fast as I could in pursuit of the truck.

Lady Luck smiled on me.

The next light was green, but the one ahead turned red for the Amazon truck. Jouncing fast along the edge of the cracked and potholed street vibrated my spine. As I pulled alongside the truck, the light turned green, and it took off in electric silence. The driver noticed me, laughed, and gave me a thumb's up. I chased the truck all the way back to Generic Groceries, where he swung into the parking lot and leapt out with an armload of boxes.

I stopped at a spot on the sidewalk with a good view of the lockers.

"Electric bikes are fast," he said as he approached. "I bought one for my daughter. After test riding it." He grinned, glanced at the bike, surely wondering why I was riding a Barbie bike but not asking, opened a locker in the group on the left, and stuffed a box inside.

To keep the conversation going I said, "They're great for getting around the city."

He opened a second locker, also on the left side. Same with the third and fourth packages.

"Got time for a question?" I asked.

"Be quick. Jeff Bezos has a stopwatch on me."

"You ever deliver packages over there?"

Without even looking he said, "Nope. Those are for a different route." He gave me a little salute. "Nice racing you. Stay safe on that thing, these streets have a mind of their own." Then he was in his truck, backing into the street, and waving goodbye.

A different route?

That gave me a fresh idea.

Markus owned the second bank of lockers.

They sat in plain sight with no one wondering about them, because deliveries came and went just like the other lockers. I did a little math in my head. A plan blossomed. In ten minutes I was back at Shianti's townhouse. Her car wasn't in sight, but she was at the kitchen table in her black waitress skirt and a white hoodie. Prof sat directly across from her wearing a short dark blue robe and staring at a four-foot paper map spread out on the table.

"A map in the age of Google?" I said.

"I am orienting myself to the terrain."

"Was Roger helpful?" I asked.

Shianti giggled.

"They left from the office this morning," Prof said. Return Monday night."

"Bus?" I asked.

He shook his head. "A bus can't get there. Unpaved roads in and out. If it rains, mud will trap them for a week. A local Jeep dealer loans them Grand Cherokees in exchange for free advertising."

"We don't have an SUV," I said, stating the obvious.

Prof squinted at me. "That's only problem number one.

"Uh-oh," I said.

Shianti said, "We have nothing but problems. Secluded like that, where to hide? How to spring her out?"

The we stood out. I kept quiet and debated what to tell to whom.

"We can get in," Prof said. "But we'll have to shoot our way out."

"Unsubtle," Shianti said.

They looked at me. My mind was playing Braden's voice in my ear. I nodded. "Other ideas?"

"One," Prof said. "Get help."

I met his eyes and recalled bullets flying at Toucan Sam's.

"Jake?" I asked.

Depends on what we're doing," Prof said. "And why."

"In my opinion, we're springing a hostage," Shianti said.

"You haven't even met Leni," I said.

"But we have shared experience dealing with older men who want to get our panties off."

Not smart to argue that one.

"How do we find out what goes on at the retreat?" I asked.

"Depends on our resources," Prof said.

I sat down at the table and instinctively started thinking about food. "Lunch?"

Prof's mouth worked as he thought before speaking.

"The place is isolated. They want the retreat attendees to be safe, but at the same time, cut off from civilization. And understand that they are cut off, so they don't try anything silly…like hiking out on their own."

"Makes getting in tough," I said.

He shrugged. Shianti made no comment.

"Only for a human on foot," he said.

"You have a plan?"

"We're not going to zoom in with Blackhawk helicopters like a bunch of Navy Seals. We know nothing about what we're going to find."

"A spy," I said. "We need a spy."

Prof looked me over. "Or a private eye wearing brothel creepers."

I went to the fridge. The OJ wasn't empty. I held up the container. Both declined. I poured a lowball glass.

"You want me to go in?" I said.

"Markus won't be there. Roger won't be there. So no one will suspect that you aren't who you say you are."

"And who is that?" I asked.

"We have to figure that out," Prof said.

I nodded agreement even though I had no idea how I would get in to see Leni, or what I would say when I did. Recalling a night scene in the alley behind Prof's house, I said, "What if she doesn't want to come out with me?"

"Respect her wishes," Shianti said. "Or drug her and drag her out."

Prof's eyes drifted to Shianti and then to me.

"Kidnapping is a felony in most states," he said.

"What about?" I began, then stopped myself. They stared at me. I sipped orange juice for a moment. "What about just guarding her?"

Shianti studied my face. "Do you mean secretly stalking her like old-school private eyes hiding in the shadows ready to pounce on the bad guys?" She laughed.

Prof suppressed a grin.

"Well, when you put it that way," I said.

"You even have creeper shoes," she said, still laughing.

"Stalking is a great idea," Prof said. "But not practical. Let me study these maps. Maybe I can find commercial satellite images of the camping area." He put his finger on the map. "They chose middle-of-nowhere Wisconsin."

Shianti said, "Giving up is harder than staying in the program."

"Positioned carefully between a rock and a hard place," I said.

"These academic papers claim a double-digit success rate after two years," Prof said. "Seems a worthy endeavor." He paused. "I wonder how it compares to Narcotics Anonymous."

"I've heard that fentanyl is super bad," Shianti said. "Multiple ODs on campus last year."

"Multiple?" Prof asked.

"Well, that made the student paper. One was a competitive cheerleader who was good at doing back flips off of muscular guys."

I could guess, but I waited for the rest of the story.

"She'd been hurt so many times from missed attempts that she was constantly on medication for pain."

"And ended up on fentanyl?" I asked.

"And OD'ed," Prof said. "Before a big game that she was anxious about."

"Homecoming," Shianti said.

"Any details?" I asked.

She shook her head. "The family wanted it kept quiet." She grew solemn. "The article said it was easy to score on campus. They even did some testing in the chemistry department to show how you can never know what you're getting on the street."

"Not Big Pharma level quality control," I said. "How old was she?"

"Twenty," Shianti said.

Leni was twenty. I imagined her in a coffin from an overdose. Anger and frustration butted heads inside my skull. But a good plan did not materialize.

Prof opened a road atlas of all 50 states and stared at one page.

"Where did that come from?" I said.

"I dream of traveling," Shianti said. "And I like to see the big picture. I fantasize late at night to avoid screen time before bed." She reached across the table and tapped the book. "No interruptions from social media or incoming text messages."

I, too, was a fan of eliminating interruptions. But at the moment Braden's news weighed me down inside like bad pizza. I had key information. But what to do with it? Who to tell? I could think of only one person who could confirm or deny—although it was possible that even she didn't know for certain. Plenty of women couldn't identify the father of her baby. There was even a TV game show that revealed DNA paternity results live.

"I have research to do," I said.

"I have to do some real work today," Prof said. "Shianti has a shift at the Pig. Regroup here tomorrow morning?"

Shianti gave a thumbs up, apparently willing to let us wreak havoc on her life for another day.

I nodded slowly, my thoughts on how much could happen in 24 hours.

◇

Minutes later I was rolling west on I-80 blasting the radio. Alone. Retracing the road I had been on when I drew The Magician from Leni's deck. I pressed the upper edge of the speed limit and ran through scenarios of what to do when I reached Leni's hometown. Probably the town where she went to school. Likely the town where she was born.

I stopped for carry-out at the Rocket Man, visited the alien girl in the silver skirt, and was back on the road before you could say 'Rocket Burger' five times fast. By the time I swallowed the last Rocket French fry, I was pulling into the parking space behind Prof's house. I knocked on the back door, not expecting an answer. I stepped into the kitchen using Prof's key.

Something felt off.

I had been there only a few nights. Possibly the feeling of edginess was simply the warning bell of the unfamiliar. I snuck through the kitchen and Prof's work area. Everything in order. Too in order. Like the maid had come to clean and moved everything, then put it back where she thought it had been. Like in that movie Girl with a Pearl Earring. A young girl cleans for a famous painter, restoring all of the objects in the still life he was working on to their exact position after dusting them off.

I checked the fridge.

The ice cube trays weren't on the top shelf. The orange juice bottle was on the left. It had been on the right. I closed the door.

The back door had been locked. The front door was locked. I stood still in the foyer and listened. No creaks or groans coming from upstairs.

Check Leni's room first.

The mattress was leaning against the wall, blocking the lower half of the window. The box springs were inverted. Whoever had been here got interrupted. They had been careful on the lower level. But not in this room. The remainder of the upstairs appeared untouched.

I went downstairs and tapped the space bar on Prof's three-monitor computer. It asked for a password, fingerprint, or face.

The screen went dark.

I stared at my reflection in the glass for half a minute. I dug a card out of my wallet and dialed the number using Prof's burner phone. Definitely more convenient than a phone booth, but not as much fun. The phone stopped ringing. No one spoke.

"Naomi?"

"Yes." Soft, guarded voice.

"Tommy Cuda here."

"Oh, hi Tommy." Not guarded. A little shy.

"I know this is super late notice, and it's a Saturday night so you likely have plans. But I just got to town a few minutes ago. Would you like to have dinner tonight? I have a ton of questions, and I think you're the best person to talk to about how to find answers."

"Hmmm. A private eye with questions? Should I worry that you'll dig into my past and find out what a naughty girl I've been?"

My fingertips tingled. She wasn't referring to Santa's list.

"You're a mind reader. I need to dig into the past. But we can avoid yours if you like."

"What time?"

"Any time you like. I'm happy to pick you up or meet at the restaurant."

"I'll pick you up at Prof's," she said. "Dress upscale-casual. I've got just the place."

She hung up.

I donned my last clean T-shirt, sport coat, black jeans, and boots while making a mental note to do laundry. I envied Jack Reacher, a fictional guy that just bought new clothes whenever the current ones got dirty. Then I sat down at Prof's computer and stared at the blank screen. I had cold-called Naomi, she might need a couple of hours to get ready. That left me time to ponder.

I recalled a method from formal logic that I had learned when a bald and graying Philosophy professor tried to teach us how to think. I was supposed to list all conclusions implied by the DNA findings. Then follow where they led.

First, Leni had sex with someone. Markus, if the video could be trusted.

That someone was her biological father. Braden had high confidence in that finding.

Accept these as true. Then who knew what?

Leni either did or did not know.

Markus either did or did not know.

Leni said Markus told her that she reminded him of someone who had been special to him. That someone was likely Leni's mother. Leni's mother, Alexxia, owned Shey's Gym.

I stared at myself in the black mirror of the monitor. What should I make as an operational assumption?

Markus and Leni both know.

Difficult to accept. But had happened many times over the course of history.

Neither knew.

Then this was the age-old student-teacher fling. Had happened a million times before.

But what if one knew and the other didn't? What if that person was Markus?

Did it matter what I assumed?

The relationship was on. Leni was being abused, but she didn't want to leave. Or she couldn't figure out how to leave. And now she was headed up north to—

The doorbell rang. I checked the time. Twenty-three minutes. Could it possibly be?

No one on the porch, but Naomi's red sled sat idling at the curb. I locked the door behind me, jogged to the car, and slipped into the passenger's seat.

"Wow, Naomi, you're fast."

She turned to face me. Gold hoop earrings danced against the smooth brown contour of her neck. She grinned.

"You have no idea," she said. The car shot away from the curb. "I scored a reservation at a place I've wanted to try forever, but I lacked a secret ingredient. Now we have," she checked a white-faced round watch covering her slender wrist, "twelve minutes to get there." She sped through an almost red light under acceleration, then slammed on the brakes with a flick of her thumb as the suspension bottomed out.

"You could be a Formula One driver," I said.

"Danica Patrick is my hero. First woman to win an Indy car race. And, and she did a photo shoot for the Sports Illustrated swimsuit edition. Amazing woman. Inspiring."

She drove wearing a classic little black dress that had ridden halfway up her thigh. If I hadn't been at the gym and experienced how hard she worked, I would never have guessed she couldn't stand up and walk away from the car. She was even wearing high heels on her unmoving feet.

"How did you—"

"Get into cars? Via powerful women. I read biographies. Try to figure out what makes them tick. And what tricks I can borrow from their lives and apply to my own."

"Any you care to share?"

She glanced my way. "With the enemy? The sisterhood wouldn't approve. After all, knowledge is power." Her laughter filled the car with joy.

"Maybe a tiny one, by way of example?"

"How about this? I'll tell you a truth that if you think about it carefully, you already know has affected you over and over again, ever since you could walk."

"You'll confirm my perspective?"

"For sure." She braked hard and swung right. The tires squealed midway through the turn. "Are you ready? Guys don't want to believe this. Even after I tell you, you will refuse to believe. And many women will claim that it's not true, fueling your non-belief."

"But it is true?"

"Oh yeah. One hundred percent of the time. Ready? Brace yourself. The truth can hurt when it comes at you fast and smacks you in the chest."

I crossed my arms to protect myself. "Ready."

"A woman, any woman, all women, will say anything to get what she wants."

I felt a thud on my chest. "Anything?"

"Pretty much. Here are a couple of favorites. 'You don't love me.' Next, 'If you loved me—fill in the blank.' And another, 'I would never —fill in the blank.' And the perennial favorite: 'I'm pregnant.' That one even shows up in the movies.'

"Not true?"

Naomi shrugged. "Might or might not be true in what scientists call 'objective reality.' But absolutely true at the moment inside the tiny world women inhabit in their heads. It's this inside world that is most important to us."

I was skating on micro-thin ice. So I kept it short.

"Your feelings?"

"OMG. No wonder you're a private dick. How observant. Ever notice that there are fewer female scientists than male? Sure you did, we just demonstrated what an observant guy you are. But why? Is it because girls play with dolls? Girls hate math? Nah, none of that shit matters. Here's my hypothesis. Are you ready?"

"Another blast of truth coming?"

"Nope. This is just Naomi's personal point of view. It has not been tested and is not supported by data. Shit." She squealed to a stop at a red light. "This light had better not cost me our reservation or I'm going to sue the mayor."

"You think that will work?

She shook her head. "No. But imagine the social media traffic. I'll make a ton of money. How about this headline? 'Mayor Gyps Gimp in Failed Traffic Management Lawsuit.'"

"Voters won't like it. But aren't you, uh—"

"Using my physical condition to garner attention? You bet your cute little white ass I am."

Naomi took off from the light, swerved across two lanes of traffic, and up into the entrance to the John Hancock building on Michigan Avenue. A valet in a red jacket started toward the car.

"Chariot is in the back," she said.

I got out. The rear hatch was rising when I got there. I lifted her chair out, punched the button to close the hatch, and rolled the expanded chair to the driver's door. The valet was holding it open with a blank expression and wide eyes.

Naomi moved fluidly to the chair, took the parking ticket from the valet, and slipped him a tip.

"Would you please call up to the Signature Room and let them know the Naomi party has arrived? I'd hate to lose our reservation now."

"Yes, Miss. I'll be sure they are ready for you." He pulled a cell phone from his belt and was tapping in a message as I pushed Naomi toward the entrance. We made it through the revolving door by careful maneuvering because Naomi wanted to see if her chair would fit. We reached the elevator bank and rolled into a waiting car with open doors. I pressed the button beside the label for the restaurant. 95th floor.

"Can we breathe that high?" I said.

"Best view in Chicago."

"Earlier, before you started telling me truths, you mentioned a 'secret ingredient.'"

"Yes, I did." She smiled, all elegance and innocence in black with a short leather jacket that had been with the chair.

"And now you have this ingredient?"

"Yes, I do."

She was holding back laughter as we rose past the 40th floor. My ears popped from the pressure change.

"You want me to share two secrets in one night? On our first date?" She smiled up at me.

"Too demanding, huh?"

"Maybe," she said.

Maybe too demanding. Or maybe she wanted a guy who would press forward and not give up.

"I think three," I said.

"Three what?"

The elevator slowed and shuddered to a stop on the 95th floor. The air seemed thin.

"Secrets. I think you should share three secrets."

"Now why would I do that?"

"Because sharing secrets is a key way to grow incrementally closer. But more important—"

"Oh, important. I'm listening."

The doors separated to reveal a mood-lit restaurant overlooking the Chicago skyline.

"I'm buying."

She laughed. "See, you discovered the missing ingredient all by yourself. Now my guard is up so you don't guess too much about me."

A hostess arrived behind a podium.

"You must be Naomi," she said. She was holding menus and wearing a translucent white dress to mid-calf, a black necklace, and tall platform shoes that elevated her to about five feet four inches. Her blonde wispy hair looked shiny, like it had just been brushed a hundred times. "Claude called. We have your table ready." She led us to a table for four but set for two beside curved glass that reached from a 12-foot ceiling down to a red carpeted floor.

"Preference?" I asked.

Naomi nodded toward a chair. I positioned it for her and she did her fluid movements using her arms to make the transfer. I met her eyes and she gave me a slight head shake.

"Is there someplace you could store this for us?" I asked.

"Certainly," the hostess said. She handed us each a menu and rolled the wheelchair away.

"This is beautiful, Tommy. Thanks for thinking of me. I feel almost…average." She smiled. Her hoops twinkled in the colored lights. "It's exciting to finally do something I've been dreaming about from pictures on the web."

"Do you dream often?

She hesitated before answering.

"Is this secret number three?" She pressed her lips together. "I don't know about other people, but I try to dream wide awake and daily about something in my life. Doesn't have to be a big deal thing. Just something to look forward to, to work toward, to make life a little bit better."

"Toyota corporation does that." I smiled. "They call it kaizen. Continuous improvement. Great philosophy."

She smiled back at me then looked at the menu, so I did too. It was filled with exotic appetizers at 95th floor prices.

"These sound huge," she said. "Want to split something?"

"Sure. Anything spelled F-O-O-D is fine with me."

"Oh, you're not going to be helpful at all," she said.

"OK. How about this? Let's try something that I've never had before."

"Aren't you getting adventurous? Like what?"

"Bacon-wrapped jumbo shrimp brie plate with dates. I've eaten each component, but never together. Have you ever wondered about the phrase 'jumbo shrimp?'"

"Oxymoronic. Like lots of people I know. Hey, they drizzle honey on the brie. Let's try it."

The hostess returned, handed me a claim check, and ask if we wanted appetizers. I tilted my menu and pointed.

"Excellent choice," she said. "The shrimp are amazing this month."

I wondered if management handed out notes to quote from for each day, or if she was improvising. She nodded and departed.

"How hard will I have to think?" Naomi said.

"That depends. The next steps might be obvious to you. Or we might have to spend hours in a local library to find it."

"OK, let's start with wine."

The list contained wine from California, Oregon, Italy, France, and a couple of vineyards in Ohio.

"You're from Ohio, aren't you?" she asked.

"That was a secret."

"Ha, ha. Want to try an Ohio wine for fun? Must be pretty good to be on this list."

"Sure. I'm mostly a beer guy. Wines sort of taste—"

"All the same to you." She tilted her Afro with the golden splash and smiled.

"Not so much the same, but equally bad in different ways."

She laughed aloud.

"Sounds like my past three relationships. Let's get a cabernet. I like that word. Makes me think of a fast car."

The waiter arrived, convinced us that an Ohio Cabernet Franc would be quite nice, left to get a bottle, returned, opened it, let us taste it, and placed it on the table along with the cork.

We admired the view out the window of architectural and engineering masterpieces that were all less than 50 years old. Barely a blink of the eye in the history of Homo sapiens.

"Doesn't this all seem unlikely?" I said. "When you think about it, why put so much stuff in one place? Millions of people. Third largest city in the entire United States. Why?"

"Tommy Cuda, private eye. You know why and I know why. Every kid who ever flunked Economics one-oh-one knows why."

I gazed at the gentle curve of her chin and waited for her to continue.

"Every brick you see out there exists because someone, at some point in time, thought they could make a buck by putting it there."

"The spires on the cathedrals?"

"Ha!," she said. "Especially the cathedrals."

"I am tempted to ask how you became cynical. But I'm afraid you'll tell me."

She sipped from the glass floating in her hand.

"Pragmatic. Follow the money. Think about it. If you don't follow the money, what the heck else would you follow?"

I was trying to follow who knew what when about whom.

Our waiter returned with tall leather-covered folding books. They described a hundred different ways to assemble a meal. Fortunately, there was no cheeseburger, so I wasn't tempted to order it. Naomi chose line-caught fish from Alaska. I kept it simple with the chef's special grilled steak. The waiter departed with the folding books.

I gazed at Naomi. My eyes drifted to the skyline, and drifted back.

"Naomi, I'm in a delicate position. I possess a modicum of sensitive information. It has the potential to destroy careers, relationships, maybe even psyches."

She pressed her lips together and frowned.

"Give me hint."

How to explain without explaining?

"I need to understand someone's past in order to understand the present."

She spread brie and honey on a piece of toast no bigger that a potato chip.

"Like a shrink dredging up your childhood to explain why you can't make a decision?"

"Sort of. But more concrete."

"You called me. This is your ball game. Where would you like to start?"

"A hypothetical situation."

"Of course," she mumbled through the toast.

"Male. Thirty-six. Advanced degrees. We know his current name but assume it's fake. We also know his whereabouts."

She nodded while sipping red wine, rocking liquid past her lips with each motion.

"We have photos of him from the Internet."

"And what do we want to know about this gentleman?"

"Real name. Where he went to high school. Did he ever cross paths with a certain individual."

She placed her glass on the table. "Woman?"

I nodded.

"Can't we just ask her?"

"Delicate. The paths crossed a long time ago."

Naomi remained silent while preparing another slice of mini-toast.

"This woman. Do we know where she was in the past?"

"Not yet. I was hoping you would ask her." I smiled.

Her knife stopped moving. She met my eyes with her shiny brown ones. I wondered what people saw in my eyes. And if the impressions we got from eye-gazing were ever accurate.

"Why me?"

"Familiarity. Trust. History."

"I know this person?"

"You work out at her gym," I said.

"Alexxia? What does she have do to with this guy?"

"Don't know for sure. But I have a suspicion."

Naomi spied me over her glass. When she placed it on the table it was two-thirds empty. I reached for the bottle, she nodded. An impish grin formed on her wine-reddened lips.

"Are you trying to get me drunk?"

"Only if you want to," I said.

"Let us observe how the evening develops. Looks to me like you're putting me to work in your spy business."

I grinned. "Only if you want to."

Naomi finished her toast.

"What do you really have?" she asked.

"An invented name. A job. A Cadillac."

"Oh, start with the car."

"Late model. Bright blue metallic sedan. Loads of horsepower."

"Penis mobile?" she asked.

"Hmmm. Maybe he just likes nice cars."

"Oh right. Bright blue. Has no intention of picking up little bronze-skinned girls like me and playing house with them."

"You're the expert," I said.

She laughed. "You private eyes catch on fast. Tell me about the job."

"Psychology professor. Prestigious university. Somewhere between well-known and famous."

She whistled. "Psychology? The man is well-armed for the battle of the sexes. You got a hot one here, Mr. Cuda. Name?"

"Markus Corolla. Doctor Markus Corolla."

"Medical doctor?"

"Ph.D. But his lifestyle doesn't seem poor or hungry."

"Starting with that shiny Cadillac. Is it paid for?"

"Don't know."

"Tsk, tsk. And you call yourself a private eye."

"Business consultant," I said. "Freelance."

The waiter arrived to clear the appetizer plates and let us know that our dinner would be served momentarily.

"OK, business consultant. Let's see the face."

I flipped to the photos I had saved from the University of Chicago website into Leni's phone. Three-piece suit. Excellent lighting. Two poses. One standing in front of a full classroom, one seated beside a podium taking questions at a packed conference. I held the phone out and rested my arm on the table.

Naomi's eye grew wide. She reached out and swiped the two photos left and right. Then used two fingers to zoom in on each in turn.

"You're kidding?" she said.

"Not so far."

"This guy is white as moonlight. I figured a Cadillac man, name like Markus, skirt chaser…" She shrugged.

"Isn't that stereotyping?"

She nodded firmly. "Sure is. But just because a stereotype oversimplifies things, doesn't make it totally wrong."

"Except?"

"Except you bring me a white guy in expensive threads driving a flashy car spouting Freudian id impulses to impressionable young ladies."

"How can we prove that?" I said.

The waiter arrived to place plates, offer fresh ground pepper or grated cheeses, agreed to bring another bottle of wine and left with "Bon appétit."

"Something bothers me," I said.

"About stereotypes?"

"No, about pepper."

Naomi laughed so loud that the four people at the next table turned their heads in unison.

"You drive an antique. Drink beer. Play raunchy guitar. And you worry about pepper?" She sputtered a bit more, then petered out.

"It's not the pepper. It's that they ask me if I want it before I taste the food. Unless I'm a frequent flyer and the chef is perfectly consistent, I won't know until after I've tried it."

"At which point," she said, "it's too late, because the waiter has already trotted off with the pepper grinder."

"Precisely."

"Good argument for condiments on the table." She sliced off a piece of fish and ate it. "So, rich white boy chases young dark meat. This is news?"

I shook my head. "Are you always so eloquent?"

"Only when dining with a rich white boy in a restaurant I have dreamed about since learning it was hiding up here on the ninety-fifth floor."

"I'm nowhere near rich."

She stared into me. "Hmmm. You got a cool car. You have your health. You have cash in your pocket. You have a job. And…you're having a lovely chat with an amazing woman."

I nodded thoughtfully. "Rich barely begins to describe it."

"See. You have to keep perspective. So, give me perspective on this Markus guy. Why did you call me?"

I sliced my steak to buy time. The knife glided through the meat. Hamburger it was not.

"Besides that you're irresistible?" She smiled but had her defenses up. "I thought you might know Alexxia well enough to convince her to talk to me."

"Why would she want to talk to you?"

The waiter returned, convinced himself that we found our dinners acceptable, swapped our candle for a taller one, and took his leave.

"To help Leni."

Naomi settled into a distant quiet for a time. As if her mind were taking a short walk. She stared out at the skyline. She looked around the room from person to person.

I broke the silence. "How's your dinner?"

She gave me a thumbs up but didn't speak.

I waited. I was asking for her help. We would do it on her clock.

Naomi met my eyes across the table.

"Is someone in real trouble?" she asked.

"Seems so. I'm trying to connect the dots."

"And Alexxia is a dot?"

"A big one right in the middle," I said.

"OK. What do you want to know?"

I wanted to tell her about the rape kit. But it seemed to me that Leni should decide who would know.

"Did Alexxia know Markus about twenty years ago?"

"A white college professor with a fake name? How do we even ask? Here, look at this photo. Ever seen this guy?"

"We could try it," I said.

"We need the right name and an old photo," she said, and scooped up scalloped potatoes.

"Do you know if Alexxia went to high school in St. Louis?"

"Sure. We all did. If you live in the right neighborhood, a couple of them are pretty good." She cut the potatoes into bite-size pieces.

"I've never been to Missouri. So please forgive me if this is the wrong question."

She held up her hand, still holding the knife, for me to stop. "I know where you're going." She gestured with the knife toward Leni's smartphone lying face down on the table. "You want to know where the white boy went to school."

"Beautiful and smart too," I said.

"Thanks. Most guys act like the wheelchair is for my brain." She paused in thought. "I can think of two, but there are more. Public, private or both?"

I replayed my brief meetings with Markus.

"Private I think. He has an air of superiority."

"Like the rest of us were put here to ensure he has a nice life?"

I laughed.

She didn't.

"You know a lot of guys like that?"

She nodded. "Most guys, most of the time. I figured it was genetic. A Y-chromosome trait favored for survival by natural selection."

"Remnants of wanting to be alpha dog?" I asked.

She shook her head. "I wouldn't say 'remnants.' Did he grow up in Missouri?"

"Unknown. I didn't notice a regional accent."

"Prep school will train that out of you. And fancy colleges. But we need a name."

"All I have…" An idea formed. "Would it be okay if I make a quick call while we are having dinner?" Her expression suggested it was very not okay. "I'd like to introduce you to my friend Chin. He's the guy who argued for the red leather interior."

She smiled and nodded.

I initiated a video call to Chin's Auto Service, a number I had used so often that I couldn't forget it. The call was answered by a video of Chin sitting in his office telling the caller his business hours and offering the phone numbers of two towing services. Then he suggested that I leave a message and he'd get back to me during business hours. I held the phone between us so Naomi could see and hear the entire conversation.

"Hi Chin, Tommy Cuda. I have a computer problem with your name on it. Time is short. Please text me at this number."

The table of four was looking our way again.

"What is it," she said, "about talking on a cell phone that irritates a bunch of people who are all sitting around talking?"

I listened briefly to a bunch of voices all speaking some form of dramatic nonsense.

"I sat next to a teenage girl on an airplane once. She swiped a credit card and talked on the plane's phone for two hours and barely took a breath."

"Annoying?" she asked.

"For about five minutes. Then I put in earplugs, donned headphones, and listened to music. If I'd had to listen to her chatter I'd probably be in jail for assault of a minor."

"That bad, huh?"

I listened to the room chatter for a few seconds. Usually there was at least one.

"Behind me at the next table. I can't see her, but she's facing our way and carrying on about how the government is banning the wrong books. She has a high-pitched nasal voice that would cause an alley cat to commit suicide."

Naomi laughed.

"The plane girl was worse because her mouth was only a foot from my left ear."

"Ouch," she said.

Leni's phone vibrated on the table. I hoped the message was from Chin and not Oleace.

Cuda! A smartphone? I am disappointed that you have regressed. I am at the office. Was buttoning up some engine work on a hybrid. Call me.

"My friend wants me to call him back."

Naomi dug around in her flat purse with a gold chain and came out with a cinema-size smartphone. She flipped open a little black case and handed me an earbud.

"We can whisper. And no one will hear your friend." She handed me her phone unlocked.

I inserted the earbud and dialed Chin. His office popped up on the screen after two rings, but he wasn't in the frame.

"Tommy? I'm filing. Be there in a minute. You got a new number. What public place?"

"Signature restaurant," I said.

"Marvelous. Does this mean that Tommy Cuda P.I. has a paying client?"

Naomi was listening through the other earbud. She covered her mouth with one hand and laughed.

"Not yet, but there is hope. I am dining with a colleague, attempting to seduce her into helping with my project. We're using her phone."

Chin glided into the frame on a rolling swivel chair. He was wearing the one-piece blue overalls he favored while working on machines."

"Naomi, Chin. Chin, Naomi," I said.

"A pleasure to meet you," Naomi said.

"The pleasure is mine. Perhaps you can reveal why, each time I see Tommy, he manages to be with a beautiful woman?"

Naomi smiled. Maybe her cheeks became rosier.

"Only if you promise not to tell him," she said.

Chin held up the two-finger scouts honor solute.

"It's the muscle car," she said. "A time machine back to the days when fast cars, fast women, and fast adventures were on the table. Those leather seats are so supple. And red—the color of true passion."

"In all modesty, it was I who found and installed the new interior. Arm twisting was required."

"Bravo," she said.

"My grandfather did the rest," I said. "He willed the car to me with explicit instructions to drive it, not sell it."

"A man of immense foresight," she said. "Go Grandpa!"

"You contacted me," Chin said into my right ear. "I surmise that you have a problem that requires my skills."

"A problem," I said softly, "without a clear solution. But I have a proposal."

Chin leaned back in his chair and put both feet on his desk, crossed at the ankle. His favorite listening position.

I kept my voice down so the foursome chattering at the next table wouldn't overhear, letting the earbud microphone do its job.

"Thirty-six year old white male. False name. We want to find out where he went to high school. Possibly a private academy."

"Social media presence?" Chin asked.

"A professional profile on the University of Chicago website."

"The big time," Chin said.

"We think," Naomi whispered, "he spent time around St. Louis."

Chin leaned his head back and stared at the ceiling for half a minute.

I ate my steak.

Naomi pushed a piece of fish around her plate with her fork. The lady I couldn't see switched from banning books to why requiring children to be vaccinated was unconstitutional.

Chin sat upright. "Send me photos, please."

I texted them from Leni's phone.

"Hmmm," Chin said. He tilted his head left and right. He raised his phone to look up at it, then lowered it almost to the floor. "What year of high school are you targeting?"

Naomi lifted her eyes to me.

"Third," I said.

Chin typed. "Give me a minute."

Naomi and I ate in silence. I tried to block out the woman behind me, but my brain had latched onto her voice like an earworm and wouldn't let go.

Leni's phone vibrated.

"First try," Chin said.

Four photos arrived. A young Markus. Face only. Same angle as my originals. He looked like a kid going to his first prom.

"Hairstyle is a guess," Chin said. "Those are common for the era."

"You did this in sixty seconds?" Naomi asked.

"AI apps can do amazing things. We do not know if these results are close to reality. But they are a place to begin, instead of trying to take twenty years off a face with your imagination."

"Thanks, Chin," I said. "What do you think about a facial recognition search of social media?"

"Wasn't much social networking back then. I'll do background, try to find a name change." He leaned forward and looked directly into the camera. "Did you find my surprise?"

I nodded. "Used it a couple of times. Makes for a great conversation starter. And sounds incredible. Thanks."

"Only the best components, my friend. Stop by when you need an oil change. Naomi, it is a pleasure to meet a lady who appreciates my innovations."

We said goodbye. Naomi put her phone and earbuds back into her sparkly black purse. We ate for a bit.

Naomi broke the silence.

"What surprise?"

"Chin did a massive restoration on my car after it was, uh, vandalized. He slipped in something unusual."

"Like a hidden locked compartment under the back seat for condoms?" She laughed with her mouth closed, containing her hilarity in enticing movements of her chest.

"You're very creative," I said.

"Have to be, or life gets boring fast."

"Hard to imagine you ever being boring," I said.

She glanced down and was quiet and shy for a split second.

"I have my moments. So the suspense is killing me. What did Chin do to your car?"

"He mounted a turntable under the floor of the trunk."

"For spinning vinyl?"

I nodded.

"That's madness! How do you change records while you're driving?" She laughed harder. The four at the next table looked our way. "Whoops."

"Only works when parked."

"Hmmm."

"You know. Like at a tailgate party before a big game."

"Oh, I'm sure that's what Chin was thinking. Hey, does it have an auto changer? I saw a turntable dropping records in a museum once."

I shook my head. "One LP at a time."

"How long does that play?"

"The average is twenty-two minutes."

Our eyes met. Even in the restaurant's low mood lighting, hers twinkled.

"Enough for most guys," she said, and choked on her wine as she drank. "Can you reach the turntable from the back seat?"

"You have to get out and go around to the trunk if the divider is in place."

"Tsk, tsk," she said. "Design flaw."

"I think Chin wants me to back the car onto a beach when I reach the Pacific Ocean and play an LP while watching the sunset."

"Wow, that will be tough," she said.

"Sitting on the beach with a beer watching the sun set?"

Her dark hair floated as she shook her head.

"Oh no, deciding what to play."

"Bad time to be indecisive. I had better start planning."

"Or."

She didn't continue.

"Or?" I asked.

"Be impulsive. Flip the proverbial coin of the big-u Universe. At the right moment of time, in the eternal now, an idea will come to you. Play that."

"You read a lot, don't you?"

"I mostly watch videos and documentaries. As you might guess, I sit around a lot." She laughed, so I laughed with her while marveling at her attitude. I had no idea how long she had been using a wheelchair, or why. I considered asking, but it all seemed…irrelevant. And maybe something she didn't care to revisit.

I opened one of the time-reversed images Chin had sent and stood it on the table where we could study it. The waiter arrived to clear plates. We gazed out over the city. Something about a thousand lights in a thousand windows made me wonder how civilization had ever arrived at this particular place. I thought about how high 95 floors was and how our ancestors never looked out at a glowing city at night and to the foreboding dark waters beyond. I briefly pondered the universal human desire to occupy the high ground when all the rivers and good food resided in the valley.

"You know what we have to do, don't you?" Naomi said.

Before I could answer a cart filled with thousands of calories in a dozen colors arrived.

"You first," she said.

I pointed.

"One triple chocolate cake," the waiter said.

"Triple?" I asked.

"Cake, frosting, special whipped cream. Blended to meld into the perfect mouth or…gy."

Naomi snickered and pointed with the index finger of her left hand. I noticed that she wasn't wearing a wedding band. There was no reason for me to have that thought, but I had it anyway.

"The first ring," the waiter said, "is four kinds of berries, surrounded by vanilla ice cream, encased in a warm pastry ring. Whipped cream optional."

"Yes," she said.

He rolled his cart away.

"What do we have to do?" I asked.

She pointed at the young Markus. "Somewhere there is a yearbook with a class photo of a guy who looks just like that."

"Somewhere is a lot of places to look. Can we narrow it down?"

Naomi gazed at the skyline for a few seconds.

"Ah," she said.

I waited.

She nodded to herself. "How much time do we have?"

"I have no idea."

The desserts arrived in the hands of a blonde woman wearing an apron over an elegant blue dress.

"Who's the chocolate?" she asked.

I raised my left hand.<

She placed a plate in front of me containing a cube of chocolate with frosting between the layers but none on top. The ring of fruit went before Naomi. The woman pulled a silver canister the size of a lunch thermos from her apron, shook it, inverted it, and covered my cake with a mountain of brown whipped cream until the cake was invisible. She then switched canisters and made circles around Naomi's pastry.

"Bon appétit," she said, and turned toward the kitchen.

"I hope you're hungry," Naomi said.

We each tried our whipped cream first. Naomi missed her mouth slightly and licked it off her upper lip. Mine was super smooth, like eating a chocolate cloud.

"Yum," she said. "I have an idea."

"Is whipped cream involved?" I asked.

Her head tilted down, eyes up. "That too. But I was thinking about our mission."

I waited to see where our mission was going to take us.

"Let's go ask Alexxia where she went to high school and who she hung out with. That will narrow our search to a prime target area."

Naomi ordered tea. I followed her lead. The hot liquid enhanced the chocolate. Naomi ate berries, purposely sensually if I had a vote. We gave up and boxed what was left, transferred to the wheelchair, and felt our full stomachs flop on the 95-story ride down. The valet had her red machine waiting. I held the wheelchair while Naomi made the transfer to the passenger's seat, insisting that I drive. I put the chair in the hatchback and tipped the valet.

He nodded and said, "A beautiful lady. Have a good evening, sir."

I slid in behind the wheel and almost broke a kneecap on the steering column. I slid the seat back as far as it would go, then stared at the levers on the wheel.

"Ignore those," she said. "The pedals all work too."

"OK. Where to?"

"Shey's Gym."

"Tonight?"

"Of course."

It would be a long drive, so I stopped at Shianti's to switch cars. Rolling west in the Barracuda, I thought about Leni at the Nature Incognito retreat. It ended Monday night. Had Prof found out anything yet?

"It's not like we have to stop for food," Naomi said with a laugh.

"Will Alexxia be there?"

"Depends. If the place is busy, she'll be there keeping an eye on it. If it's not busy, she might have gone home."

"We could call her," I said. "Send a photo electronically."

I felt Naomi's eyes on me.

"Not the best way to get information?" I said.

"You're the private dick. What do you think?"

"There's nothing like face-to-face."

"Yes. Do you have a good cover story?"

"No."

"We could try the truth," she said.

"I've heard that works sometimes."

Her laughter filled the car with joy.

We reached Shey's Gym well before midnight. Sitting on the sidewalk across the street, we still didn't have a plan.

"Improvise?" I offered.

Naomi stared into the gym. "Sometimes that's the best way."

Inside, a dozen people were sweating into expensive, well-fitting, colorful athletic attire.

"Dress to be seen," I said. "I feel like a pauper."

"Imagine how I feel," she said. "They'll think I'm trying to show off."

"Wait until you tell them about an exclusive restaurant on the ninety-fifth floor of a skyscraper."

She punched my arm.

Alexxia entered the gym from the back carrying a dumbbell the size of a football in each hand. She saw us and waved by slightly raising one dumbbell. We headed her way.

"Hi Naomi, your skinny friend looking to join the gym?" She smiled broadly.

"Alexxia, this is my new friend, Tommy Cuda. He's staying with Prof. He helped me workout yesterday."

"I was wondering who you dragged in here, girl. Nice to meet you, Tommy."

We shook hands business style. I was confident she could have crushed my fingers, but she didn't.

"Pleasure to meet you. You have an impressive gym here."

"Thanks. Took a decade to get it this far. Hardest part was to convince these steroid-hyped testosterone lumps to stop fighting with each other over who has the biggest whatever."

"An impressive feat," I said. "Have you considered running for president?"

"That lousy job?" She paused, thoughtful. "Although being surrounded by those buff secret service types might be fun."

"You can't date the staff, Alexxia," Naomi said. "Imagine the scandal."

"Impeached in the first week," Alexxia said, with a laugh.

Naomi glanced at me and back to Alexxia. "Can we talk for a minute?"

A shadow descended over Alexxia's eyes. She might trust Naomi, but she sure didn't trust me.

"The three of us?"

"If it's okay with you," I said.

"I won't know until we start talking." She gestured with her head without taking her eyes off me—like I was a Russian spy. She led us through the back door into a storeroom, out a side door, down a hallway with green linoleum and a flickering LED, a bulb I thought was supposed to last forever, and into a 10 by 10 office containing a metal desk, a dark gray laptop and two chairs that made me think of an interrogation room.

"Pardon the accommodations. I don't get many visitors. All the selling goes on out front." She looked to Naomi. "What's up?"

"Lenore," Naomi said.

Alexxia was quiet. Her eyes distant.

"We don't talk much since she went off to that fancy school. Busy student and all. She having man trouble?"

I had planned to keep my mouth shut, but Naomi remained silent, so I had to fill the space.

"Why would you say that?" I said.

We waited until Alexxia decided what to say to the white boy who had just arrived on the scene.

"That girl has had man trouble ever since—" She glanced at the wall. Her eyes found a framed photo of a girl holding a baby. "Ever since she knew what a man was."

"Definitely man trouble," I said. "Maybe worse."

"I told her and told her. Only thing worse than a man is drugs. Combining them can be the end of a person."

She looked at Naomi, then at me.

"Have a seat," she said to me. Then she sat down in front of the laptop. I took the guest chair. Naomi rolled up beside me so we were both facing Alexxia. The wall behind Alexxia was covered with posters of Olympic weightlifters. All black. All female.

"Which is it?" she asked.

"Maybe both," I said.

"That poor kid. So much talent. So much ambition. So little patience for the endless steps of hard work necessary to build anything useful." She spoke to the laptop. "What can I do now that I haven't already done a hundred times?"

"Tell us who her father is," I said.

"She doesn't have a father."

The room was cool and quiet. Grunting from the gym reached us.

"Literally? Like an anonymous donor?" I ventured.

Alexxia grinned slightly. "Something like that."

"Do you know where he is now?" Naomi asked.

"Don't know. Don't care."

"Is he white?" I asked.

Alexxia hesitated. But only for a moment. She held up her arm.

"You could guess that by how light she is compared to me."

"Meet him at school?" I asked.

"No. Well. Sort of. I was a cheerleader. Damn good one too." Her face hardened. "Long ago. Long time ago." She stopped.

"Cheerleader?" Naomi said. "I bet that was fun."

"Go Wildcats," she said, and laughed.

"Did you get to travel?" I asked.

"Oh yeah. We performed at every game, rain or shine. Near froze my booty off in that skimpy little outfit."

"Did Lenore follow in your footsteps?" I asked.

"Cheerleading? No way. She's too busy tapping at a stupid smartphone to do anything real with her life. They should call those 'dumb-fuck phones' with what they do to a person."

"Funny you should say that," Naomi said. "Tommy doesn't like dumb-phones either."

Alexxia looked me up and down. "You're young to be a Luddite."

"I prefer to view it as enlightened. I don't think the Buddha would have carried a dumb-phone."

Alexxia laughed, releasing some of the tension in the tiny room.

"Closest I ever got to nirvana," she said, "was the last four rows of a concert. "Buddha with a smartphone. You are too funny."

"Thanks for talking with us," I said.

"Sore subject for me. I don't allow myself to think about it anymore. I've wasted enough time imagining alternate paths in my life. It's over and done. Can't change it now." She stared into me. "Life's a one-way street you know. Don't you ever forget that."

"Thanks," I said, forcing myself not to think of my past.

Alexxia walked with us to the front door without saying another word about Lenore, her father, or the past.

One-way street.

No rain outside. But an abundance of clouds.

"Look at that," Alexxia said. "How old you think that heap across the street is? It looks like a Tonka toy, all square and edgy."

I gazed through a window painted on the inside with the image of a weight machine.

"About nineteen sixty-five," I said. "I bet it's got a Hemi."

Alexxia's eyes widened, brightening her face.

"That yours? I figured you for a hepcat with modern wheels."

"My grandfather was a hepcat. I'm trying to get a little to rub off on me."

Alexxia nodded, apparently agreeing with my goal.

"Speaking of rubbing," Naomi said. "Don't you owe me a shoulder massage?"

Alexxia laughed outright. "Don't let her get away with that. She tries it on all the new guys."

"Not all," Naomi protested.

"OK. Only the ones that can walk and chew gum."

Alexxia and I laughed, but Naomi pouted.

We said our goodbyes. Naomi remained quiet until were were situated in the Cuda and the Hemi was idling.

"I'm not that bad," she said.

"I'd be honored to give you a massage. But first, a treasure hunt?"

"Where?" she said.

"A library that carries local papers. Do you know when Leni's birthday is?"

"Um…June, I think. Around the beginning of summer."

I said, "Football."

CHAPTER 29

Naomi and I cruised to her place in silence, each of us lost in our thoughts. Every few minutes, she would breathe out a long deep sigh that made me think of giving up on civilization and going to live deep in the Amazon forest. But then without warning she would smile. I wondered what was going on inside her head, then remembered the old adage: Be careful what you wish for.

I pulled to the curb in front of her high-rise and turned off the engine. It stumbled to a stop.

"Thank you for helping me on such short notice," I said.

She met my eyes. "My pleasure." Hesitation. "Did you find what you were looking for?"

"Not yet. Tomorrow, the hunt for details begins. If I can find an open library."

"School libraries will be open. It's cram for college entrance exams season. Some stay open 24 hours so students have a quiet place to study."

"Study all night? What a concept." I smiled.

"We pushed for more study space for years. Teachers expect everyone to have a nice, quiet, supportive environment at home."

"Not reality for some," I said, remembering futile attempts to study while my roommates played euchre.

"For most," she said. "TVs blaring. Siblings arguing. Mom wants help, complaining: 'Why do you have your nose in a book all the time?'"

"The voice of experience?"

"Oh yeah. And that doesn't even begin to address the so-called friends who want to party every day."

"And rock and roll all night?" I said.

"Been there?"

I recalled my days at Oberlin College. "On both sides of the table."

Naomi considered me, her eyes scanning my soul.

"I see it. First you have to sit around in solitude and learn to play the guitar. But then, once you reach a certain level—"

"You spend all of your free time in clubs playing high-energy music."

"So everyone else can party," she said. "Kind of a Jekyll and Hyde existence. No wonder so many musicians use drugs."

The word drugs pulled me back to my treasure hunt.

"I guess we should get some sleep before the hunt begins."

Her eyes held mine. "Are you sending me a coded message?"

I shook my head slowly. "I just feel tired."

"Sugar crash from triple chocolate cake," she said, and laughed. "What time are you picking me up for breakfast?"

"Naomi, I've imposed on you far too much. I don't expect you to sit in a library and scan old newspapers."

She stared at me for what felt like back to back commercials on YouTube.

"So, you're cutting me out of the action just as things get interesting? You know it's not nice to leave a girl hanging."

"I figured you have better things to do."

"Isn't that my decision?"

Her eyes didn't let up.

I nodded slowly. "I would appreciate your help. You're a local. You know useful stuff."

"You bet I do, Tommy." Her smile reached all the way to her eyes.

"How's eight o'clock?"

"Perfect," she said. "Dress library casual."

I retrieved her chair from the trunk, held the car door open while she refused assistance and made the transfer, then pushed her through the main entrance to a bank of elevators whose shiny black doors reflected us together in the hallway. I pushed the up button.

"Let's say goodbye here, Tommy. My nosey neighbors have loose tongues."

"Don't like seeing you with a white guy?"

"Late on a Saturday night? Rolling me towards my apartment? Oh, no. They think that because I can't walk, I should become a nun."

I squatted so our eyes would be at the same level.

"Thanks for helping me out tonight."

Her smile emerged slowly.

"Thank you for a lovely dinner. Now I know why the Signature way up on the ninety-fifth floor is so popular."

She reached out with one hand and took hold of the lapel of my sport coat, then pulled me toward her until her lips were an inch from my left ear.

She whispered, "I owe you ninety-five kisses, Tommy. Here's the first one."

She leaned away for a moment, then placed her lips against mine in slow motion. Soft. Warm. Moist. Heat rushed up my back.

She pulled away.

The elevators door spread apart.

"Goodnight, Tommy Cuda." She rolled herself into the elevator car. The doors glided closed as she waved to me over her left shoulder.

I remained squatted, breathing slowly. My lips recalled every sensation of the past thirty seconds. Then I rose slowly, my heart rate above normal. Without meaning to, I wondered where those next 94 kisses would take me.

◇

I drove to Prof's place in the middle of a hazy fatigue dreamscape. Alcohol, sugar, and caffeine vied for dominance in my brain. I didn't touch Leni's room. Prof might want to examine it. I checked my phone service. Nothing. No Leni, no Prof, no Shianti. Was nothing happening? Unlikely. But maybe with Shianti at the Pig and Prof working, there wasn't much to talk about.

I took off my boots and jeans and laid back on the bed where I had spent my first night in St. Louis. The night Leni had snuggled up against my back.

Three nights ago?

I double-checked Leni's phone. Her fans were impatient. They wanted to chat. They wanted private time. They wondered if she had quit Oleace. Or been fired. A few offered support if she was going through hard times. Hohoman25 asked if she was okay and getting help? He advised, 'You don't have to go through this alone.'

I replied to each message carefully, using the emojis that Leni favored—especially the dancing hot dog. Then I kicked back on the bed, glanced at 2:07 A.M. and drifted toward sleep.

Chirping birds woke me at 5:40, shivering from being too dumb to crawl under the blankets. I set an alarm for 7:20, pulled the covers over me, and hid my eyes under the edge of a spare pillow. Before I knew what had happened, the alarm was chirping along with the birds.

I called my service. No messages.

I showered, shaved, and was rolling toward Naomi's apartment at ten till eight. She was full of surprises and I'd bet breakfast that she was punctual in a land of people texting "Sorry, I'm running late" like a mantra.

When I pulled up, she was parked in her wheelchair on the sidewalk in front of her apartment building looking at her wrist—even though she wasn't wearing a watch. It was 7:58 A.M. As I was walking around the trunk to open the door for her she said, "Get stuck in traffic?"

"Haha. I'm early."

Golden morning sunlight splashed on her face as she exited the shadows of the high-rise.

"Early bird catches the worm," she said.

"Ugh. Please. Not before breakfast."

Sections of yellow and orange in her black yoga pants glowed in the sun. Her multi-colored French-cut T-shirt appeared tie-dyed, but had probably been printed by an AI trained on Woodstock posters. A yellow sweater that matched the yoga pants was draped over her shoulders.

"You're looking sunny today," I said.

"You mean as opposed to Tommy Monochrome?"

"Makes doing laundry easy."

She shook her head. "No slave to fashion you."

"I have a red leather interior."

"Only because Chin twisted your arm. Maybe twisted both arms."

"I was sort of attached to the original black."

"Black in a…what do you call it?"

"Turbo-bronze metallic. Black was the only interior option in sixty-five."

"Turn right," she said. "Wait until you see what I found."

Naomi guided me through town like a nav system.

Get ready to turn right.

OK. Right at this light.

Get in the left lane.

Hurry, this is your turn.

I stopped in a parking lot facing a coin-operated meter. The two-story building of beige brick had black steel bars over the windows.

"We're visiting a prison?"

She threw a soft punch into my arm. "It's a historic building. The bars are to protect the precious contents from evil people."

"What evil people?"

"The kind who would steal priceless documents that carry the stories of ancient tribes to us."

"This is a library?"

She nodded vigorously. "Wait 'til you see the third floor."

The access ramp to a building constructed in the 19th century was around the back, cleverly disguised as an inclined walk through a garden maze. Once inside, the unmistakable smell of dusty old books pervaded the space. Naomi studied a directory on a silver stand and guided us to a hallway where an elevator had been grafted onto an outside wall of the building.

"Imagine, Tommy. If we came here in 1890, you'd have to carry me up the steps."

Over a hundred and thirty years ago. "Do you think we would have been educated enough to read books?"

She frowned. "You maybe. White male living in the North. Not me. Back then, no one wanted a child of, uh, mixed ancestry." She hesitated. "I guess there's been a lot of progress in a few generations, hasn't there?"

"Seems slow. But in the span of all human history, progress is being made."

"Here," she said.

Gold block letters bolted to the wall above double doors declared THE ARCH CAFÉ. We entered a room that would seat 50 people in a clinch, but there were only six scattered at tables along the right wall. It reminded me of a high school cafeteria except the food smelled good. It also had a row of tiny cubicles right out of the Steelcase catalog across the back. Each had two chairs, a table, a computer, and a microfiche reader.

"Microfiche?" I said.

"The world existed before computers," Naomi said. "Check out that corner."

Behind a diagonal desk sat a woman wearing a librarian costume: black-framed glasses, severe hairstyle tight to her head, mid-calf skirt, black shoes with thick heels.

"She's a research assistant and will bring materials directly to our table."

"I hope the food is good," I said.

Naomi reached up and punched my arm in nearly the same spot as last time. Then she selected an empty cube between a tall, narrow window and the assistant. I woke the computer. It said it was running Linux, had access to the library's digital archives, and would I please enter my name and search. I typed Tommy Cuda and a search for a high school friend who was 35 or 36 years old and had recently had a heart attack and passed away. Then I moved a chair out of the way for Naomi.

A food menu popped up on the computer screen. It took an order of quiche and coffee for Naomi and blueberry pancakes and bacon for me, plus two orange juices. I checked the box for crispy on the bacon.

Ready in six minutes.

"They've updated this place from the nineteenth century," I said.

"Website says they got a Google grant to invest in 'library access people will actually use.'"

A text message popped onto the screen.

"Hi, I am Kristen, your library bot. The lady in the corner is Dorothy. If I need help, I consult Dorothy. Please tell me more about your friend?"

"Dorothy," I said to Naomi, gesturing toward the woman in the corner.

Naomi smiled.

I held a key down and spoke to the computer. "Hi, Kristen, it's nice to meet you. I am interested in the football schedule for a high school team in the St. Louis area whose mascot is a Wildcat."

Text of my words appeared on the screen as I spoke. The avatar of a dark-haired female bot named Kristen spun.

"William McKinley High School. What year?" Kristen asked.

"Twenty and twenty-one years ago," I said.

The avatar turned away like she was walking down a hallway to find my book.

A white woman with Dolly Parton blonde hair arrived pushing a silver cart. She checked a printout and placed the quiche in front of Naomi.

"You don't look like a quiche guy," she whispered.

"Coffee," Naomi said with a smile.

"Everything else," I said.

The woman nodded. "You're for sure an everything kind of guy. Ever eat the kitchen sink?" She guffawed a little, then gestured toward the screen. "Tell Kristen if you need anything else. The strawberry pie is excellent if you're in the mood." She gestured again. "Kristen can will your credit card when you're ready." She stared straight at me. "Don't get sneaky and try to leave without paying. It already took your photo and our security boys like to mess with crooks."

"Thanks for the tip," I said.

Naomi snickered under her breath until the waitress disappeared into the kitchen through a pair of swinging doors.

"Must be your honest face," she said, then burst out laughing. When she stopped, she tasted her quiche and declared it excellent.

Two schedules appeared on the screen, twelve games per season, home games in bold. Same opponents both years, just in a different order.

Naomi leaned in for a closer look.

"One chance in twelve," she said.

"Eight point three percent," I said.

She stopped chewing and stared at me.

I pressed and held a key. "Thanks Kristen. Can you show demographics of each of the twelve schools?"

"Sorry, Tommy. I do not have that information available."

"Kristen, can you show the county where each school is located?"

"County?" Naomi said. "What do counties have to do—"

County names appeared beside each school. Some were in the same county, so there were only seven unique names.

"Any idea what's where?" I asked Naomi.

She sliced quiche with her fork, sipped coffee, and gazed at the screen.

"I don't think in counties," she said. "Are they important?"

"They contribute dollars to education. Usually through property taxes."

"You said he's a professor," she said.

I nodded and ate a piece of pancake soaked in melted butter and maple syrup.

She placed her black cup on the table. A picture of the library building was printed on it in gold. The building looked a lot better on the cup.

"So," she said. "We want a white-boy prep school."

"Isn't that racial profiling?"

She shrugged. "Call it what you want. I'm going with the probabilities. The math says this guy did not attend a ninety-eight percent black school in the heart of the ghetto."

"Unlikely," I agreed.

"Precisely." She slowly and precisely, poked quiche into her mouth.

"Kristen, tell me which presidential candidate each county voted for in the last presidential election."

The bot turned away, making me think of animated emojis.

"Clever," Naomi said.

The results popped up followed by a reference to the data source: a dot gov domain with a long name.

"Two red," Naomi said. "That narrows it down."

"We're making massive assumptions."

"Are we now?' She smiled.

"OK," I said. "Following probabilities."

"We might find nothing. But at least we're looking."

"Want to do more math?" I asked.

She sipped her coffee before answering.

"I love math. It's like magic. You push symbols around on a piece of paper like a demented Tetris junkie and WHAM-O! you can predict the future."

I asked Kristen for the distance between the two red schools and the Wildcats. Three miles and twenty-three miles. I looked at Naomi.

"Ease of access matters to high school kids," she said. "Just across the river makes it easy to sneak off and be alone."

"Brothers of St. Francis it is. Now what?" I asked.

"We ask Kristen for pie. I need to fuel my workouts." She smiled.

The same lady came with the silver cart to deliver two slices of strawberry pie covered with whipped cream. She cleared the breakfast dishes. "You young folk took my advice. Most kids just ignore the dumb old lady working as a waitress in a library. But you'll see." She rolled her cart away.

"Nice lady," I said.

"Unless the pie is stale and she gets paid extra to pawn it off on unsuspecting strangers," Naomi said.

"Cynical."

"Realistic. We live in a capitalist's paradise where profit trumps everything. Especially the truth."

I tasted the pie. It was amazing but I made a bad-taste face. Naomi paused with her fork in midair, then pushed it into her mouth.

"You're lucky I can't kick you under the table," she said.

I chuckled and enjoyed more pie.

"What's next, Mr. Cynical?" she said.

"We visit the target school. You said the library might be open."

"I was thinking of public schools obeying government regulations. Not so sure about the Brothers of St. Francis on a Sunday."

"Lord's Day. Day of rest?"

"Or." Her eyes locked on my face. "Day of priests molesting altar boys in the name of the Father, Son, and Holy Ghost."

I shook my head slowly. "Definitely not cynical."

"Imagine your shin being kicked by the toe of my sneakers."

"Ouch." I rubbed my leg with the palm of my hand. "Let's go visit." I began to stand, but a fresh thought stopped me. "Give me a minute." I strolled over to the corner where Dorothy was reading a hardcover book whose name was obscured by her hand.

"Hello, Dorothy. I'm Tommy."

She smiled ever so slightly.

"When a person legally changes their name, what happens to the old name?"

"Birth certificates are issued by state governments. Then there is the federal registry of social security numbers. So procedures vary." She captured me with beautiful brown eyes behind her thick black frames. "That complicates things for librarians."

"Does the person get all new numbers?"

"Generally, yes. Otherwise they would be easy to find. And, not to be judgmental, but not being found is often the reason people change their names."

"If I have a person's new name, how do I find the old one?"

She straightened and blinked, then smiled. "Usually it's the other way around. My experience suggests you find someone who knew them before the name change."

"That's tricky without knowing the original name."

She shook her head slowly, like a teacher sinking into despair that a student will never learn.

"Not anymore. Thousands have contributed DNA to online databases. It's easy to find almost anyone. Or their sibling, or parents, or cousins in Miami." She smiled. Her eyes sparkled. "Sorry, old song that I like. It's as if we have all carved our initials into an ancient pyramid that reaches from here to Mars."

"We're all connected," I said.

"Very philosophical. But yes, we are. Only the connections used to be invisible and undiscoverable."

"Sounds sort of—"

"Spooky," she said. "Nothing is private anymore. Not even our genes."

Spooky was right. "Thank you for the tip, Dorothy."

"My pleasure. Kristen handles most of my job. I'm really here for the personal touch when needed."

I flagged down a human to pay the check with cash and we headed for the car. We were riding down the elevator staring out at trees when Naomi broke the silence.

"What did she say?"

"Old names aren't connected to new ones. Best option is websites that do DNA analysis."

She nodded. "Good idea."

"We don't have DNA in hand."

"I'll think about how to get some."

"Did I detect a twinkle in your eyes?" I said.

"Maybe one eye."

Naomi played turn-by-turn navigation girl and guided us to a narrow parking lot between the Brothers of St. Francis school buildings and the lacrosse and soccer fields. The school was in a town of houses built on acre lots that created open, green space everywhere. There were no other cars.

However, there was a lone electric bicycle locked to a curved rack along the side of the yellow brick building.

"Looks dark inside," she said.

"I vote door and window alarms. Motion detectors."

"Hmmm," she said.

"I'll go take a closer look," I said.

"Take me with you. I don't want to be sitting here alone when a cop pulls up and asks what I'm doing."

I hesitated, trying to determine which cop scenario would be worse.

"Let's go, Tommy. This is one of those time is of the essence situations."

I pushed her along a concrete sidewalk that ended at a pair of ten-foot doors. I tugged gently. They were indeed locked.

Naomi pulled my ear down to her lips and whispered, "Let's find the library."

We circumnavigated the building with Naomi rolling silently along the sidewalk under her own power and me working close to the building, occasionally pulling out a weed near the brick wall, pretending to be the gardener. With each squat I took a good look into the low windows that let light into a floor that was half-buried like the living room in a garden apartment. As I turned a corner that brought the football field into view a humming sound caught my attention. I placed my ear against the window. A machine was running inside. And someone would be running it.

That electric bicycle.

I gestured to Naomi and snuck around and checked the door closest to the rack. The left side was locked. But the right swung outward toward the parking lot. As it did, the humming grew louder. Naomi pulled up beside me and peered through the open door.

"Give me five minutes," she said. "If I'm late, come rescue me." She pushed a metal rectangle and the door swung all the way outward like a welcoming arm.

"What are you going—" I asked to her back as she rolled silently through the door and down a hallway covered in gray tiles with the image of a medieval shield on each one. She stopped at an intersection and pointed at a column of black plastic signs on the wall. She tapped the last one.

LIBRARY

I gave her two thumbs up and checked the time on a white-faced wall clock with a sweep secondhand.

10:10 A.M.

I didn't think she could do much in five minutes, but her plan wasn't up for discussion.

Time is of the essence.

I put my ear against the glass door. The humming continued. While considering what kind of machine would make that sound, the answer appeared from the floor of the hallway Naomi had just traversed. The floor was shiny. So shiny that I could read the reflection of the LIBRARY sign on its surface.

Someone was working over the weekend when the school was closed to polish floors.

Naomi came flying around the corner, wheeling the chair at a frantic pace. I opened the door so she could blast through to the outside. She panted out words between quick inhales.

"Found the library. But the door is locked."

"The bicycle rider is in there waxing floors," I said.

She nodded. "I know. We have to get the door open."

I pulled out my wallet and extracted two small tools that looked like crooked metal toothpicks.

"Chin gave me these as a private eye gift. But I've only ever practiced in his garage."

"Trial by fire," she said. "Here's the plan. You pick the lock, follow me in, duck out of sight, and keep watch. I'll search."

"That would be breaking and entering a government building."

"The Brothers are private. And we're going to burgle it too. But we have an emergency trying to save Leni. The judge will go easy on us. Let's go!"

She pressed the square button to swing the door open.

Her chair rolled in near silence. I crept along behind her, my shoes living up to their name. She turned left. The humming grew louder. She turned again. It grew softer.

She stopped.

A half-glass door had a LIBRARY plaque just below the glass.

"Go, go, go," she whispered.

I slid the first tool in along the bottom edge of the keyhole and positioned the second tool on top of it, the jagged edges pointing up.

"Try the knob," I whispered.

It wouldn't turn.

I wiggled the top tool up, down, in, out, feeling for pins.

"Now," I whispered.

Nothing.

I recalled what Chin had told me about imagining the inside of the lock being touched by my picks and tried again. The lock turned in her hand, twisting the tools in my fingers.

We stepped in.

Overhead lights automatically came on, spilling white everywhere, including out the door into the hallway.

Naomi whispered, "Shit."

I pressed every switch in a row of eight beside the door. The lights went off on number six.

"Duck," she said.

I dove for the door and pressed my back tight against it. Naomi wheeled herself into the stacks.

The humming grew louder. And louder. I could feel the throbbing of the polishing wheel through the floor. The edge of the wheel rattled against the other side of the door.

It felt like two hours, but the wall clock only registered twelve minutes. The sound from the polisher was down to a distance thrumming. Naomi emerged from the darkness with a pile of books on her lap.

She said, "Let's get out of here fast."

We retraced our silent steps to the door nearest the bicycle and verified there wasn't a cop waiting at the Barracuda. Then I pushed Naomi down the sidewalk fast with her clutching the booty to her chest.

Door. Chair. Trunk. Fire up the Hemi. Move. Move. Move.

I didn't start breathing normally until we were five miles from the Brothers' school.

Naomi hummed a melody I didn't know.

"You okay?" I asked.

"Super OK. We were like Tom Cruise in Mission Impossible."

I laughed.

She glanced at me, then laughed too.

"It sort of felt like that," I said.

"My heart stopped when those lights came on," she said, breathless. "I could hear some fat, smelly cop saying, 'The jig is up!'"

"The jig?"

"Yeah. Game over."

"Haven't heard that in a long time."

"You don't watch enough movies," she said. "Especially old ones. You ever watch old movies? I find it fascinating to watch decade by decade. Skirts get shorter. Violence is more graphic. More real. Directors evolving the art form."

"Sounds like studying musicology," I said.

"Exactly. People talk about Bach and Beethoven. Or all those painters with the different styles. But most people think of old movies as worthless junk. My friends are all into the latest action flick. Not me. History is important. To me, I mean. As a means of dealing with life."

"That's how I feel about the blues. It transcends generations. And geography. And cultures."

"Can you define it?" she said.

"Uh. It has its own forms and harmonic structures. And themes of loss, including the loss of relocating."

"What do you like about it the most?"

"The way it makes me feel. One with fellow humans. All of us experiencing the same heartbreak. Sharing the pain of the human condition."

"Wow," she said. "Don't stop."

"I like the way blue players who have never met can walk on a stage together, and through a shared understanding of the genre spontaneously create unforgettable music with nothing written down or a single rehearsal."

"That's amazing," she said.

"Jazz players take it to super complex levels."

"And?" she said.

"I get to meet great people who come together with respect for the music and each other. People like Jake, who probably wouldn't even talk to me if it wasn't for the blues."

"And the guitar," she said. "Don't forget those six strings."

"Any instrument can play the blues."

"I know. I just like the guitar. Those flying fingers. And the facial expressions. You can't play electric guitar without your face."

I laughed. "You've noticed that, huh?"

"For sure. It's part of the instrument."

"I hadn't thought of it that way." I gestured to the books still in her arms. "What did you find?"

"Facebooks," she said. "Every high school has them for alumni. There must have been fifty in a row. Conveniently for me, on the bottom shelf."

"You stole their books?"

"Borrowed."

"Won't they miss them?"

"I pushed the rest together so there's no visible gap. No one will notice unless someone needs one of these three years." She grinned. "I took three just to be safe."

No one had called on the burner. No Prof. No Leni, who was possibly out of cellular range at the retreat. I had been so focused on finding out about Markus, I was neglecting the primary objective. I was also doing a lousy job of being Sally on Oleace.

I pulled to the curb. "Are you hungry?"

"Only a little. But I'm thirsty. Burgling is hard work."

I fed a parking meter and wheeled Naomi to a corner Starbucks that seemed more spacious than I remembered them being.

"Why is this place so huge?" I asked.

"Location. Today is Sunday, an off day for a downtown hot spot. On a business day, we'd be standing in line for twenty minutes."

We ordered Grandé Americanos and almond scones. Naomi paged through our stolen merchandise while I answered messages from:

Loverboy300

Bandit400

Showme101

Trampluvr69

Hohoman25 asked how he could help. Good question. If this ended up in court, could he testify as a virtual eyewitness?

I called Tina, but got the bot. The first message was from Braden.

"Kelsey. I've got something. Stop by."

He probably meant Monday morning with donuts. No, he might be working now. I replayed the call. It was two hours old.

The second message was Prof whispering.

Shianti is a crazy cat. Tommy, drive to these coordinates. Come in from the east with your lights off. And hurry. We got ourselves a situation.

I replayed the message and handed the phone to Naomi. She wrote down the coordinates beside the facebook page numbers she had been recording on a napkin.

The third message was from Tina saying that she wouldn't be in until noon on Monday and leaving a number where she could be reached.

The fourth message was more whispering from Prof.

"Tommy, bring Narcan. At least two. More if you can get it."

"What's Narcan?" I asked.

Naomi frowned, tapped her plus-size phone, and read.

"An opioid inhibitor. Can reverse an overdose." She studied my face. "Why?"

"Prof wants me to bring it to those coordinates."

She looked my way but didn't speak.

I drank my Americano and frowned as I imagined what was happening to Leni.

"Tommy…what's going on?" Naomi asked in a thin voice.

I shrugged. "Don't know. When I left to meet you, Prof was at Shianti's apartment looking at maps."

"If he needs Narcan," her shaking head made waves in her afro, "it's serious."

She rotated an open facebook toward me. The page was covered with inch-high thumbnails of an entire class. She pointed with a sparkling pink fingernail.

"Michael Carnes," she said.

She placed Chin's AI age-reversed pictures on either side of the photo. His hairstyle was longer than our estimates. He had a crooked tooth on the upper left that Markus didn't. And the photographer's lighting had washed out details of his forehead.

"A solid maybe," I said.

She checked the notes on her napkin and flipped pages to a half-page color photo of the football team. Everyone, including both coaches, was white. Not so unusual. There were lots of all-white schools. Whites were, after all, over 60% of the population of the Unites States of America. Just not in Missouri.

Naomi didn't point this time.

I pulled the book closer, studied Chin's pictures, then scanned the team.

"Middle of the second row," I said.

She read from her notes. "Sixth from the left."

I checked. "Yep. That's him." I read the caption for the second row and counted six names.

"Michael Carnes," I said. "M.C. Just like Markus Corolla."

She motioned for me to turn pages. "Thirty-four."

The back section of the book was filled with candid photos of events like bonfires, roadside clean-up days, Toys for Tots drives, homecoming.

Homecoming.

Photos of after game celebration on the field. Two teams mingling. Michael Carnes standing on the sidelines with four cheerleaders.

"Is he signing autographs?" I asked.

"Or getting someone's phone number."

"But—"

"Check out the cheerleaders."

I did. "They're all from McKinley."

"Yes they are," she said.

"The Brothers of St. Francis played McKinley at homecoming that year?"

"You private-eye guys are masters of observation."

I studied faces. Hers was smooth and dark and youthful and full of the smile of an unlimited future.

"Third from the right. With her hand on his—"

"Today that would be assault." She laughed. Then became serious in an instant. "Sorry. I have no idea what Alexxia went through, so I shouldn't joke." She looked at the book. Then at me. Then the book. "OK," she said. "This football player is your Professor with the shiny

new name. He and Alexxia were touchy feely back in high school."
She shrugged. "So?"

"When was this football game?" I asked.

Naomi checked the spine for the year and did math in her head.

"Twenty-one years ago, give or take a few months. A long, long time."

"And how old is—"

"Holy Toledo! He's Leni's father?"

"Toledo?"

"It's a song," she said. "Green Day. Was in a movie. Isn't she, um…"

"In his class at the university? Yes."

"Holy…never mind. She's not. I mean. Please don't tell me she's pregnant."

"Don't know," I said. "Topic never came up." But it sure was a possibility after dating for five months.

"Wait a minute," she said. Naomi sipped coffee and broke off pieces of scone with her fingers. Her lips started to form a word, but she stopped them. Then she leaned across the table and whispered. "Does Leni know?"

"I don't know that either. You saw how Alexxia won't talk about it. I think Leni has never heard of Michael Carnes."

"Why didn't you tell me?"

"I wanted to discover the truth without biasing the data."

"Could have given me a heart attack," she said. "This isn't exactly evidence. Fake AI photos. A high school book. It's going to take a lot more than that."

I finished my scone. "To do what?"

"To convince Leni she's sleeping with her father."

I eyed the second half of Naomi's scone. She pushed it across the table towards me.

"You sure?"

"I'm sure she won't believe us, and yes, you can have the rest of my scone. I'm thinking that I want a fruity drink while we figure out where to get Narcan." She slid a napkin with numbers on it towards me. "And where in hell this is."

The legs of a chair scraped behind me. A deep male voice followed.

"Peter's Pharmacy sells Narcan over the counter. Big chains won't touch it because of the snowflakes who think it promotes drug use. My daughter was doing street drugs. Just a typical stupid high school kid. I had Narcan on me all the time. And in her purse. And in the glove box of the car. Anything to keep her alive."

I turned around to speak with him, but his chair squeaked back into place at the neighboring table. I said, "Thank you," to the back of his gray sweatshirt. Seemed too warm for the outside temp, but it was freezing inside Starbucks. He had used the past tense. I had Narcon on me. Not, I have Narcan on me.

"Peter's has one location," Naomi said, while staring at her phone. "According to this map we passed it a few miles back.

"Are they open on Sunday?"

She tapped and scrolled and I wondered at the power to answer questions so fast from a brick in your hand. Then I wondered what constantly being fed information was doing to the human brain.

Naomi placed a call.

I took a bite of her scone.

"Hi, do you have Narcan in stock? Thanks. How late are you open today? Super. I'll be there shortly."

"Alexander Graham Bell would be proud," I said.

"Graham? Like the crackers?" she asked.

"Yes. The guy who invented the telephone, enabling millions of hours of conversation that wouldn't have occurred otherwise."

"Oh him. I can't imagine living without a cell phone."

"It's not impossible," I said.

"Just boring."

I smiled. "Not with friends like you."

Her cheeks turned rosy.

"You know the history of the Graham cracker?" I asked.

"No," she said. "Tell me s'more." She giggled.

"Good one. It's ironic that this cracker became part of an enticing marshmallow and chocolate treat."

"You're going to tell me that bland little cracker has some deep purpose?'

I waited.

"Go ahead. Ruin s'more's for me."

"Dr. Sylvester Graham had an idea in the mid 19th century. He thought that the path to heaven was paved with minimized stimulation, including masturbation in teenage boys, and a vegetarian diet."

"So he invented a cracker?" she said. "And the world named this anti-masturbation device after him?"

"More or less."

"You're making this up."

"Just to ruin your s'more experience."

"Wow, you're not kidding. A doctor no less. What happened to his oath: Do no harm?" She laughed hard and raised a hand to cover her mouth. "Sorry."

"Humans do weird stuff," I said.

"Yeah. Lie, cheat, steal, form religious cults, outlaw pleasure, and invent anti-fun crackers." She laughed again, but not as loud. "Maybe Peter knows a good smoothie place."

"Ready to hit the road?"

She nodded. I finished her scone in one bite. Naomi held a coffee in each hand while I pushed her to the car.

CHAPTER 30

eter's Pharmacy had a whole shelf of Narcan and three other brands of naloxone. I bought two Narcans and one each of the others for backup. All were nasal sprays administered as a single blast into one nostril. Amy, the clerk Naomi had talked to on the phone, had an addicted cousin who was saved by a firefighter armed with Narcan. She directed us to Heavenly Smoothies about a mile north.

Naomi was taking orgasmic delight in a concoction containing fresh strawberries, bananas, vanilla ice cream, and chocolate syrup blended into the consistency of a milkshake. For fun, she had them sprinkle crumbled Graham crackers on top.

"Yum," she said. "Amy was right about this place."

I sipped a chocolate shake made with organic vanilla bean ice cream and fair-trade cocoa beans. It was heavenly too.

Naomi poked at maps on her phone. "Faster if we bypass Chicago."

I thought of Braden. "But I should respond to this meeting request. I doubt it will take long."

"Once we battle our way there," she said.

"Piece of cake on a Sunday."

Which was normally true. But it was summer. Increased tourist traffic. Construction, sometimes in two lanes at the same time. And it was hot. The kids in the back seat were noisy and distracting, mom and dad were tired from too much driving. It all added up to accidents blocking traffic every 30 miles.

Finally, I pulled up near the copper-topped church. Their parking lot was overflowing with vehicles.

"Over there," she said.

"We'll block that pickup truck."

"I'll handle it if anyone shows up. But this is a festival. They'll be at it until dark." She turned in the red bucket seat to face me. "You're going to be fast, right?"

I eased the Barracuda into an angled opening that blocked one vehicle and left me enough room to squeeze out of the driver's door. But Naomi was trapped.

She sipped her smoothie and winked at me.

I jogged to Braden's office holding a bag of scones I had grabbed on our way out of Starbucks. I ran around the corner from the elevator into the hallway to find his door closed. The frosted glass was glowing from light inside. But it was still daylight and might simply be the sun on its rounds. I knocked. No answer.

I called my service. No new messages. I thought about Naomi trapped in the car. I knocked again, just to be sure. I tried the door.

The knob turned.

Braden wouldn't go home without locking his office. He wouldn't go anywhere without locking it. A manila envelope lay on his desk. No label. No markings.

I sat down and noted the time on his desk clock. I'd wait five minutes. I stared out the window knowing that Lake Michigan was in that direction, but saw only cuboid office buildings and a steeple. I uncrossed my legs. I crossed them in the opposite direction. I watched the minute hand, trying to perceive its motion.

Four minutes gone.

I checked messages with the burner phone.

"Kelsey, I'm indisposed. Damn taco sauce will burn a hole in your insides. The way the universe works, you'll probably show up while I'm in the crapper. The envelope on my desk is for you. They're copies. But keep this to yourself. Call me if there's a crime I can get credit for solving. Lots of people think us old guys aren't necessary. Somehow, a kid with a smartphone and an AI app is going to crack the big cases of the future. Gotta go."

The message ended. I placed the scones on his desk and picked up the envelope. It was fastened with a string wound around two buttons. I started to unwind it, noticed the clock, and double-timed back to my car. When I opened the driver's door, Naomi stared at me over a wrap sandwich she was eating with two hands.

"Hi, Tommy."

I smiled. "Let me guess. After I left, a nice person stopped over to ask if you were all right. You said, 'Yes, just a little hungry.'"

"And he explained how this was a Greek festival and there were many kinds of traditional food," she said.

"So you have," I peered at her sandwich, "a gyro in your hand and a bag at your feet."

She nodded with the sandwich half in her mouth.

"And in the bag," I said, "is the TNT we're going to use to blow this case wide open."

She chewed and half-laugh-snorted through her nose. She handed me the bag using just the thumb and index finger of her left hand. When I touched it, she said, "BOOM!" through a mouthful of meat.

I handed her the envelope and started the car. We had places to go.

"What did he say?" she asked.

"He wasn't there. But he left that for me. I haven't opened it yet."

There was no dynamite in the bag. But there was another gyro sandwich and four pieces of baklava. We ate slowly while reviewing the two sheets of paper and rolling down the highway.

"Your detective friend put some DNA data he has into 23andMe?"

"Seems so," I said. It had to be from the rape kit. Braden didn't have anything else to work with.

"And he got a match with someone named Belinda Cercus?"

"Is she married?"

"Doesn't say." A pause. "Maybe she changed her name."

I selected a piece of baklava and returned the bag to Naomi.

"Why?" I said.

"She's hiding something."

"Then why provide DNA to a private, for-profit, capitalist enterprise like 23andMe? Because there is something she wants to know? Like is she Irish, or French, or there's a Chinese way back in her past."

"Or African," Naomi said, staring out the window at the passing fields. "White people want to know if there's a slave ancestor hiding in their past. And they're depending on genetics to tell them."

"What possible difference could a paper report of your genetics have? Are the tests even reliable?"

"Imagine that you're a white supremacist and you find out you have eight percent African heritage. How does that make you feel?"

I shrugged. "I am what I am. Can't change it. I don't even understand how they figure that out."

"But what if you hated blacks?"

"And now I am one? That's something people want to know?"

"No," she said. "They spend money to have science tell them they are clean. That there is no detectable people of color in their body. That's what they want to know."

"Hmm…"

"I'm not being cynical," she said, and punched me.

"I wonder how many white people are surprised by their ancestry."

"More than a few," she said.

"What about the other direction?"

"You mean blacks finding out if their great-great-grandfather was white? Happens all the time. White men liked slave girls. Just ask Thomas Jefferson."

"The past is complicated, isn't it?"

"And brutal," she said.

"How about the present?" I realized too late that was not something to ask a woman using a wheelchair.

"The present ain't perfect," she said. "But it's worth fighting for." She dug into the bag for baklava.

"What should we do about Belinda with no address?" I asked.

"We're delivering Narcan. No time for her."

"We? Naomi, you don't have to risk the wilderness. Prof will help me."

"And what do I do?"

"Go find Belinda?"

"Trying to get rid of me?" she said. And she wasn't smiling.

"No way. You're a great navigator. But I don't know what we'll find in the backcountry."

She chewed and stared my way for a few seconds. She rolled the bag closed and placed it between her feet.

"Answers," she said.

◇

Brittle scrub grass, brown and half dead from lack of water, covered the center of the dirt road rolling under the Barracuda. I swerved regularly to avoid the deepest potholes.

"We could walk," Naomi said.

"Who carries the cooler?" I asked.

She laughed. "Good point."

"And your suitcase?"

"I only brought essentials."

Her four-wheeled pink suitcase, possibly the largest ever made, sat sideways across the back seat filled with the essentials I had raced into a pharmacy, a boutique, and a Walmart to purchase . My duffel bag and a new cooler filled the trunk. The road crisscrossed its way up a hill. We had traveled north after leaving Braden's office, and were now headed due west, slowly approaching Prof's coordinates. I stopped at the top of the hill.

"Uh-oh," she said.

Our little road disappeared into a hardwood forest.

"You forgot your hair dryer," I said.

"Nothing so simple. This map shows a river ahead. No way this goat path has a bridge."

"Maybe there's a ferry."

"Aren't you the funny one."

We rolled carefully down the hill into the forest. The world became dark and damp. The forest floor was covered with anything that could survive on traces of sunlight filtering through the canopy.

"Where's the road?" she said.

The growth in the center had spread. A flick of the headlights revealed grass the width of tires bent away from us.

"Recent tracks," I said.

"How did they get across the river?"

We rolled in near darkness over the forest floor for the better part of a minute.

"They didn't." I pointed. "Two o'clock. Through the trees. Look carefully. Silver vehicle."

Naomi stared at her smartphone. "We're super close to Prof's coordinates. I don't have a cell signal." She rotated her phone between portrait and landscape. "Nothing. You drove into a black hole."

"We're trapped." I smiled. "Nothing gets out of a black hole."

She stared at me. "I dozed off in physics class."

"OK, no more physics jokes. What now, master navigator?"

She pointed at the silver splotch hiding among the trees.

"Over there."

"But the road goes that way."

Naomi looked over her shoulder and frowned. "We have no choice."

I inched forward. The road took us away from the silver splotch into thick forest that stopped abruptly at the edge of rushing water. Not whitewater, but not still either.

"Our river," she said.

"And something else."

I backed up until we were in the trees again. We studied the opposite shoreline.

"Tents?" she said.

"I count ten."

"And two SUVs."

"Seven passenger max. Could mean fourteen people."

"Two employees, a cop and a cook," she said.

"Or a cop and a nurse and the attendees do their own cooking as part of the experience. Each tent has a fire ring."

"Give up drugs and do your own cooking in the same weekend? Hardly seems fair." She laughed lightly.

"No buildings. Outdoor shower or they bathe in the river?"

"Brrr. Now what?"

"You're the navigator."

"My instrument went blooey."

I checked my borrowed phones. No signal. "That silver vehicle got there somehow."

"You think we're on the wrong road?"

"Tires crushed the grass recently."

We stared out the windshield at the rushing water. The near shore was covered with smooth rocks the size of golf balls.

"You okay here alone? I'll go take a look."

"I'll beep the horn if a bear shows up. You come and save me."

"From a bear?" I said.

"Metaphorically."

The sun was low in the western sky. Blazing yellows and oranges streaked the horizon. I put on my black leather jacket, stepped out of the car, and eased the door closed. Naomi leaned over and pressed the button to lock it. She waved to me with a smile and a thumbs up.

I felt the chill of being alone in a strange place. No way to communicate. I realized people felt this way all of the time before cell phones existed. I walked toward the river and stopped at the last tree, then turned and moved upriver in the direction of the silver vehicle, one tree at time. Stones and water to my left. Undergrowth trying to trip me. The stones showed no signs of car tracks. I moved to the next tree and examined the banks for any sign of disturbance. I bent low and moved close to the water. One slow step at a time.

Twenty yards later a clump of grass growing up between the rocks near my right foot was bent forward. I stacked some rock into a pyramid to mark this place. Then I dropped to my hands and knees and looked for more patches. The next two were upright, but the third was bent. I crawled in the direction of the bend until I was back in the forest. Except for the tracks in the grass weaving around trees, there was no road. I made my way back to the car, one tree at a time. A campfire came alive across the river, a spot of orange against the coming night. Then a second one.

Naomi unlocked the driver's door. I slipped in.

"Have a nice stroll?" she asked.

"Found tire tracks. We can drive in."

"We have a problem."

"Noise?" I said.

"Correct. We need an electric. We could whoosh away. What are you thinking?"

"We don't want to be seen."

"Will they come after us?" she said.

"Or break camp and disappear."

"We're probably trespassing. Which could get us arrested," she said. "So?"

"We wait. They'll have dinner. We have dinner. They'll turn in at some point and zip up their tents. Unless they have someone stand guard. Let's hope they feel safe enough out here that they don't post guards."

"Uh, I'll need help when nature calls," she said.

"Just tell me what to do."

She smiled. "Telling guys what to do is my hobby." She laughed, then covered her mouth with one hand to muffle the sound.

We watched tiny figures in the distance mill around more campfires. Shadows drifted over tents. No sound reached us.

"Does your camera have a zoom?" I asked.

"Sure. Check this out."

She propped the phone on the dash and selected a campfire. The zoom revealed three females. I looked for Leni without luck. I plugged Naoni's phone into the cigarette lighter to preserve its battery. The door of the fourth tent from the river fell open.

"New tent," she said.

"Watching."

A girl crawled backwards out of the doorway and carefully zipped the tent closed—like it would explode if she wasn't careful. She turned away from us and walked toward the nearest campfire.

"I want to hear what they're saying," Naomi said.

A crow swooped low over the group and kept moving. I couldn't identify the girl.

"They seem to be moving slowly," I said.

"The whole point is to relax. Remote location. Quiet. Water. Sky. Trees."

"Not helping me relax," I said with a smile.

"We're on a mission. Their fight is internal."

We shared a submarine sandwich with peppers. Afterward, Naomi climbed on my back and I carried her to a spot between two trees. Once she was on the ground she shooed me away. She called me back with a whoop-whoop fake bird call. I squatted, she clung to me like a human backpack and I deposited her back in the passenger's seat.

One by one the girls across the river crawled into a tent and didn't come back out. Light glowed through orange or green or yellow ripstop nylon shells.

"Wouldn't that be boring?" Naomi said.

"Living in the wilderness, cooking over a fire, fishing in a roaring river? Did you expect something unusual?"

"You mean like being parked in a forest miles from civilization watching female zombies prepare for the apocalypse?"

I laughed. "Were you a drama major in high school?"

"No, but I was on the debate team. Colorful narratives can be very convincing."

"Remind me not to argue with you."

She made her eyes big and batted her eyelashes.

"Why would you argue with a sweet little thing like me?"

I burst out laughing. She clamped a hand over my mouth.

I said, "Sorry," into her palm.

"Shh."

The green tent where the girl had come out backwards stopped glowing.

Over the next 30 minutes, all of the tents went dark. All except for the one farthest from the river. It wasn't a plain color like the others, it was green and tan camouflage.

"Weird color," she said.

"Hunting maybe. Or military surplus."

"Or someone finds camo fashionable. Let's them stand out from the crowd in a subtle way."

Two bodies emerged from the camo tent, both wearing camo fatigues. Both wearing a wide black belt with attachments.

"Women with guns?" she said.

"Can't be sure from this far away. Might be a taser. Or pepper spray in case a hungry bear shows up."

Naomi cast her gaze my way.

"I'm sleeping in the car." She tapped her phone. "No signal. Does Wisconsin really have bears?"

"Chicago Bears are close," I said, and grinned. "I bet they have mountain lions too."

"Thanks. I feel better now."

The pair of camo-clad figures walked from tent to tent, stopping at each entrance. Possibly having a good night conversation that we couldn't hear.

"End of day formality?" Naomi said.

"Make sure everyone is where they should be. Can't be easy overseeing addicts who have never been out of the city."

"Do you think they tell everyone about bears and mountain lions? And wolves? I bet there are wolves."

"Lions and tigers and bears, oh my," I chanted.

"What's that?"

"Very old movie. My Mom's favorite."

"I'd need a tranquilizer to sleep out here in a tent," she said. "Were there wolves in the movie?"

"Nope. Tin man and a scarecrow. Oh, and flying monkeys."

She stared at me. "Your mom is into some weird shit."

"Witches. There were witches too."

"Sounds like it should be banned. Did she let you watch this as a little kid?"

"Do you want to hear about the wizard?"

"No thanks. Flying monkeys are scary enough."

The sentries visited the last tent. I crossed my fingers that no one would stand guard. That would make our magic trick harder to pull off.

One camo figure crawled into the camo tent. The other stood at the entryway, looking up at the sky, sipping from a cup. Clouds had rolled in. I could see only two stars.

"Tommy." She waited until I stopped stargazing and faced her. "How loud is your stereo?"

"I think Chin designed it as a DJ system for outdoor block parties. You have an urge to party?"

"I have an idea. Can we play from my smartphone?"

"Knowing Chin, the amplifier probably has Bluetooth."

I snuck quietly out the driver's door into the woods I had backed into. I lifted the trunk and opened the compartment housing the turntable. A wire from the table ran across, down, back up. The amp was made in Sweden.

"It has Bluetooth for amplifier controls. I don't know if it will accept audio. Wait. Chin put the manual behind the amp.

"He knew," she said, "that eventually a Luddite would need the manual."

I read by moonlight and remembered my father using what he called my "young eyes" to read the fine print on contracts. I realized now that he could probably read it just fine. But he used the experience to educate me about the world of finance, contracts, and life in general.

I pressed buttons on the amp while Naomi tweaked settings in her phone. A few minutes later we had her phone playing through the speakers at a super low volume.

When I returned to the driver's seat, the sentry was gone.

"Where's the guard?" I asked.

"I think she's in the camo tent with her partner. Where else would she be?"

"She could be afraid of wolves and is sleeping in one of those SUVs."

"Or," she said. "She's in one of the other tents."

I hadn't considered sex. But the situation was ripe. Someone with power. Someone else vulnerable and strung out. Drugs handy.

"Are you going to share your plan?"

"Do you remember the children's story about the boy who cried wolf?" she asked.

"Wolves are bugging you, aren't they?"

"Not yet," she said. "But they made me think of the story. We use your stereo to make a jet engine noise. With us parked in the forest and the sound bouncing off the clouds, they'll think it's a plane overhead."

"And the third time we play the jet, I start the car and idle along the shore and duck into the forest where I left the marker."

Naomi smiled. "Think it will work?"

"It's a lot better than starting a Hemi in the middle of a silent night with our fingers crossed."

She high-fived me.

With both doors and trunk wide open we played the sound of an A320 Airbus taking off. One sentry came out of the camo tent and looked up for thirty seconds. A yellow tent glowed from inside for a minute, then went dark.

We waited twenty minutes to give everyone time to doze off.

The second time no one came out, although light flashed around inside a red tent like a mini-spotlight.

We waited, chewed gum, fought off flying insects, and hoped the cloud cover would reflect and jumble the sounds.

◇

At 3:10 A.M. the wind had picked up and was blowing the waves on the river directly at us, carrying sound away from the campsite and into the forest. This time we closed the doors, rolled the windows down, but left the trunk open. I looked at Naomi and saw the same anxious anticipation on her face that I felt in my stomach.

We gazed across the river.

I couldn't see stars for the clouds. All of the tents were dark and flapping in the wind.

I said, "Ready?"

Naomi lifted her phone. I wrapped my fingers around the ignition key and pressed in the clutch. Roaring jet engines filled the car. As they crescendoed toward takeoff, I turned the key. The Hemi jumped to life and rumbled right along with the jets. I eased out the clutch.

We rolled toward the river. I squinted to find the water's edge and made a hard right where waves washed river rocks. I scanned for my pyramid marker. The rocks complained with scraping sounds.

"No lights," Naomi reminded me.

I jumped at the sound of her voice. My eyes followed the riverbank as I realized the waves could have destroyed my marker. The jet engines faded away, exposing us.

"There!" she said, in a load whisper.

A wave covered my stone pile, then revealed it. I waited until the front bumper came even, then turned away from the river, dodging a tree stump a foot wide, being careful not to touch the brakes and spill red light into the black night.

Naomi twisted around and stuck her head out the open window. The jets were nearly gone. The Hemi pulled us deeper into the forest on an invisible road. Naomi reached toward me with her left arm and made an OK sign with her fingers. The grass was knee high but bent where a vehicle had meandered through. The Barracuda waddled over uneven ground like a happy duck. We curved left, deeper into the forest.

"Can you see the tents?" I asked.

She twisted the other way in her seat.

"I can't even see the river."

I stopped and closed the trunk, glad it didn't have an internal light. A squadron of mosquitos dive-bombed me. I waved them off and high-tailed it back to the car to roll up the windows and flick on the AC.

We sat idling in the forest. I could barely see Naomi's smile.

"Nice job, Tommy."

"Thanks. Your jet engines did all the work."

"Now what?" she said.

"This had better lead somewhere. We can't backtrack."

Our eyes locked. Gentle idling of the Hemi filled the car. The shared experience, a dark moonless night, isolation…

I whispered, "Shall we make it ninety-three?"

The nod of her head was barely perceptible.

I twisted in the bucket seat and leaned across the Hurst shifter. As our lips touched and my eyes were almost closed the inside of the car filled with white light. I pulled away.

"Did you see that?" I said.

"I felt it," she said, smiling. "But that didn't count. It wasn't long enough."

I kissed her again, longer, with my eyes closed, concentrating my entire being on the warm pressure of her lips. The insides of my eyelids flashed orange. I pulled away slowly.

"Mmm," she said.

"Wait a minute."

She leaned closer. "I'm not good at waiting."

I stared at a black tree amid shapes and shadows shifting in the wind. A white dot blinked through the trees.

"What was that?" she said.

"I hope someone trying to signal us."

I slipped the car into first gear and eased out the clutch. We crept toward where the dot had flashed. The shift knob vibrated against my palm. Naomi placed her hand on mine. Hers was warm and soft and squeezing me gently.

The white light flashed again, lit the inside of the car, and revealed that we were ten yards from an RV sitting in the forest on monster truck tires. A three-pronged Mercedes logo faced us. The vehicle could have been any color out there in the darkness, but I'd bet it was silver.

No lights. A curved sunscreen inside the windshield blocked the view into the interior.

"Who, what, when, where?" Naomi said.

"You're a mind reader." I switched off the engine. Silence enveloped us.

"Now what?" she said.

"We wait or we knock. Are we at the right coordinates?"

She checked her phone. Tapped. Swiped. Shook it like she was erasing an Etch A Sketch.

"Don't know. It won't hook up to the satellites."

"I'm feeling isolated," I said.

"At least you can run when the bullets start flying."

Her brave voice was tinted with fear. Which made perfect sense. She barely knew me. Couldn't roll out of here. And couldn't drive my car. She'd have to crawl out.

I leaned over and kissed her. "Ninety-two to go."

She punched my arm but was smiling.

I checked both of my phones. No signals. I sighed.

"Let's knock," she said. "They know we're here. There's no lightning in the sky. That light had to be coming from the RV."

A hooded figure wearing black emerged from the depth of the forest behind the RV. It moved slowly toward my front bumper. The hood shifted left and right, answering no to an unspoken question. I reached one hand into the pocket of my jacket for Prof's insurance. The figure came along the side of the car, head low, hands hidden, bent forward, and turned to face me through the glass.

"BOO!"

Naomi laughed away her tension. I cranked the window down.

"Hi, Prof. Why the high drama?"

"Was surprised to see Naomi. Made me wonder if there was a guy lying across your back seat holding a gun on you."

"And if there was?"

He removed his hands from the kangaroo pocket of the hoodie. Each held a handgun.

"Things are weird here, Tommy," he said. "If this was Denmark, it'd be rotten. Notice that your cell phones don't work?"

"Yeah, a ways back."

"Jammers. Good ones. Maybe military grade. Blocking phone frequencies and GPS frequencies. Took me a long time to find an open channel."

"For what?"

"Let me show you." He lifted his eyes. "You need a hand with the gym rat?"

"I got her." I gestured toward the RV with my head. "Nice wheels."

"Shianti insisted we rent the best. Turned out she was right. Getting close to that Incognito crew without being seen was a lot easier from this side than just rolling up the sorry excuse for a road they used. C'mon in."

With Naomi on my back I followed Prof to the rear of the vehicle. Barn doors stood open wide, revealing a luxurious interior of wood and metal, a microwave, and a bed across the front seats. With Prof's help, we got Naomi situated at a little dinette table with seating for two.

Prof said, "Naomi, my friend Shianti. Shianti, my friend and gym buddy Naomi."

The girls smiled and nodded and said nice to meet you the way strangers do when they're introduced.

"That last half mile is sketchy," I said.

"Would have warned you, but I didn't know when I left the message. And once we parked, no communications."

"How are we going to watch Netflix?" I said.

"We've got more exciting things going on," Shianti said, as she rolled out a piece of white butcher paper. On the hand drawn map I could pick out the location of the tents, the river, the Jeep SUVs, the forest, and the Mercedes RV I was sitting in. While we watched, she sketched in the Barracuda.

"What made you decide to come up here?" I asked.

Prof folded his slender height into a corner seat.

"Me getting drugged. You springing me. What you found in the boxes. The accounting records. It all adds up."

I looked from Shianti's freckled nose to Prof's poker face to Naomi's eager eyes. No one said anything, so I asked the obvious.

"My math is rusty. What's it add up to?"

"A con," Prof said. "Ponzi scheme. Prestidigitation accounting. Something sneaky behind the curtain."

"And Leni in the middle of it?"

"Smack dab," he said. "Look at this recording." He pulled a laptop out of a drawer and lit up the flat screen TV mounted on the wall across from the dining table. Colored tents drifted across the screen.

"You have a drone?" Naomi asked.

Prof nodded and grinned. Of course he would have a drone.

Shianti opened a cabinet and placed a model of a bird on the table. A four propellor black drone in a cage was strapped to it like a backpack.

"Gives new meaning to the term 'carrier pigeon,'" I said.

"Crow," Shianti said. "Most birds are afraid of crows, so they stay away from the drone. The camera is inside the open beak."

"Did you know," Prof said, "that a crow is one of the few birds that will attack an eagle?"

"Sounds suicidal," Naomi said.

Prof shook his head. "Crows are smart. They clamp onto the eagle's back and peck at its neck."

"That'd hurt," I said. The recorded drone images zoomed in, revealing faces and eyes and expressions. "There's Leni."

Prof froze the picture. "Fourth tent from the river."

"Orange," I said.

"Yes."

"Are all the tents the same?"

Prof pointed. "That camo one has two military types in it. They carry pepper spray and tasers." He paused. "I'm betting they might be hiding a sidearm. And a couple of AR-15s in the Jeeps isn't out of the question. The rest of the tents are singles."

"Isolate the addicts?" Naomi said. "Is that smart?"

"Makes it more difficult to conspire," Prof said.

I studied the frozen frame.

"Why so much firepower? Are addicts dangerous?"

"I think," all eyes turned toward Shianti, "the camo girls are protecting a three-day supply of opiates for the entire group. Beaucoup street value."

"Why so many drugs for a retreat?" I asked.

"The million-dollar question," Prof said. "So far, we haven't seen anyone swallow a pill, or shoot up, or even sniffle funny."

"But you ordered Narcan?"

Prof nodded. Looked to Shianti and back to me.

"We have an unconfirmed hypothesis." He restarted the video. The bird-drone looped around a campfire. Its camera found faces in the flickering light, then rose to show a bird's eye view of the entire area. Some girls were eating. Some were wandering from campfire to campfire.

"Why so many fires?" I asked.

Prof answered. "Two thoughts. First, teach them survival skills to occupy their time. Second, keep them apart, just like the solo tents."

Shianti said, "Notice anything unusual?"

I had, but I thought it was my imagination.

"Everyone's exhausted," I said. "Not sleepy from hiking far. But frantic tired, like they've been working against a deadline and haven't slept well in a week."

"Wired," Naomi said. "Zombies."

"Or drugs," Prof said.

I studied the video as the bird-drone made its dive-bomb rounds.

"Has anyone noticed your drone?"

"A camo girl shot it with a finger. Leni pointed at it once."

"Why give people drugs on a rehab retreat?" Naomi said.

"The skeptical part of me," Prof said, "thinks these retreats are really stay high and don't get arrested weekends."

"People would pay for that," Naomi agreed.

I nodded.

"Or, being cynical," Prof said, "there's a hidden agenda that wants the rehab effort to fail."

"Drug addicts are gold mines," Shianti said. "Mommy and Daddy pay for college. Tuition, room, board. Big investment. Maybe the retreat tries to wean the kids off the hard stuff."

"Crazy enough to work," I said.

Prof exhaled hard. "Maybe this is only one type of retreat."

I shifted on my cushioned chair. "And there are others, each with a different agenda?"

Naomi frowned. "What agenda?"

Prof grinned.

"What am I missing?" she said.

Prof opened the drawer that had held the laptop and pulled out a sheaf of papers. He eased them across the table to Naomi. I recognized a title. She shuffled through the stack, reading a bit here and there.

"Academic research papers?"

"That they are," Prof agreed.

Naomi read and shuffled. "Immersion in nature as a drug intervention?"

"Like the group in the tents across the river," Shianti said.

"But they're all high," I added.

Prof grinned. "Control group."

CHAPTER 31

I considered the people around me. I had only known them for a few days. Shianti's fine features and golden curls. Naomi's streaked afro and smiling dark eyes. Prof's somber concentration. I said, "In summary, we assume the attendees are consuming opioids and have impaired function. They are also sleep deprived from regimented activities."

"What do we assume about the watchdogs?" Naomi asked.

"That they have strict orders," Prof said. "Secrecy at the top of the list. And they're dangerous."

"You and Shianti acquired this incredible RV and had me bring Narcan," I said. "You have a plan?"

Prof gestured to Shianti, who cleared her throat and took a sip of water from a plastic bottle before speaking.

"We know the layout. If we grab Leni and get her across the river before they know she's gone, we have a good chance of disappearing from the grid."

"Or they wake up and use us for target practice," I said.

Prof shook his head. "Too much downside. Incognito would never create an incident like that."

"I hope those guards know that," Naomi said.

"Then what?" I asked.

Shianti said, "We hightail it out of here. The time they need to cross the river gives us a good head start."

"If it's calm, a good swimmer could be across in a couple of minutes."

"Not much margin for error," Naomi offered.

"Assume success," Prof said. "The guards can't chase us because their SUVs are on the wrong side of the river. We're rolling down the highway. What do we do with Leni?"

"Hide her," Shianti said.

"We tried that at Prof's place," I said. "Markus found her. And she left with him."

"Um," Naomi said. "What makes you think that she'll even come with us?"

Prof and Shianti exchanged glances.

I said, "I don't really know Leni. But maybe she likes being an addict."

Shianti shook her head. Prof shrugged. Naomi stayed quiet.

"We need options," I offered. "Get to Leni in her tent. Administer the Narcan. How long?"

"Two minutes for the initial effect," Prof said. "No more than ten. Shouldn't need a second dose. Note, if we're wrong and Leni isn't on opioids, Narcan is safe and won't have any effect."

Naomi raised her hand like a schoolgirl.

"If she comes with. If we escape. If we hide her successfully Then what? Those people can't just lose a client in the middle of a forest."

Prof steepled his long dark fingers and lowered his forehead down on the tips. "They'll fabricate a cover story about Leni and continue with the weekend like nothing happened. Meanwhile, they send word to Markus and he puts out an underground all-points bulletin to find her."

"How?" I asked. "Nothing works out here."

" Prof said. "I need to do research, but I can't get to the Internet."

"Which sucks," Shianti added.

"Like being trapped in a classic movie from the twentieth century," Prof said. "So I experimented. If I walk far enough east, I get a signal. The drone works at radio frequencies way below the ones cell phones use."

Naomi's eyes registered surprise. "They're jamming cell phones so no one can call home?"

Shianti nodded vigorous agreement.

"What if," I said, "Leni wants to stay in her tent and return from camp to please Markus?"

"We have a problem," Prof said. "We can still help. Supply her with Narcan and food and water so she can stay straight and understand what is happening around her." He paused. "Assuming she wants to."

"Maybe set up a rendezvous once Leni's not under surveillance," I offered.

"If she even wants to meet," Naomi said.

"I suddenly feel," Prof said, "like we're trying to help someone who doesn't want to be helped right now."

"Not uncommon," Shianti said, smiling a smile I couldn't interpret.

"What if we do nothing?" I asked. "That's sometimes the best path."

Prof considered. "Leni stays with Markus, addicted and abused."

"Which is what she was trying to escape when I met her," I said.

They looked at me. I couldn't recall who knew what.

"Leni was telling fortunes at a rest stop on I-80 west for five bucks. Said she was trying to raise bus fare."

"And you became the bus," Naomi said.

"I drew a card. She began to talk about it. Then saw something behind me, grabbed her stuff, and ran into the restroom."

"What did she see?" Shianti asked.

"Markus's blue Cadillac."

"So he chased her?" Prof said.

"No doubt." Looking from face to face made me think that we were all wondering what we were doing here. And I was sitting on a crucial piece of information. But I wanted to tell Leni first, let her decide who should know. However, all of us were volunteers helping out a friend. Shianti barely even knew us, yet I'd bet she was paying for the RV. More information might change things.

"What?" Naomi said.

"What what?" I said.

"Tommy, your eyes broadcast when your brain shifts gears. You're thinking about a secret."

"Are you a psychology major?" I asked.

"I'm a woman."

"Much more dangerous," Prof said.

"You better believe it," Shianti added.

I sighed. "OK, here's the situation. I am in possession of possibly relevant, highly personal information about Leni. It's unclear whether she even knows."

"Who does?" Naomi asked.

"Me and detective Braden." And Naomi had guessed.

"Markus?" Prof asked.

"I don't think so."

"Well, I don't know," Prof said.

"Who else might know?" Shianti asked. "Who else is she close to? Her mother?"

"I think Alexxia does not know the details."

"My appetite is very whet," Shianti said. "When is the main course?"

I was stuck in the rock-hard place conundrum. "It stays in this group until Leni says otherwise."

They all nodded.

We hooked our fifth fingers together and made a pinky promise. I felt the spirit of a little league team about to play the championship game.

"I can't think of any way to ease into this."

"What's your level of confidence?" Prof said.

"I'm as confident as the science."

"I can deal with science," Prof said.

"Me too." Shianti.

"And me." Naomi.

Six eyes drilled into me.

"DNA evidence shows that Markus Corolla is Leni's biological father."

Forest insects filled the silence.

Shianti whispered, "DNA."

Prof's mind was working, but his face and hands were still.

All eyes were on me.

"Leni's version of the story. She dated Markus for months. But recently, he raped her. She filed a Jane Doe rape kit at the school dispensary."

"But…" Prof began.

"Right. A Jane Doe would not be processed without a formal request. I called in a favor."

"Some favor," Shianti said.

"You were trying to identify the rapist," Prof said. "This paternity thing fell out of the sky."

"Leni says it was Markus. But I can't prove it."

"Why lie in a Jane Doe filing?" Prof said.

"She didn't identify the guy. She was angry and wanted documentation. Just in case."

"Just in case," Naomi said. "Wow!"

"You have to tell her now," Shianti said. "If she already knows, nothing changes. But what if she doesn't?"

"I read a book once," Prof said. "Won a Pulitzer Prize."

We waited. Prof read lots of books.

"Young GI in Vietnam gets it on with a local girl. Goes home. Builds a life. Life falls apart. He goes back to 'Nam seeking some kind of closure from his time in the war."

"OMG," Naomi whispered.

"Meets a beautiful young woman who carries him back to his past. They fall in love. She becomes pregnant."

"No way!" Naomi said.

"They go to a village to find her mother. Want her to bless their marriage."

"And he recognizes the mother," I said.

"Exactly."

"Damn, Prof," Naomi said. "What happened?"

"Sure you want me to tell you? It'll spoil the ending if you read the book."

"Good point." She frowned. "What's the title? I'll get it when I get home."

"Something with Mountains. I'll look it up when we return to civilization."

Shianti sighed and said, "We need a new plan."

◇

At ten after four in the morning I was beside the Barracuda working a hand pump to inflate a stand up paddleboard. I was perspiring by the time the board was stiff along its entire twelve-foot length. The idea was to stand up on it. But with the waves and the pack I needed to carry, kneeling seemed a wiser option. I shortened the adjustable paddle, hoping the board would behave like the canoes I had piloted at summer camp.

Shianti came out the side door of the RV carrying a black backpack that matched the shirt, pants, boots, gloves, and face paint I was wearing. The only thing that wasn't black was the board. It was gray.

"This should be everything," she said. "Do you want to go over it again?"

I shook my head. "I'm ready."

"Not tired?"

"Buzzing. Like I'm about to start a gig and the energy from the crowd is surging through my veins."

"I hope you can focus it," she said.

"I'm trying to channel Tom Cruise in Mission Impossible."

She hummed the famous theme, so I joined in. Then we laughed together quietly. She helped me slip the backpack on and secure it, then stood facing me.

"Narcan?" she said.

I reached back with my left hand, flipped open a side pocket, and came out with the sprayer. Unpackaged and ready to go.

"Gun."

Right and back to the bottom compartment, hand on grip, finger off trigger, point it at the ground.

"Revolver. No safety. Just—"

"Pull the trigger," I finished for her.

She smiled. "Two hours to sunrise."

"I'll be back long before."

She kissed me on the cheek.

"Break a leg, Tommy."

"Thanks." I picked up the board in one hand and the paddle in the other and slogged through the bent grass my Barracuda had left behind. Shortly I reached the smooth river rocks. Across the river, the colorful tents sat gray in the darkness. I left my boots on the shore and piled rocks over them, then waded barefoot into remarkably cold water. I knelt on the board, pointed the nose at the tents on the other side, and started paddling.

The moving water carried me downstream, so I angled the board and paddled faster. The wind turned the nose. Waves washed over the board, soaking my knees. I paddled harder. The wind and waves worked against me, holding me in a zen-like state of suspended animation. I worked hard for a couple of minutes, but the tents remained far away.

I abandoned my crossing plan. Walking to the tents seemed like a better idea.

I brought the nose perpendicular to the shoreline and focused on paddling as fast and quietly as possible. Stabbing the water and pulling hard crunched the nose onto rocks in a few short minutes at a point where there was no forest to hide me.

The camp was far to my left.

I dragged the board away from the river so it wouldn't be washed away. Walking the rocky shoreline in bare feet, I worked my way upstream until I was across from the orange tent. I knelt and ran through the plan. I considered that I didn't have an escape plan if things went wrong, or a good explanation as to why I was here. I would have to improvise. I took a slow, deep breath and worked my way to the rear of Leni's tent.

No voices.

No movement inside.

I crawled on my elbows around the tent to the entrance. The zipper tab hung at the lower right edge. I pulled it. In the quiet, it sounded like a beast growling. There was no other way in. I moved it a few more inches and it growled some more. I relaxed my arm and moved the zipper in slow motion. The growl became a ticking. A quick calculation estimated two minutes to open the door. Not long, but it felt like holding my breath underwater.

The door fell inward with a light swish.

Nothing happened.

No motion. No sounds. No lights. No guards.

A figure lay on her left side. Spine toward me. Couldn't confirm it was Leni.

I crawled in, my wet knees scraping across the ripstop nylon floor shattered the silence. I longed to hide us behind a closed door. But that zipper would slow me down.

I opted for speed.

I reached for the Narcan and leaned over the sleeping girl. Straight black hair covered half her face. A silver necklace with a tiny copper key dangled. Leni had worn it to the Toucan. I positioned my thumb on the plunger and reached over her shoulder without touching her, glided the tip of the sprayer into her left nostril, and pressed.

One dose.

I yanked the sprayer away.

Her body twitched and both eyes flew open. She sniffled and stared blinking at the side of the tent. Rolled onto her back. Saw me. Her mouth opened.

I clamped my hand over it and whispered, "Leni, it's Tommy. Please be quiet."

Her breath puffed against my hand. She struggled slightly. Her eyes glued to my face didn't seem focused.

"Easy, Leni. Relax," I whispered. "Just wait a minute. Be calm. I'm going to remove my hand. Please don't scream."

I relaxed my fingers and slowly withdrew my hand. She panted like she had been running. I held eye contact. Hers seemed to dance in the dim light.

A humming sound made me whip around toward the door. A hovering bird was staring at us and tilting from side to side.

"Stay quiet," I said to Leni.

I crawled to the open entrance and peered out. A guard was stepping out of the camo tent at the end of the row. I slid back until our faces were two inches apart and stared into Leni's eyes.

"Who am I?"

"T…tom…Tommy," she said.

"You're being drugged with fentanyl. I gave you a blocker. How do you feel?"

"Like waking up. Woke up fast. From a nightmare." She panted. "And it hasn't stopped."

"There's a guard coming. We—"

"Don't let them see you."

I looked around the tent. The best I could do was sit beside the doorway behind my backpack. But the door was open. I unzipped her sleeping bag in one swoosh, the sound like a giant mosquito flying through camp. Leni was wearing a yellow Nature Incognito T-shirt and white panties.

"Leni, go pee."

"What? I—"

"Leave before the guard arrives. Make sure she sees you."

Gears gnashed behind her eyes. She swung her legs off the low cot, stepped into running shoes, and crawled out the open entrance with her shoelaces trailing behind her. She waved a greeting to the guard.

A guard who might check her tent. Or wait around to chat. Or tuck her back into bed. The vastness of a forest and I was trapped in a nylon cage smaller than my car.

Leni's jacket had been tossed on a pile of clothes in the corner. I lifted the pile, shoved my backpack into the corner, then dropped the pile on top to hide the pack. I considered options, then pulled the pistol out and held it in my right hand. If I absolutely had to protect Leni, I had it. I tilted the cot up, crawled underneath, and let it down over me with my head below her pillow and my toes poking up into the fabric.

"You okay?" Voice outside the tent. Not Leni.

"Yeah. You make us drink so much water, I have to pee at night."

"What's your target?"

"Four bottles a day," Leni said. She crawled into the tent moments later.

The voice of the guard was close. "Be sure to meet your water goal. We're outdoors. Dehydration is a real danger."

Leni rolled onto her cot and hesitated when she felt my body under her. Then she slipped into the bag and stretched out on top of me. I breathed quietly through my nose as her body weight compressed my chest.

"Sleep well, Lenore. Full day tomorrow," the guard said.

The door zipped shut in three quick bursts. Footfalls of boots on grass moved away. Leni lay frozen in place. I breathed shallow so my chest wouldn't rise.

The night settled into forest quiet.

Leni giggled, her body shaking against mine. She rolled to the edge of the cot, removing some of her body weight from my chest.

She whispered, "Romeo, Romeo, wherefore art thou, Romeo," and giggled some more.

Occasionally the beam from a flashlight would pass over the tent: the guard making rounds. Finally we heard a zipper in the distance and held our breath until it sounded again.

Leni rolled onto the floor and lowered her head to gaze into my eyes.

"This is so romantic. I have a backdoor man and no back door." She stifled laughter.

"I bet it's the water," I said.

"They're crazy about hydration here."

I tried to shake my head, but it was trapped by the cot.

"They're delivering fentanyl."

"What?" she whispered. "I never use Fenty. It's too easy to OD."

"That's why the water allotment. Did they weigh you?"

Her eyes widened as random data became knowledge inside her head.

"Yeah. Getting into the SUVs. Had to take my shoes and jacket off."

"Don't drink the water," I said.

"I'll die. We're in the middle of nowhere."

"I brought a filter for you. You can drink river water. But use their bottles. How do you feel?"

"Better than yesterday. What did you do?"

"Shot an opioid blocker up your nose. I have more if you need them. But you have to act not fine."

"You look silly holding up my cot."

"Had to hide."

"They're really drugging us?"

My neck was cramping so I rotated it back and forth, shifting the cot with it.

"Yes on this retreat. But there is a bigger agenda."

"That includes me?"

"Includes hundreds of people."

"Do you mean my delivery job, or something else?"

"Both," I said. I had a debate in my head: Was now the time to tell her? "Leni, there's something else."

"Not now. My life is complicated enough."

"It can wait until you're back home. But you need to know before you see Markus again."

She stretched out on the floor of the tent and rested her head on her arm.

"Tommy, I'm lost in the middle of this world. I want to have a regular life where I work and accomplish things and earn money and love and be loved."

"Education?"

"It's my best shot. Look at the average income of doctors and lawyers and engineers compared to the average high school kid."

"Giant difference over a lifetime."

"Yeah, millions of dollars. I'm smart. I work hard. I don't want to be a drug addict or somebody's ho."

"Meaning?"

"I have to keep my act together and finish college with grades that will get me into medical school."

"So it's about money."

"I need to make it or borrow it and pay back fat loans." She fell quiet. Her eyes drifted away from mine. "I'm scared, Tommy. I'm scared the young me is going to let down the future me."

We were alone. I could tell her now. But if she freaked out…

"How about escaping with me? Tonight."

"That will cost me my job, my boyfriend, and my college mentor who can open doors for me."

Harvey Weinstein came to mind, blocking the acting careers of women who refused to have sex with him. Allegedly.

"High price," I said.

"Sky high. I'm only at this retreat because he pressured me. Now you tell me this is fueling my addiction. What's going on, Tommy?"

"I have guesses. Not facts."

She met my eyes before whispering.

"That doesn't stop most people."

◇

Four of us were sitting in the RV at the mini dining table. I had returned from the river only minutes ago.

"Where are your boots?" Naomi asked.

"Had the wind behind me, pushed me downstream. I hiked upriver, but couldn't find them in the dark. Didn't want to be seen, so I cut the search short."

"Good call," Shianti said.

"How's Leni?" Prof asked.

"Sober and scared," I said. "I asked her to come back with me. Answer was no. Marcus made it clear that if she runs away again, he'll make her regret it."

"Prick," Naomi said, her eyes narrowed like she was planning a murder.

I smiled to show appreciation for her attitude.

"How did she react?" Shianti asked.

"Fuzzy brained at first. But totally cool when we had to deal with security."

"I mean about the DNA news."

I took the time to swallow. "Didn't tell her."

Everyone stayed quiet.

"She's fragile. I was concerned that her reaction would summon a guard." I paused. "I know she deserves to know. But in a safe, supportive environment."

"Good point," Prof said. "How do we arrange that? And when?"

"And how do we get out of here?" Naomi said, her eyes dashing from one end of the RV to the other. "I feel trapped."

"The way we came in," I said.

"They'll see us."

"It's now early Monday morning," Prof said. "Third day of the retreat. We have food and water and are well hidden."

"We wait?" I asked.

"Wait and sleep. Rest up for whatever the future is going to throw at us."

Shianti took the foam bed across the back. Prof slept on a specially shaped air mattress that covered the two fronts seats. I slept on the lowered kitchen table while Naomi chose to sleep in the aisle on an air mattress. Close quarters, but comfier than a tent.

◇

A scream shocked me awake. Shianti scrambled out of bed, duck-walked over Naomi and pulled the drone out of its charging pod directly above my head. Prof's face poked between the two captain's chairs up front, his eyes half-closed. Shianti sat on the edge of my bed and launched the crow-drone out the side door.

A second high-pitched wail ripped through the RV. It wasn't close, but it wasn't far away either.

Shianti put the drone's camera feed on the wall monitor. She piloted it along the path I had driven, staying low. When she reached the river, she climbed.

Thirteen girls were skinny dipping in the morning sunshine. One guard stood on the shore facing the river, statue-still. A tall redhead I hadn't seen before tossed a black object into the air. A spume of water trailed it. A dark-haired girl leapt for it. When she caught it, half of the girls screamed, while the other half descended on the catcher.

They weren't all skinny dipping. One team was wearing panties.

"They're playing a game?" Prof asked in a rough morning voice.

The dark-haired girl tossed the object.

Another catch. More screams.

Shianti zoomed the drone's camera as it did a fly-by. She leaned toward the screen, and started laughing.

I was on my back in bed looking straight up at the monitor.

"What are they throwing?" I asked.

Shianti said, "An engineer boot like bikers wear to Rolling Stones concerts."

I lifted myself onto my elbows. A boot flew through the air. The receiver missed the catch; the entire group moaned. The girl who missed the catch dove underwater.

"This nature therapy sure is something," Naomi said from the floor. "Who thought we'd all be getting naked?"

"Hope springs eternal," Prof said, then dropped back onto his bed.

"Since the drone is up," Shianti said. "Is there anything we want to know?"

"Is Leni still sober?" I asked.

Shianti turned the drone around and flew low to the water like a bird searching for surface insects. Leni's eyes locked onto it. When it grew close, she smiled and winked.

"Did you tell her about the drone?" Shianti asked.

"Not a word. But a little bird warned us about the guard's approach last night."

"One plus one," Naomi said. "At least she knows someone is watching. That should be comforting."

The boot flew. Girls screamed. More frolicking through calm waters now that the wind had dropped.

"Which leaves us," Prof's voice rose from the front, "with what we do today."

"Sleep," I said.

"Scheme," Shianti said.

"Eat," Naomi added.

"Here, here," Prof chanted.

We took turns watching the drone, and otherwise ate and slept at will, preparing for whatever the next day would bring.

I brought the drone back for fresh batteries. Then flew high overhead to watch the entire camp. The camo tent collapsed. The sentries were going first. Ten minutes later, their gear was packed onto the roof of the Jeep nearest the tent. The two sentries moved down the line to the next tent. Now three people were working and the tent was smaller. It and its cot were rolled and roof-topped in minutes.

The sentries did the lion's share of breaking camp. Everyone else seemed to be hearing a slower drummer. Leni moved at the pace of the others, wisely not showing bursts of energy that would generate suspicion.

One sentry checked the fire rings, pouring water on each, and stirring the ashes with a tree branch.

Leni's smartphone beeped.

I removed it from the charging drawer. Oleace had 38 new messages. I checked the most recent—from choochoomagoo3.

Sally, Sally, wherefore art thou, my Sally?

If the guy knew, he'd run.

Prof crawled out of the front compartment.

"You got a signal?" he asked.

"Two bars," I said. "Messages are coming in."

"The jammers are down." He looked at the feed from the drone. "I bet they're on the roof of an SUV."

I returned my attention to the drone, suddenly aware that I was driving fast and had taken my eyes off the road.

The guards lined up the clients beside a Jeep and handed each a bottle. I moved the crow closer. Everyone drank. Leni looked at the bottle, and up into the sky. She lowered the bottle to her right side and glanced at the sentry who was closing the rear door of the SUV, then to the other, who was shaking open a garbage bag. She dropped the bottle.

She said something that looked like, "Whoops."

The sentry shaking the bag looked up.

Leni squatted and came up with a bottle in her left hand, twisted off the top and started drinking.

I rewound the video and watched in slow motion. She opened the bottle the guard gave her and drank.

No.

Pretended to drink. No air bubbles. No change in the level. Then she dropped the bottle. It disappeared into ankle-high grass. She bent low and came up with a bottle. But it was capped.

She wrapped her hand over the top and cleaned it with a rubbing motion and suddenly there was no top. Then she drank like everyone else, sipping a little at a time. Chatting.

I returned to the live feed from the drone. The first girl to finish drinking tossed the empty into the waiting trash bag.

"More water?" Prof said.

"The last dose maybe. It's only a couple hour drive."

"I wish I had one of those bottles to test," he said.

I reached into the drawer where Leni's phone had been charging, pulled out a bottle, and stood it on the counter.

"You dirty dog, Cuda. You copped one last night."

"The least I could do."

"Who can we get to analyze it?" he said.

"I was thinking of multiple opinions."

He grinned. "See who lies to us? They test the water. We test them."

"Were you a spy in a previous life?" I said.

"I'll take over." I handed the game controller to Prof and moved out of the way. Since we now had a cell tower I located my burner phone and checked my service.

"Hi Tommy," Tina said. "Do you know a Detective Braden? He's such a gentleman. He asked me to give you a message the moment you called in."

"Sorry, I haven't had cell coverage."

"No problem. But he is not a patient man. The message is, 'Kelsey, where are the donuts?' Does that make sense? It's not my business, but who is Kelsey?"

"It's a code we use in case someone is listening," I said. Which was almost the truth.

"Oh," she said and waited a couple of beats. "Do you mean someone like me?"

"No, Tina. I mean a bad guy who wants to mess with us."

"I see," she said.

"Any other messages?"

"Two hang ups. Why do people do that? Call an office and hang up when I answer?"

"Probably shy." Or avoiding a data trail with a live witness.

"They don't want to be recorded?" she said.

"Some people hate answering machines," I said. "Thanks for the update. I'll pick up the donuts tonight."

"Don't delay. He seemed sort of…desperate. You know how nasty sugar addicts can get."

"The voice of experience?" I asked.

"Twinkies. Bye, Tommy."

I laughed at the thought of sweet Tina getting bitchy because she needed a Twinkie fix. Then I dug empty water bottles out of the trash, rinsed them, and divided my one 16-ounce bottle equally among four bottles. I found a Sharpie in a drawer and labeled them A, B, C, D, like exhibits in a murder case.

I hesitated.

Why had I thought of the word murder?

CHAPTER 32

"Why can't I go with you?" Naomi asked, pouting.

"Too many unknowns. Don't know what he wants. The donuts mean it's important."

"Do cops really like donuts?"

"Everyone like donuts." I laughed. "But in this case, it's a code. The more donuts, the more important we talk soon."

"What about the kind of donuts? Is that code too?"

"Yeah, for the mood he's in."

"But I—"

"Naomi, I don't know if he'll talk if you're there. And I can't leave you just sitting in the car alone for I don't know how long."

"Afraid some guy will come by and sweep me off my feet?"

I tensed at the metaphor, but she didn't seem to care.

"Concerned for your safety."

She said nothing.

"You'll be the first to know what we talk about."

She smiled.

"OK, I could use a nap in a real bed. Those blow-up plastic things are never soft in the right places. How the heck do they make dolls out of that stuff?" She laughed.

Monday evening traffic was light so we made good time. I dropped her at Shianti's place, where her car was hidden in the garage.

"The neighbor's are going to wonder about us," she said with a smile.

"Same guy in and out. Tongues will wag."

She stuck out the tip of her tongue and fluttered it. "You bet they will. Bye, Tommy. I can get in through the garage by myself. Remember," she stared at me, "tell me first."

She rolled away with both arms pumping like she was at the gym.

I stood in the street waiting as the garage door went up. No one so much as glanced at either of us. She tossed me a little wave with one hand as the door rattled back down.

I drove to Braden's office and parked at the church. The lot was empty, so I chose a spot where the Barracuda wouldn't be visible from the street. I slipped a bottle into my jacket pocket and started walking.

I had forgotten the donuts.

I ran back to the car, drove to the Pig, and bought six of the 'Scone of the day' from the cashier. I didn't see Shianti. Back to the same parking place at the church. It was after six, but daylight saving time made it feel like midafternoon.

Braden's door was ajar. I knocked with one knuckle.

"If it can wait until tomorrow, come back then."

I opened the bag so the aroma of fresh cranberry scones could escape.

"Advance and be recognized."

I followed the Pig logo through the door and closed it behind me.

"It's about damn time, Kelsey. Good thing the patient isn't on his death bed, you'd be late for the funeral."

I unpacked the coffees and scones. "Fresh today."

He tested a scone and didn't complain. Then dumped sugar and cream into a coffee. He pushed a single sheet of paper across his desk —all the way to the edge closest to me.

I pulled the guest chair forward and read the page without picking it up. It contained the address of a Ms. Janet Doerington.

I looked up.

"I loaded mystery man into our Stretch system. Which I shouldn't do because there's no one to bill." Braden gestured with his head. "She popped up."

"Should I guess?"

"Go ahead, it'll be fun."

"DNA search. Doerington is related to mystery man."

"Good that the obvious jumps out at you. A useful skill in a private dick."

"I'm not—"

He stopped me with a raised hand. "If it walks like a dick, and it quakes like a dick…"

He was right. I was a PI in everything but the license and getting paid.

"Have you talked with her?" I asked.

"Not my job." He bit into his scone.

"OK if I—"

He stopped me. Plausible deniability. He was leaking information. He didn't have an open case. Yet.

"Anything you can tell me about Doerington?" I asked.

"Mr. Kelsey, do you have any idea how many rapes are reported in this country every year?"

"I could only guess."

"Don't bother. Call it three-quarters of a million. But that's an estimate. Probably over a million if we knew about them all."

"That's a lot of crimes. But why…" I watched his eyes. They were examining his coffee.

"She was raped?"

"Sadly, yes. Over 20 years ago. Full report. Completed kit. The whole nine yards."

"They get the guy?" I asked.

He finished his first scone. "Nope."

"Technical error?"

"Nope."

"You know what happened?"

"Nope." He reached for the bag. "Case vaporized."

I took time to eat and sip so I could think.

"How can that happen?" I asked.

"Couple of ways. Usually the injured party refuses to press charges. Complaint is withdrawn." He paused to finish his coffee. "Or there's a plea deal."

"Can I review what you just told me?"

"Go ahead."

"A database somewhere thinks Doerington is related to the mystery man we think is Lenore's father."

He nodded. "Doerington was raped. Test kit says so."

"By the mystery man?" I asked.

"Test kit says so."

"Case never went to trial?"

"Not that I can find," he said.

"Question?

He fired at me with his finger.

"Can your Stretch system determine the relationship between Doerington and the rapist."

"At varying levels of confidence."

"What's the most probable?"

He broke a scone in half and sprinkled sugar from a paper packet onto it, took a bite, and chewed.

"Mr. Kelsey, do you have any siblings?"

<>

Naomi stared at me across the remains of a pineapple and chicken pizza, sipping a zero-caffeine cola drink I had never heard of. I was on my second beer.

"No way," she said.

"That's what Braden said. Or implied. The only hard data is a name and an address."

"Where?"

"A little lake up in Wisconsin."

"Lots of lakes in Wisconsin. Does being on a lake mean anything?"

"It's a long way from St. Louis," I said.

She eyed the last slice of pizza. I gestured for her to take it.

"I'll split it with you," she said.

"I'm full. But I'll eat half if it will make you feel better."

She cut the pizza slice across and gave me the tip.

"I eat alone too often," she said.

We each took a bite.

"Maybe," I said, "she moved far away from what happened long ago in St. Louis."

"Ain't no running from that kind of bad. The planet Mars would be too close. And it's a hundred and forty-two million miles away. Light takes twelve minutes to get there."

"New surroundings eliminate reminders." I drank some beer. "Do you think she'll talk to me?"

She shook her head. "No way. But she'll talk to us." She smiled.

We finished eating, recycled the box, rinsed the plates. Shianti and Prof still hadn't returned.

"We can be there in an hour," I said.

She ran her left thumb back and forth across her lips as she thought. She had painted her nails a different bright pink since returning from the forest.

"It'll be after eight by then," she said. "Strangers showing up, asking questions." She shook her head. "Let's leave after early rush hour tomorrow. Get there mid-morning. Much better vibe."

"We're not cops," I said. "Why would she talk to us?"

"Because we're clever and persuasive." She smiled. "Now. We had a nice dinner. How about a movie? Shianti has streaming galore." Her eyes seemed bigger and rounder than I remembered. "And our kiss countdown needs attention."

◇

"You'd think," Naomi said, "they would have paved roads."

"At least pave the one that circumnavigates the lake," I said.

"But the houses are on the water. And the road is way back there."

"Think of this as communing with nature," I said. "Lumbering along dirt tracks like the Pilgrims in covered wagons."

"Fun," she said. But she didn't mean it.

"There's the lake."

I drove slowly along a dusty road with tall marsh grass growing in the water on both sides. Narrow and potholed kept the Barracuda at a walking pace. The mound of road expanded into a natural island with a row of six cottages planted at the edge of the lake. They all needed paint. At least one needed to be bulldozed and replaced.

"I bet these lakefront places are worth a lot," Naomi said. "Why are they so run-down?"

"Cash flow. Been in the family for years. Kids can't agree what to do with it. Taxes. Upkeep. No one takes responsibility. These were probably built as fishing shacks for grandpa after returning from the war to end all wars."

"A wee bit cynical today?" she said.

"DNA data can do that to a guy."

She grew quiet. Then whispered, "You've been thinking about that too, huh?"

"Hard not to."

The road ended at a T-intersection with three houses in either direction.

"Which one do you think?" I said.

She pointed. "That place way down on the end looks like it's going to fall into the lake. I hope it's not that one."

"You jinxed us," I said, turned left, and stopped by a mailbox on a metal post tilted backward as if a tornado had attacked it. Leftover adhesive marks on its side indicated 4 Lowwater Rd.

Naomi said, "I hate being right."

The weeds in the yard were halfway between green and brown and the height of the doorknob. A dirt path barely six inches wide meandered up to a porch with a single Adirondack chair recently painted sky-blue.

"You think someone really lives here?" she said.

I shut off the car and we cranked down the front windows. Birds, outboard motor whining on the lake, wind waving marsh grasses. I stepped out on gravel. No sound from any of the houses. An aluminum row boat plunked against the dock of the house next door. Boards were missing from the dock.

"There's a boat next door," I told Naomi.

"Probably leaks," she said.

Both windows of the house were covered with drapes aged to fog gray. The entrance had once had a screen door that was now standing beside the house, held upright by the height of the grass. The front door had been bleached by the sun. I started thinking Naomi was right, no one had lived here for a long time.

A finger poked between the drapes nearest the front door and opened a space for one eye.

"Left window," I whispered. "Someone's watching you."

"Place looks like it's waiting for the next victim to enter."

"You want to stay here while I check it out?"

"And get attacked by a swamp monster? No way."

"You could lock yourself in the car."

"Hmm," she said.

"I'll leave the gun for you."

"Oh yeah, get me thrown in jail for protecting your butt."

I looked around at my ass.

She laughed.

"If you stay here, the house won't collapse on you."

"But if the interview goes well," she said, "I'll miss the whole thing."

"And your innocent look and clever repartee may be required to get us inside."

"Who wants to go inside?"

The front door swung inward with a screech like a gull burning its feet on hot coals. A frail woman in a flower print apron over a gray dress stepped onto the porch. She was wearing pink flip-flops. A black and white tabby cat circled her feet.

"You can't park there. The mail truck needs to get to my box."

"We'll just be a few minutes. When does the mail come?"

"Thursday," she said, "at noon."

"But it's—" I stopped myself.

Naomi cranked down the passenger window.

"We are hoping you will help us," she said.

The woman stared straight at Naomi and scowled.

"Why would I help a darky?"

I froze. But Naomi didn't even blink.

"It's a family thing," she said.

"I got no family."

I kept my mouth shut.

"Are you Janet Doerington?" Naomi asked.

"No."

"We're journalists doing a story on the history of football at the Brothers of St. Francis Academy."

"I don't give two hoots about football. Then or now." She looked at me across the roof of the car. "You can't park here."

"Yes, Ma'am," I said. "I'll move right away."

"Your brother played for St. Francis," Naomi said.

Janet retreated a half-step into the shadow of the house but didn't close the door.

"I got no brother."

I stooped low, still standing beside the open driver's door. Naomi was looking at me through the car.

"This isn't going well," I said.

Naomi nodded her head enthusiastically. "It's going great. She's still talking." She turned back to the house.

"Michael played a couple decades ago."

"I don't care," she said, fading further into the house. "And he sure don't care about any nonsense you write."

"We can make him famous in history," Naomi said.

Janet shook her head. She seemed to be in her mid-40s, but her hair was already graying. The tabby sat down by her left foot.

"He still don't care."

"The story might win a big award," Naomi said.

"He could win a million dollars," Janet said. "He still won't give a tinker's curse."

Naomi was making it up as she went along. But at least Janet hadn't slammed the door.

I straightened and over the roof of the Barracuda said, "Why wouldn't he like a million dollars?"

"Because, sonny, he's dead. Been dead a long time. May he rot in hell for all eternity."

For the first time, she smiled broadly, showing slightly crooked and nicotine-stained teeth. Then she chased the cat inside and slammed the door behind her with another gull screech.

I slipped behind the wheel.

Naomi said, "You can't park here."

We laughed, but our hearts weren't in it.

On a hunch, I crouched low and snuck around the front of the car. I crawled on my hands and knees from the bumper to the tilted mailbox, reached up and swung the rusted metal door open with a creak. I lifted my head to peer in. The box was half full of mail, all slid to the back because of the steep angle of the post. I reached in and grabbed a handful.

The first two were for Resident.

The third was addressed to Belinda Cercus.

None were for Janet Doerington.

I stuffed them all back into the box.

I raced to the driver's seat and backed up along the earthen path to the T-intersection. The finger and eye between the curtains watched us go. I backtracked through the swamp, reached pavement, and drove around the lake. Waterfront cottages lined the shore. White capped waves popped up on the lake.

"I'll bite," Naomi said. "What is she talking about?"

"What's your impression of Janet?"

"Hmm. If she's the sister, she wouldn't be more than ten years older. So forties? But parts of her look closer to sixty. Hair. Scrawny. Weak. A few stairs missing."

I laughed. "What?"

"Not quite right in the head. Lives in this isolated place all alone with a houseful of cats. Worries about getting her mail on Thursday. It's only Tuesday. Yet the mailbox is full."

"Maybe cars sit around a long time out here." I slowed and eased into the gravel parking lot of an ice cream shack.

"Have you ever driven past a diner and not gone in?" she asked.

"I hope not," I said.

That got us laughing again.

"Real food or ice cream?" I asked.

"Both."

We read the hand-printed menu hanging over the service window and ended up with coney dogs, sodas, and two hot fudge sundaes packed to go.

"Are these called coney dogs for the reason I think?" she said.

"How can I know what you think?"

"I mean, they have something to do with Coney Island. That's in New York, right?"

"Big amusement park a hundred years ago. Someone poured chili on a hot dog."

"Good idea. Hot dogs are boring."

I laughed.

"What?" she said. "They taste bland."

"True. The fun is in the…eating."

Her face went blank and she stared at me. Then she slowly shook her head.

"Blues player. Is that all you guys ever think about?"

"Sometimes I think about amplifiers. And strings, and—"

"I get it. Hey, I have an idea." She sat there and smiled.

"Is it a secret?" I said.

"Uh-huh. For me to know and you to find out."

I chuckled. "Isn't that a little childish?"

"Yes," she said. "But back to our homework. Janet is frightened of her shadow. And fear led her to live in isolation where no one would know or care who she is." She paused, then said, "Isolation produced stress. And if you allow me to speculate, I bet she's an alcoholic. One of those who forgets to eat."

"Not much data to support that," I said.

"There are other explanations for what we saw. That's just a highly probable one."

"Do I want to know the others?"

"Next most likely. Cancer."

I had nothing to add to that, so we rode in silence with our coney dogs sealed in a bag and our ice cream sundaes melting.

"Let's park by the lake," she said. "And make a plan."

We followed wood signs with letters carved into them to a county park with a single boat ramp and two picnic tables under a gazebo.

"I like watching the water," she said. "The motion is hypnotic. Can we get close?"

"Can you swim?"

"I can float. But not for long."

We were alone in the tiny park, so I swung toward the lake and eased down the boat launch until the front bumper got wet.

"Close enough?"

"You're a little crazy, aren't you?" she said. But she was smiling.

"In a conservative sort of way." I shut off the engine, shoved the transmission into first, and pulled the emergency brake.

"This is delightful," she said. "The lake seems massive from down here close to the waves. Makes me think of ancient sailors in the middle of an ocean with no land in sight."

"Lost," I said. "Mostly they were lost before the invention of a clock that could keep time on a moving ship."

"And look at what we have. A phone in our pocket that can hear satellites." She stared out over the rippling water. "Seems like a dream."

"It was once," I said. "Someone has to dream it first before anything gets invented."

She looked up into a mostly blue sky.

"How did anyone ever think of Global Positioning Satellites? It just seems so weird."

"They wanted to know where their army was."

Naomi dug into a white bag and extracted a coney dog.

"That's right," she said. "Technology trickles down to us lowly consumers from the Department of Defense, doesn't it?"

"For sure. Most of modern life can be tracked back to a military project. Especially the granddaddy of them all."

"Nuclear energy?"

"That too. But I was thinking of the Internet."

"No way!"

"Oh yes. The challenge was to find a way to keep the big wigs of command and control in touch with each other even if the Unites States infrastructure was under attack. Now it connects almost everyone."

"For better or for worse." She sighed and began to unwrap her hot dog.

I laughed. "Funny way to put it. But we are married to it, aren't we?" That had been rhetorical. But she answered.

"Don't have to be. Just press the off button."

Sunlight flickered from the tops of waves. I attempted to see patterns in the lights the way people see shapes in clouds.

"I'm trying," I said. "But it's harder than it sounds. Everyone expects me to be available at the touch of a button. And if I'm not, there's no backup system. You know, like stopping by my place. Or running into me at the malt shop on Friday night like my grandfather did with his friends. Half his stories started out with a chance encounter at that shop."

"What was it called?"

"The Malted Way."

"Sounds like a philosophy," she said with a laugh. The she bit off the end of her hot dog and dribbled chili sauce down her chin. I tried not to laugh, but failed.

"How about you?" she said.

"Me what?"

"Do you want everyone available at the touch of a button?"

I considered. "No, I want to sit around the malt shop once or twice a week and catch up and make simple plans and lead a simple life."

"You sure? Sounds boring."

We ate in silence. I wasn't bored.

Finally she said, "So, what was in the mailbox?"

◇

Naomi napped in the passenger seat while I drove a road that was becoming as familiar as my driveway back home. I hadn't planned on commuting between Chicago and St. Louis, but the problems wouldn't stay in one place.

And Janet was a new problem. Her DNA in an old rape kit and in a database at a genetics company. Belinda Cercus in her mailbox. And believing that her younger brother was dead even though his DNA was alive and well in a Jane Doe rape kit?

Naomi stirred and blinked at the sun facing us as it floated near the horizon.

"Can't you go faster?"

"Yes, a lot faster. But the highway patrol frowns on it."

"Party poopers," she said.

I laughed. "They're trying to keep our highways safe."

"Then get the drunks off of them. And those pinheads who text while driving."

"Hard," I said. "Especially in a country where alcohol is more popular than water."

"You think we worship alcohol?"

"Ever been to a party that didn't serve it?"

"Sure, lots of times."

"I mean after high school."

"Oh," she said. "Only once. And before you ask, it wasn't around here."

I waited for more.

"Utah. No alcohol. And no caffeine. That was bad. Can you imagine a world without coffee or tea or Pepsi? And no Red Bull or Monster Energy! What are they thinking?"

"That caffeine is a stimulant drug best avoided."

"How silly. Who came up with that?"

"Hmm, same place all religions come from," I said.

Naomi stared at me and waited. Then she laughed and changed the subject.

"Do you think he's really dead?"

"Not if our DNA evidence is correct. But I'm no geneticist."

She stared out the window at Route 66 gliding under our tires for half a minute before speaking.

"Assume he's alive. Assume our yearbook research is correct and Markus Corolla is really Michael Carnes. She said she wasn't Janet Doerington. Her mailbox suggests she's Belinda Cercus. What is going on? And why did Janet slash Belinda say he's dead?"

"Maybe she's wanted him dead for so long that she believes it."

Her lips rolled and pursed and twisted in thought.

"We need answers," she said.

"Yes. And gas."

I pulled off the road into a one pump station under a flying red horse. A paper note taped to the front of the pump read:

CASH ONLY — PREPAY!

The roof over a single pump attached to a building the size of a hotel room. Inside, a yellow counter of cracked Formica held a mechanical cash register. Shelves along the walls were filled with automotive products with the horse logo and rows of Route 66 souvenirs.

Behind the counter, a man with a gray beard was sleeping with his head against the glass window and the rest of him balanced on a three-leg stool. A newspaper on his lap declared itself the Norman County Clarion. A sign taped flat on the counter with masking tape advised:

DO NOT RING BELL

IF I'M SLEEPING

PRESS THIS BUTTON ==>

AND LEAVE CASH

I waited, but he remained immobile as wax.

I pressed the indicated metal button and heard the gas pump outside reset. When I reached the car, Naomi was engrossed with her phone. I leaned against the rear fender as the ancient pump delivered gas in slow motion. I called my service. Tina Retrina didn't answer, so I listened to recordings. The first tried to sell me a new cell phone service. The second was five seconds of silence and a hang up. The third was Prof. He was working at Shianti's place. She had gone to the Pig to keep her job. He wanted to know the plan.

Nothing from Leni.

I went back inside and left cash on the counter beside the bell. The man was snoring. The upside down headline on the Clarion shouted:

Gas Prices Jump 11% in Norman

Slow news day.

Remarkable, though, that this little station could exist. If this guy owned it, he could be a historical landmark. But how did the Clarion live on in the Internet world of 24-hour instant news in your pocket?

I returned to the Barracuda and slipped in beside Naomi.

"How would a county newspaper survive now?" I asked.

"Local focus. Low overhead. Some kids with pickup trucks distributing. Ancient, paid-for printing technology. But the secret ingredient is getting harder to find."

"People who read?"

"Yeah. People like video. And talking heads in suits and pretty dresses."

"So what's the secret?" I asked.

"Just my opinion. I can't back it up with statistics."

I started the car and pulled away from the lonely pump as quietly as I could.

"Point taken."

"The secret ingredient to anything is someone who wants it. Loves it. Is passionate about it. Behind every local newspaper is a newshound who is thrilled by the scoop, the angle, the rolling presses, the shouts of 'read all about it' on the street corner."

"Does anyone shout anymore? It'd be kind of exciting."

"An algorithm figures out your news for you now." She stared at me. "Or it would if you had a smartphone and some social media accounts so it could track your behavior. Instead, you live in the past in an old car on a road no one uses anymore."

"I'm seeking a way to live in the modern sea of information, disinformation, and outright lies that is conducive to my personal happiness. A journey of discovery that will bring fulfillment."

"You sound like a fortune cookie," she said.

"That was too long for a fortune cookie."

She laughed. I joined her.

"But you have an idea," she said. "I can tell by the way you start beating around the bush, as if you're trying to scare the idea into running out so you can capture it."

Insightful girl. "If Janet, um, Belinda's brother is dead, where would we find a story about it?"

"Depends on what happened," she said. "Heart attack while running a foot race. Car crash. Concussion, coma, death from a football game. They'd all be local news, but not for long."

"Should we go look?"

"Sure, I love the smell of microfiche. But let's try the Internet first."

I drove. Naomi stared at her phone for several minutes.

"There's nothing on Michael Carnes. It's like somebody erased his entire life."

"Any ideas who?"

"His father," she said.

"I thought fathers wanted a son to carry on the family name."

"Only when they are proud of them. Screw up and you're scratched out of the will and never spoken of again."

"Harsh," I said.

"It's a dog-eat-dog world. Or haven't you heard?"

I recalled being punched by a guy while picking up my car from the valet at the Pink Monkey for talking to the wrong girl.

"I see your point."

"I have another idea," she said.

"You're an idea machine today. Google should patent you."

"I'm one of a kind," she said. "What about your famous guy?"

"Markus? The university professor?"

"Yeah. Politicians cover up youthful blunders. Why not a professor?"

We made it to the library 30 minutes before closing time. The microfiche lady was happy to see us back, but frowned at her watch when we asked for archives of local newspapers that had been active 20 years ago. Still frowning, she brought us multiple trays. Naomi and I worked separate readers to process pages faster. With four minutes to go, the librarian started clearing her throat every 30 seconds.

Three minutes.

Two minutes.

The librarian collected all of the boxes we had been through.

"I'm sorry," she said, "you'll have to come back in the morning."

I replaced the fiche I had been viewing with weary eyes. The printer whirred behind me. Naomi grabbed the pages and folded them into her purse. She put her last fiche back and put the box on her lap, then wheeled to the librarian's desk and placed the box on the counter.

The overhead lights flashed three times.

"Thank you," Naomi said.

The librarian nodded with tight lips.

"Come back anytime," she said.

Naomi was quiet as I pushed her wheelchair back to my car. We got her comfortable and stored the chair. I hopped in behind the wheel and reached the key toward the ignition. She grabbed my wrist with her left hand and held it tight. With her free hand, she fumbled in her purse, pulled the printed pages out, and stuffed them into my hand. Then she released me and stared straight out through the windshield. Her expression unreadable.

I unfolded the pages.

The St. Louis Morning Star showed me a headline.

Football Hero Dies in Car Crash

I looked at Naomi. She didn't look back. I read the entire article. Twice.

Single vehicle accident. Open alcohol bottle found on front seat. Fire in engine compartment consumed the cabin, the tree the car had hit, and two more trees near the accident site.

"He stole his father's car?" I said.

She nodded, but didn't look at me.

"And his father's whiskey?" I said.

Another nod.

I looked for a date. Four months before Leni was born. No ID had been found in the ashes, but a ring and a knife had been discovered. Father refused an autopsy. The cause of death was obvious.

"So…" I began.

"Was it really him?" she said.

"Belinda thinks so. His father appears to agree."

"Explain the DNA your friend analyzed."

"There's likely some percentage chance that the test is wrong. A good lawyer would use that to cast doubt into the minds of jurors."

Naomi's face snapped toward me. "What do you think?"

"I don't think anything with confidence. But my intuition is screaming."

"Mine too," she said. "It says this Markus cat is smart, tricky, and evil."

"Isn't that a moral judgement?" I said.

"Sure is. If half of what I think is true, I'm right."

"Shall we sit here and go through out list of suspicions?"

She shook her head. "Let's go to my apartment. It's set up to make things easy for me."

I turned the key. The engine came instantly to life.

"Prof is waiting for a plan," I said.

"Me too. And Leni, although she might not know it."

At the mention of her name, Leni's phone vibrated in my pocket as if it had been listening.

Check Cuda Freelance messages

I called my service with Prof's burner. Two new messages. The first was another hang up. The second was from a breathless Leni.

"Tommy, I'm in Chicago. You were right. I feel different. I'm trying to act like my old self, but he'll know if he sees me. I want to run away. But if I leave town…" She paused for seconds. "I need to get lost. Really lost. To a place where no one can find me." Another long pause. "Forever."

"Leni is on the run in Chicago," I said. "Wants to disappear. She added 'forever.'"

"I can relate," Naomi said. "Some days things feel so impossibly hard and complex my brain rebels." She glanced my way. "What does 'forever' mean?"

I shrugged. "I think she's super frustrated. Leni's too ambitious to contemplate suicide. But I'm not a professional. What do you do on bad days?"

"Drop out. Hibernate. Recharge my batteries by not using them."

"Prof is still in Chicago."

"He's a smart guy. Tell him the problem."

I dialed from the burner.

"This had better be important," he said. "I prefer text."

"Leni is back," I said. "She recently made a call, I think from a phone booth within running distance of Nature Incognito. She wants to be lost."

"I got the E-ticket ride to obscurity. What's her number?"

"I have her phone," I said. "Don't know if she has another."

"We'll do it old school," he said. "I'll do concentric loops with the RV. When I find her, I'll grab her off the street. Where do I take her?"

"Hide her in the RV. I don't think Markus knows about it."

"I'll be in touch," Prof said. "We still need a plan."

"I'm analyzing new data tonight."

We wished each other luck and ended the call.

"He's going to kidnap her?" Naomi said.

"You heard that?"

"Deduced," she said.

"Leni will go willingly. But making it look like a kidnapping might help if word gets back to Markus. She needs to be safe. Disappearing is a good start."

I headed for Naomi's apartment.

"Are you driving back to Chicago tonight?" she asked.

"I don't think so. I need time to think about how this car crash fits."

"It doesn't," she said. "But Belinda and the reporter both believed it."

I pulled up in front of her high-rise apartment building.

"But you're not so sure?" I asked.

"Oh, I'm sure. I just can't prove anything."

I retrieved her wheelchair from the trunk and held the door while she made the transfer. I locked the Barracuda with a key and pushed her to the elevator, where she whispered to me.

"You know Markus faked his own teenage death. An innovative way to avoid responsibility for fathering Leni. And erase the black mark—" She froze for a moment, her face blank. "…that having a child with a black woman would permanently attach to his shiny prep-school record. All that after raping his sister."

"Seems like an extreme solution."

"The elite crowd is insular and self-interested. And self-protective."

"How could a high school kid pull it off?"

She reached out an arm to push the up button.

A dark-skinned man in blue jeans and white sneakers walked up behind us. A woman pulling a three-year-old by the hand arrived. The little girl was licking an orange sucker and staring at me.

Naomi rolled herself away from the closed elevator door and back toward the main entrance.

"What's up?" I asked.

"You'll see. Wait here with me."

The doors opened and ingested the three people. Naomi rolled back to the elevators.

"He can't," she said.

"Who would help a kid fake—"

"His self-serving prick of a father."

"To protect the family name and fortune and ensure his son's gilded future?"

"That would be the good-old-boy pitch," she said. "Can't let some black whore bring down his fine upstanding boy."

"But they would—"

"Have to find a body. That's what I've been thinking about. And I think I've got it."

"You should be a private eye." I smiled.

"Ha! Are you carrying a cell phone?"

"Two of them."

"Are they turned on?"

I nodded.

She shook her head. "Easy to track."

I pulled out both phones and turned them off. But thought about my Barracuda parked outside. It was easy to track too.

Naomi smiled. After the elevator doors were fully open, she rolled herself in and spun the chair 180. She pressed the door-close button the moment my feet were in the car.

"What's the hurry?" I asked as the doors glided soundlessly closed.

"I want to be alone to work on our project." She reached over and grabbed the sleeve of my jacket and pulled me toward her. "Let's see if we can get down to ninety."

I dropped to one knee and felt the warmth of her lips on mine as she pulled us together. The next clear thought I had was the chime of the elevator arriving at her floor. She pushed me away. I stood up fast.

"That should count for more than one," I said.

"Oh no, you're not going to get away with reinterpreting the rules. Ninety-one to go."

I followed her along mauve carpet with a swirl pattern, passing identical doors on both sides of the hallway. Each door had a number above a peephole. She stopped at 833 and raised her wristwatch to the doorknob. The latch whirred and clicked. The door swung inward under its own power.

"Isn't technology wonderful?" she said.

"Convenient."

"Little things help a lot when you have to roll through a walking person's world."

Her apartment was soft pastels and lacked the clutter of coffee tables or cabinets that would hinder movement. It had a flat screen TV mounted opposite a La-Z-Boy lounge chair. There was no other seating in the room. But there was a dinette set near the kitchen with a full setup of silverware but no chair. One straight back chair sat opposite the setup. Sagging white once-fresh flowers adorned the center of the table.

"What's the plan?" she said.

I was standing in the foyer on a shiny hardwood floor that seemed recently polished. She faced me from her metallic red chair. Martin Luther King stared at me from a hubcap.

"Find out if Prof found Leni."

"And we do that how?"

"Check my answering service."

She frowned and shook her head. "We shouldn't turn on any cell phones. Those things are blabbermouths with data."

I considered the burner and whether someone might have grabbed that number and be tracking it.

"Where's the nearest pay phone?"

She pointed. "End of the hallway past the elevators. The owners left them in because our cell phone coverage is quote: 'frequently interrupted by unscheduled outages for which management is not responsible.'"

"How thoughtful," I said.

She laughed and rolled to a desk in the foyer. It was covered with green alligator skin and had gold legs. She opened a drawer and reached in.

"Open your hand." She dropped a bunch of quarters onto my palm. "You can't get much for a dime anymore. When you get back, knock nine times in a row so I know it's you."

"OK," I said, and turned to head out.

"Hey."

I glanced back to see her gesturing 'come here' with one finger. I bent over and gave her a quick kiss on the lips.

"I'll be back in a couple of minutes. Ninety."

"I'm not sure that one counts."

I headed out the door and found a pay phone next to the stairway exit. There was a silver holder, but no phone book inside. I tried Prof's number direct and got a robot message that the number was no longer in service.

Hmm.

I checked the number, dialed again to be sure. Same result. I dialed my service. Three messages.

A hang up. Third time now. Maybe someone wanted me to answer the phone. I hesitated. Or someone wanted me to call in to retrieve messages so they could determine my precise location.

But why was I important?

The second message was Prof whispering.

"I picked up the package. It's damaged. Going to see the sights. Will send you an update in the morning."

I hung up. Why whisper? He was in public and not on his cell phone. In fact, his cell phone was no longer in service. Therefore, he was going deeper into hiding. And the packaged was damaged. How badly? And where would he take Leni?

Nowhere in Chicago. Even St. Louis wasn't safe; we had been found there. And shot at. Hmm. No place that I would know, because Markus would probably know too. I listened to the last new message.

"Mr. Cuda, a close friend of mine has disappeared. She has... special needs. I am extremely concerned for her welfare. I would like to retain your services to assist in finding this individual. Your fee will be very generous."

The caller recited a phone number twice. I looked around for a way to scribble it down, found nothing, so repeated it in a whisper over and over. I was still whispering in an empty hallway when I knocked nine times.

Nothing. Nine more. Nothing.

I turned the knob. The door opened into an empty foyer. Naomi was nowhere in sight. I locked the door behind me with the deadbolt and started to call her name but stopped myself. Instead, I took off my boots and snuck through the apartment.

The light beside the La-Z-Boy was on, and the kitchen table was covered with maps. Three circles had been penciled on: Wisconsin, the Upper Peninsula of Michigan, and Canada.

North was a good guess.

It bothered me that Markus had a working arrangement with guys in Missouri with red lights under their cars. But what better way to find drug addicts than through their suppliers? I unlocked a sliding door and stepped out onto a patio barely wide enough to stand on. I wondered if Naomi ever came out here. I reached for my cell phone out of habit. It was off.

I backtracked to the pay phone in my socks, this time with paper and pen, and dialed the number from memory. It rang five times. A male voice I didn't recognize answered.

"Go ahead."

"Returning a call that left this number."

"What about?"

"A retainer to help find someone," I said.

"Hold."

A minute became two. I debated hanging up because Naomi was alone, probably sleeping, and the door was unlocked. The phone clicked. I thought it had gone dead, but the same voice spoke.

"Locker B14. Code 1699."

The phone clicked off.

CHAPTER 33

I wrote the message down word for word, added the phone number, and tried to think of something to do right now to help Leni. The blue smoke bomb on my Barracuda came to mind. And the fact that I wasn't getting closer to the Pacific; I was merely rolling up miles on my car and combusting dead dinosaurs.

I returned to the apartment, locked the door, and headed for the kitchen.

"Tommy?" floated from the bedroom.

I flicked off all the lights. Naomi's door was six inches ajar. I eased it open.

"You OK?" I whispered.

"Waiting for you," she said.

"I…uh…had to return a call. Prof said he'll call in the morning. I'll stretch out on the couch."

"Come here."

I slipped through the opening. She was on the far side of the bed, lying on her side, facing me. Pink pajamas showed above a white blanket. She slipped both arms out from under the covers. I couldn't see her eyes well enough in the moonlit room to read what they were saying.

She whispered, "Let's work on our project."

◇

Dust particles in the sunbeam drifted in slow motion. I was still wearing my street clothes. Naomi's pajamas peeked out from under the lightweight blanket. Her chest rose and fell slowly. The last number I could recall was seventy-seven.

Her kisses could last a long time.

I needed a plan.

Some philosophers claimed it was not possible to be happy without well-defined objectives. One must define success or they will be forever chasing moving rainbows and never achieve bliss.

I started with a low bar.

Search my car for another bomb.

Find locker B14.

Open locker without being blown apart.

I moved on to the harder stuff.

Find Leni.

Deal with whatever is in the locker.

Free Leni from Markus.

And maybe even…

Bring Markus to justice.

That last one was too vague. The philosophers wouldn't approve.

Naomi's slumber continued. She hadn't moved more than an inch since the sun woke me up. I wondered if I ever slept so peacefully. Waking up regularly with blankets wrapped around me suggested no.

I tiptoed out of the room and started the shower in the guest bath. Then I turned it off and went down the hall to check my messages from the pay phone. There was only one.

We are on the road. Will send destination soon. Buy gas.

Prof was warning me of a long drive. But he probably thought I was still in Chicago, not St. Louis. I wondered why no destination and the obvious occurred to me: He hadn't chosen it yet.

I restarted the shower and let the puzzle pieces that were Markus Corolla shift around in my head. The clearer I saw him, the more one idea persisted.

Con artist.

The flowing hot water relaxed me in places I hadn't known were tense. The hissing rush of the spray tuned all voices out of my brain. The warmth brought back the feel of Naomi's lips and the touch of her finger for me to not talk, just kiss.

The room filled with steam. The mirror fogged over. I breathed warm, wet air. I lathered and tried to think like Marcus about the nuances that needed to be under control to keep his shell game afloat. Possibly the most important aspect of the scheme was his reputation. It opened doors with money behind them. Nothing could be allowed to taint it. Anyone who tried must be silenced.

The blue smoke bomb came to mind. Someone had to find me. Place it. Arm it. All to let me know that shey could get to me at will. Therefore, I was perceived as a threat.

The door banged against its stop, revealing a pink-clad Naomi in her shiny chair.

"You going to use all the hot water?"

"If I can," I said, as I rinsed and shut it off.

She was laughing.

"Something funny?" I asked.

"I have a continuous water heater." She lifted a light blue bath towel off the rack and handed it to me. I stood in the shower stall and toweled my hair toward dry. Her image, blurry through the frosted glass shower door, remained in the doorway. I poked my head around the edge of the door. She was gazing in my direction, hands folded on her lap, steam rolling past her into the hallway.

"Are you, um, going to sit there?"

She licked her lips. "Let me ask you a question, Mr. Cuda. If this situation were reversed, would you want to sit here and watch?"

Easy answer. "Only if you wouldn't let me dry your back for you."

◇

I hoped the blue smoke bomb was a one-time warning. But I searched my car anyway. The sun was slicing across a clear blue sky when I finally saw it. A black wire, no thicker than a paper clip, hiding under the cable running from the positive terminal of my battery.

A wire meant something needed electrical power that a simple battery couldn't supply.

I traced the wire down low and back to the firewall. It ended in a plastic box that looked like a voltage regulator, but smaller. The cover had Plymouth stamped on it. Plymouth had manufactured the

Barracuda, but the brand had been defunct for years. My first guess was that it was tracking whenever the car was moving. And it completely powered down with no lithium battery to find when the car was off. But that was an assumption. Perhaps it didn't track me. Perhaps it listened. Or it was a trigger.

Whatever else Markus was, he was serious.

I crawled under the car to check the fuel tank for wires or boxes or anything that looked newer than 1965. Finding nothing, I dragged myself from under the car to find Naomi sitting there in a tight black top that reached her throat but left her arms and shoulders bare. Yoga pants that had a silver dragon printed along the shin on her left side completed her outfit.

"Are you going to Shey's Gym to work out?" I said.

"No, I'm going with you."

I shook my head slowly.

She stared down at me, lying in the street at her feet.

"Seriously, Naomi. It's dangerous. Someone wired my car with a box full of electronics."

"What does it do?"

"I have a couple of guesses."

She waited, her expression calm yet demanding.

"I know it can set off a smoke bomb near my fuel tank. Which implies—"

"That it could also make it go boom," she said.

I sat up and brushed off my jacket.

"Correct. Second guess is that it's tracking the car. And therefore me. Us."

"Doesn't have to be that way," she said.

"Chin could remove the box. But he's back in Chicago."

She shook her head. "Don't you watch movies?"

"Not recently."

"If you remove it," she said. "Then they come gunning for you because they know you are onto them."

I dusted off my pants. "What does Naomi 'Holmes' suggest?"

"Depends on where we need to go. Remember planes, trains, and automobiles? We could even use a motorcycle with a sidecar." She smiled.

I stayed quiet.

"What?" she said.

"I don't know where Prof is. But Leni is with him. I think. He may have stashed her someplace."

"Yes, and…"

"And I was prepping my car for a trip of undefined length to an unknown location."

"And you found the electronic thingy."

I nodded. "I was thinking about how to remove it when you showed up."

"Don't," she said. "It might blow up." She watched me for a moment and said, "Misdirection."

"We put the car someplace we're not?"

"Correct. We show them the zag, then we zig."

<>

I moved the Barracuda to a numbered slot in an underground garage, hoping being below ground might interfere with the box's signal. Obscurity made me think of the forest, and river, and tents and jammers. And if their jamming had jammed their own secret box.

I grinned. Serves them right.

Naomi insisted I stay out of the way while she packed her car for the undefined trip. So I stretched out on the La-Z-Boy to become Sally. If the Markus crew was tracking Leni's phone, they wouldn't be surprised to find it close to the Barracuda. The Oleace messages were endless. Leni must spend hours responding every day.

Magnetman500

Sally I miss you. You know I can't live without you.

TriumphAnt13

I need you like I need air. Come back.

hot4more

Are you okay? You've never been gone so long before. Send up a smoke signal.

phoenix1000

Please write. I can fix whatever the problem is.

MasterBlaster10

Don't leave me hanging bitch. Get your ass back to work.

DoitagainJack

Be ready for a hard spanking.

Pain2pleasure threatened long, slow torture if he ever got his hands on Sally.

Oleace had thousands of women online ready to fulfill every male primal fantasy—for the right price. Each member starring in his own movie.

"A penny for your thoughts?" Naomi said.

"The male of the species can be…um…peculiar."

"Becoming more self-aware while meditating in my La-Z-Boy?" She laughed so hard her wheelchair squeaked. "Something specific get your attention?"

I stood and stretched my legs. "Have you ever wondered where desire comes from? Not in general, but specific desires? One guy likes redheads. Another likes brunettes but not with short hair. You know the old leg-man versus breast-man kind of stuff."

"And the guys who have to beat up their girlfriends to get it up. Don't forget them."

I knew better than to ask. So I stuck with a simple question.

"Why such different…tastes?"

She rolled to the kitchen and loaded sodas, water bottles, and beer into a small cooler with an electric cord dangling from it. "Easy," she said. "Evolution requires diversity and mutation. It contributes to the survival of the species. Doesn't give a hoot about the individual experience. It's all about the reproductive outcome."

"In that context—"

She slapped the cover down on the cooler.

"Rape is as good as love. Maybe better. Because a rapist is violent and can protect the offspring. And the rapist gets the advantage of reproducing with a female who would never choose him. So he's pulling himself up the evolutionary ladder by his jockstrap."

I lifted the cooler off her lap and carried it.

"You're saying his genes are successful through violent domination of the female."

She rolled along beside me towards the elevator.

"We're talking about our ancestors. We're only hundreds of years out of the jungle. An eye blink in evolutionary time."

"That explains the messages."

"Oh, online is worse. In the virtual world, people are anonymous. No social pressure. No sense of duty. More like," she chanted, "Sack that village, rape and pillage." She paused before adding, "Eat, sleep, repeat."

"But civilization," I protested.

"Which part? Slave ships? Dungeons? Witch trials? The guillotine? Black lung disease? Asbestos? Or my favorite, the Supreme Court."

We were quiet as the elevator descended toward the parking lot. Naomi was breathing hard through her nose, like she had gone a round with Mohammed Ali. The door opened. Cool, damp air flowed over us.

"Is there hope for Homo sapiens?" I asked.

"Sure. Springs eternal."

◇

By noon we were in Chicago parked at the Generic Grocery between a silver BMW SUV and a Ford pickup truck with tires as high as Naomi's head.

"Why do they do that?" she asked.

"Do what?"

"Jack the truck up so high. I'd get a nosebleed."

"So they have the ground clearance to traverse the rivers and rocks and canyons of downtown Chicago."

"I think it's the same reason most people like to live at the top of a hill."

"To keep their basement from flooding?" I said.

"Ha ha. So they can look down on everyone else and feel superior. And conversely, so everyone else has to look up to them."

"People prefer tall leaders. CEOs. Presidents. They're all above average height."

"Dumb," she said.

"Yeah, tall vehicles tend to roll over and kill the occupants."

She smiled. "Thanks. Now I feel smart about my little car."

"You are," I said.

She looked at the center of the steering wheel and blushed a little. We had parked away from the Amazon lockers, in case someone was watching them.

"How do you want to do this?" she asked.

"If they're watching the lockers, they'll see me pick up B fourteen."

"I could get it."

I shook my head. "You're already too close to this. If they see you grab it, they'll sneak a tracker onto your wheelchair."

"Then at least hide your face. And limp."

"Limp?"

"Prevents them from using how you walk to identify you."

"Movies, right?"

"Of course. Where else can you learn stuff?"

I almost said 'books' but thought better of it. I ended up wearing a black hoodie under a red umbrella and limping by locking my left knee straight. On an 80-degree day. I limped around the left side of the building, being careful to keep my face between the low umbrella and the wall. I could see bushes and a few feet of pavement in front of me, hoping that if I couldn't see them, they couldn't see me.

I tilted the umbrella toward the security cameras. A blonde girl of perhaps 14 retrieved a box from the A bank, let the locker door slam, stood, and dropped the package into a handlebar mounted basket. She pushed her bike toward me.

"Umbrella?"

I whispered, "Slows aging. Just ask the Koreans."

She pfft'ed and rode away. But maybe she would look up aging and sun exposure and go buy herself an umbrella. I smiled inwardly at the thought, then remembered why I was there. I slipped on nitrile gloves and moved in close to the second bank of lockers. Number 14 was near the top. I had to deal with an umbrella, a code, the contents, and a spring-loaded door.

To free my hands, I tucked the shaft of the umbrella between my shoulder and chin like a journalist using an old-school desk phone. I pressed the first two digits of the code and froze. Would a bomb be wired to the code, the door, the box, or opening the box?

I moved sideways away from the door as far as possible and still get a finger on the keypad. I entered the last two digits and moved further sideways as I pulled the door open. A familiar Amazon box sat in the center of the locker. I looked down to hide my face, folded the umbrella, and prodded the box with its tip from as far away as possible.

The box was heavy.

I opened the umbrella, dragged the box out with one hand, and caught it like a football against my chest with one arm. The locker door slammed shut. I was now carrying illicit drugs or illicit cash. I backtracked around the building, eyes down, the umbrella up, knee locked, feeling like I was flying blind on a night raid. I slid into the passenger's seat beside Naomi, tossed the umbrella over my shoulder and lowered the box between my feet. Then I leaned forward until my forehead touched the dash to get out of sight.

"Let's get out of here," I said.

Naomi pulled away carefully. "Where to?"

"Toward the beach." I moved the box around on the floor and found a white envelope taped to it. T.C. had been scribbled across the envelope with a blue felt-tip marker. I didn't recognize the handwriting. I peeled the tape back to free the envelope and thought of the anthrax murders. Then I decided I was being paranoid. Whoever sent this had far easier ways to get rid of me.

"What'd you find?" Naomi said.

"An envelope with my initials on it. Should I open it?"

"No. We should burn it and forever wonder what this is all about."

"Impatient are we?" I said.

"Just trying to keep you moving. Guys have a one-track mind. And if they're not on that track, they wander all over the place."

I tore off the end near the C. "There's a sheet of paper inside."

"Perhaps we should read it."

I slid it out of the envelope with two fingers. "It starts 'To whom it may concern.'" I read the letter fast, dropped it on the floor, and tore open the cardboard box. It was filled with blocks wrapped in brown paper. I pulled out the top one and unwrapped it.

"A thousand dollars in twenties," I said. I counted. "Twenty packs."

"Someone likes you," she said.

"Someone wants to know where Leni is and they think I can help find her."

"The letter mentions Leni?"

"No. It says that they are looking for a missing person and offer the enclosed as a retainer for my services. It's signed by Harvey Constantine ESQ."

"Who uses a lawyer to hire a private eye?" she said.

"Someone who likes using the client-attorney privilege to keep information out of court."

"OK. Who would do that?"

She jack-rabbited off as the light turned green.

"In my limited experience, anyone who can afford it. Multi-national corporations. Governments. Organized criminals."

She slowed to the posted speed limit. "Which is this?"

"We're thinking Markus has a good delivery business going," I said.

"Yes. But you're worried about something."

"Why not put the note in the box?"

"Because they wanted you to read it before you knew what was inside," she said.

"There's a pay phone," I said.

Naomi signaled, slowed, and pulled to the curb without the slightest squeal of rubber.

"Smooth."

"Thanks. I'm trying to not attract attention. Feels a bit foreign."

I hopped out, chatted with Tina, listened to the single message three times, then got back into the car. Naomi blended into traffic.

"A one-word message from Prof."

"And the word is?"

"Fudge. I listened three times. Nothing before. Nothing after."

"Mean anything to you?"

"Not yet. But it gave me an idea. Let's find a donut shop."

<>

The Donut Vault wasn't just a little spot for breakfast. It was the high art of combining dough and sugar suitable for the Louvre. I went in for a dozen but came out with two. Braden could take a few home, and Naomi and I needed some for the road— if we ever figured out where were supposed to be going.

Naomi drove past the church, through the intersection, and pulled up in front of Braden's building.

"Do you want to go in with me?"

She shook her head. "You're only asking to be nice. I am keen to know what you find out. But talking to a cop with me present as an unknown won't help. Besides." She smiled. "I have shopping to do. When should I pick you up?"

I considered the upcoming conversation, the two large coffees, and the bag of donuts.

"About an hour."

"Let's call it ninety minutes. Shopping requires commitment. If I'm not right here, walk down to the church and check the parking lot."

"Got it." I met her brown eyes. They glimmered with excitement. "Thanks."

She pulled me to her and pressed her lips to mine.

"Seventy-four," she said. "Good luck, Tommy. I hope your cop friend can help Leni."

I stood on the sidewalk as she pulled away and waved at the rear window. She flashed the brake lights three times. I headed to the elevator in a daze, trying to sort my thoughts. I was still sorting when I reached the closed door to Braden's office. No lights shone from inside.

I crackled the bag open and waved it back and forth until the hallway smelled like the Donut Vault. I sipped my coffee. The knob turned and the door opened.

"Come on in," Braden said, almost friendly. "I'm finishing up paperwork on a morning homicide."

I tried to imagine chasing murderers for a living. Day in. Day out. I couldn't. I had nothing in my experience to help me picture what it would be like. What kind of internal compass would be required to remain stable? I placed the donuts and coffee on his desk and closed the door. The afternoon sun filled the room.

His shirtsleeves were rolled up to the elbow. Maroon tie loose. Hair disheveled from running his hands through it too many times. He seemed tired. Or sad. Or a bit defeated.

"Is now a good time?" I asked.

He harrumphed, which passed for his laugh. "This is Chicago. There's never a good time. What d'ya got?"

I knew he meant information. But I pushed the donuts across the desk.

"New supplier," I said.

He dug around in the bag and came out with a fried cake with pink frosting.

"I think the Jane Doe rapist raped his sister twenty years ago, like you thought."

He chewed for a moment. "Ain't DNA wonderful?"

"But the following year, he died in a single car, drunk-driving crash."

"Clever trick," he said. "How did they ID the body?"

"Bad fire. Not much left. No autopsy."

"Dental?"

"Not mentioned in the newspaper article I found."

"Drunk kid crashes daddy's car isn't front-page news." He considered his donut from three angles, then placed it on his desk on a paper napkin. "Let's work forward in time. Kid rapes his sister. Father finds out. Next thing, the kid is dead. Accident, murder, suicide?"

I shrugged. "This is shortly after he fathered Jane Doe. Wait. No. It's before Jane is born, but he would have known she was on the way."

"Fourth option," he said. "None of the above. The accident was a plan to disappear."

"Seems like it worked," I said.

"Have a donut," he said. "Much as I would like to, I can't eat a whole dozen."

"Ever try freezing them?"

"Ugh. What a horrible thing to do to a delicacy of the baker's art."

We both managed to smile.

"Crash boy has reappeared in Jane Doe's rape kit. How?" he asked.

I studied the donuts in the bag, but couldn't decide.

"Fake death to protect boy's Great-Gatsby future," I said. "Aided and abetted by wealthy father who thinks his son is just a red-blooded American boy sowing his wild oats."

"Friday night lights stuff," Braden said. "The end justifies the means." He finished his first donut. "These are grade A work."

I gave him a thumbs up.

"So," he said. "The disappearing act worked. Then Jane Doe shows up. Tie this all together for a jury."

"I'm no lawyer."

"Lucky you. Counselors are the grease necessary to make our justice system work. But they aren't the system. Although a fair number of them think so."

I removed a half-empty water bottle from my jacket and placed it on his desk.

"You know me well enough," he said, "to know that the only way I drink water is if there is whiskey or coffee in it. What's this about?"

"Lab test."

He frowned and waited.

"I suspect fentanyl at a dose to keep a dozen addicts happy but functioning."

"Do I want to know how you got that?" he said.

"A local business hosted a retreat. I stopped by their campground and got thirsty."

"You drink beer when you're thirsty." He studied the bottle but didn't touch it. "All of them?"

"Not the armed guards. Two of them."

His right eyebrow lifted.

I said, "Tasers, pepper spray, pistols, rifles."

"For a retreat?"

"Three days."

"You said local business."

"Nature Incognito runs rehab retreats. Three days to two weeks."

He frowned and studied the bottle again.

"They provide all food and," I nodded toward his desk, "drinking water."

He pulled a donut out of the bag. It had dark brown sprinkles on bright green frosting.

"Rehab programs have doctors," he said, "who prescribe meds. They focus on careful management rather than cold turkey."

"This seemed like a group of zombies who didn't know they were zombies."

Braden drank some coffee. "Involuntary?"

"They pay to attend." I took a bite of a chocolate-on-chocolate donut and thought about who knew what. "The retreats are academic experiments. No one should know what they are getting. Might even be double-blind studies."

"Science. Necessary, but not sufficient. So, our Jane Doe is a zombie?"

I nodded slowly.

"You ever wonder," he said, "who the bigger pushers are? The thugs on the street or the guys in white coats who went to medical school?"

I recalled a pharmacy student trying to sell me uppers he swore had come from big pharma.

"What else?" Braden said.

"I got a strange phone call."

"Welcome to my party. If a day went by that I didn't get a strange phone call, I'd think I was dreaming."

"Not my business," I said. "But do you ever get up in the morning and wonder why you do what you do?"

"Nope." He sipped his coffee in the quiet room.

"No, you never wonder?"

"Correct. I don't have to wonder. I know why I do what I do."

His donut was half gone.

"Is it a secret?"

He chewed for a long moment. "Not really. But mostly no one is interested in why. They just want me to succeed." He paused. "Or fail. Depending which side of the law they're on."

"I'm traveling Route 66."

"I know. Trying to find meaning, your calling, how to live, a philosophy that will survive the burning hot sun of rational inquiry."

"At least a job that I like."

He shook his head. "Wrong goal."

I stuffed the chocolate donut into my mouth and kept quiet.

"You have to respect it. Believe in its purpose. How it fits into society. In short, you have to give a shit. If you care deeply, sincerely, about what you do—some people call it passion—you can survive the furnace fires of a hundred hells."

He drank coffee with one finger in the air telling me to wait.

"But if you don't truly care, no matter how much you like your job or its perks—money, fame, women, big houses, fast cars, yachts, motorcycles—it won't matter to you and you'll wonder why you are wasting your life doing what you're doing. Worse, you will try to find that answer in a bottle—booze, pills, injections—that trick your mind into everything-is-alright for a little while."

"So you care?" I said.

"Sure do," he said, in a calm, even voice. "I care every damn second of every damn day that some motherfucker ended someone else's life and is walking around free bragging about how he got away with it."

"Justice?"

"Can be no justice for a murder. You can't bring people back to life. What compensation can there be for the death of a loved one? I want a society where it's unacceptable to kill people. At least an eye-for-an-eye. They die, you die."

He hadn't raised his voice or showed the slightest hint of emotion. Yet he had an upon this rock I will build my church intensity that I had never seen before.

"Thanks for the clarity," I said.

"Anytime. And good luck."

From a second bag I pulled out the Amazon box I had hid under the umbrella. I hadn't resealed it. I placed it on his desk.

"A message on my answering service directed me to the Amazon lockers by Generic Groceries. It also provided the code to open it. This was inside, sealed. I tore it open."

"Anyone else touch this?"

I shook my head.

"Good. We won't find any prints, but it's worth checking. Criminals make mistakes like anyone else. It's usually how we catch them." He reached in the middle drawer of his desk and pulled out a dagger-shaped letter opener. I couldn't see the handle, but the blade was black. He used the point to rotate the box and lift the lid so he could peer inside.

"How much?" he asked.

"How much what?"

He stared at me, his eyes unmoving.

"Twenty thousand," I said, "if they're all the same as the one I opened. But how can you tell it's money when it's wrapped? It could be blocks of soap."

"Soap stinks. But more important, government agencies have standard ways of doing things. It's the only way they ever get anything done."

"Do you think—"

"This is an FBI trick. One of many I've seen. Bills are fifties or less. They avoid the oft-counterfeited hundred. What was the message?" He held up a hand. "Wait. First contact. Twenty grand. They want to buy information that is important to them, but maybe not so important to you."

Braden not only cared, he was good. Maybe the two went hand in hand.

"They're trying to find Jane Doe," I said.

Braden leaned back and placed his coffee on the desk, though he didn't remove his hand. He stared over my shoulder. The sweep second hand on his wall clock jumped from second to second for a full minute.

"You know what this means, don't you?"

"I have a hypothesis," I said. "But it seems far-fetched."

"This is the twenty-first century. A hundred years ago, New York City had a horse manure problem. Now little glass slabs in our pockets connect billions of people who use them to watch puppy videos. Everything is far-fetched."

"I think Jane is an informant with important information. And she's missing."

"Maybe," he said. "Then this box of cash is a finder's fee. I think she's a threat."

"You have a guess?"

"Kelsey, have you ever wondered how we know how much illicit drugs are coming into the U.S. across the border from Mexico?"

"I've heard estimates. Never thought about where they come from."

"Fortunately," he said, "Most people don't." He leaned forward and drank coffee. "To know for sure, you have to count it. To count it, you have to know where it is. How is that even possible?"

"You buy information?"

He shook his head. "Not reliable."

"You seize some, then estimate what percentage of the total traffic you got."

"Good idea. But if you've never known the total traffic, what would you base the percentage on?"

I hated even thinking this thought. "You back calculate from the number of overdose deaths."

"Another good idea. You could be a cop. But the count varies too much based on the quality of the incoming product, not the quantity."

"I give up. You need a checkout counter like a grocery store."

"Essentially. There's a known bottleneck. Getting the stuff through checkpoints and into the United States. A middleman is required who picks up product from the producer in Mexico, smuggles it across the border, and delivers it to the distribution dealer in the states."

I guessed. "You bribe the middleman?"

"We would. But they know if either side finds out, they're dead.

"I'm stumped."

"Easy," he said, and waited. When I didn't hazard another guess, he said, "Become the middleman."

Reality smacked me on the side of the head.

"You mean actually move drugs illegally across the border for the very cartels that you are trying to stop from moving drugs across the border, just so you can count it?"

"We were quite accurate for a number of years."

I tried to imagine myself as an undercover FBI agent moving drugs for the people I was trying to lock up. And what would happen to me if my cover was compromised, like that CIA agent in the movie Fair Game? Those agents must have cared a lot.

"So the FBI has something going on that Jane Doe might interfere with?" I gestured toward the box of money. "And they pay me to find her?"

"Maybe." He shook the donut bag. "Or maybe they scare you, follow you, grab her, and steal their money back."

"Then they have it all."

"And we still won't know what it is." He looked in the bag for a moment, then rolled it closed. "You know, rumors float around police stations all the time. You hear about a hair-brained project some politician started. Or juicy details of an active case. All good fun to share a story while waiting for the morning coffee to brew."

"I bet you hear most of them."

"I'm a detective." He unrolled the bag. The frosting on the third donut was sky blue. "These should be a controlled substance." He took a bite and washed it down with coffee. "This city has a drug problem."

"Hasn't it always?"

"Yeah, since before women got the vote and passed the eighteenth amendment in nineteen nineteen. But this time, it's one drug."

"I can guess."

He nodded.

"Fentanyl," I said. "It shows up in every article about overdose fatalities."

"For good reason." He held the blue donut in front of his face and rotated it. "I bet they make hundreds of these. Each one perfect. The right amount of sugar. The ideal thickness of frosting."

"Quality Control," I said.

"Exactly. With fentanyl, there isn't any. Not in China, Mexico, US distribution. Nowhere." He bit into the donut.

"Seems crazy," I said. "Ingesting substances without knowing what's in them?"

"You're serious? The general population has been trained from birth to take the pill the doctor prescribes. Dizzy? Sad? Tummy ache? Put something in your mouth. For an addict, the problem-solving doctor is simply replaced by the problem-solving dealer."

I contemplated the last of my chocolate donut and doctors as government-sanctioned drug dealers.

"Not so different," I said.

"In my experience, addicts pay more attention than the average patient. Without an insurance company footing the bill, they want good value for their money."

Value made me think of Naomi's shopping trip. I checked the clock. My 90 minutes wasn't up.

"Value translates to a better high for your money," he said.

"Which can translate to overdose." I paused. "And now, you're hearing rumors?"

He nodded while biting.

I sipped coffee and tried to be patient.

He finished chewing and said, "Mister Clean."

"I thought a cleaner was a professional assassin. Do you mean murders by fentanyl?"

He shrugged. "I only heard the name in conjunction with fentanyl. Could be murder. Could be a code name for a project. Could be someone's idea of a joke."

"Cops joke about murder?"

"When we're not joking about domestic abuse, the homeless, or drunk drivers. Mr. Clean is an all-purpose household product. Bald guy, white clothes, big muscles. He was around before that ancient piece of tin you drive. Do you still park at the church?"

"Yeah, we cut a deal."

He almost laughed. "You know what the Madison-Avenue crowd calls Mr. Clean?"

“Haven’t the slightest.”

“Genie in a bottle.”

CHAPTER 34

Naomi wasn't in the church lot, so I waited outside the station with twenty thousand dollars inside my jacket pressing against my chest. I freaked out a couple of times thinking that the guys who wanted Leni had ID'ed Naomi and dragged her off the street. I calmed my fear by checking messages every five minutes, attempting to formulate a plan to find Leni, solve her problems, get the FBI off my back, put me on the road to California, and update my friends back in Ohio. And call Mom.

Naomi screeched to a halt six feet from where I stood. She was smiling from between two gold hoops I hadn't seen before. I pulled the handle to open the passenger door. It was locked. She waved for me to wait while she found the right button. The lock popped. I slid inside.

"Sorry. I travel alone most of the time."

She sounded happy, though traveling alone most of the time sounded sad. But I also traveled alone most of the time. It had advantages.

"Learn anything?" she asked.

"Chicago has a chronic drug problem."

"Why pick on Chicago? Tiny towns in the hills of West Virginia have a chronic drug problem. Everywhere has a chronic drug problem."

She eased through an intersection and swung onto Lakeside, heading north.

"Why do you think that is?" I asked.

"Because life is mostly the same everywhere in the U.S."

"And people are the same everywhere?"

"Well, not exactly the same. But drugs solve a load of problems."

She accelerated to the speed limit and beyond.

"Seems like drugs cause them," I said.

"That's part two of the novel of life. In part one you feel very, very good for awhile. Maybe a long while. Days. Weeks."

"But—"

She held up her hand. "Have you read Brave New World?"

"Uh, Huxley, right? It's been a long time."

"Published in the nineteen thirties. Remember the drug?"

All I could remember was a society divided into alphas, betas, and epsilons.

"It had a special name," she said. "Remember the plot?"

"Lots of things were illegal," I said.

"Yeah. Like family. And monogamy. It was supposed to be a utopia to cure the ills of society."

"It sort of worked, didn't it?"

"If you like orgies."

"Don't know," I said. "Never been invited to one."

"Would you use Soma to relieve all discomfort?" she asked.

"Is that what Huxley named the drug?"

"Sure did," she said. "But Soma is a plant-based intoxicant used in Hindu Vedic rituals. It's called the drink of the gods."

I laughed. "You must watch a lot of documentaries. I never thought of the gods being drunk. That would explain a lot."

She gave me a playful slap on the thigh. "The gods are fiction, silly."

"True. But the people who invent them aren't. So what was the downside of Soma if it made people happy?"

"More like comfortable zombies. But it had a major drawback."

Her car buzzed north toward a destination we were waiting for Prof to reveal. I plumbed the depths of my memory.

I ventured, "Something about aging."

"Bravo! Everyone died at sixty. Or earlier from accidents and stuff. But no one lived longer."

"Heck of a trade-off," I said.

"Our drugs have that feature too. So, tell me more about Chicago's drug problem."

"Plenty of demand. Boatloads of uncontrolled fentanyl. Lots of dead users."

She stayed quiet, touched a few buttons, and placed her hands in her lap. The car cruised along as if she were still holding the wheel.

I broke the silence. "My friend thinks the FBI is involved."

"What can they do? Arrest everyone?"

I shrugged, though she probably couldn't see me. "The United States has been fighting a war on drugs for a long time."

"And losing," she said.

"We have Narcan now."

"Better living through chemistry," she said. "And before you ask, yes, I have lots of experience. Some of it even legal."

Her icy tone froze my questions in their tracks.

"There's something else," I said.

"I bought some cool stuff." She glanced my way. "I'll show you later."

The car in front of us slowed. We did too.

"Is this car driving itself?" I asked.

"Mostly. I just sit here so it knows it's not alone."

"Do you like it?"

"Better than an Uber driver selected at random by an opaque algorithm."

"What did you buy?"

"You have to see it to appreciate it," she said. "You mentioned 'something else.' You sounded worried. So I changed the subject."

"I'm worried about Leni. I think Prof is with her, but I don't understand his message."

"Is that the something else?"

"No. The message, the box of money, the letter seeking Leni's whereabouts."

"I thought that donut bag was awfully big." Naomi stared at me for a long time. The car beeped a warning. She moved her eyes back to the road.

I said, "Someone really wants to find her."

"Or they're rich and don't care about a bit of cash."

I wondered how much the FBI cared about cash, but I kept my mouth shut. The car drove along for a few miles. Finally, Naomi interrupted the humming of the tires with a highly relevant question.

"Where are we going?"

<>

I thought hard for the next 30 miles. I had a long-shot guess where Prof was going. But I hadn't heard another word from him. I was confident Braden's lab would find fentanyl in the water sample. But who or what was Mr. Clean? I asked myself why I wasn't rolling down Route 66 and got a lot of answers.

Leni needed a solution to her multifaceted problem.

I was seeking adventure and was knee-deep in it.

Markus required a justice adjustment.

Naomi.

There were others. Like fear of returning home having learned nothing. Going back to being a Walmart mechanic around friendly faces. A safe life of numbness, following a hidden agenda designed by capitalists to extract as much economic value as possible out of me.

I was becoming more cynical than Naomi.

Yet, I had no reason to be negative. Since leaving my new Chicago friends a few days ago, I had made more friends—Leni, Prof, Jake, Naomi, Shianti—and an enemy named after a Japanese car: Markus Corolla. Not a bad balance sheet for an unemployed guy driving a relic down an obsolete highway to find an America that was no longer there.

"A farthing for your thoughts," Naomi said.

I laughed. "Farthing? The bid is starting low today."

"I'm on a budget."

"How would you like an all-expense paid vacation to a Midwestern treasure like you're never seen before? Except we have to use your car."

"You paying for gas?" she asked.

"Of course."

"Will we have Wi-Fi?"

"Most of the time."

"Too bad, I was hoping to get us isolated." She tossed an air kiss my way. "Where to?"

"North."

"Our destination is secret?"

"Barely a guesstimate," I said. "Do you want me to tell you?"

She watched the car drive itself for half a mile.

"Surprise me. Why this place?"

"If Prof is alone with Leni, he'll choose a place where he can protect her if Markus shows up." I considered the letter and the money and Braden's FBI comments. She stared at the inside rearview. The car beeped another warning.

"What happens if you ignore the warning?" I asked.

"It pouts and pulls to the side of the road and stops."

"We've got a long ride," I said.

"Long like a hundred miles, or a thousand miles?"

"Halfway in between."

"The car will help us if we give it a destination."

"Give it Tahquamenon Falls State Park."

"You spell it."

I managed to get it into the navigation system on the third try.

"We're going to Michigan?" she said. "I've never been there, what's it like?"

"Invented Motown. Early punk. Iggy and the Stooges. The MC5. And the Motor City madman himself, Ted Nugent."

She wagged her Afro. "No, no. I was thinking of nature."

"I know just the place. But it's farther than Tahquamenon."

"The car wants to turn around and go back through Chicago."

"Too risky. Let's take the long way."

"OK, but it's going to be grouchy." Naomi took control and continued north. The nav system told her repeatedly to turn around. Eventually it gave up and she let it drive itself again.

"Are we in a hurry?" she asked.

"Not enough to get thrown in jail for speeding."

She laughed. "You think a cop will put me in jail?"

"No. They'll put me in jail as the accomplice."

She kept laughing. "Are we stopping for the night or driving straight through?"

I tried to figure timing if my guess was right.

"We'll need to be fresh tomorrow. Let's stop for dinner and start out early in the morning."

"Where?" she said.

"Can your car find a good Mexican restaurant when we get close to the falls?"

She tapped buttons on the steering wheel and spun a knob she called her 'wonder wheel.' Shortly, she had three choices on the dashboard.

"Hotel-motel preference?" She asked.

"A place where we'll be hard to find, even if a government agency is looking for us."

Naomi tossed glances my way while twiddling the wonder wheel. Options popped up on the dashboard. "Do you prefer the obscurity of a chain? Or the obscurity of a Ma & Pa standalone?"

"Chains have more rooms. And employees who are less likely to notice us."

"The family places notice everyone," she said. She hesitated. "Was the money a bribe?"

"Reward for information about a missing person."

"Who? What? Did you tell them? Who is them?"

"They didn't leave a business card. But Braden had a suggestion."

"Are they after Markus?"

Braden and I hadn't discussed Corolla. "They didn't name names."

"You assumed Leni?"

"Yeah."

"Why?"

"Because Prof nabbed her, so they lost her."

The car drove itself around a long sweeping turn, staying perfectly in the center of our lane.

"How do they know?" Naomi asked.

"Know what?"

"Anything. Especially, how do they know that you know where she is?"

"I have no idea how I got on their radar. But it troubles me. I don't want to me important enough for the FBI to even know my name."

"And you think it's because of Leni?"

"I lead a boring life. What else could it be?"

"Surveillance cameras at the campsite. A fingerprint. Contact DNA match. Anyone in your family put their DNA online?"

I sighed. "My mother wanted to know if she was Irish."

Naomi looked at me and smiled.

"Yes, a little," I said.

"May the luck of the Irish be with you," she said, and laughed.

"We need all the luck we can get."

She grew serious. "I agree. We're on foreign soil."

Her comment gave me an idea.

"Let's find a pay phone."

"And a bed," she said.

◇

We drove longer than planned because we were both feeling good, finally locating a pink hotel in the shadow of a giant crucifix. Naomi sat on the king bed reading travel brochures. I used the hotel Wi-Fi to respond to messages, trying to act like Sally from a tiny desk that kept whacking my knee.

"The cross is made of redwood from Oregon," Naomi said.

I wrote to GeneralCuster2. He wanted Sally to dress up in buckskin and fulfill his rape fantasy. It was important that she resist with just the right phrases, which he listed. I asked what shade of buckskin and should it have fringe.

"The statue on the cross is bronze," she said.

"Does it say anything about why it's out here in the woods?"

"Tourists. Apparently, hundreds of thousands of them. Look at this. The hill the cross sits on was constructed of steel and concrete, then covered with grass."

She turned pages.

I told mellowyellow69 that no, he could not meet me for dinner in Paris even if he sent a first-class plane ticket.

Naomi held the magazine at arm's length

"That's a huge bridge," she said. "It was spooky driving across it. It's like a magnetic force reaches up from the water and makes you wonder what it would feel like to drive over the side and skydive your car straight down into the water."

I looked up from Leni's phone where I had two bars of strength on PinkNet, login password 55foot+.

"Good thing the car was driving."

"The human mind is a curiosity generator," she said.

"Yours is. Most people just wonder what's for dinner."

"Maslow's hierarchy," she said. "I'm just way up the pyramid." She tossed her magazine on the nightstand and flicked off her reading light. "How long are you going to play with that thing?"

"Eleven more messages. Then I should call my service."

She sighed. Extravagantly so, it seemed to me.

"I offered to get separate rooms," I said.

"I feel safer here."

Sleep tugged on my eyelids. I answered messages. Then I checked in with my toll-free number using the phone in the room. The bot told me I had two messages.

"Fudge maker."

Prof's second hint used a synthetic voice and a blocked number. He was getting more and more cautious.

"You picked up our gift. You have our number. We expect to hear from you soon…with helpful information."

"What are you staring at?" Naomi said.

"The wall. Focusing on a single point reduces the amount of data the brain must process. Helps me concentrate."

"Don't yogis stare at candle flames?"

I turned off Leni's phone and considered turning the burner on in case Prof called. But if Prof was sending two-word coded messages, he wouldn't call. I was flying on a hunch, but needed something to tell the maybe FBI. I pulled the chain to turn off the light on the desk and headed for the bathroom by the glow from the Pink Inn street sign leaking through the curtains. Automatically, I stopped and peeked out to check on Naomi's car. One car was parked in front of each room.

No one visible in the lot. The sky was the kind of overcast that promised to bring rain.

I released the curtain.

Naomi had crawled under the beige bedspread and closed her eyes. I tiptoed to the bathroom in stocking feet and brushed my teeth by the half-moon nightlight Naomi had stuck into a power socket. The guy staring back at me in subdued monotones looked like he had stayed up all night studying and then failed the exam.

I took a slow breath in. And let it out.

I rinsed the brush and leaned it against my dopp kit to dry. I flossed because my mother made me do it every night as a kid to ingrain the habit. I should call. Let her know I was doing okay.

I hung my pants and shirt on hooks on the back of the door and tucked my socks into a pocket so Naomi wouldn't see them lying on the floor. I put both hands up against the mirror and gazed into my own eyes. If I was wrong about Prof's clue, I was lost. No backup plan. No way to contact him. Corolla out there somewhere. The FBI asking me questions. I crossed the fingers of both hands for luck like I had done since it had worked in generating my first kiss.

"Good luck, Cuda," I whispered.

I eased the door open, checked the parking lot again to see if anyone had staked out the room, made sure the door was locked and that the little dangling chain that wouldn't stop a determined cub scout was in place.

Naomi was lying on her right side facing the center of the bed. In the low light she radiated the angelic nature of a child who'd had a super fun but exhausting day. I slipped under the covers and lay on my back staring at a textured ceiling that probably contained asbestos. My mind wandered down Route 66 until it reached Los Angeles. The feeling of 'What are you doing out here in northern Michigan?' floated over me.

Naomi's fingers found my left forearm. She pulled my arm toward her until she could cuddle it with both of hers–that angelic child hugging a stuffed toy.

"Tommy?" she whispered, stretching my name like a 45 played at 33 and a third.

I gently squeezed the part of her arm lying on my palm. She pulled my arm closer. Her breast pressed against me.

"Naomi, I—"

"Shh. Stop thinking. Our bodies need to talk."

Her hand stroked slowly up my arm and down my chest. Then along my neck until I could kiss her fingertips. Out of the corner of my eye I saw her lips lift toward a smile.

"Where were we?"

I would have bet my car that she knew exactly where we were. But I answered anyway. "Seventy-two."

She pulled me close and kissed me.

"Seventy-one," she said.

At sixty she took my hands in hers and pressed my palms against her neck. Then moved them ever so slowly down her body all the way to her knees and up the side of her legs, making it clear that she had forgotten her pajamas.

"Naomi—"

"Shh." She expertly guided my palms to her breasts. She sighed softly, eyes closed, then pushed my hands lower and whispered.

"Tommy…think about the firm and delicate ways your hands touch a guitar…think about us. Play me."

◇

In the morning Naomi wanted to give thanks for the good things in her life. So I wheeled her along a brick-red path of paving stones to the foot of the giant crucifix for a dawn service. It was performed in Latin, which made me think of Bach and Brahms attending essentially the same service hundreds of years ago. Naomi and I sang along with the hymns as best we could.

She smiled slightly during the entire thirty-eight minutes. We waited while the other dozen or so attendees departed.

"Do you think he's right?" she said.

That was a question with a hundred faces.

"Who? Right about what?"

"This professor guy you're after. Is he right about our friend Leni? You just heard the 'judge not for ye shall be judged' stuff."

403

We started down the walk. "Right is complicated. But if Corolla is forcing her to do things against her will." I shrugged. We reached the end of the walkway.

"It's so beautiful out here in the forest," she said. "Doesn't feel at all like St. Louis." She gazed at the sky where puffy white cumulus clouds were lit by morning rays of gold.

"Leni went back by choice," she said. "Why?"

"She's intent on changing her life through education."

"Hmm…"

"Maybe," I said, "it's as simple as Newton's first law. She's following the momentum of her life."

Naomi twisted around in her wheelchair to meet my eyes. "Is that why we're here?"

"Naomi, I'm not even sure that we're in the right state. I'm just trying to find Leni and Prof. He shut down his phone and left cryptic messages for a reason. In short, I don't know what's going on. But I'm glad you're here helping me find out."

She held up her arms for a hug. I dropped to one knee and held her while birds chirped around us and I marveled at the churning inside of me her touch could generate.

"What do we do first?" she asked.

"Boat ride."

She pushed me away. "I can't swim."

"Ferry boat," I said.

A short drive and a thirty-minute wait brought us to a ramp covered in black sandpaper. It angled upward onto the deck of a ferry built like a tour bus: enclosed seating below and open-air seating above. I backed up the ramp with Naomi in tow. She assured me she could stop the chair if I slipped.

"Can we sit on top?" she asked with pleading eyes.

A narrow steel staircase was the only way up. But she didn't weigh much over a hundred pounds. I tipped the ferryman to stow her chair so I could carry her piggyback up the stairs. The ferryman laughed and commented that though he had never seen it done, he wasn't aware of any law against it.

"This is so cool," she said as we clanged to the top.

I deposited her on an empty bench. She immediately scooted to the outside rail and looked straight down at the water. I sat beside her.

"I feel like I'm in the sky," she said.

The boat rocked slightly from an incoming wave and she threw both her arms around me.

"Have you been on a boat before?"

"Not one this big. Or with so much water around it." She gazed off at the monstrous Mackinac Bridge that we had driven across the night before in a driving rain and crosswind that reminded me why I prefer heavy, powerful, muscle cars.

"We'll be fine. This boat has made the run across open water hundreds of times."

"There's always a first time for things to go wrong."

"Odds are against it," I assured her.

"Did you study mathematics?"

"Just the standard stuff," I said.

"Math seems like magic to me. You move squiggles around on a piece of paper according to the rules of a game someone made up hundreds of years ago, and you figure stuff out about the real world that are actually true."

"The universe follows certain laws. Our species just has to discover them."

"Unlike people," she said. "We know what the laws are. We just don't follow them."

Monster engines fired up far below us and the wooden seat began to vibrate.

"Nice," Naomi said, and wiggled her butt on the bench.

I laughed. "You're teasing me, aren't you?"

"Yes. Is it working?"

I pretended it wasn't. The half-full ferry floated sideways, giving the impression the dock was moving away. Then the engines came alive.

Naomi white-knuckled the back of the seat in front of us.

"Holy moly," she said.

The ferry rushed forward, lifted onto a plane, accelerated, and settled into a fast, easy cruise with a giant rooster tail of foam shooting into the air behind us.

Naomi swung her head around. "What's that?"

"Exhaust water from the jets. Makes people think they're going faster than they are."

"This is fast enough."

The ferry drove through the waves without visible effort as hundreds of horsepower jetted water into the lake.

Naomi held tight to the seat in front of us.

"Where are we going?" she asked.

"To the hotel."

"And later?"

"We have a few choices."

"Good, I like choices," she said. "Making them allows me to use my advanced knowledge of probability." She laughed into the wind.

"First option," I said. "Sit tight at the hotel and wait for Prof to find us."

"But that gives the bad guys time to…um…do bad stuff."

"Option two. Drop off our luggage and go ride around the island in a horse and buggy."

"What? Why?"

"Cars aren't allowed on the island. If we want to nose around like good private eyes, it's horsey time."

Naomi released her grip from the back of the seat in front of her and held onto me instead. In short order we arrived at another dock. I carried her down the steel stairs and deposited her in her waiting wheelchair. I pushed the chair with my duffel strapped across one shoulder and her dragging her wheeled luggage with one hand. The weather was pleasant enough that we decided to walk. We approached a hotel with a super long porch, built on the side of a hill facing the water.

"We're staying here?" she said, her voice incredulous.

"I think Prof is too."

"I saw this place in a movie. It's even better in real life. Superman traveled in time in that movie."

I wracked my brain but came up empty. "Superman?"

"The actor who played him. What's his name. Cute guy." She grabbed the wheels and stopped the chair. "That movie was so romantic. I can feel my heart throb just looking at this place."

I leaned over and kissed her on the lips. I said, "Fifty-two," thinking of a deck of cards. And Leni. And the Magician. And that 95 kisses weren't really all that many.

She smiled. "What a grand hotel."

"Longest porch in the world."

"So amazing. Can we cruise the whole thing?"

"Sure. Let's check in."

The hotel with the longest porch in the world, sitting on the island famous for Mackinac Island fudge, also had the longest wheelchair ramp I had ever encountered.

"Reservation?" a girl asked. She had long, wavy red hair and was wearing a name tag with Bobbie handwritten on it in blue ink.

I gave her my name, cash, and Naomi's credit card. She gave me a map and two brass keys. We wandered up to the room. As the door clicked behind us Naomi grabbed my sleeve and lowered the count to 49.

"Let's go see that super porch," she said. "The vibes from that movie are buzzing inside of me. Maybe we can even travel back in time."

She laughed. I laughed. But part of her wasn't joking.

◇

We made our way to the end of the 660-foot porch with the best view of the water and gazed out on Lake Huron.

"I thought watching the Mississippi river was interesting," she said. "This is mesmerizing. Blue water. Breeze. Sunshine speckling the surface with little silver spotlights."

"The view dives right down into the primal brain and comforts it," I said.

She intertwined her fingers with mine. "Gives primal thoughts."

I squeezed her hand until our palms touched. "You really want to see the entire porch?"

"Yes. And I'm going to do it under my own power."

Her tone left no room for debate.

She rolled forward, eyes on the lake hundreds of feet below us. Every few yards we would pass a pillar that threw a shadow across our faces. Naomi didn't speak; she just rolled steadily along in a kind of trance. Tourists passed us going in both directions.

"Can you feel the energy?" she asked.

I mostly felt concern that I had misunderstood Prof's clues.

"You can tell?" I asked.

She shook her head. "No, not really. But if I think about superman standing on this very porch, and the story of lovers lost in time, the building starts to speak to me."

"I went to the Rock and Roll Hall of Fame in Cleveland one time. The guard let me hold a guitar that Hendrix had played. It felt like shaking hands with Jimi."

"The mind works in mysterious—"

A hunched over man walking with a cane in his left hand banged into my left shoulder, fell forward, caught himself on the arm of Naomi's wheelchair, muttered a sound that might have been 'sorry,' and continued down the steps of the main entrance. Gray in his dark hair put him somewhere in his 50s. I never got a look at his face.

"Even here," she said. "People are in a hurry."

"Habits are hard to break. Like right now, I'm thinking a drive around the island would be nice. But behind a horse? I'm not so sure."

"I got a weird vibe from that guy," she said.

"Cane. Graying hair. Trench coat. What's that tell you?"

"Rich guy came over on his yacht, looking for investment opportunities. Or, a fugitive from justice hiding here because no one has cars. How do they police this place? Horses?"

I shrugged. "Golf carts?"

"I bet you need a special permit for those," she said.

"Electric bicycles?"

She nodded. "Great idea. Oh wait, I know. I bet that guy is a famous movie producer and he's here scouting the location. I love this place. I hope he shoots his movie here."

"If they do, maybe we could watch them make it."

She stopped rolling. "You had better mean that, Mr. Cuda. I would love to see a movie get made."

"Maybe they'll need a pretty girl."

"You're teasing me. But it's okay. I like it."

We reached the far end of the porch. Naomi spun her chair and faced the lake. She sat up straight, took in a long deep breath, held it… held it…held it. Then let it out. After a few cycles of this, she rolled herself to the railing and squeezed it in her outstretched hands.

"Damn," she said. "Beauty flows into my veins like good alcohol."

"Is there bad alcohol?" I asked.

"Ha!" she said.

"The brain reacts to water, sky, high on a hill—"

She interjected, "Being with someone you trust."

I smiled and rested my hands in the pockets of my jacket. My left pocket wasn't empty. I pulled out a strip of paper torn from Grand Hotel stationery and read it aloud.

"Somewhere in time. 6:16 P.M. tonight."

CHAPTER 35

Naomi wanted to traverse the entire porch a second time. I pointed out that four times 660 feet was 2640, exactly half a mile. She asked if we could do a mile. I countered with a suggestion.

"How about lunch at the Cupola Bar on the fourth floor? I bet it has great views."

"OK," she said. "But I have to change shoes." She was wearing light blue sneakers that looked great with her white capri jeans.

"This is a lake-side resort. You could wear lime green flip-flops and no one would care."

Her face sagged. "You're right. People see the wheelchair and not the girl in it."

"No. I meant that at a casual resort, being casual is the whole point. You can wear whatever feels good."

Her smile returned. "Good. I have just the thing."

"Should I wear boots or creepers?"

"Creepers. At least they have laces."

I followed her off the elevator and pushed along the hallway to room 409. Which made me think of the old Pontiac GTO. Not only was the GTO gone, Pontiac was gone too.

Naomi was quiet.

I stopped at our door and dug out my key. As I started the automatic motion to insert it into the lock, I heard a voice. My mind thought 'television.'

"Did you hear something," I asked softly.

"Your breathing," she said. "Are you hearing voices in your head? Is it from the past?"

"All the time. But it's usually mine."

I unlocked the door and opened it with my backside as I pulled Naomi through. I turned around to face the room and she screamed.

"Easy," a tall black guy said. Short hair. Large biceps. Gray shirt with red ovals around the sleeves. He was sitting straight legged on the bed holding the remote. "It's just us."

I didn't see anyone else in the room. I was about to back up into the hallway when I recognized him as the guy who had arranged for me to perform at Toucan Sam's that night.

I ventured, "Is Jake with you?"

He nodded. "He's, uh, busy right now. But he'll be along." His eyes drifted to Naomi.

"That cute redhead at check-in," Naomi said. "Jake hit on her."

"How do you know that?" he said.

"His reputation precedes him," she said.

He laughed. "That it does, that it does. I'm Ramone. Jake said to wait here, you'd be by."

I nodded. "And Jake has a key to our room?"

Ramone nodded.

"Did he sweet talk that girl?" Naomi said.

"He didn't need to do much talking from what I saw. But I think he stole the key."

I laughed. Ramone laughed. Naomi scowled at us and rolled to the closet.

"We're headed to lunch," I said. "Want to join us?"

"I better be here when Jake arrives. He gave me the key. And he'll be hungry. Plus, I'm supposed to be the lookout and deliver a message."

"Let me get something to write on."

"You won't need it."

I sat at the foot of the bed, wondering how other people's problems found me.

"Shoot," I said.

The door to the room opened.

"Shoot who?" Jake said.

Naomi's face registered 'no comment.'

"I was just about to deliver your message," Ramone said.

Jake nodded and checked that the door behind him was locked.

"Mr. Clean," Ramone began, "is well known as a concept, but not an individual." He looked to Jake, who pulled out a chair from the kitchenette and dropped into it backwards. Ramone continued. "He seems to be everywhere, and has an endless supply."

Not wanting to jump to conclusions, I said, "Of what?"

"One product," Ramone said. "One configuration."

"But," Jake added, "the quality is excellent. And more important, consistent."

Naomi said nothing, but was listening intently.

"What would that take?" I asked.

"A relationship with a reliable foreign lab," Jake said. "Hard to find. Or a private lab stateside buried deep enough that the narcs can't find it."

"Sounds hard," I said.

"And expensive, which drives up prices. Leaves room for the China-Mexico road to go low market. Odd thing. Mr. Clean has competitive prices. I doubt the Chinese like him."

"You sound like my economics professor," Naomi said.

Jake smiled broadly. "I could teach your professor plenty."

"Any trouble?" I asked.

Jake patted his pocket. "Not even a metal detector on the ferry. We're ready for anything."

Naomi's eyes flashed at me.

"Last resort," I said. "Bullets cause problems."

"When they don't solve them," Jake said.

Ramone nodded agreement. Jake looked around the room like he was trapped and searching for a way out before a bomb exploded.

"Where's Leni?"

"Don't know," I said. "And right now, don't want to. Got an anonymous phone message asking questions I don't want to answer."

"Ignorance is bliss," Jake said.

Naomi added, "Plausible deniability."

"I want to answer honestly," I said.

"Better not to know," Jake said, bobbing his head. "Is she OK?"

"Word from Prof was yes twenty-four hours ago," I said. "Anything else on Mr. Clean? Location? Fingerprint? DNA sample?"

Jake laughed and tossed a sugar packet at me. It spun like a tiny Frisbee into my left hand. Not sugar. A sealed white package. My fingers said there were two caplets inside.

"Marketing sample," Jake said. "I have been assured the supply runs deep."

That conversation lull where everyone stops at once happened. The spell was broken when Naomi rolled to the closet and came back wearing gold sandals that framed her sky-blue pedicure.

"Tommy and I are headed to lunch. You guys want to join us?"

Jake checked a device strapped to his wrist that I had no doubt was too capable to be called a watch.

"Our rooms should be ready. I think I'll call room service."

"Room service wouldn't have red hair, would it?" Naomi said.

Jake tossed a wide smile her way. "Now what makes you think that?"

"You were late," she said. "You're passing on an incredible lunch in my marvelous company for room service. Can only be one reason a guy like Jake would do that, and it rhymes with wussy."

Jake laughed and shook his head. "You got strange ideas about me, missy."

"And," she said, "a hundred girls to back them up."

"Tsk, tsk. You could only find a hundred?" Jake guffawed on his way out. Ramone followed him with an apologetic grin.

"Wussy?" I said.

"Guys like Jake use women."

I waited. She stewed but didn't elaborate.

"And vice versa," I said.

"You're defending him?"

"What's to defend? He likes the redhead. She likes him well enough to let him steal the key to our room and play hanky-panky in a closet on her break."

"And she'll jump into his bed tonight," she said, "and not be sorry tomorrow."

"Or vice versa," I said.

"Que sera sera," she said.

"C'est la vie," I added.

She shook her head, but she was smiling.

"Please push, Tommy. I'm hungry."

◇

The view from the Cupola restaurant—indigo water and wind pushed whitecaps, stark white billowing clouds against a sky I knew wasn't really blue, but only looked blue because of Rayleigh scattering in the atmosphere, gold sandals wrapped around petite bronze feet—I was again struck by how much my being relaxed in the presence of natural wonders.

"A farthing," she said.

"Nature is incredibly beautiful."

"And humans are part of nature. And I am human. Therefore."

"Therefore, you will fish for compliments." I laughed.

She punched my shoulder from across the table with a wide, straight-armed swing. Shrimp arrived along with a vegetable tray with three dips including hummus. The bar even had Mexican Coke in glass bottles. They didn't have Dr. Pepper or I would have ordered a Bronze Jeep.

"Does Mexican cola taste better?" she asked.

"Mucho."

"They truck that all the way from Mexico just so you can drink sugar?"

"Oh yes. Instead of high-fructose corn syrup produced by government handouts to corn growers."

"But think of the fuel needed to move that glass bottle just for," she picked it up, "twelve ounces of sugar water down your throat."

"It has caffeine too." I took the bottle from her and swigged. "Think of the poor people in Mexico who now have jobs manufacturing and transporting this precious fluid." I gazed into the dark liquid. "It even sort of looks like oil, the crucial lubricant of our great society."

She shook her head. "You're crazy."

"Free-market capitalism. If no one bought it, they would stop importing it. Let the market decide after removing farm subsidies."

"Your market clearly needs regulating." She dipped her shrimp, bit into it, and dripped sauce on her plate.

A dark thought entered my mind. "That's the heart of the overdose epidemic. The market for street drugs make dirty fentanyl attractive now that Oxycontin is no longer available."

Naomi stared at me. "You really think that's the problem?"

"No. The problem is that people want to take drugs. And these drugs have been made very expensive by government regulations."

She carefully spooned sauce down the length of a jumbo shrimp and moved it to her mouth.

"Tommy, do you think narcotics should be legal?"

I shrugged. "Not sure. But I think they should be taxed like cigarettes and alcohol. And the proceeds used to help users." I paused. "The present system flows the biggest money to the criminal risk takers."

"You mean like in Silicon Valley?" Her face was blank, then she burst out laughing, then turned serious.

"What are we doing here, Tommy?"

"Waiting for a cheeseburger."

"You're very lucky that I can't kick you under the table."

She was serious.

"I will consider myself kicked. Ouch!" I bent over and rubbed my shin. "We're here because Prof's clues led here."

"You figured that out from the fudge?"

"Mackinac Island fudge is famous."

"And you knew that?"

"I grew up in Ohio. Everyone knows that."

She stared at me with a question in her dark eyes.

"But how would Prof know?"

"He ingests Wikipedia faster than an AI."

"And this mysterious note in your pocket?"

"I can think of a couple of options. At least one of them is good." I smiled.

Naomi licked her lips. "I won't ask."

"I can't tell you much anyway. Most of what I think is barely a conspiracy theory."

She winked. "This is a nice romantic island for a nice romantic vacation."

The waiter arrived with my cheeseburger and the chef's special lobster, macaroni, and three cheese casserole for Naomi. His handwritten name tag read David.

"Hi, David. I'm Naomi. What do you think of if I say 'somewhere in time?'"

He blinked a couple of times and appeared to be considering the question carefully.

"Well, first, I would hope you were suggesting a meeting." He smiled sheepishly. "Then I would figure you were referring to the movie shot here ages ago. Lots of people come here seeking that kind of romance for themselves." He glanced at me, then at my burger. I nodded approval. "But here in the hotel, you are likely referring to our special suite of that name. It's decorated with memorabilia from the movie. Not the real stuff, the filmmakers took most of that with them. We also have a Jane Seymour suite right out of the movie."

"You have a suite named somewhere in time?" she said.

"Oh yes. But it's often booked months in advance. If you want it," he looked around, "you'll probably have to bribe someone to get it." He grinned.

"Thank you, David," she said. "It's so nice to know you are keeping the movie alive. I really loved it."

"Me too. It's why I work here. I came for a weekend once to see where the filming took place and saw a job opening. This is my third summer."

I cleared my throat.

They both turned my way.

"Based on your experience. Does the romance last?"

His smile came on slowly, like he was pumping air into it.

"Well, brother. That depends on the people involved. As for me, I signed up for next summer too."

After he departed, Naomi blew on a forkful of cheese-smothered lobster and looked into my eyes.

"Told you," she said.

◇

"Black," Naomi said.

I said, "Should I ask why?"

"Only if—"

"I want to know. OK, why black?"

"It's dramatic. Makes us look sinister. More formidable. And if we have to escape, we'll be harder to see."

"I thought the bad guys always wore black."

She nodded vigorously. "And now you know why." She grinned.

So we both wore black. She even removed the pink hubcap, opposite the MLK portrait, from her wheelchair. She debated on MLK, then removed him too. Where I had expected spokes were solid carbon-fiber wheels.

At 6:10 P.M. we placed a room-to-room phone call but no one answered. We headed out the door. At 6:14 we stood in front of a door with a simple metal plaque.

Somewhere in Time

I knocked three times.

The door was opened by the gray-bearded guy in his gray trench coat that had bumped me on the porch. He was wearing sunglasses. He waved me aside, stepped into the hallway, and stared down it for many seconds. Then he turned and stared in the opposite direction. He waved us into the suite but remained in the hall. Shortly, he entered and double-locked the door behind him. He motioned for Naomi to move into the main sitting area that included a glass-enclosed fireplace with a purple light glowing inside. He gestured for me to follow him into the kitchen. Once there he wrote on a white pad of paper with Grand Hotel letterhead using a Grand Hotel ballpoint pen.

Are you wearing a wire?

I shook my head no.

Does Naomi know about the water at the retreat?

I shook my head no.

Do you know about Mr. Clean?

I held my thumb and index finger about an inch apart.

Know who he is?

I whispered, "Maybe a person. Maybe an organization. But if I guessed, Markus."

No proof.

I borrowed the pad and wrote.

Don't need it.

I couldn't see his eyes behind the glasses. I wrote.

Forget about Mr. Clean. Let's get Leni what she wants.

He met my gaze through the sunglasses. Maybe. It was hard to tell. I didn't know what she wanted either. Or how she would react to what I needed to tell her.

Can I meet with her?

He took the pad back.

Ferry dock at midnight.

He glanced at Naomi in the next room admiring the bits of movie magic decorating the suite.

Just you?

I nodded.

Were you followed?

I shook my head, pointed at Naomi, and made a steering motion with both hands.

The old man shuffled to the balcony with his notepad. Naomi and I let ourselves out.

"Let's cruise," I said.

We stepped into an empty elevator car and waited for the doors to close.

"Who is that guy?" she asked. "And why all the hush-hush spy stuff?"

"We're involved with a rapist, drug dealers, and cops."

She took my hand in one of hers. "Plenty of reasons to be careful."

"Not only for us," I said. "They all want Leni."

"And Leni wants Markus," she said.

I hesitated to elaborate. But Naomi had seen the camp. "She might also want a supplier."

"Less complicated if they're both the same guy."

I wondered if she was speaking from experience.

The elevator dinged its arrival at the first floor. The doors parted. I held the OPEN button while Naomi rolled out, released it, and began to follow, but the space suddenly filled with two men in light gray suits entering the car. One turned to the control panel. The other blocked my exit.

The doors glided shut.

I tried to classify them as dealers or cops, but they were as blank as a pair of store mannequins. Both about six feet. Both white. Both faces halfway to a scowl with vacuous eyes focused on nothing.

The elevator began its ascent.

"Where is she, Mr. Kelsey? A great deal depends on us finding her soon."

"Are you going to identify yourselves?"

"Sure, he's Tick and I'm Tock, and we have the authority to arrest you if necessary."

I leaned back against the wall of the car just to put space between us.

"What would make an arrest necessary?" I asked.

Tock said, "Us not getting what we want."

"Lenore?"

"Correct."

"You won't believe me, but I don't know where she is. The last time I saw her was at a Nature Incognito retreat in Wisconsin." I decided on offense as the best defense. "All the attendees were high on fentanyl-laced water."

"You are right," Tick said. "We don't believe you."

"You can verify my story with Detective Braden of the Chicago Police Department. He has a sample of the water."

A quick visual exchange convinced me that they didn't want Chicago cops involved. I couldn't tell if the water was a surprise.

"You had better be lying," Tick said.

"Nope."

"Shit," mumbled Tock.

"Minor complication," Tick said. Then to me. "How do we find Lenore?"

"Follow Markus Corolla," I said.

Another glance between them.

"How do you know Corolla?" Tick asked.

"Met him in a bar near St. Louis." Time for more offense. "Turns out he raped a friend of mine."

They each grabbed an arm to immobilize me.

"Slandering a famous person will get you into trouble."

"Slander requires making a false statement," I said.

"Correct," Tick said.

Tock's eyes danced around. "OK, Kelsey. Spill."

I looked from one to the other. The elevator reached the fourth floor. Tick sent it back down without opening the doors.

"You won't believe anything I tell you, but here goes. Markus has DNA in two rape cases. An old one that is probably beyond the statute of limitations. And a recent one."

"DNA doesn't prove rape," Tock said.

I nodded. "For that you'll want a witness. His sister in the first case. Do you remember The Girl with the Dragon Tattoo? How she brought down the psychologist?"

Tock frowned at what was clearly new data.

"Video?" he said.

"Markus hasn't told you about the recording of him raping Lenore?"

They ignored me and stared at each other. Whatever passed between them was invisible. Tick nodded.

"Why are you involved?" Tock asked.

"Friend of the family."

"How long have you known the little cocktease?" Tick said, releasing my arm.

"Almost two weeks."

Tock released me too. The elevator stopped on the first floor. Tock locked on my eyes. His were pale blue.

"Do not leave this island until we tell you to."

They stepped off.

I pressed the door close button and waited for my breathing to return to normal. When I stepped out, Naomi was waiting six feet from the elevator.

"Two more minutes and I was calling the cops," she said.

"Those were the cops."

Her face sagged. "How did they find us?"

"They didn't volunteer their methods. But given the timing, I suspect they followed Jake."

"Of course. Known associate. What did they want?"

"GPS coordinates for Lenore."

She studied my face. "What did you give them?"

"Markus."

"Wow. The fan is starting to spin, isn't it?"

"Faster and faster. Probably okay to use our cell phones now. The bad guys know where we are."

"Speaking of Jake, he called. His new squeeze, his word not mine, knows the booking agent that schedules entertainment on the island. Bobbie, the squeeze, is trying to get you guys a gig."

"Us guys?"

"You and Jake."

"Did he bring—"

"Nope. Just you two. Guitar and drums. Like the White Stripes."

"Did Jake happen to mention little details like equipment or a rehearsal?"

"In fact, he did. No rehearsal. Thinks it'll destroy the spontaneity of the moment. Bobbie is tracking down instruments. Jake thinks the guitar will be easy, but he's worried he won't be able to find all the drums he wants."

"There aren't that many drums in the state of Michigan."

She smiled, then turned serious. "How about Prof?"

I thought back to the fingers I had seen writing on the notepad in the Somewhere in Time suite.

"I think he's with Leni." I didn't like keeping secrets from Naomi. But if the goons grabbed her, the less she knew the better.

Naomi checked messages on her phone. I fired up Leni's phone to do the same. No new messages in the Oleace app. I frowned without meaning to.

"What's wrong?" she said.

"No new messages. Maybe I don't have an Internet connection." I opened the browser and visited Dodge's website to see if they had introduced a new Barracuda. The Internet worked fine.

But Sally had no unanswered messages. I opened the chat for a member named JJ331. The last message to him—a selfie from the ferry dock—was an hour old. I checked magnetman500. Same ferry picture, thirty minutes old. A photo on the porch of the Grand Hotel showing Sally in a mint green sundress had been sent to goodvibrations69 with the message:

I miss you madly. We must video chat ASAP.

That was two hours ago.

Leni had a new phone. Leni was being Sally. Leni was on the island.

And so were the cops trying to find her.

"You're frowning again," Naomi said.

"Worried about Leni with cops on the island."

"Is she here?"

"She was recently. But I don't know if she is now."

I felt like I was tossing a coin four times in a row and betting they would all be heads. I turned on Prof's burner phone and called my service.

"Enjoyed chatting in the elevator. There have been no indictments or convictions. You are clearly mistaken."

I clearly was not. But they weren't interested in reality. They were interested in Leni.

Next message.

"Received overnight samples. Lab boys say it's the same stuff as the gift bottle. I'll pay a visit to the supplier. I think I know where to find him."

Braden eliminated one guess. The drugs in Leni's box springs matched the water and matched the caplets Jake had given me.

"Should I order red or black lingerie?" Naomi asked.

I glanced sideways. She was staring at her smartphone.

"Any other choices?" I said.

Her eyes rolled up to meet mine. "Like what?"

"Shiny bronze," I said.

I expected her to laugh, but she said, "Hmm," and returned to scrolling.

I turned off both of my phones and tucked them away in pockets. But carrying them still felt like a beacon, asking to be found.

"I'm going shopping," Naomi said.

I looked at the phone in her hand. "Aren't you shopping now?"

"It's not as much fun." She rubbed her thumb and first finger together. "Some things need to be touched."

We went down to the lobby. Naomi made me wait while she whispered to the redheaded Bobbie at the main desk. Bobbie opened a half door so Naomi could go behind the counter with her. Then they both disappeared down a hallway.

I stepped out onto the 660-foot porch and gazed toward the ferry dock, trying to recall the details of that area. The long black bumpers for the ferry. A small building for luggage. A trail where the carriages lined up to pick up passengers. The smell of the lake and horses. The empty silence of no cars.

I focused on the absence of internal combustion engines. Absence of airplanes. Absence of the doppler sound of a motorbike racing past. Absence of sirens. Voices on the wind was the most prevalent sound. And the occasional horse complaining about his job.

"What're thinking?" Naomi asked. She had finished with Bobbie and rolled quietly onto the porch beside me. A brown paper bag rested in her lap.

"Our arrival on the island," I said.

"Magical, isn't it? This is better than Disneyland."

"I've never been."

Her eyes went as wide as Minnie Mouse's. "You've never been to the Magic Kingdom? That's almost child abuse."

"I got to act in a Disney play with our local theatre group. Does that count?"

"Were you a princess?" She laughed.

"I had two roles. A horse pulling a carriage built on an antique hay wagon with bicycle tires. And a locomotive that pulled a train filled with dancers."

"What did you use for train cars?"

"Grocery carts painted black."

"They danced inside a moving grocery cart?"

"We had other dancers around to catch them. Only one fell. And I still think she jumped because she wanted a certain guy to catch her."

"Did Mr. Locomotive get to smoke?"

"A bucket of dry ice and a battery powered fan that I would switch on and off made puffs out the smokestack."

"Wow. Special effects. I bet the Magic Kingdom would hire you."

I gestured toward her lap.

"Is there a shopping mall hidden inside the hotel?"

"Not exactly," she said. "But this is designed for romance."

"Something about a fantasy movie shot here?"

"Romance," she said.

"Fantasy. Every romance movie is a fantasy." I laughed.

"OK, Scrooge McDuck."

Jake and Ramone approached the main entrance of the Grand Hotel. Jake was carrying brass cymbals the size of extra large pizzas. He was a big ripped guy with powerful muscles, partly from the way he played the drums. But with a brass disk in each hand he looked like a superhero coming to save the world with his magic weapons.

"Yo, guitar man." He gestured to the side with his head. "Huddle."

Naomi nodded at my unasked question. I followed Jake along the porch's white railing toward the lake. He placed the cymbals on the porch and leaned them against the railing.

"Important stuff first," he said. "We got a gig. I've always dreamed of playing on an island. Although I thought it would have palm trees and chicks in bikinis on motor scooters." He laughed and held up a palm. "Don't ask, dude. I almost got the gear issue covered. It'll be different than Sam's, but we'll bring the blues anyway." He looked me up and down. "You okay? You're looking even more white than usual."

I smiled, but my heart wasn't in it.

"Cops visited today. They are keen to find Leni. Didn't care to talk about Markus and rapes."

Jake frowned. Not like he was confused. But like he was going to have to shoot someone. "Plural?"

"Yeah. Raped his sister back in high school. Then died in a car crash."

"Now he resurrected, huh?"

"DNA test says yes."

"Not a brother or cousin or eff-up in the lab?"

"Can't be sure. Looks like a bit of a cover up going on."

"Oh yeah. This bad stuff can never happen in honky-land. Would spoil the boy's chance at his legacy seat at Hah-vard." He laughed harder than the first time. "What kind of cops?"

"Suits. Didn't show badges. Light physical restraint."

"That's because you a white boy. It'd been me, they woulda cuffed me on the ground and choked me."

"You speak truths that shouldn't be reality. What do you think is going on?" I asked.

"You're messing with Feds. They don't care if they're in Missouri, Illinois, or Michigan. It's all their territory."

"Why wouldn't they care about rape?"

"Because something more important is going on. You got a head cold and you win the lottery. You forget about the head cold fast."

"So our plan is DOA?"

He took a few steps and sat down on a white bench.

"Cuda, you got a couple things happening. What's important to Markus and his shiny career ain't necessarily important to your FBI boys. Can tell you this for sure, it's an either or situation. Markus has the power, or the Feds have the power. Then Markus be a pawn."

"Care to guess?"

"Pawn," he said.

"So he's vulnerable?"

"In a dozen ways. We just have to find one." He reached inside his leather jacket. "And this might be it."

"Did you have any trouble?" I asked.

He shook his head. "No. My guy thinks he's the Lincoln Lawyer. The moment he found out that he was helping a half-black girl put the screws on a white guy, he was all ears."

"Not to be nosey…"

"He's white. Just trying to do his bit for racial equality." Jake laughed and handed me a sealed business envelope. "He does have a thing for busty black girls." Another laugh, but short.

"Should I read this?" I asked.

"Only if you want to be a lawyer. The key element: he pays. Once she has the cash, she has 30 days to comply with the details."

"Jake, you ever study law?"

"Only from the wrong side of it." He stood and looked down at me. "You got it set up yet?"

I shook my head. "By tomorrow noon, I think."

Jake stared down the incredibly long porch. Naomi was sitting alone in the sun.

"Nice girl," he said.

"Sure is. I think maybe she likes me."

"Naomi's friendly," he said. "But she doesn't like most men. Careful you don't get chewed up in the grinder of her…not sure what to call it. Unique existence."

"Thanks. We're going slow. Forty-four kisses left."

"You count them?" he asked, without looking at me.

"A game she invented. We started at ninety-five."

He laughed. "You were on the ninety-fifth floor I bet." He shrugged. "I play lots of games with women. Counting kisses is as good as any." He turned to me. "You want help with delivering that contract?"

"Yes, for sure. Once I have a time and place, you'll be the first to know."

"OK."

"Can I ask your advice?" I said.

"Cuda, fellow blues traveler. For you, advice is free." His smile lit up the porch.

"This situation. Women involved. Feds. Elite power player with good lawyers. Would you use a place with loads of people around to constrain their shenanigans? Or an isolated location to free up ours? With no recordings?"

He rotated until he was gazing out over the blue water of Lake Huron.

"Trade off. Better if he's alone." He paused. "And we're not."

"The Feds will follow at least one of us."

"Lose them," he said.

"OK, thanks."

"Time to go," he said. "Native girl will be getting restless."

Far down the porch Naomi was waving. Probably wondering what was taking us so long.

CHAPTER 36

Jake set off to hunt for more equipment to fulfill his island dream. Naomi and I rode up the elevator. I was contemplating shoot-out locations when she interrupted my thoughts.

"Will you watch the movie with me?"

"What movie?"

"Tommy Cuda, are you not paying attention? Bobbie says it's free to stream in any room. I want to relax."

I nodded. I needed to relax too. But a movie wasn't going to help. Remarkably, popcorn, Junior Mints, and Squirt were all on the room service menu. So we snacked, held hands, and watched Christopher Reeves and Jane Seymour pretend to love each other on screen.

"Oh, that chemistry!" Naomi said. "I can feel it in my toes. And I can barely feel my toes even on a good day."

At the part where Reeves self-hypnotized his character back to 1912, Naomi was cross-checking a hotel brochure.

"Aha," she said. "They had an affair."

"Who?"

"Seymour and Reeves fell in love while making the movie. I bet right here in this hotel." She leaned across the popcorn bowl between us.

"Forty-three," she said, and held my hand for the rest of the movie. As the credits scrolled, tears started down her cheeks.

I squeezed her hand. She pulled it away and dried her eyes.

"It's so sad," she said.

I waited, confident she would share.

"What if your one true love was born in another time?"

"That would make life tougher," I said.

"Think of them, separated by time."

"It's a romance movie. Time is the obstacle that kept them apart."

"But they lost," she said.

"They had one night. And each other in their hearts. That's a lot better than nothing."

She blew her nose into a napkin. Even in the dim light from the screen her eyes were red.

"I wonder why Chris and Jane didn't last?" she said.

"Faking emotions for a living seems awfully complicated to me."

"Would sure mix me up."

"And…" I said. Our eyes met. "When the shooting was finished, they left this magic island."

"You think this place is enchanted?"

"Sure seems so," I said.

She pulled me over for a kiss, then moved the popcorn bowl and leaned against me. I started the movie over with the sound off. In a few minutes she was crying again. Shortly after that, she was sleeping with my arm around her.

I turned off the TV, carried her to bed, and tucked her in without removing her street clothes.

It was nearly 11 P.M.

I fingered the business envelope that Jake had given me, wondering just how long of a long shot this was.

<>

At twenty minutes before midnight, I poked my head into the hallway to check for all clear, then eased the door to 409 closed behind me. I pressed the down button to call the elevator and hustled into the stairwell, down loads of steps to the first floor, and into the restaurant kitchen. Twenty bucks and a story about hiding from my wife got me a silent pass to a back door from a young guy with a blow torch preparing desserts.

The night sky was filled with diamonds.

The clouds had moved on. Island lighting was minimal. Even wearing all black and my creepers I felt exposed. Vulnerable. I tapped Jake's envelope for the umpteenth time to be sure it was still inside the kangaroo pocket of my hoodie.

Absolutely nothing was moving. Not one carriage. The last ferry was long gone. I strode across groomed lawn toward the main road. I flipped up the dark hood of my sweatshirt and pushed my hands into my pants pockets to hide anything not black.

I crossed the road.

I crossed a beach strewn with rocks.

I walked on hard, wet sand.

The ferry dock area was gray, quiet, foreboding. Slow waves rose and fell against the concrete. Further up the shoreline boats in the marina bumped in the night. A single yellow bulb over the door lit the entrance to a small building painted white. A sign over the door read LUGGAGE. The door was locked. The building was empty. I leaned against the door, seeking a place to hide from as many eyes as possible. Then I realized I shouldn't be standing. I ducked and crossed the pavement to a park bench. I sat on the bench. Then I laid down on the bench. Then I crawled under it and stretched out on the ground on my back. Stars were visible between the slats of the seat.

I listened to waves breaking.

Blood pumped hard in my ears.

Lines slapped against sailboat masts over in the harbor.

I turned my head to watch for approaching feet.

I waited.

Footfalls arrived from the direction of the road. Soft and quick. The person approached, but the bench blocked my view of their face. White sneakers. Blue jeans. A small purse swinging on a chain. No socks. Brown, slender ankles.

She sat on the bench directly above my feet, apparently unaware of my presence. I closed one eye to peer between the wood slats. She lifted a smartphone with one hand. The screen lit and illuminated her face. The phone recognized her. The tones changed from blues to reds, making her face appear darker. Leni held the phone at arm's length and took a selfie.

I tried to relax my body with slow, silent breathing. She opened her purse, put the phone in and removed an object. The part of the object I could see between the slats wasn't definitive. She rotated it.

The barrel of a revolver pointed out at the open water, its grip firmly in her right hand.

"Psst. Leni."

She looked up, eyes roving

"Don't move. It's Tommy."

She sat frozen, staring out over the dark water.

"I'm under the bench."

Leni pulled out her smartphone and held it to her ear as if she had just received a call.

"Hi, Tommy," she said into the phone. "Thanks for coming all this way to help me."

"You're welcome. Why the gun?"

She placed it on the bench beside her. "I'm afraid. Of everyone. I haven't felt right since you stole my water bottle." She paused for a few seconds. "No, I don't want it back. No, no."

"Markus?"

No response. I shifted slightly so I could see her face better. The hard ground pressed against my shoulder blade. She was crying. She whispered into the phone pressed to her ear.

"I'll never be safe from him. Unless I kill him."

Bad idea.

I rolled out from beneath the bench, palmed her pistol as I got up, and held out my hand to help her stand. I put my arm around her and pulled her close. She took the clue and leaned into my shoulder—two young lovers walking by the sea. I guided us toward the marina, the land of a hundred floating bank accounts. We strolled among yachts more luxurious than my suite at the Grand Hotel. A few had lights on in the cabin. But most were dark, their occupants asleep or staying at the hotel.

We walked out the longest dock, sat down at the end, and dangled our feet toward the water. The yachts formed a wall between us and the shoreline.

Out of sight.

"Tommy, why does bad shit happen?"

"Something to do with the laws of entropy. And decline into disorder."

She sighed and swung her feet back and forth in the air.

"I have something to tell you," I said. "Been waiting for the right moment."

She stopped swinging and faced me. Her eyes were still wet.

"More shit?"

"Let's just say it might be a surprise that could complicate your life."

"It's already too complicated."

She found a pebble on a dock plank and tossed it. The splash was barely an inch high.

"Remember Jane Doe?" I asked.

"I stopped thinking about her."

"There's something about Mr. X that you need to know."

"No, I don't. I want that pig out of my life." She was quiet but breathing fast. "Without destroying my future."

"You will find this hard to believe," I said.

She tossed another pebble. "My whole life is hard to believe. There's nothing normal about it."

"Jane and Mr. X are related."

Her body tensed under my arm, but she didn't pull away.

"Go on," she said.

"The DNA analysis—"

"What DNA analysis? They said only cops can run a test."

"The cops did."

"Those bastards are trying to clear that piece of shit."

"No. Trying to confirm."

"And did they?"

"They confirmed that Mr. X is your father."

She jumped away so fast that I had to grab her with both hands to keep her from falling in the water. Her mouth started forming words but froze open before anything came out. I got both of my arms around her to prevent her from jumping off the dock.

She closed her mouth.

Her eyes hardened. "Impossible."

I provided details. Cheerleader mother. Academy footballer. Game schedule. Yearbook photos. Timing.

She stared at me in disbelief while I spoke. Then slowly leaned away until she was on her back gazing up at the stars, her feet still dangling toward the water. She raised her right arm, pointed, and started drawing in the air with her finger.

"He said I reminded him of someone from his past. Only I was smarter and more beautiful, so fate meant for him to wait for me." She continued sketching, I knew not what, with her finger. "I figured it was a long line of royal B.S." She lowered her arm and hugged herself as if a cold breeze had passed.

I picked a cluster of stars to stare at and waited.

"Now what, Tommy? I just lost a pig-hearted lover and gained a pig-hearted father. What in hell am I supposed to do? Send him to prison for rape and then go visit him?"

"Which path leads to happiness for Leni?"

"Not ever having met the…" She didn't finish. She didn't cry. She just stared up at the sky from her supine position on the dock.

"Life's a one-way street," I said. "There's no going back."

"If only."

"Is Oleace part of the Markus world?" I asked.

She shook her head slowly.

"No way. He'd stop me if he found out. He wants to own everything around him. Especially women." She tossed a pebble. If it splashed, I couldn't hear it. "I faked my ID and started doing Oleace in high school. Say what you will about cam girls, but it's safe, efficient, and you make your own schedule." She grunted a little laugh. "You ever think about all the unfulfilled sexual desire in the world? It seems out of balance."

"You mean like too many people want cheeseburgers at the picnic, so some have to eat hot dogs?"

Her gentle laugh rolled out over the dark water.

"More like a guy wants a spicy burger with double cheese and extra mayo, and he can't make it for himself, and he can't find anyone willing and able to make it for him."

"Frustrating."

"For everyone," she said. "But you meet some nice people. A few are even male. And boy is it the mother lode for a psych student who wants to find out what makes humans tick."

Which reminded me of Tock, and where he and Tick might be now.

"What do you want most?" I asked.

"Independence," she said. "I want to be free from the desire of males."

"How can you do that?"

"M.O.N.E.Y. Or more accurately, income generating power."

"Thus, college."

"But jerk-off is going to blacklist me. Block my financial aid. Vaporize my future with his ray gun. He'll never stop making demands because he thinks he owns me." She paused for several breaths. "Damn we're small compared to those stars." More pause, then, "In a way, he does. Now you tell me this narcissistic Godzilla is my father. Even my dream of finding my dad and being a real daughter goes up in smoke."

She sighed. But had stopped crying.

"And…" she began, but didn't finish.

"And you're addicted to fentanyl."

"Almost a year," she said. "It makes the world feel so damn good."

I tried to think of something to say to counter that, but failed before she continued.

"Now you come along and show me the real Leni. I don't like her. Screwing her teacher. Running boxes and pretending not to know what's inside. Becoming a victim. An addict. A fucking addict instead of studying. Thinking I'm in love with the famous psycho psychologist. Fantasizing a blossoming career for the little half-and-half girl from Missouri. All totally dependent on him." She sat up and looked down at the water. I got ready to stop her. "And now I'm trapped by the consequences of my own decisions. How's that for independence?"

"Traveling back in time would be ideal. But I have two ideas," I said.

"Markus gets hit by a fast-moving bus. Doesn't survive. What's the other one?"

"Do you remember Donald Trump, Stephanie Clifford, Karen McDougal?"

"For sure. White misogynist swings prick and pays women to be quiet about it."

"Or buys the rights to the story and buries it," I said. "Money changes hands so the women won't talk."

"I haven't talked," she said. "Only a few people know what happened."

"Including the guy who recorded the video."

She frowned. "Do you think Markus would pay me to keep quiet about us?"

"If he won't, Tick and Tock might."

She asked the question with beautiful, silent deep blue eyes.

I said, "A couple of cops stopped to chat with me. They're desperate to find you."

"About Markus?"

"About what you know about Markus."

"The boxes?" she said.

I shrugged. "I told them about the rapes, but they don't want to arrest him."

"Rapes? With an S?" she said.

"At least two."

"Oh my god."

"They claim that he's never been indicted or convicted."

"Doesn't mean he didn't do it," she said.

"His sister while in high school."

"Holy Jesus," she whispered. "His sister?"

"Incest is in the dictionary for a reason."

Leni sat up, swinging her dangling feet to and fro, staring at her sneakers as if they were the most interesting thing in the world.

"Tommy, tell me your ideas."

I removed the sealed envelope from inside my shirt and handed it to her.

She laughed almost to tears. "You keep your ideas in a sealed envelope?"

If only life were that easy.

"Jake and I asked Jake's lawyer to construct a hush contract that might interest Markus. The lawyer doesn't know what you're keeping quiet. Just that there is a secret to be kept."

A splash to our left drew our attention. I looked behind us down the empty dock. The boats were all dark. The docks were empty.

"Should I open it?" she asked.

I waited, suppressing a smile.

"I know. Only if I want to know what it says." She carefully peeled off one end. It wasn't exactly a contract. It was more like a one-page term sheet without the legal mumbo jumbo. She whispered the words as she read.

"A quarter of a million?" she said.

"That enough?"

"I think so. Let me read the rest."

"He gets the video recordings?" she asked.

"It says he gets all videos that are in your possession."

"And I agree to never talk about what happened. Even if subpoenaed and under oath. Is that even legal?"

"You can invoke the fifth amendment."

"Thou shalt not incriminate thyself?" she said. She read some more. "This says Markus must essentially forget that we ever met or this contract terminates."

"The lawyer is trying to keep Markus honest."

"Feels like blackmail," she said. "Is this legal?"

"Maybe it's one of those fifty shades of gray. But a good lawyer wrote it. Jake doesn't mess around."

She folded the paper back into the envelope, stuffed in the little piece she had torn off the end, and handed the envelope back to me.

"Reaction?" I asked.

"Money is okay, but he can afford more. I think there needs to be a detailed hush clause for him. And some kind of huge financial penalty if he violates it. But—" She tossed a pebble.

"Where are you finding the stones?" I asked.

"In my pockets. I've been saving pretty ones I find on the beach. I walked the far side of the island for hours. Almost no one goes there except for a few carriage rides. There's not even a tour bus here."

"Don't you want to keep them?"

"Not anymore. The more I forget about the past year, the better."

"So?"

"I think letting him off with a quarter million dollar fine is a slap on the wrist."

"Funds your education. Protects your reputation."

"But nothing happens to him. He puts up some money and this all goes into the dump heap of history. If I agree to this contract, he'll never stop doing what he's doing. If it's not me, it'll be some other young girl as dumb as me."

"That's a different goal. What are you thinking?"

"Put him in prison."

"If he doesn't make money, how can he pay you?"

"Sell his Ferrari," she said.

"A college professor has a Ferrari?"

"And a cabin on a lake up in Wisconsin. And an airplane, or part of one. And a fabulous condo in Chicago."

"I bet none of it is paid for. More important, you will have your freedom, money, support from a psychologist already in the club, and a secret that you both keep."

"I would always wonder," she said.

"About?"

"How many more lives he manipulates. Maybe a girl who doesn't have friends to help her find a way out. So she stays. Sinks into depression. Despair. One day she pulls the trigger on her life because I didn't send this jerk to prison when I had the chance."

"Whopping cost if you go public. Remember what the world did to Monica Lewinsky? An intern gave a rich, powerful guy a blow job. And when it all hit the fan, he threw her under the bus."

She was quiet, swinging her feet and staring into the dark water.

"The woman gets blamed a lot, doesn't she?"

"Ever heard anyone blame Adam for eating that apple?"

◇

Leni and I dangled our toes a yard above the water for a few more minutes. A pair of bright lights appeared in the sky to the east. We watched them approach across the water.

She nudged me with her shoulder. "Look, a foo fighter."

"UFO wouldn't be my first guess."

She laughed a little and pretended to toss pebbles at the lights. She shifted toward me until our legs pressed together and warmth flowed between us. The lights grew closer and lower to the water.

And lower.

We both reflex ducked as a plane passed over the harbor and roaring jet engines woke anyone sleeping on a yacht.

"Loud," she said.

"Who would fly in so late?"

"Rich guy with his paramour. She wants to see the island. His cover story only works for one night away from wifey and kids. So he has to get in and out fast." She paused. Silent. "So to speak."

The jet engines faded behind us. We both laughed.

"Sorry," she said.

"Feeling cynical?"

"I thought that was rather romantic. Jet away to an island portal to forbidden love." She gazed up at the stars.

I was reminded there were always multiple ways to look at any situation.

Leni tossed another invisible stone, said "splash," and stood up. I got to my feet.

"Would you like me to walk you back?" I said.

She shook her head slowly. "Prof said I should hide and not tell anyone where."

"Good advice. How can I reach you?"

"I'm watching Oleace. I figure even if they eavesdrop on my account, they'll never be able to sort through the traffic. Pick a handle."

"Um...how about...turbo bronze?"

She smiled. "Sounds like an old guy with a suntan who thinks he can keep it up all night." She grinned. "Turbo bronze 65 has been used. You be sixty-six."

I held out her gun that I had lifted from the park bench.

She stared at it for a long moment, then reached out with one hand and slipped it back into her purse. "You never know when a vicious animal might attack." Then, she walked silently away on the wood dock and into the darkness beyond the ferry landing. I wondered if she was staying in the Grand Hotel. Then realized she might be in a tent on the other side of the island in a hidden cove. No one to see her face. New cell phone number.

Now that I had dropped the DNA bomb on Leni, what next? She took it in stride. Or she hadn't processed it yet. Or she was in shock. Maybe still in shock from the rape. Whatever she was feeling, I wasn't going to get anything done standing on a dock.

Before I took a step, two figures on bicycles rode straight at me. They were towing a third cycle between them that had no rider. Everything was black except for one guy's hair. I could run, but I was trapped on a dead end dock. I could swim. Or I could wait.

Tick and Tock pulled to a stop in front of me.

"Gentlemen," I said. "You wish for me to accompany you?"

"We do," Tock said. "Even brought you wheels to speed things up."

"Markus wants to see me."

Tock studied me before speaking. "This is way bigger than Corolla. My advice to you is, don't get cute."

I nodded, mounted the spare bike, and followed Tock down the dock with Tick close behind. Riding along a dock in the dark with a drop-off to the water on either side should have been easy. But it felt like riding on a tightrope stretched across a canyon.

We approached a ninety-degree turn. Tock made a sweeping arch with no problem. I looked down at the water where the two docks met, caught the front tire in the gap between them, and wobbled toward Tock. Tick was probably laughing at me. I looked up and braked hard with both hands, but still rammed into Tock, who had stopped where the dock dropped off to a gravel path.

Tock managed to stay upright, but I ended up on my left side staring at two figures pointing guns at Tick and Tock. I sat up and brushed gravel off my hoodie. The two men were wearing ski masks. Their double XL size gave me comfort.

"What do you guys want?" Tock said, both hands still on his handlebars, making no move for the weapon I was sure he was carrying.

"A trade," the shorter masked guy said. He gestured toward Tick. "Me for him."

"And why would I do that?" Tock said.

"Because you boys are messing with Tommy Cuda. Maybe you're taking him against his will on your little government-issued wheels. But no uniform, no badge. Maybe you're legit. Or maybe you're rogue. Or maybe you're big, bad terrorists and Cuda might be in the kind of danger he don't know how to get out of." He smiled wide behind his mask. "So here we are."

"And if I don't agree to the trade?"

"We take Mr. Cuda and leave you two hogtied to your toys to be found in the morning by a little kid waiting for the first ferry. Then you explain to the Michigan Department of Tourism why you out here scaring away money-spending tourists."

Tock studied the masked men.

"Do you know who I represent?" he said.

"That I do. No one. Without ID and proper procedure, you're nobody. And we are, of course, recording the proceedings to prove it."

I didn't see a camera. But I was confident Jake would know how to use clandestine equipment. Or, he was bluffing.

"You'll regret this," Tock said.

"Not as much as you will if we don't make a deal."

I sat motionless on the ground, trying not to think about stray bullets.

Tock nodded to Tick and began to dismount. Simultaneously they threw their bicycles forward like spears and chased in after them. Tick's bike bounced off Ramone like it had hit a boulder. His non-gun hand shot up and Tick ran his face right into it.

Jake sidestepped Tock's bike and hammered Tock in the groin with what I'd call a martial arts move if I saw it in a movie.

Tick and Tock both went down.

Ramone removed four firearms from the two probable agents, but found no wallets or identification, just a thousand dollars in cash between them. No phones. Not even a Mastercard.

"Where?" Jake asked.

I looked at Tick and Tock on the ground. One curled into a ball moaning, the other apparently unconscious. "Do they need medical attention?"

"Not right away," Ramone said.

I wondered if my friends had just improved or worsened the situation. But I was breathing easier.

"The luggage shack."

In a handful of minutes, Ramone had opened the shack, tied the men with cables intended to secure luggage, and closed the place up. Standing outside the shack, Jake pulled off his ski mask.

"How do people wear these things?" he said, rubbing a hand over his face. "Feels like ants eating your skin." He looked to me. "Where were they taking you?"

"Never said. But a couple minutes before they showed up, a jet flew over."

"How do you want to do this?" he said.

"I'm in over my head. I'd appreciate your expert advice."

Another grin. Even bigger without the mask. "We leave these two for the vultures. I go with you. Ramone hangs for back up."

The three of us mounted the bicycles and followed the signs toward the island's airport. A mile later we entered a Michigan State Park and approached an airport with a small tower and one runway. No glowing lights. Closed for the night.

Except for one plane.

In a row of parked private planes, each with a single propeller, light showed from the windows of an aircraft with two jet engines near the tail. We stopped as a group in the moon shadow of the tower.

"Thoughts?" I said.

"Fat cat," Jake replied. "Drug dealer. Saudi oil prince. U.S. Government."

I removed the revolver Prof had loaned me and showed it to Jake, careful to keep my finger away from the trigger.

He nodded. "OK. If you need it, do not waste time trying to pull it out of your pocket. Just point and shoot. We can get you a new sweatshirt."

I nodded while trying not to conjure a scenario where I would need it.

"Before we go," Jake said. "Lay out the land for me."

"Option one, drug dealer and rapist Markus Corolla wants me to stay away from Leni and has flown in to give me a personal reminder."

Jake nodded understanding, but didn't comment.

"Option two, Markus is a cog in a bigger wheel. Somehow, Leni is throwing sand in the bearings. Those guys back there, who might be FBI but never identified themselves, are probably a part of the wheel. Possibly, the second author on Markus's research papers is another cog. He's a chemist."

"How convenient," Jake said.

CHAPTER 37

A bronze plaque on the side of the tower told me that the airport was built in 1964 and moved to flatter land in 1978. I tried to imagine moving an entire runway, then focused my attention on the sleek aircraft spilling light out through its cabin windows.

The stairway was up.

"What do you like?" I asked Jake.

"Walk up like we own the place. Keep your hand on your gun."

"I'm not used to this kind of thing," I said.

"Good. It ain't something you ever want to get used to." He tilted his head for me to lead the way.

I gave Ramone a thank you salute and walked straight toward the door of the jet. I passed through a light beam that flashed in my eyes. Jake's footfalls followed me. I stopped at the spot I thought the steps would touch the runway if they swung down. No one was visible in the cockpit.

Jake stopped beside my left shoulder.

"We wait," he said. "Let them do whatever checking they want to do. Get comfortable we ain't a threat. Ho ho ho."

Stars twinkled beyond the plane. A light breeze touched my ears. I silently repeated the letters and numbers on the side of the plane so I wouldn't forget them.

A metallic snap punctuated the night air. I squeezed the grip of my pistol without meaning to while forcing myself to remain standing stoically beside Jake. A motor whirred, the door lowered. More light spilled onto the runway. I got a glimpse into a wood trimmed cabin.

No people.

"Be my guest," Jake said with a smile.

I walked up the steps, resisting the urge to look back and be sure Jake and Ramone were still there. At the top, I stepped into the cabin. The expected double rows of seats were missing, replaced by four first class lounge chairs at the front and an oak conference table surrounded by six seats behind them. A man sat at the head of the conference table, facing me. Papers and colored folders covered the table. A black laptop sat to his right. Neither of his hands were visible.

Jake stepped into the plane behind me.

The man looked up through round, silver spectacles that made me think of John Lennon. His gray hair touched the tip of his ears. His face was suntanned. He was a bit overweight, or maybe just stocky. Perhaps stronger than he looked. Light gray suit, white shirt, maroon tie.

He studied us for a moment, then said, "I was told we have two undercover agents on this island." Dry, rough voice. The kind that gave orders instead of asking questions.

"Partner is outside guarding the perimeter," Jake said.

"That means this white boy is the one causing all the trouble."

I felt Jake stiffen beside me.

"Tommy Cuda," I said, "At your service." The pistol grip was getting hot in my hand.

"Welcome. Sit down."

I sat at the opposite end of the table to face him. Jake sat between us to my right, likely with his gun pointed at the guy's stomach. The man shuffled papers until he found something he wanted. He looked at me.

"Why are you in the proximity of our person of interest? You have been told repeatedly to stay away."

I took a slow breath to make him wait.

"Mr. Clean raped a friend of mine."

Jake suppressed a grin, the effort rippling the muscles of his jaw.

"Allegedly," the man said. "No one bothered to file a charge."

"She's afraid."

"Aren't they all," he said.

"With good reason."

He stared at me, so I continued.

"She stands to lose her scholarship, her job, the support of a key professional, and maybe her career if she files charges. All this, even though she's not the one on trial."

"Rape case," he said, "everyone's on trial. He said this, she said that."

"She has a video."

"One of those, huh?"

"Coincidence," I said. "She happened to be on a video conference on her phone at the time of the assault."

He studied me for a moment. "Tell me about Mr. Clean."

"So you can know what I know?" I shook my head. "You have the jet. How about you tell me about Mr. Clean?"

A grin almost made it to his lips. "Mr. Clean isn't important."

"Then why protect him?"

The almost grin faded. "There are bigger issues. Thus far, you haven't caused real trouble. I'm here to prevent you from interfering."

"Prevent sounds like a threat," I heard myself say before thinking of how he might react.

He shook his head. "I'm simply giving you a way out before things escalate."

"You sound like a godfather protecting territory."

This time the grin reached his lips. "Something like that. Why don't you take your girl and her wheelchair and just go away?"

"Why don't you arrest Mr. Clean?"

He placed both elbows on the table, brought his fists together in front of his mouth, and stared at me.

"He's doing important work."

"Raping co-eds?"

"There's been no—"

"Formal complaint," I said, cutting him off mid-sentence.

He met my eyes for the first time. His were like a panther hunting a gazelle. I glanced toward Jake, who still had both hands in the pockets of his black jacket. I wondered for a moment if he had two guns.

"Do you know who I am?" the man said.

"A guy in a flashy jet who works with Mr. Clean."

"Has no one explained the situation to you?" He paused. "Within confidentiality limits."

"No one has even bothered to identify themselves. They just want me to tell them where Leni is."

"Leni?"

"Lenore. The girl who was raped. Allegedly."

He leaned back and took a deep breath. It worked like a fountain of youth elixir, relaxing the muscles of his face. He looked a couple years younger.

"What do you want, Mr. Cuda?"

"I want Mr. Clean to pay for raping Leni. But not by rotting in a jail cell while she struggles to build her career. Here's one option. Full-ride scholarship. Admittance into an Ivy League school. Money for graduate studies."

I waited. He waited.

I added, "And Mr. Clean's unrelenting support of Leni's career. Kick open as many doors as possible."

He stared past me as if someone had walked out of the cockpit. I glanced at Jake. He gave me a slight nod that everything was okay.

"Trivial," the man said.

I hoped that meant he would do it.

"And Mr. Clean stops having sex with students. Not just raping them, actively avoiding them."

"He needs to…interact with them. But he'll do as I say."

"Godfather card?"

He grinned again. "I can be quite persuasive."

"Lastly, shut down Nature Incognito."

He reached below the table. Jake tensed. I felt for the trigger in my pocket.

His hand came up holding a whiskey bottle then disappeared again. Came up with a glass. He poured a splash into the glass and returned the bottle to its hiding place. But he didn't drink.

"Can't do that," he said, dropping sheets of paper on the desk. "Well, actually I could, but doing so would be counterproductive." His hand brought up a single printed page. He handed it to Jake, who handed it to me without even looking at it.

I read fast. "A one-way non-disclosure agreement?"

"Correct. You cannot repeat to anyone what I am about to tell you."

"What about you?"

"I can do anything I want."

Jake grinned ever so slightly.

I said, "But that company is…well, you know what they're doing. And Markus…Mr. Clean is drugging—"

He held up a palm. "Read and sign."

I read carefully. I was agreeing to keep silent about whatever he told me. There was a place for a second signature.

"Is this legal?" I asked.

"Absolutely," he said.

"Is it necessary?"

"Not if you're willing to leave it alone."

"What does 'leave it alone' mean?"

"Disappear," he said. "Don't ever think about Mr. Clean."

"And Leni?"

He shrugged.

"But if I sign this you'll do those things for Leni?"

Slow nod.

I said, "Including controlling Mr. Clean?"

Faster nod.

I signed and dated the document, then pushed the paper toward Jake, who reached out and passed it down with one hand, the other still in his pocket.

Leni's phone vibrated in my pocket.

I debated for an instant, then realized it might be Leni.

"Excuse me for a moment," I said, and pulled the phone out. Seventeen messages for Sally. One to the turbobronze66 account I had recently created.

T. I saw him on the sidewalk. I'm at a B & B on Mahoney. It's painted blue. Registered as Sally. Called Prof. I'm scared. —S.

My thoughts spun. "Where's Mahoney Street?"

The man lowered his silver spectacles. "Why?"

Jake tapped his phone. "Near the marina."

"Markus saw Lenore," I said. "Grabbed her."

"We don't know that," the man stated calmly.

"Operating assumption," Jake said, as if on cue in a movie.

A black smartphone appeared in the man's hand.

Jake and I waited.

He lowered the phone. "Mr. Clean does not answer. He knows it's me. And he knows to never not answer."

Jake stood. "His hands are busy. Give me the location of his phone."

"I'll put someone on it. But it can take a bit."

Jake headed for the door. He stopped at the top of the stairs.

"How do I reach you?" he said to the man.

"Through channels."

Jake stared at him, both hands back in his pockets.

"You think that'll be fast enough to stop Clean from raping her again? And this time he thinks maybe it's a good idea to shut her up for good?"

The man rattled off a ten-digit number.

The stairs shook as Jake ran out of the plane.

I ran after him. A voice behind me shouted for me to stop, finish the deal, do not interfere with a government agency. It wasn't much. But it was the first admission that professionals were involved.

Jake, Ramone, and I jumped on the bicycles and headed for downtown. Jake shouted over the wind.

"Guesses?"

"We were in the marina," I said. "Leni left just before the agents grabbed me."

"I saw her go," Jake said.

"Maybe Markus did too."

"Yacht," Jake said. "He'll drag her onto it and split."

"She might be at the B & B," I said. "But I have no idea when she posted that message."

Jake looked at me, then at Ramone.

"Registered as Sally Holiday," I said.

Ramone nodded and headed toward a blue B & B on Mahoney.

Jake and I peddled hard toward the marina knowing Markus was closer to Leni and had a head start. When we finally arrived panting and sweating, we hopped up from the gravel trail to the dock and split up, looking for any boat with activity.

The riding a tightrope feeling returned with a vengeance.

Most boats were dark and resting at their moorings. I finger-crossed that Markus wasn't already at sea. The guy in the jet could send a chopper after him, but what would happen to Leni before it got there? Then I remembered her promise and the gun she was carrying. If she pulled that trigger—

Movement on a flybridge caught my eye. No interior lights. No deck lights. If the engines were running, their sound was hidden under the wind rushing past my ears.

Light and shadows shifted on the bridge. I couldn't tell who, but someone was moving. I slowed, made a tight turn onto the correct dock extension, peddled faster, and reviewed what Jake called operating assumptions.

Leni onboard against her will.

Markus on the bridge.

Dock lines had been cast off.

The yacht backing out of the slip.

The yacht could reach open water in minutes.

I shouted, "Wait for me!"

The face that turned toward me was Markus. Maybe. Eighty percent confidence. He ignored me and turned toward the stern.

The yacht glided further out of its slip.

I rode to the very edge of the dock nearest the yacht's rail and slowed until we were moving at exactly the same speed. I stepped over the rail onto the deck with one foot, then the other, keeping both hands on the bike. I was now standing on the deck near the bow and pushing the bike along the dock. As the dock ended, I grabbed the frame, lifted with both arms, spun in a full circle as fast as I could, and tossed the bike at the flybridge like a shot-putter. A tire clipped the windshield. The bike stood up, shot over the flybridge's windscreen, and slammed into the back of Markus's head.

I reached into my hoodie and wrapped my hand around Prof's gun. Jake's voice filled my head, "Don't waste time pulling it out of your pocket." I ran across the roof of the cabin, leapt over the windshield of the flybridge, and landed with both feet on the spoke's of the bicycle's rear wheel. The prone figure under the bike was wearing a white suit.

The collar was stained red. He wasn't moving.

Peripheral vision told me that the yacht was.

I looked up as the words Holy Toledo! emblazoned across a sleek sailing yacht came closer. I freed my foot from the bent spokes, spun around, grabbed the wheel, and pushed a pair of throttles toward center.

The engines dropped to an idle.

Holy Toledo! came closer.

I pushed the shifters up into neutral, then forward. A red light blinked as the port engine stalled. I pushed both throttles forward.

The yacht slowed and turned and slammed into the back of Holy Toledo! with a massive crunch of splintering fiberglass. The impact halted the yacht's progress and tossed me backwards. I tripped over the handlebars of the bike and off the flybridge. My right shoulder hit the deck first, then my head, and finally my right hip. Pain shattered my thoughts, but I remained conscious. The second engine rumbled as it tried in vain to separate the two yachts.

My right hand found the grip of the pistol, in case Markus was conscious. My left searched for the burner phone.

I called 911.

I managed to stand. My right hand worked okay, even though my shoulder was burning inside.

Jake waved to me from the dock.

"I'm okay." I pointed to the flybridge. "Markus."

He nodded, both hands in his pockets, no doubt ready to sacrifice his sweatshirt.

I considered whether or not to help Markus. Decided a possible neck injury was best left to professionals. The emergency team should be fast, even on an island with no cars.

But what if?

I climbed the ladder up to the flybridge using my left arm. A quick search of his body revealed a Glock in a shoulder holster. I took it, and I made my way down the ladder to the cabin door. It was padlocked from the outside. I stepped back and kicked repeatedly, making an incredible racket in the late-night silence, until the latch gave way and the hatchway access to the cabin could be opened.

Leni was in the master stateroom on her back, arms above her head, mouth taped, ankles roped together, her naked body stretched diagonally across the bed. Her cheeks were scratched and bleeding. Her eyes projected a mountain lion about to defend itself.

Then she recognized me.

I removed the tape carefully, avoiding her lacerations. She took a few deep breaths..

"I couldn't do it," she said.

'It' left a lot of room for speculation. I thought she might cry, but her eyes shone like she was working on a hard math problem. While I untied her wrists, she talked nonstop.

"I felt trapped in the B & B. Wanted to be someplace where I could run. He jumped me on a dark section of beach. Threw himself on top of me and pinned me down. He likes holding me down while doing it." She breathed harder with the memory. "I had one chance. A free hand while he unbuckled his belt. I had my finger right on the trigger."

I worked to untie the rope around her legs that was so tight both ankles were bleeding.

"I knew I had him. Could end his life right then, and never have to worry about him again." She stared at the ceiling.

I imagined the 'but.'

"I didn't need to ruin the rest of my life to prove I could kill him. I knew I could. I had the opportunity, the will, and the power." She smiled, cracking the dried blood on her face. One laceration started bleeding again.

"So I stopped struggling," she said.

I helped her sit upright on the bed.

"As soon as I didn't resist, he lost his erection. Then he got really mad and beat me, dragged me here, and shouted how he owned me and I would never amount to anything without him."

"The cops will be here soon. Where's your gun?"

"He found it and threw it into the ocean. I never even fired it."

"Did you tell him about the DNA?"

She stiffened head to toe. Her lips pressed together into a thin line.

"He doesn't deserve to know."

Clamoring on deck announced the arrival of someone with heavy boots. I left Leni to get dressed and prepare for a hundred questions. I crawled up from the cabin, saw no one. I found two EMTs on the flybridge moving the bicycle.

"We need to talk." A voice from behind me.

I turned around to see the gray-haired man with silver spectacles standing on the stern of Holy Toledo!. A female EMT called down from the bridge.

"Vitals stable. Unconscious. ID says Markus Corolla."

The man stepped across to Markus's yacht and made his way to the ladder. He went up one step at a time, dragging his left leg after the right.

"Yeah, that's him," he told the EMT.

He made his way down with the same one-at-a-time method. When he reached me, he stopped and met my eyes for a long time.

"He better live," he said. "And not as a vegetable." He put both hands into the pockets of a gray trench coat that seemed too warm for the weather. "My plane in fifteen minutes." He turned and glanced at the hatchway to the cabin. "Is the girl here?"

I nodded slowly. "She was tied up below."

He raised an eyebrow. I guessed the question.

"Tried to. But was unsuccessful. Beat her up instead."

He gazed at the stern of the sailboat, said, "Holy Toledo," softly, then stepped across to its aft deck, looked up at the moon, then down at his watch.

"Fifteen minutes."

"On my way," I said.

"Alone. This is for you and me to work out."

"Can I bring Leni?"

He thought for a moment. Shook his head. "Bad idea."

He walked away.

Leni agreed to go with the EMTs so a doctor could examine her. Ramone went with her, just in case Markus had friends on the island. I walked a dozen yards down the dock with Jake.

"He wants to talk to me alone."

"Keep your hand on your piece. I'll be outside. I smell anything weird, I'm coming in."

"Thanks." I pulled out the Glock. "Found this in a shoulder holster."

Jake took it, looked it over, made it disappear inside his clothes.

"What Glock?" he said, and faded into the darkness.

I called my service with the burner phone. Braden.

"Found the bakery through the baker. Nice shop. Very clean. High quality ingredients. Big pharma would be proud. Haven't told the baker yet." He ended with, "Imagine a smiling emoji here."

I shut the phone off, stuffed it into my hoodie opposite my gun, and headed out to ride to the airport. Jake was waiting with Ramone's bicycle. We rode halfway in silence.

"Remember," Jake said. "Gig tomorrow."

I thought about the pain in my right shoulder, the pounding in my head, and the ache in my hip every time I spun the pedals. I released the handlebar and flexed the fingers of my right hand. The show must go on.

"You found equipment?"

"On the way," he said, as if our roadies would be here any minute to construct a stage for us.

"Where are we playing?"

"I got an idea. The other party has not seen the light of day yet. But I will convince them before noon tomorrow."

We pedaled along for a hundred yards.

"You're going to tell me," I said, "that we start at noon tomorrow?"

"That's my plan."

"But we don't have equipment yet."

"We will."

"And no rehearsal or sound check on this equipment?"

"This is the blues, man. Rehearsals are for people who write shit down. We are on a live adventure into the unknown. What the computer jocks call 'real time.'"

We pulled into the shadow of the airport's control tower for a second time.

"I'll be close," Jake said. "You need anything, make noise."

I nodded my thanks and held out my hand. We shook in silence. For no particular reason, I wondered how many times Jake's finger had needed to pull a trigger.

I took a deep breath and headed for the plane.

The boarding staircase was again folded up into the plane. I massaged the pistol grip in my right hand, appreciating the texture of the handle, and the cell phone in my left, wondering, when all was said and done, which technology presented the greater threat to society.

The door whirred down before I reached it, spilling the inside lighting over me. Again the cockpit was empty. I wondered if the gray man was his own pilot or if the pilot had been sent away. I took the steps slow and easy, favoring my hip and trying to clear my mind of assumptions and hypotheses to be ready for whatever was coming my way.

I reached the top.

The staircase whirred up and sucked tightly closed against the fuselage. Jake had no easy way in. And I had no easy way out. Fatigue crept into my body even as it went on high alert.

"We are in a private plane," he said from his former position at the far end of the conference table. "No recordings. No witnesses. A meeting that never happened to solve a problem that doesn't exist, because the reality can't exist." He gestured for me to sit. "Officially."

I took Jake's chair. Closer. Better chance of hitting the target if the world went haywire.

"Why me?" I asked.

"Because you are the thorn that must be removed from the lion's paw."

He leaned back in his chair, put both hands into his pants pockets, and sighed.

"The person you know as Markus Corolla is a valuable asset."

CHAPTER 38

The word 'asset' covered a lot of ground. But the most important part of an asset was: Who owned it?

"Doesn't make him innocent," I said.

He moved several papers around on the conference table like a player reviewing his cards.

"No argument. But it does make guilt or innocence irrelevant."

I breathed in slowly through my nose. "Not to Lenore."

"That troublemaker must keep her mouth shut," he said. "Allow me to propose a way to end this nonsense."

I double-checked the location of my pistol. Though I couldn't imagine using it, I was heeding Jake's words.

"First," he said, "scholarship, graduate school admission, graduate funding."

"In a way that she doesn't have to trust anyone."

"Agreed. However, she must sign a non-disclosure agreement. And she will be watched for…some time into the future."

"Fair enough." I hesitated. "Corolla?"

"She will have his complete cooperation for career assistance. Otherwise, he will disappear from her life."

I shifted slightly in my chair.

"And if he doesn't?" I asked.

He rubbed his palms together before saying, "I will deal with Mr. Corolla."

A humming started somewhere in the plane.

"Godfather," I said.

He smiled slowly. "Perhaps."

"What about the others?" I asked.

He made no reply.

"Leni wasn't his first conquest," I said. "How many others has he drugged and raped?"

He shook his head. "They were already addicted."

"He keeps them supplied."

He nodded but said nothing.

"How is that acceptable?"

He looked into me with a strange warmth in his eyes. "It is better than the alternative."

I looked down at the table and felt my palm sweating around the pistol grip. He slid a sheet of paper across the table toward me. It contained a 24-month graph. A red line had been climbing. But 14 months ago, it plateaued and had been dropping ever since. The vertical axis was labeled:

OD/100,000

"This shows," I said, "a drop in overdose deaths." His gray eyes agreed. "Something happened about fourteen months ago."

"Precisely."

I stared at the line. The reduction over the past year was phenomenal.

"And that something is classified?"

"Of course."

"Mr. Clean?"

His gaze crystallized for the briefest moment. He sat in silence.

"And I should have figured out by now that Mr. Clean isn't a person," I said, "it's a huge project with lots of moving parts. Corolla is a tiny wheel inside of it."

"I can neither confirm nor deny your supposition." He hesitated. His gray eyes no longer looked threatening. They looked sad. "It took years and millions of dollars to put that narcissistic jerk in place."

"It's really that bad?" I asked.

"What's that?"

"The Chinese fentanyl coming up through Mexico."

He looked around the interior of the plane like he had just entered a museum and was admiring the paintings.

"Let me tell you a story about the American Dream. Two brothers, Rick and Maurice, traveled across America by automobile. 'See the USA in your Chevrolet' and all that happy family stuff. They noticed that sometimes the food at a diner was very good. Maybe even had pretty girls on roller skates take orders and hang them from your car window. But other times, the food was barely edible. So eating while traveling was a hit and miss gamble every single day. The brothers decided to start a chain of restaurants where the traveler could be assured of quality every time."

"Who were these guys?"

"Richard and Maurice." He paused. Cleared his throat. "McDonald."

I stared at the graph and recalled Amazon boxes filled with pills. Scooter girl picking up and delivering. For cash. A co-author with a state-of-the-art laboratory. Research papers showing the efficacy of treatments from a company called Nature Incognito.

Incognito => True identity concealed.

"You're kidding," I said. "The government clamps down on OxyContin sales, creating a huge demand on the street for opioids. In rush dealers with Chinese chemicals. The fentanyl is good. But inconsistent. Sometimes too good." I shifted in my chair again. It was a fine chair, but no position felt comfortable. "So you created the McDonald's of fentanyl suppliers. Clean. Consistent. Cheap."

"And always available," he said.

He motioned toward the graph. "There are similarities to McDonald's. And some major differences."

"But consistency is key," I said. "Addicts have habits."

His head bobbed slightly. "What happens if the system doesn't support those habits?"

"Addicts use whatever they can get."

The conversation stalled. I tried to read the other pages lying on his desk. But they were upside down and too far away.

"Leni is a threat to this, uh, project?"

"Mr. Clean is key to its success," he said.

I put my left elbow on the table to brace myself and turned toward him. "You're telling me that if Leni exposes Markus your carefully constructed secret supply chain will collapse. The fentanyl supply becomes polluted. More addicts die, not fewer?"

Without hesitation he said, "Without a doubt."

"So you keep Leni quiet, and your Mr. Clean project continues to fill in for Purdue Pharma?"

"We have much better control than they ever did. Quantity. Quality. Delivery chain." He didn't smile, but he wasn't frowning either.

Breathing felt hard. "OK. I understand the deal on the table. Can you do something for Corolla's sister? She's living in a shack by a swamp in Wisconsin."

"Uncle Sam will send monthly checks. I will fabricate an appropriate reason. Anything else?"

"What if Leni won't go for it?"

"I will arrange for her to be hidden away from the eyes and ears of the public."

I considered. But not for long. "So this is an offer she can't refuse?"

"Acceptance would be the wisest path for everyone involved."

"Hell of a trade-off you've got going."

"Welcome to the messy, no-obvious-solution but you gotta do something real world, Mr. Cuda."

I studied the graph. Thought about what number of deaths per 100,000 population really meant.

"Are you sure this data is real?" I asked.

"Mortuary statistics are generally quite accurate."

I pushed the page back to him. "So, the U.S. government is in the drug business."

"I have not presented any documents that would indicate I am from a government agency."

No records. Just like he said.

"You might be the Blackwater of the drug world. One more problem outsourced to a private firm by public servants."

"Could be," he said. "But another irrelevant detail. The U.S. government has been in the drug business since Prohibition. The FDA makes all the rules."

Of course they did.

"How does this deal happen?" I asked.

"I send a few messages and," he made a magician's motion with his right hand, "voila."

"What do you need from me?"

"Convince the girl to take our generous offer." He paused and his eyes shifted. Without looking at me, he said, "Don't let her be a hero. There is too much at stake from our side."

"In plain English that means you would be forced to neutralize her by other means."

He swept his papers together into a neat stack, but didn't confirm or deny.

CHAPTER 39

Jake and I stood back and watched a team of horses pull a wooden flatbed wagon along the street fronting the Grand Hotel. Jake tapped a rhythm against his thighs, syncopated against the clop of the hooves on the pavement.

"I wanted to set up on the porch," Jake said. "Management nixed it. Even with Bobbie vouching for us."

"So we play on the street?" I said.

"Busking at its finest."

"I don't see electrical outlets on that wagon."

He gestured toward the luggage cart borrowed from the hotel and stacked to the nines with gear.

"Behold. Amp, PA system, drum machine. Everything runs on batteries. We can play anywhere."

"Did you rob a music store?"

"Cuda, I'm insulted." He smiled. "Do you think I would lower my standards to petty theft?" He laughed deeply. "This island has a DJ. Does weddings. Corporate hoo-ha. Rented me his stuff."

"The DJ had a guitar?"

"Borrowed that from the doorman. Turns out, he's from Cleveland. Visits the Rock and Roll Hall of Fame like a church. Comes up here summers for the tips and chicks."

"Tough life," I said.

We dragged the luggage rack to the wagon and waited while the driver unhitched his horses and led them away. My right hip and shoulder were bruised and stiff. But my fingers all worked. And Jake had provided a little something to dull the pain while keeping my mind intact.

"Tommy!"

Leni's voice floated down to us from the porch. She was wearing a bright orange top and leaning over the white railing waving. Her face was blotched with bandages and the arm that wasn't waving was wrapped in white gauze from palm to elbow. She was smiling broadly and gesturing for me to come over.

To reach each other one of us would have to walk the 300 feet to the stairs that went up from the street to the porch. I left Jake with the cart at our makeshift stage and crossed the street until I was looking straight up into Leni's smile.

"Guess what?" she said.

"I need a hint."

"I can stay in school."

"You won the Michigan Mega Millions lottery?"

"Don't be silly." She dug with her un-bandaged hand into the front pocket of skintight yoga pants that ancient yogis never envisioned, unfolded a piece of paper with one hand, and waved it above her head. "I got a scholarship. And, and…advanced admission to, are you ready? Harvard!"

The gray man was quick.

"That's amazing." I opened both arms in an air hug. "Mega congratulations."

"I'm sooooo haaaaappppyyyyy!"

She blew me kisses with her good hand, dropped the letter, disappeared behind the railing to retrieve it, and popped back into sight. "I can't wait for your concert."

"Thanks." I extended my fingers. "Ten minutes." I waved goodbye, feeling good about Leni's smile, and hoping the gray man would make good on his promise to control Markus. I crawled up on the wagon and helped set up the smallest amps I had ever seen on the raw planks of the wagon stage. Jake didn't have a drum kit; he had a drum machine the size of a dinner plate and a keyboard with about two dozen black and white keys, each as long as my finger.

My amp was covered in brown vinyl and had only one knob. It didn't go to 11. In fact, there were no numbers at all, just the word OFF in the lower left.

"You sure about this?" I asked.

"Be confident. Use what you have. Channel Robert Johnson with a broken string, not Jimi Hendrix."

"Do I have to sign a deal with the devil?"

As I jokingly referenced Robert Johnson at the crossroads, I felt the isolation inside that jet aircraft and saw the gray man's eyes.

Jake grinned. "From what you told me about last night, the ink is already dry." Jake handed me a metal bucket.

"You're not going to use this as a drum?"

"Ha ha. Tips, my man. Tips."

"But we don't really need the money," I said.

He stopped preparing and stared at me.

"First, my friend. It's not for us. It's for the fans who get a good vibe from making a small donation to the starving musicians with the little…" he grinned, "amps. Second, we'll give it all to Leni. That girl has been through trials and tribulations."

I stretched out prone on the rough wood of the wagon platform, reached toward the ground, and dropped the bucket the last foot to the pavement. Applause rose from the grand porch of the Grand Hotel. Prof was standing beside Leni. They were both clapping. Shianti stood near Prof's other shoulder. Very close, their hips pressed together into an airtight seal.

I waved hello and went over to the guitar case containing a guitar I hadn't seen or touched. Plenty to worry about. So much could go wrong with a guitar that wasn't maintained. I hoped for at least all six strings.

I flipped open five brass latches on a case dented and torn like it had experienced baggage handlers on a hundred flights. My expectations sank as I recalled the song trilogy United Breaks Guitars by Dave Carroll. I lifted the cover, my heart racing, to reveal a glistening black ES-355, favored by none other than B.B. King, reflecting my astonished face back at me.

"The doorman?" I said. "Are you sure he's okay with me playing this?"

"I told him you could channel Hendrix, so don't make me a liar."

I tuned, plugged in to the tiny amp, and warmed up with The Thrill is Gone. Jake sang, brought in a drum part halfway through, and a bass line from his pint-sized synthesizer during my guitar solo.

The guitar was pure, buttery brilliance. The setup was so perfect it almost played itself. And I had so much tonal control from the guitar, I didn't need any from the amp.

That amp screamed its tiny heart out into the afternoon sky with a kind of little-engine-that-could attitude. A small crowd formed on the porch across from our stage. Near the left end of the group, right up against the railing, Naomi was standing, yes standing, beside a pillar and hugging it with both arms. Our eyes met at the climax of my solo while I was bending strings to find B.B.'s blue notes as carefully as I could.

While the guitar wailed and Jake made the tiny drum machine cut a groove a mile wide, Naomi lifted her left hand. She glanced up and down the railing. All eyes were on the band. Then she slowly unzipped her hoodie to reveal a shiny hot pink bra.

She smiled.

She mouthed a word that I thought might be 'tonight.'

She pointed at me.

The clang of the bucket broke my trance. I looked down to see the gray man in his gray trench coat dropping a gray envelope into the bucket.

He pointed at me too.

◇

The elderly driver wearing blue coveralls led his team of horses toward our stage. The hotel management had approved only a single 45-minute set. But the crowd insisted on two encores, the second of which consisted of Jake rapping over a slowed down, funked-up version of Fire by Jimi Hendrix.

The horseman insisted that the hotel had already paid him when Jake tried to give him a hundred-dollar tip. He said that we needed the money more than he did, and added, "You young fellas are OK. Keep practicing." So we bought his metal bucket for fifty dollars.

We presented the bucket to a smiling Leni at a going away dinner Prof hosted in the 'Somewhere in Time' suite, this time without his trench coat costume. Jake and I helped Leni count, slipped some of our own cash in, and ended up with over a thousand dollars to help her get back on her feet. I also dropped in the $95 IOU she had given me at the rest stop. But she counted out 95 dollars, and made me take it.

Leni grew tired early. I walked her to her room and hugged her goodnight. I wanted to explain the gray man's promise about Markus, but there would be a better time. With a full scholarship and admission to Harvard, she would do fine without him—if he just stayed out of her way.

Back in Prof's suite, I tried to pay Jake for his assistance and my share of the equipment. He refused. Told me I needed the money more than he did because he, like Prof, had an excellent income stream. Then he thanked me for adding some excitement to his weekend and invited me to stop by Toucan Sam's to play anytime I was in town. I thanked him again for the sticker on my windshield.

I said goodbye to Prof and Shianti, who seemed anxious for the party to wind down so they could be alone.

Now I was sitting beside Naomi on the couch in the connecting suite she had insisted on because she hated being alone in a new place. We were watching Christopher Reeves attempt time travel through self-hypnosis. Admittedly, it wasn't something I had ever tried, but it seemed delusional. Naomi was engrossed in the movie and squeezed my hand at every high-anxiety moment.

The gray envelope from the tip bucket brought back visions of the gray man pointing at me. Reminded me too much of the old Uncle Sam Wants You posters.

It was lying beside me. Unopened.

Naomi noticed my attention drifting and tapped the remote, freezing Reeves and Seymour with their lips two inches apart. She picked up another piece of the Mackinac Island fudge she had insisted we try. This one was called S'more Please and combined chocolate fudge, marshmallow bits, and crumbs of the famous Dr. Graham's crackers.

"Who is Janet Doerington?" she said.

"Where did that come from?" I asked.

"Belinda said it wasn't her. But your cop friend found that name."

"On a…" I froze as the obvious hit me. "It was on a police report. And I bet that report was filed by Belinda Carnes father before she changed her name to Cercus."

"Then why?" Her brown eyes stared at me and I almost forgot the conversation we were having.

"Drop the T from Janet," I said. "And take the first three letters of the last name."

She frowned. "Damn, her father filed it as a Jane Doe way back when." She shook her head and pointed to the envelope. "It's not going to open itself." Then she smiled and pulled the zipper on her hoodie down to her navel. The bra was very pink. And satin. And shiny.

I reached for the envelope. Sealed. No markings. A question popped out of nowhere.

"You never talk about your past," I said.

"Only now is important. Absentee fathers, drinking mom's who run off with boyfriends, boyfriends who get too friendly with the daughter, foster care, damaged legs that don't work right. It all teaches you the same thing. Depend on yourself. Do as much as you can with what you have left. And, baby, oh baby, carpe diem."

I tore the end off the envelope, expecting detailed instructions that I wasn't allowed to disclose to anyone. I extracted a half sheet of paper with two fingers, then on impulse, handed it to Naomi without looking at it.

She studied it carefully for some seconds.

"Who is Thomas Kelsey?"

"The name on my birth certificate." And the name I had signed on a non-disclosure agreement.

She folded the page until it was the size of a credit card and tucked it into her hot pink bra. Then she leaned my way and kissed me until my ears felt warm.

She whispered, "We have forty-two kisses to go. Have you read The Hitchhiker's Guide to the Galaxy? This number is the answer to life, the Universe, and everything." She placed a hand on my thigh and squeezed. "Come. Let me show you what I can do with what I have left. And when you find the hidden treasure, you will be fifty-thousand dollars richer. Payment for, and I quote, 'Services rendered to the government of the United States of America.'"

She met my eyes and fluttered her eyelashes.

"Unquote."

THE BRONZE JEEP

INGREDIENTS:
2 oz. Jameson Irish Whiskey
4 oz. Dr. Pepper (with cane sugar, no HFC syrup)
1 Slice of lime

THE MIX:
Fill Old Fashioned glass (or lowball glass) with ice. Pour whiskey slowly over ice. Add Dr. Pepper (up to 6 oz. for a sweeter drink). Rim glass with lime and affix wedge to lip.

Enjoy.

ACKNOWLEDGEMENTS

My heartfelt thanks to all who made contributions to this novel both big and small. They include, but are not limited to, my long time editor Robyn Russell and my ever reliable first reader R. Many thanks to Rachel Hansen (@Rach_22h) for posting insights of her life on two wheels. Check out her artwork at rachellovesdesigns.etsy.com. And last but not least, thanks to Michael at the Riva Grill in South Lake Tahoe for his assistance in the creation of the Bronze Jeep.

ABOUT THE AUTHOR

JOE KLINGLER is the author of eight award-winning novels including the London Book Festival winner Missing Mona and Tune Up – Best Thriller Beverly Hills International Book Awards. His novels include *Nomad Thrillers* featuring Damon, *The Qigiq Detective Series* featuring Qigiq and his partner Kandy Dreeson, and *Tommy Cuda Mysteries*, with accidental private eye, Tommy Cuda. When not writing he meanders on a motorcycle between Nevada, California, and his native Ohio doing research for his next novel.

9 781941 156179